CARI MOSES

JUDITH TYLER HILLS

authorHOUSE®

AuthorHouse™ UK
1663 Liberty Drive
Bloomington, IN 47403 USA
www.authorhouse.co.uk
Phone: UK TFN: 0800 0148641 (Toll Free inside the UK)
    UK Local: 02036 956322 (+44 20 3695 6322 from outside the UK)

Published by AuthorHouse 04/22/2021

ISBN: 978-1-6655-8831-7 (sc)
ISBN: 978-1-6655-8830-0 (hc)
ISBN: 978-1-6655-8832-4 (e)

Library of Congress Control Number: 2021907308

CONTENTS

SYNOPSIS

When the multiply disappointed Karen discovers Cari Moses, she sets about making her the epicentre of her life, unaware of the devastation her action will leave in its wake. Careers are made and broken, and family life is regained and ripped asunder, while the evil that has been set in motion proliferates before the final terrifying crescendo.

This is a psychological thriller in which the personal grief and deception of one young woman is inextricably linked to the activities of a serial killer who harbours a fascination with pregnancy. Set among the rambling inland waterways and heaving anonymity of cities, the narrative unfolds through the drama of hospital life, from midwifery to ICU, to a nationwide police alert, to the tenuous nature of relationships, as it charts the inexorable progress of the protagonists towards discovery and retribution.

It is a story of beginnings and endings, of ruthless ambition and professional shortcomings, where the dubious skill of the amateur is pitched against the inconsistent efficiency of professionals and where the harsh reality of rural poverty and life on the streets is set alongside the power and corruption of the wealthy. The players inhabit a dark world of contrasts where the hopes and aspirations of youth become enmeshed in despair and depravity and where the evil, working through the generations, encounters moments of rare courage and the possibility of redemption.

Above all, *Cari Moses* is a story of human frailty and the ordinary, often extraordinary people we are.

Disclaimer: No part of this story relates to actual occurrences, and the people portrayed are entirely fictional. Specific references to hospitals and procedures are similarly mere imagination, and some of the geographical detail has been altered or embellished to fit the plot.

PROLOGUE

The late afternoon sunlight cast long shadows across the pretty garden with its beds of riotous colour: a vibrant display of dahlias, roses, and fuchsias jostling for space, attention, and maximum effect. No serried rows of formal, rigid planting here; rather, a mass of glorious confusion, heady with the scent of lavender, spilling out from the flower beds over the crazy paved path down to the grassy area at the far end of the long garden. Here tail ferns grew in abundance under the wizened branches of old apple trees bordered on three sides by mature oaks and the dense foliage of conifers beyond.

Distracted now, the girl found herself looking at the jumble of pretty pink apple blossom and thinking about how it replicated the tangle of intertwining roots beneath the ground. This was something she knew well from previous futile attempts to separate the fragile root systems of the tiny wild cyclamen from those of the pale primroses, their marginally more robust neighbours, in an endeavour to move some of these plants to another part of the garden, namely the little raised bed which her father had painstakingly constructed for her from old railway sleepers and had further embellished with a carefully painted sign—her sign, her name, and her very own garden. Hers was a miniature garden within the much larger, sprawling garden beyond which had been the playground of their youth.

It was here that the girls had amused themselves throughout their childhood, acting out their imaginative little dramas, their dolls and teddies variously becoming patients in a well-ordered hospital ward, recalcitrant children in an old-fashioned schoolroom, or an appreciative audience at a talent show hosted and performed by their young owners. Always the girls were in their dominant roles—doctors, nurses, teachers, or celebrity performers. And always Megan was the principal character: Megan the at the familiar land mass behind her. She felt the cool contours of the rail beneath her hands, iron on stone, as solid and intractable as the mercurial water beneath, which was endlessly shifting and changing. The permanence of the rising pillars of the stanchions, the arches firm and starkly defined in the moonlight, emphasised the utter frailty she felt when confronted by such powerful reminders of time gone by, maybe a time that never was.

Climbing above the handrail now, looking down, glancing away, forever drawn to the vista below, she saw the seething mass of froth and foam splashing ineffectually against the mighty pillars. She watched the black waters rising and falling, the perpetual motion of the swell, the incessant rhythm of it all. She wanted to shut it out, to clasp her hands over her ears, fearing as yet to release her tenuous grip upon the ancient stone structure. Resisting the urge to scream, she bit back the bile rising in her throat. She was poised now, a leap—no, not even a leap—away from the oblivion she craved. No "Giant leap for mankind" here, she thought; one tiny stumbling step would be all it would take—one step to end a lifetime of deception and lies.

CHAPTER 1

The Man on the Bus

The man on the bus was watching her. He was still watching her. Having first caught sight of her in the bus station café, he had begun to watch her then, slowly sipping his tea as she was served with some frothy concoction topped with whipped cream and marshmallows. The sight of that, even though she was sitting a few tables further inside the café than he was, made him gag. He felt the wave of nausea hit him and then recede, but still he could not avert his eyes from her. He had watched her waiting in the queue to board the bus and had followed her, selecting a seat two back from hers so that she would not be aware of his surveillance.

He had thought then that she was the one. The irony of this had caused a wry smile fleetingly to contort his pale, scarred lips. What, if after all his recent searching, here she was, working in the same town as he, catching the same bus home?

He had judged her to be four or five months gone. Her pregnancy was showing, but her figure was still firm. Probably her first, he thought. She was wearing a smart dark dress and a faux-leather jacket left undone. No doubt it would be beginning to strain over her bump, he speculated excitedly. She had neat ankles and wore low-heeled sensible shoes. Looking at her, he knew that she was still working and that he would see her again.

He could feel the beginning of an erection and swiftly pulled down his donkey jacket to conceal this from the woman on the opposite seat, whom he had already figured as a nosey old bag, when the young woman he had been watching pressed the bell button on the upright strut in front of her seat and prepared to alight. He had hoped that she might be travelling further, not only because in her presence his sexual arousal was increasing, but also, on a more prosaic level, because he knew that he would not be able to follow her—not this time.

He would have to plan this carefully. He would need a van. His own was in the lean-to next to his house, the recent respray he had given it still drying out. October was a bad time of the year to have done that, he knew. It would have dried out quicker in the summer. But it had had to be done. As it turned out, it had done him a favour. That was why he was using the bus tonight. That was how he had come to see her.

He wondered about using the van he drove for work, but that presented more of a challenge. He would have to sign it out overnight, inventing or manipulating the following day's sequence of deliveries as the pretext for starting from home. He did not dare to risk a repeat of today's fiasco. He had had to account for the extra mileage on the clock, fabricating a traffic problem which had resulted in a lengthy detour along unfamiliar country roads, where he had become rather lost. The work van was one of the older models and had no integral satnav installed. He was glad now of his earlier insistence to the transport manager that because he knew the locations of all his various drops, he could see no reason to carry one himself.

That excuse had explained the additional miles and the mud-spattered bodywork of the van. Although he knew that it would not hold up under scrutiny, he was pretty confident that the bored depot manager who had booked his vehicle back in would have more pressing concerns, not least the desire to finish his shift and go home, than to authenticate the story about a traffic accident. It was a stupid story now that he thought about it. Why hadn't he just said that there was a broken-down car blocking his way, or a herd of cattle holding everything up—anything that could not be checked? He felt uneasy, sure now that an RTA would be reported and recorded somewhere official.

He did not usually make such elementary mistakes. Over the years he had covered his tracks well, seldom operating in the same area for long, moving to a new job in a new location, all the time keeping his old house, locked up now, should he ever need a more distant bolthole, albeit an unappealing one. Always the same type of work, though. He was not an ambitious man. No, he was definitely not ambitious. Not any more. He had had that kicked out of him—surgically excised. And that was the pattern of all the work he had had over the last few years, the work he had now. A driving job. Deliveries. It was a job that took him round the country, one where he could follow his hobby.

The more he thought about it, the more annoyed with himself he became. As an excuse, his story was far from watertight. Whilst it supported the extra miles and some of the journey time, it was hardly a sufficient justification for the prolonged delay in returning the vehicle, which was due back at the depot by 4p.m. to allow ample time for it to be cleaned and loaded with the next day's deliveries. As it turned out, it was almost six by the time he had pulled into the cleaning bay.

It was company policy that the interiors of the vans should be cleaned each day. Because of the sensitive nature of some of the products being transported, it was essential that a good standard of hygiene be maintained. This usually involved little more than discarding any split packaging then sweeping the floor, particularly in wet weather, when dirt may have been carried in on the drivers' shoes. Once a week the walls would be wiped down with cleanser, but that was generally a weekend job when there were fewer deliveries to be made. The exteriors were routinely hosed down at night so that the vans would emerge the following morning with the firm's logo clear and bright.

He had never really minded cleaning the van. At a basic level, it was an established routine, one that appealed to his latent sense of order. Furthermore, the contents of the split packets were never stringently accounted for, and over the months he had managed to acquire quite a few useful items that supported his absorbing hobby, smuggling them past the security desk in the inside pocket of his jacket.

Today he had done a more thorough cleaning than usual for a week night. Having been aware of the manager's presence in the bay for some of this time, he hoped that, rather than being irritated by any unprecedented delay in processing the vehicle, he would be impressed by such conscientious behaviour. He would have done even more, but the evening packers had arrived and were anxious to stock the waiting vehicles with the following day's deliveries. As it was, he had missed the earlier bus home and had had to wait for the next one, killing time in the bus station café. Killing time. He almost chuckled aloud at the inappropriateness of the phrase. How could anyone kill time? he wondered.

Still, the wait had been providential. It was then that he had first noticed her, and the time had passed (Passed, not been killed, he thought) quickly indeed, intent as he was in his watchfulness. It could have been meant. As she boarded the same bus as him, he knew for sure that they were destined to meet again.

CHAPTER 2

Karen

The day had been truly awful. At least that was Karen's summation of events. Far from cementing their relationship, or even beginning to address the insidious creeping realisation that this was really going nowhere, Karen had begun to suspect that the sooner she and Ben began their separate lives, the better.

"Oi, Karen, landlubber, are you in a trance or something?" Ben's imperious, condescending shout echoed across the narrow concrete chasm that formed the sides of Marton top lock, a late nineteenth-century construction, one of several single locks scattered along this stretch of the Llangollen Canal.

"Landlubber, indeed," harrumphed Karen quietly to herself, wondering for the umpteenth time whatever must have possessed them to embark upon this two-week out-of-season break on one of the country's more isolated canals. At least that was how it felt to her now. It was late October, and the tourists—couples, families, and the occasional group of raucous young people on stag or hen parties—seemed to belong to a distant and idealistic world of travel brochures and posters. It was an image of sun-drenched days and the happy chatter of fellow boaters helping one another through the locks—people in holiday mood, laughing together about the privations of their temporary floating homes and the idiosyncrasies of boatyard etiquette, lock paddles, windlasses, temperamental ovens with gas cylinders running out at the most inauspicious moments in the middle of cooking supper, floating key rings, and pump-out loos. That was how she and Ben had first perceived the notion of a canal holiday getaway, back in the summer, long before the coldness had set in. And it was not just the coldness of the encroaching winter, underscoring as it did the slow paralysis of their one-time affection for one another, feeling for all its worth (she shivered as the comparison arose unbidden) like icy fingers beginning to crush the very warmth and humanity from Karen's soul.

"Come on, landlubber," echoed again from the depth of the lock. "Do close these gates and fill it up with water. I don't want to spend all day down here."

Grudgingly, Karen complied, feeling her mounting irritation at what now seemed the futility of it all, particularly with Ben and his silly commands, strutting, posturing, and bossing her about like that. He had really shown her up a couple of days ago, going through the staircase locks at Grindley Brook, where, as usual, it was Karen who had jumped onto the towpath, wielding the windlass, while Ben steered their hire boat through the rising levels. Here it was that she felt most ashamed and embarrassed by what they had become. For at Grindley Brook, the boaters' progress was assisted by an official from the Canal and River Trust, a modern-day lock-keeper no longer living in one of the picturesque lock-keepers' cottages they had passed on their trip, long since sold into private ownership, but someone who travelled daily to his work and his role in helping to maintain the smooth running of this more demanding arrangement of locks. At the height of the holiday season, he would alternate groups of boats, three or four at a time, between the top and bottom lock, easing the way for uninitiated boaters and portraying a level of calm and implied safety to which Karen felt drawn and by which she had been oddly comforted.

Here, though, Ben had really let her down. Thank goodness theirs had been the only boat being guided through the locks and there was no one else to witness their charade. If only he hadn't insisted on addressing her as "landlubber". Just how puerile was that? "Ahoy there, landlubber" indeed!

And he was wearing that stupid pseudo-naval jacket with gold braid on the cuffs and sparkling epaulettes, for which he must have scoured the fancy dress costume shops near to their home, and a cap proclaiming him to be the captain. She had refused point-blank to humour him and wear the matching "Galley Slave" cap he had bought for her. What were they, five-year-olds?

"Don't let him get to you, love." The lock-keeper looked at Karen with a warmth and sincerity that she had so long felt lacking in her life. "They all think they're Lord Nelson," he said, chuckling.

If only he knew. Her feelings towards her personal Lord Nelson had become more antagonistic and remote as the holiday progressed. She felt so very unsure of herself now and of any remaining affection for Ben.

She had heard it said that a grief shared brought couples closer together. She doubted it. Their own personal tragedy seemed to have driven a wedge between them, which only became more firmly divisive as the weeks went by. Perhaps it was only Karen who felt the weight of the tragedy. True, in the beginning, Ben had seemed almost as distraught as she was. They had sobbed together and rocked in each other's arms. There had been no niggling doubt in her mind back then. Ben was as traumatised as she had been.

But was he? Now, as she pondered it, she wondered if it was more of an act for him even then. Or had his grief, real enough at the time, begun to diminish imperceptibly, relentlessly even in those early days after the "meltdown"? That was what he had called it. She was remembering that now, meltdown. "Something just wasn't right, love. It had to go into meltdown." That was what he had said. She had salvaged a shred of comfort from that at the time, but she was seeing it in a different light now. She saw him as callous, uncaring, trivialising *her* personal tragedy, her failure, as though it was something they could dismiss as easily as minor storm damage to their house, as casually as he might regard a prang to their already battered old car.

"Heh, landlubber, if you don't get a move on to get us out of here, I'll have you walk the plank!" Still speculating on the gaping difference which had opened up between them, Karen returned to the present as Ben's call cut through her musings. She tugged the bottom lock gates closed and, moving lethargically from one side of the lock to the other, used her windlass to open the top paddle and fill the lock. Ben, wearing his captain's cap at a jaunty angle, rewarded her efforts with a slow handclap as Karen swung the gate open. Gripping the tiller now, he began to manoeuvre the narrowboat out of the lock into the wider channel of the canal.

CHAPTER 3

Ben

Ben wondered for the twentieth time that day how he could have got it so wrong. He had hoped that this holiday would give them both a much-needed boost. Work had not been going very well since their problems earlier in the year. He had lost a lot of time there, and with it, he felt, the respect not just of his immediate line manager but also of the MD who had appointed him, and even perhaps the two young apprentices assigned to him as part of their college day-release programme. Still, it did no good worrying about that here. That was a problem he would have to address honestly and with as much enthusiasm as he could muster on his return home. Here there was the much more pressing and immediate problem of Karen, of her unhappiness and the distance this was creating between them. If only he could cheer her up.

He had loved Karen for as long as he could really remember. Arriving at the start of the fifth form, Ben, whose father's frequent job relocations had meant repeated settling and unsettling of his three school-aged children, had been a newcomer to King's High School. Of the three of them, Amy, now thirteen, had taken this most recent upheaval to their life and her education, badly. "Ah, Dad, you're taking me away from my bestest friend ever!" she had wailed, reverting to the sort of babytalk that she hoped might win him over. "I hate you. And I hate your horrid job. No one else keeps on having to go to new schools like we do. I hate you. I really do."

The familiar refrain was met, as usual, by a stony glare from her mother. "You know your father's work comes first. After all, may I remind you, young lady, that it is your father's job that pays the bills and keeps you provided with all the things you like to have."

And their father, as always, would look defeated and mildly distraught as he sought yet again to cuddle and cajole his youngest child into agreeing that it might not be too bad and that there might well be other *brilliant* friends just waiting for Amy to find them.

Andrew and Ben, sixteen-year-old twins, identical in everything but attitude, reacted differently. Andrew seized upon the opportunity which every move presented to sort his belongings out, ruthlessly consigning outgrown games and his collection of trump cards to his mother's permanent charity box in the hall and flogging anything he had of value on eBay.

Ben, always the more measured of the three of them, would begin to draw up his "moving list," working out which of his possessions he still needed (nearly all of them) and consigning very little either to the charity box or Andrew's eBay offerings. Always a rather timid boy, Ben had faced up to the previous three moves by attempting to render himself invisible, hoping that by failing to attract anyone's attention in his new surroundings, he might just be able to cope with the challenge of a new routine; a different journey to school with the attendant nightmare of the inevitable bullies on the school bus, and the alien approaches to once familiar subjects on the timetable. Worst of all was the prospect of PE and each soul-destroying wait whilst all those around him would be selected before him for the various teams. Unknown by his peers, and unremarkable in physique or physical attainment, Ben knew that it was always his role to be last picked and first out.

But this time, he had resolved, it would be different. It had to be time to break the mould. Elevated now by virtue of his age, to the rank of fifth former, he knew that the competition among his fellows would be more keenly pursued than ever. And he also knew that, in the way these things inevitably play out, he could not hope to compete on equal terms. So, shy and reserved, and certainly not the greatest scholar the King's School fifth form had ever known, Ben Aldiss determined that his new role from now on would be as class clown.

Instead of his previous deprecating behaviour and quiet acceptance of a classroom existence always on the fringe of things, Ben started as he meant to proceed. Throughout the long summer holiday between schools, he had practised a commanding, almost aggressive pose. He had mastered the art of repartee, constantly bandying words with his twin and even, if she was feeling agreeable, with Amy. Towards his mother, his behaviour never really wavered. She never had been the most approachable of people and manifested a certain intolerance and almost disregard towards her children. Fiercely loyal and unflinching in her support of her husband, she viewed the domestic trivia of a life providing for the physical needs of their three growing children as her portion of the contract that being his wife involved. "We all have a cross to bear," she was fond of repeating both to herself, when her children's behaviour drew an unusually high level of reproach, and to her neighbours and associates in whichever Women's Institute or charitable concern had attracted her allegiance during the course of their many house moves.

But towards his father, Ben felt a new kinship and regard. When the developing banter was gently reciprocated, he began to hone his repartee and practise a more mature and wittier repost than was possible with Andrew or Amy.

CHAPTER 4

Karen

At fifteen, Karen had known that she was luckier than most. Not only had she the intelligence to have succeeded in almost all her subjects up to now, but also in her choice of future A levels that had delighted her parents, both of whom had always harboured academic ambitions for their only child. Over the years her school reports had been consistently excellent. The parental dream was for her to achieve a place at one of the top universities in the country.

The teachers at her secondary school had encouraged this, recognising the girl's potential and appreciating her lively contributions in class. They had known Karen since she started there as a slight, quiet ten-year-old, seemingly permanently overawed by her presence, courtesy of a late August birthday, in a form of girls many of whom were not only almost an entire year older but also taller and far more well developed for their age. Gradually the shy little girl began to attract the grudging admiration of her peers. Although unable to compete with the willowy height of her classmates on the netball court, Karen proved herself to be a competent athlete in all but the high jump, excelling not only in track and speed activities but also in the school gymnasium, where she showed a measure of fearless determination. She was a fierce opponent on the hockey field, a characteristic which was to surface in her later battles with her parents and eventually even with Ben, the only boy she had ever really loved.

Now, at fifteen, Karen was proving to have a keen intellect and a real enthusiasm for learning. Not that she was seen in any way by her colleagues as a swot or teachers' pet. Nor did they seem unduly envious of her classic

English rose good looks: perfect white teeth (without any need for the orthodontic braces which bedevilled the appearance of so many girls her age) and a mass of curly fair hair. Something in her personality seemed to elevate Karen beyond such petty jealousies. Life was good for her, and she could envisage no reason why it should not always be so.

CHAPTER 5

Leckie

Leckie had had a troubled childhood. But that was nothing in comparison to the sort of trouble she would be in now if they ever found out.

Leckie was not her real name of course. She'd been christened. At least she liked to believe that someone back then had cared enough to have her christened, or at least given her a special naming day or whatever, something more to show than the tatty birth certificate she had carried around for years in the deepest pocket of her rucksack, until that too had been stolen from her while she was asleep somewhere in a shop doorway months ago. That certificate had proclaimed her name to be Felicity Evangeline Zabot. Why on earth would anyone have given her such an awful name, the initials spelling fez indeed? What could possibly have possessed them?

Not that she had ever called herself Felicity—not since that day, barely remembered now, when she was still been part of a family and she had her little brother, Gregory Matthew—the lucky one, she thought, as his initials didn't spell anything. It was Gregory Matthew who had whooped with delight when their mother, in a rare moment of attempted bonding with her somewhat elaborately named children, had tried to teach him to say his older sister's name. "Fel-ic-it-y," she repeated—"Fel-ic-it-y"—more patiently than Leckie could ever previously recall.

"'Lectricity," whooped little Gregory, "'ike a 'ight 'witch." Gregory was having trouble with the beginnings of words. Leckie had liked it instantly. Not so their mother, who had snorted with disgust, turned away, and abandoned any further attempt to encourage the younger child to speak.

But Leckie herself had grasped the possibility, even then, of escaping from her formal nomenclature, already the object of ridicule amongst her classmates at St Stephen's primary school. "Felicity, Felicity. Smells like a lavatory," they chanted on the days when she actually made it to school, on a Monday morning, usually wearing the same clothes she had worn all the previous week. Mortified by their taunts, she would dab furtively, futilely at the miscellaneous food stains and assorted grime, whilst pushing her other fist tightly into her eyes so that her tormentors wouldn't see her starting to cry.

Why couldn't she have had a mummy who sent her to school looking clean and fresh with her long hair brushed and shiny in neat little pigtails like Katy-Lou Aspinall, instead of a permanent matted tangle? Katy-Lou was the closest thing Leckie had ever had to a friend. Katy-Lou, who never joined in the daily catcalling and persecution Leckie received from the rest of them, stood quietly at the edge of things, sidling up to Leckie when it was all over to give her the beginnings of a hug, or if, as Leckie suspected, the smell was too strong for that, an encouraging high-five.

None of it was Mummy's fault, of course. She was too tired or too sick to care, always a bottle of the vodka medicine not too far away, hidden from Leckie's bullying, bruising father, but in some place where Leckie and even little Gregory could find it and fetch it for her when she called out for it. The older children in the family, two boys, and a sister Leckie could hardly remember at all, had long since left home. The two boys were out at work somewhere and never came by to say hi to their mother and younger siblings any more, not since their father had come home late one afternoon to find them in the kitchen, sipping tea together. "Bloody parasites!" he had yelled at them. "You don't live here any more. Buy your own fucking tea!"

The youngest child, still a baby, her father hardly seemed to notice at all, unless she cried. A dummy usually calmed her. If their mother wasn't feeling well, Leckie would find a dummy for the child.

Margarita, the oldest girl, was seldom mentioned except when her father, in one of his rages, would shout her name and call her all those wicked things he said their mother had turned her into—a prossy, a whore, a feckin' cripple. Young Leckie didn't understand the words then; she just knew that they were bad and made her mummy cry and want her medicine. Now, of course, she understood those words only too well, but

14

what she still did not comprehend was what had happened to Margarita. Their mother never talked about her, not even that last time, about two years ago now, she supposed, when Leckie had hauled her tatty rucksack all the way up into town to visit Mum in St George's hospital.

"No place for you, ducks," her mum had said, so much nicer to her daughter now that they were giving her proper medicine. Not that that had really helped much. She had left it too late, they said. Should have sought help about her drinking years before. "Liver shot to hell, girl." That's what Mum had told her then.

"Can't get yer life back. Not as 'ow I'd want to, most of it. Wish I could've though. Never 'ave let you and Gregory go into care that year. They took the little 'un later on. Kept 'er with me for a bit though. You two was only seven and three—'ad to let you go. Yer dad was lacin' into the pair of you by then. I couldn'a take no more."

Leckie flinched at the memory that this brought back, not just her dad "lacing into her", but also the other things, the unspeakable things he and his mates had done to her then. "Got to teach you the facts of life, young lady. You'll thank me for it when you're older."

And if she didn't do just what he wanted, she'd get a beating for it.

That was when the woman from the social got called into school, she remembered. Mrs. Mont had seen the bruises even though Leckie had tried to do as her father always told her and keep her legs and arms covered. The school secretary had kept her back at the end of the afternoon and given her milk and biscuits while they waited for the social worker to collect Gregory from their house. By bedtime, the two children had been separated and placed in emergency foster care.

Leckie didn't get to see Gregory much after that. Or her mum and dad either. When Dad had stormed up to her latest foster mother outside Morrison's that day, demanding his rights to have his little girl back where she belonged, a truly frightening scene ensued, with her father trying to pull her away from her foster mum, who had abandoned her trolley and was doing her best to get Leckie and Ethan, another child in her care, into her car. Leckie didn't know whether to be sad or relieved to see her dad cautioned by a security guard and then handcuffed and dragged towards a waiting police car.

"You'll suffer for this!" he had yelled. "She's mine, and don't ever forget it. She'll turn out just like her sister, a cringing, whining whore. Discipline is what she needs." And that was the last she heard.,"Discipline the little whore," as he was bundled unceremoniously into the back seat of the police car.

CHAPTER 6

Pam

Pamela Manning was having a bad day. Recruited in a "back to midwifery" drive at forty-three, and mother to two demanding teenagers, she was finding the pattern of alternating twelve-and ten-hour shifts exhausting. How the younger members of the team on Bunting ward managed to combine professionalism, the unremitting encouragement of their charges, and the domestic demands of babies, toddlers, and little children was quite beyond her. But then, she rationalised, probably none of them had a husband with quite such a taxing job and the inevitable pressures this places on a wife and on the marriage.

Ted Manning, at fifty, an imposing six foot three and with a shock of steely-grey hair, presented a distinguished demeanour matched only by his similarly distinguished and much-decorated career. A double first from Oxford had launched his rapid progression through the accelerated promotion scheme to become one of the youngest detective chief superintendents in the country.

Pam, as a young midwife, had fallen immediately under his spell and had revelled in her role as his wife and then as the mother of his children. However, as the years progressed, a niggling discontentment began to form. At first she had been flattered and charmed by Ted's insistence that she should stay at home to look after him and the children. "After all," he had argued, "I draw a very generous salary, and we have a lovely home; you really have no need at all to work" She had been childishly pleased by his acknowledgement that it was entirely her influence that had transformed "a very good substantial property" into the "lovely home" they shared.

And when he said that at the end of a trying day he wanted to come home to an atmosphere of calm and serenity with a handsome meal and his beautiful wife waiting for him, she had felt that no woman could possibly ask for more.

Over the years, two boisterous sons dispelled any air of serenity the moment they burst through the doors at the end of the school day. The lovingly prepared meals too often were left to dry out in the oven as Pam turned the heat down lower and lower in attempt to keep the food palatable for her husband, delayed yet again because something important had arisen at work.

The socialising of their early days among fellow police officers and their partners had largely disappeared, to be replaced by fewer and vastly more formal dinners, at which Ted would most frequently occupy a lead role. Pam had felt herself outstripped and outgrown by all of this. Although she was still a slim and attractive woman in her early forties, these occasions left her feeling both dowdy and uninteresting. Seated next to other high-ranking personnel and among their witty, sparkling partners, she had little to offer by way of original conversation.

She felt dull. Her clothes, although unfailingly elegant, seemed dated by comparison with those of her fellow diners, always more daringly cut or more vibrantly coloured. Her conversational repertoire was similarly stilted. What was lacking, Pam thought, was a job—no, a *career*—of her own, one in which she could take pride and where, in turn, she would feel society's approbation and a wider recognition of the value of her role in their midst. So, at forty-one, this is what had spurred her to answer that advertisement for a "back to midwifery" refresher course at her local university hospital.

Ted had scoffed at first, then grudgingly conceded that it was within her rights to do this, if she was sure that it was what she really wanted (And as long as it does not impinge upon any of his creature comforts, she had thought, but did not dare to express).

But it *had* impinged upon their home life. Pam would be the first to admit it. Dirty dishes stacked haphazardly in the sink greeted her return from work, the boys long since having adopted their father's approach to anything associated with domesticity. And by the end of the week, the piles of dirty laundry threatened to overwhelm them all. There were heaps of discarded socks and jeans, and muddy sportswear, tracking from each of the boy's bedrooms and along the landing, rarely making it to the laundry basket in the bathroom, itself an overflowing jumble of Ted's work shirts and the family's underwear. Pam's work clothes were here too, but more often than not, theirs was a fleeting presence, the need for them to be clean again for the next duty shift meaning a hasty succession of wash and dry cycles most nights of the week.

Home-cooked meals still happened, but mainly as a result of Pam having had a gargantuan food preparation session on her days off. Frequently now, though, the boys opted for takeaway pizza or fried chicken, either at their friends' houses or on their way back from school. Not infrequently, Pam and Ted's own meal had to be hastily defrosted in the microwave before she could cook it, Pam having failed to rescue it from the freezer before leaving for work that morning.

If Ted noticed, and surely he must have, he never commented on this unpredictable state, about as far from the calm serenity he had once espoused as Pam was from the docile acquiescent young woman he had married. His only condemnation, it seemed, was that she "smelt of hospitals", an excuse too readily voiced on his behalf and too eagerly accepted on hers, effectively ending their already diminishing sex life.

CHAPTER 7

Sandy

Sandy Bostock wondered, not for the first time that day, what had possessed her ever to have wanted to become a police officer. Ribbed by her colleagues for her short stature and ample figure, criticised by her superiors for what they perceived as a careless impetuosity and lack of conformity, Sandy stood out as the only woman, not in the department as a whole but in the office she shared with five other officers. She often felt that she drew the short straw when the work was allocated. Always the more "girly" tasks fell to her lot to accomplish. Hers was the fallback position when the mounds of paperwork threatened to engulf them all and bury their desks for all eternity. It would be left to her to impose some sort of order on the chaos, sorting and prioritising items needing completion, pursuing colleagues for their signatures when often that was all that was needed before their typed notes could be filed, and ensuring that the printer was loaded with paper. This she did uncomplainingly, if not enthusiastically. And sometimes, overwhelmed with the sheer quantity, she resorted to a more radical approach, stuffing the papers in the appropriate folders but in no chronological sequence, hoping that there would be no call for anyone to open the files again.

Still, she did not get asked to make the office tea and coffee any more. Early on in her tenure, she had voiced her resistance to such overt sexual stereotyping, her forthrightness producing an amiable respect amongst most of the other officers. Over the years, there were some who appeared less than friendly towards her, and although this was never said to her face, she suspected that the reason for this had little to do with her efficiency or otherwise as a police officer but, instead, was a product of her chosen lifestyle. It was common knowledge that Sandy was gay and in a long-term and very loving relationship with her partner Helen. And despite antidiscrimination policies having an established place in the doctrine of the force as a whole, these being prominently displayed on the noticeboards in the public areas of the station, she knew that individual prejudices were not that easy to eradicate.

It amused Sandy to confound the expectations of her colleagues. She would be seen gathering up the assorted mugs with the not infrequent deposits of mould beginning to appear on the surface of the half-finished contents, tackling these herself rather than expecting the cleaners to do this for her and her fellow officers. In fact, she preferred to wield the soap pads and bleach herself, rather than having to face another day searching for the one possible clean beaker that might remain.

Other aspects of her role were more of a given. In the aftermath of a fatality on the road, it would be Sandy who would be despatched to break news of the tragedy and offer immediate support to the bereaved family. Incidents involving children and young people were her province too. Shoplifting, truancy, and patients with dementia absconding from their care homes at night were seen as her forte. On a more mundane note, appearances at school career evenings always seemed to fall on her watch. For the most part, Sandy remained remarkably equable about this. After all, she told herself, this is what I trained for. Or, on the more dispiriting days, she'd think, At least I'm not on traffic!

And she did have her moments of real excitement. Three days ago there had been an attempted abduction, and because a child seemed to have been the intended victim, Sandy was pulled from her job of cleaning the streets ("human detritus—needs sweeping out of the way" was how her immediate superior had described that particular role). So much for antidiscrimination, thought Sandy. However, her delight at being involved in the immediacy of a "pursue and find" was short-lived, the suspected perpetrator having gone to ground somewhere in the sprawling city streets.

But today had been a real bummer—Sandy's own acknowledgement of events. It had not started well. She had had something of a run-in with the desk sergeant, Shorty, the nickname courtesy of some station wag years ago. At six foot seven, Shorty presented an imposing figure in uniform.

He had accepted his current role grudgingly, only too aware that the front of house could be undertaken by a community support officer or even a civilian working for the force. It was the only feasible job he had been offered, light duties having been recommended by Occupational Health as the sole alternative to early retirement following an injury sustained trying to control an unruly crowd at an antifracking rally. The thought of retirement, albeit with a decent pension and probable compensation for his injury, appalled him. The force was his life. He had few friends outside and no hobbies (there had never been time for that), and since his wife had died, his home life was unutterably dull. He conceded this fact now, with a pang, as he recalled their early happy days before she fell victim to an aggressive breast cancer that that had taken her from him so cruelly, still in her thirties.

Shorty was a particular man who had exercised order and control in every aspect of his police career to date. He was also a grumpy man, suffering a degree of chronic pain, the legacy of his injury, and missing the drama of police work outside the station. Sandy's somewhat slapdash approach to timekeeping and disregard for protocol and the established sequence in which to present the burgeoning paperwork spawned by every recorded incident irritated him. He had chided her about a missing form from several days ago, and she had responded in kind: "Missing? More likely misfiled. Not my job to chase that one up."

The remainder of the day was pretty predictable. She had spent the best part of it moving on reluctant street beggars and homeless people who had spent the night rough-sleeping in the local parks and shop doorways, a role demanded by the new right-wing city council. It was nothing more than a cosmetic exercise in Sandy's opinion. After all, what harm were they doing? But under this latest regime, nothing would be tolerated that in any way detracted from the city's tourist appeal.

Sandy knew where *her* sympathies lay. She had herself felt the full weight of discrimination against a perceived underclass, at the hands of her domineering stepfather, with his muttered threats against "gays and poofters" and, after she had come out to the family about her own sexuality, his final shouted goodbye: "I'll be pleased to have you out of my house, you dyke. I want no bloody queers and lezzies under my roof!" Sandy's mother's attitude had not helped. A timid woman at the best of times, she had been unable to withstand her new husband's frequent criticism, both of her and of her rebellious daughter. Fearing that this second marriage, so soon after the death of Sandy's father, had been a mistake, she had withdrawn from any potential conflict with him and effectively cut herself off from her previous in-laws.

It could all have gone so horribly wrong for her then, she reflected, but for the unexpected generosity shown to her by an elderly aunt. This was someone Sandy had secretly rather feared as a child, the aunt's stern and formidable exterior concealing any trace of the kindness she later showed herself to be capable of.

Sandy's Aunt Julia, her father's oldest sister, had watched this partial disintegration of the family with dismay, maintaining the only sort of watching brief possible by occasionally meeting Sandy after school and taking her for coffee and cake in town. These meetings were necessarily slightly furtive, Sandy had felt, providing the occasions with an added spice. She did not even bother to devise some credible excuse for being late home, confident that her immediate family would merely assume it to be evidence of yet another detention. Despite this, she had never really opened up to her aunt, finding her to be an undemonstrative woman, and was both surprised and relieved to receive the offer of a temporary home with her, before taking up the place she had already secured to start her training at the police academy.

Aware that such introspection had occupied her for a large part of the morning in her dealings with the city's population of vagrants, Sandy knew that she had coaxed and encouraged, rather than insisted that they should move. She knew most of the regulars by sight, stopping to ask how they were doing and to pat their attendant dogs. She also knew where many of them slept and, where it was appropriate, had congratulated them on choosing a less obvious location, one which would offer them a degree of safety, out of the way of late night thugs and bullies, fuelled by alcohol, who saw beggar-baiting as a new sport.

Returning to the station mid afternoon, she had hoped to deal with some of the accumulated paperwork and get away on time for once. Instead of this, she was immediately confronted by Shorty, in no better mood than he had been earlier, who began to badger her again about the missing form, implying that if they were all to adopt her slapdash approach to work, they might just as well pack up and go home now, and leave the city to the devices of all the criminals *she* would be allowing to flourish. Infuriated, she repaired to the office and set about turning all the intrays upside down, determined to locate this one troublesome piece of paper. Engrossed in her work, she had failed to notice the sounds of conversation outside the door, and was only dimly aware of its opening. That was when that arrogant new DI, Niall Upton, asked what on earth she was doing. Still smarting from Shorty's criticism, she had found his question and his tone unduly patronising, calling her "dear girl" indeed! It was only once she retaliated with an uncharacteristic riposte of her own, "Fuck you, Upton," that she had become aware of the other figure who had entered their office with him.

"God, it couldn't have got much worse." She flinched at the recollection as she left the office and made her way to the changing room. It had to have been that supercilious prick Ted Manning, who, he claimed, just happened to be passing through on one of his regular inspections and had overheard it all. Bang goes my chances of getting in on any of the plum action now, Sandy thought, slamming the door shut on her locker, pocketing her car keys, and heading for home.

CHAPTER 8

Ben

"Hey, new boy, show us what you're made of. Can you throw a punch?"

It was break time during Ben's first day at King's School, and already the taunts had begun.

"Come on, new boy. Throw us a punch." Jason, the largest and apparently most aggressive of his new colleagues, squared up to Ben, fists at the ready.

"No way," Ben responded, his outer practised calm belying his intrinsic fear. "The only way I'd throw a punch is if I wanted to get off with his Judy."

"The guy thinks he's a comedian," scoffed another of the boys gathered round Ben and his opponent in a swelling, surging ring. But to their amazement, Jason, the hard man of the group, backed off with a chuckle. "Good answer, new boy. But you'd better not be thinking of getting off with *my* Judy."

"Hell, leg it, here comes old man Sharp." The head of upper-school mathematics came into view round the corner of the chemistry block. As one, the boys fled. Among them, and content to be so, was Ben.

Thus the grudging acceptance by his form mates began to occur, with Ben playing out his adopted role as the class funny man. True, it did not get him a great deal of regard from most of the staff, but it made his life during the school week a whole lot easier. The more Ben fooled around, the greater was the admiration of his peers. The fact that "new boy" even exchanged the same sort of witty retorts with a few chosen, generally more amenable members of staff earned him even greater accolades from his band of followers.

It was not just the boys who developed an admiration, however misplaced, of Ben's foolery. Most of the girls in his form liked this quick-witted young man who did much to lighten the most tedious of school days. They rated him as fit and vied with one another to capture his attention, hoping to get a date. Amongst these newfound disciples was the pretty, curly-haired girl sitting across the aisle from Ben. Karen could not disguise her pleasure at his antics, and for his part, Ben was equally smitten.

CHAPTER 9

Karen

Now, as she winced at his constant use of the silly nickname "landlubber", Karen wondered what she had ever seen in Ben. During their time in the fifth form, they became known to their friends as an item, Karen facing mounting displeasure from her parents, particularly her mother, who had disapproved of their association from the start. Ben's dubious reputation had reached the ears of a number of her fellow parents, with the mothers of the other girls openly relieved that *their* daughters were not involved with this clowning boy.

When Karen announced her intention of quitting school at the end of the year, both her parents were inconsolable, her mother becoming incandescent and uncharacteristically incoherent with rage. Her father had cajoled then pleaded, resorting to the childish pet name he had given her, "Karen Cariad", a fleeting acknowledgement of a distant Welsh heritage. "Cari Karen, we just don't want you wasting your life."

Intransigent, she had stood her ground, steadfastly refusing to entertain the prospect of King's School sixth form, despite the potential for good grades in her GCSEs and the hopes her parents had entertained for her to get into university. As the arguments at home escalated, Karen's grades plummeted; these earlier parental aspirations on her behalf became a distant and receding hope. Karen was determined to follow Ben's example and leave her schooldays behind. And while Ben's parents seemed resigned to their son's acceptance of a place at the local FE college as an apprentice mechanic, Karen's parents made no effort to disguise their profound disappointment with their daughter's chosen path. Alternate threats and bribery at home, and the attempt by her teachers to persuade Karen to rethink her plans, failed. Karen's mother had no difficulty in apportioning blame for this. She had never liked Ben, a view coloured, perhaps, by his reputation at the school gate as a joker and a charmer no girl could resist. Once she realised that the relationship between the two young people had gone way beyond mere friendship, the rows with her daughter became even more vitriolic.

Their once quiet and compliant daughter had become unrecognisable, flaunting her disobedience in as many ways as she could imagine: outrageous hair colouring; nose, tongue, and eyebrow studs; and, seen by her mother as a final insult to her, a tattoo on her shoulder. It was a starkly simple design, its impact immediate—a latticework heart enshrining the single word Ben.

CHAPTER 10

Ben

Watching Karen's desultory approach to closing the lock gates behind him, Ben, too, wondered about their relationship. He had never stopped loving Karen, at first marvelling at her refusal to follow the parental expectation and delighting in her support of him and his choices. Together they had attended college, Karen, much to her mother's chagrin, training as a hairdresser, and Ben completing his course and starting work in one of the larger mechanical engineering firms in their area. By eighteen, they were living together, and although they sometimes talked of marriage, Karen's by now distant relationship with her parents hardly encouraged this. That was the only real disagreement they had had in those early days. Ben secretly would love to have had his father's approval and even to have seen his mother happy at the occasion. He had long suspected that his mother's lack of warmth towards Karen had more to do with what she had seen as the girl's bad influence on her son in taking him away from the carefully constructed and maintained unity of their family than with her more obvious distaste at the choice of hairstyles and facial adornment. Ironic really, Ben thought, given his schoolboy reputation for immaturity and clowning about. Now that there were no longer any battles to be won, both he and Karen had settled down. He had the promise of a steady career, and Karen wanted nothing more than to make a home for them both and dream of the family they might have.

Ben wondered again when it had all begun to go wrong. What more could he have done? He knew, of course, that Karen's initial hopes of their starting a family of their own had suffered from the repeated anguish of

29

three early miscarriages, she constantly bewailing her inability to carry a baby to term. Ben was more pragmatic in his approach to this perceived disaster, feeling that, at only twenty-four, they had years ahead of them in which to have their children. He was disappointed, of course, but mostly his concern was for Karen, feeling impotent in the face of the devastating effect this was having upon her. When, six months ago, the most recent pregnancy had failed to be sustained beyond the first trimester, Karen was distraught, pleading with their GP to recommend an immediate course of IVF. When the doctor had gently suggested that, as Karen seemed to have no trouble in conceiving, there were other investigations which might be more appropriate, her distress was manifest. Being cautioned to wait for a few months for "things to settle down" before the couple could begin the series of tests which may or may not suggest the suitability for them of a course of assisted fertilisation, Karen's distress had turned to anger.

That much of this anger had been directed at him baffled Ben. He had tried to comfort and console her, but again and again Karen had berated him, firstly for not having stood up to the doctor and then for not caring as much as she did, for not grieving as deeply. This last time, Karen had insisted, she had done everything in her power to preserve the pregnancy. The moment she suspected that she might be pregnant again, she had taken a test kit home, and when this was shown to be positive, she had immediately handed in her notice at the hairdressing salon where she worked.

Apart from booking an antenatal appointment with the midwife, and not wishing, as she said, "to tempt fate", Karen had told no one else that she was pregnant. They had been such a self-contained unit for so long that neither Ben nor Karen had any real friends outside the marriage, and without the interest and support of either her erstwhile work colleagues or her family, from whom Karen was by now effectively estranged, their grieving when this pregnancy, too, ended in miscarriage was inevitably a very private affair. Karen had baulked at any suggestion he might have made of bereavement counselling or miscarriage support, and due in part to this intransigence on her behalf, Ben had felt unable to confide in anyone else about their latest failed attempt at parenthood.

Much as he would have liked to have talked this through with his father, he had respected Karen's wishes and determined instead to find some way to lift her spirits. After two previous miscarriages, it was not as though this was unfamiliar territory to Ben, but somehow everything seemed different this time. After the other two "misses", Karen had hurled herself back into a frenzy of lovemaking just as soon as her immediate physical pain had abated. It was as though she were desperate to become pregnant again as soon as possible and she would give Ben no respite from her demands until he complied. He had been both touched and alarmed by this—happy that she still seemed to want him so much, but scared by the intensity of it all. He worried that it was hurting Karen, even perhaps contributing to further failure to carry a child to term.

But this time her grief had been much more profound and her bitterness had turned against him. She seemed to Ben to have withdrawn into a sad, apathetic world of her own. She no longer worked or wanted to work. The cheerful ordered home that she had derived so much satisfaction from establishing gave her no pleasure now. Chores were left undone: their clean clothes were pushed to the back of the airing cupboard unironed, house plants were left unwatered, and dust accumulated on every unused surface. Little original cooking occurred, with a growing reliance upon ready meals. Even what food shopping there was had become spasmodic. It seemed to Ben that he was being despatched to the corner shop for forgotten items quite frequently these days.

Their sex life was as nonexistent now as in the immediate aftermath of the miscarriage. He told himself that it was only natural, that it was something only time could cure. He had begun to research clinical depression online, convinced that this was the cause of Karen's continued unhappiness, but her refusal to see their doctor or even tell her midwife about the miscarriage had defeated him. Aware that a yawning, gaping rift was developing between them, he had come up with the only idea he could think of: a holiday.

He brought home armfuls of brochures and cut out all the pages of holiday advertisement in their local paper. Nothing had sparked Karen's enthusiasm at all until, surprisingly, she seemed intrigued by the description of a narrowboat holiday. Relieved that he had found something which had seemed to attract her, Ben lost no time in organising this. He had accrued plenty of annual leave entitlement, having saved it for when he anticipated that their baby would be born. The holiday was booked. Delighted to have found something he thought Karen would enjoy, Ben celebrated the reduced rate for hiring a narrowboat out of season by shopping for what he saw as fun accessories. The naval blazer in a charity shop window had caught his eye. Having purchased it for very little money, he happily sourced a captain's hat to complete the outfit, and got a complementary one for Karen from the local fancy dress supplier.

Buoyed up by the prospect of repairing the rift that had developed between them, Ben was envisaging this as the holiday which would restore normality to their lives and rekindle their former happiness together. Now, five days into the holiday, he was not sure that this was going to prove anything but an unmitigated disaster. The real narrowboat had failed to engage the same enthusiasm from Karen as had the advertisement. She was less than impressed with the compact galley and small, but well-appointed, wet room. She complained about the lack of light in their cabin, due in part to the porthole windows there, but not aided by the gloomy weather they had encountered on their approach to Wales. She stood beside him on deck but so far had steadfastly refused to operate the tiller. She had not actually complained about having to work the locks but seemed to be deriving very little pleasure from the whole experience of cruising along the canal.

As for restoring any harmony in the bedroom, Karen had made it abundantly clear that this was not going to happen. Not only was the bed too narrow for comfort (although, as Ben recalled, it was commodious compared with the single bed at her parents' home where they had first surreptitiously made love all those years ago), but also her energies were entirely exhausted from working the locks.

As every attempt to lift her from her depression failed, Ben felt his own mood deflating. True, he had persevered with his jocular "captain of the ship" approach, but even that seemed to be becoming a source of resentment. If only he didn't love Karen so much, he speculated, then perhaps none of this would matter. Christ, he thought, I'd do anything to have her back as we were.

CHAPTER 11

Sandy

The rush-hour traffic was beginning to build up as Sandy turned into the small arcade of neighbourhood shops. She knew that Helen would be working late at the solicitor's office on the other side of town, so it was Sandy's turn to get their evening meal. Today was the anniversary of the date they had moved in together two years ago, and she had it in mind to buy something a bit special to commemorate this, having earlier decided that arranging a restaurant meal was unlikely to be a success given the vagaries of both their working hours. Two good thick rump steaks, fresh salad items, and a jar of the creamy peppercorn sauce Helen liked provided the basis for a meal that was both celebratory and relatively easy to prepare. Sandy was debating over whether to buy some baby potatoes or to ignore their joint attempt at a weight loss programme and treat herself and Helen to some frozen chips, when her mobile phone rang. Thinking it may be Helen, possibly delayed further at the office, Sandy glanced at the display. Bugger, it's work, she thought, recognising the number, before stuffing the phone back in the pocket of her jeans. No way was some query about work going to spoil the evening she had planned. I'm off duty now and my time's my own.

Adding a bottle of Shiraz and a bag of chunky oven chips to her basket, Sandy proceeded to the checkout, stopping only to pick up a packet of frozen profiteroles (Sod the diet for once). As an afterthought, she added a bunch of flowers, not roses but red carnations. They'll have to do, she thought. Stopping by the news stand next to the checkout, she wondered about buying an evening paper, but pushed the thought aside, knowing that Helen was likely to have bought one on her way home from the office.

CHAPTER 12

Leckie

Huddled now in the rear doorway of the ironmongers on the high street, Leckie pulled the old coat down as far as she could over her legs, hugging her arms across her chest, in an attempt to ward off the effects of the plummeting temperature, which, by this time in the evening, was already threatening an early ground frost. She was safe for the time being as this door was never used. Deliveries to the shop were made from the high street, and the refuse bins stored at the rear were accessed by another, smaller door to her left. She would wait for them to lock up the shop, and when she heard the owner's car pull away from the parking bay, she would make her way out onto the main street and take up her usual position in the front doorway, hoping that at least some of the commuters hurrying by would drop her a coin or two so she could get herself a cup of tea. Maybe, if she was lucky, there would be enough to buy a burger from the van on the corner.

Pity she hadn't had the balls to go through with her plan the other day. Her mate Rosie had made it sound so easy. She'd started telling her weeks ago that what she needed to get by as a beggar was something to draw the punters' sympathy: "Like the soppy dog the Big Issue seller in the market has, wrapped up in a blanket by his master's feet. It always seems to work."

Leckie hadn't been so sure. Her only experience with dogs was a salutary one. Her dad had had a dog when she was small—a mean-tempered pit bull, she thought now. It was mean anyway, but that wasn't helped by the way her father kicked out at it in his many rages. He had threatened to set the dog on the kids too, if they didn't toe the line. In

Leckie's case, that usually meant doing those horrible things with him. Then one day they woke up and the dog was gone. "Dad, where's Bruno?" she had asked, not from any particular concern over what might have befallen the beast but rather to alleviate her own anxiety about where the animal might be lurking.

"None of your damned business, Little Miss Nosey. Stick your nose in where it's not wanted and you'll end up like your sister, the fucking whore." Her father dabbed his face with a bloodstained rag. Serves him right if he's got a nosebleed, bad-tempered bully, the child thought.

Leckie hadn't asked again, and anyway, it wasn't long after this that she and Gregory were themselves taken away from home. Wonder what happened to the baby? she pondered, ashamed now that she could not remember the name of her little sister. They had just called her "the baby".

Leckie had pondered quite a bit about what Rosie had said that day though. Before they left the Smoke, she and Rosie had worked the long approach to one of the busiest Underground stations, hoping that the suited commuters, and the affluent tourists making their way to the museums and galleries in South Kensington, would provide them with enough money for food and the occasional bit of weed. Leckie had been galled to see how much more successful at begging was the whining Roma woman with the scrawny little kid in her arms. Although she fled from sight the moment transport police appeared, she still managed to pocket a weighty cache of coins during each uninterrupted stint. "More pulling power than a dog," Leckie and Rosie had agreed.

Well, she had left London now, after that last run-in with the police there. Although she half thought it was not strictly illegal, she had been moved along and cautioned for street begging several times, then for soliciting twice. How she had hated that, but a girl had to live somehow! Leckie cringed at the memory. She had resorted to that only because it paid better than shoplifting. If she shoplifted for any other purpose than to get food for herself, then she still had the problem of selling the stuff on, knowing that all the time it was in her possession, she could be picked up by the police.

She prided herself that she had never been caught nicking things from the stores. True, she had had to dodge security a fair few times, but she was fast—deft in her hand movements and even faster on her feet. The stuff was no sooner in her pocket than she was out of the shop and legging it away from the scene. But then her luck had run out. And she was so nearly caught, not just stealing the things but also trying to sell them on. It was only by dint of her quick reactions and even speedier running, dodging this way and that amongst the shoppers, that she had escaped capture that time.

That was when they had fled up north and, she reflected, was one of the last times she had seen her friend. This was despite the fact that the choice of their new venue had been dictated by Rosie's assertion that she still knew a lot of people and had some family up here who would look out for them.

The train journey had been a lark, though. Well, mostly. Not having any tickets or the money to buy them, they had adopted their practised look of innocent vulnerability and sweet-talked the railway official into opening the barrier to allow them to struggle through with their rucksacks, newly lifted from a luggage stall on Camden Market and stuffed, in Leckie's case, with the bare necessities for survival on the streets: an old sleeping bag, a few items of underwear, a packet of tampons, plastic sheeting she could use as a makeshift groundsheet or as a cover for herself and her meagre possessions in the rain, chocolate and biscuits stolen from WHSmith on the station forecourt, and a screw-cap bottle she could fill with drinking water from public conveniences or taps in the park.

Once on the train, the two young women had dodged from carriage to carriage to avoid the guard inspecting tickets, cramming themselves and their luggage together in the tiny lavatory when his approach appeared inevitable. There was scarcely enough room to breathe, she recalled, but they had managed it, smothering the tide of giggles that their ludicrous situation provoked.

There was one awful moment on the journey though, when Leckie had spotted someone she recognised, someone she never wanted to see again. Pulling the baseball cap down over her eyes, she had fled to the other end of the carriage and sought sanctuary among the bicycles and prams in the guard's van. She fervently hoped that the man, Martyn, had not seen her. He was one of her father's old contemporaries, and even though it had happened long ago, she could still recall every single horrible time she had been forced to go with him. Martyn, she knew now, was a user and a dealer. Back then she just knew that he always smelled funny. She knew the smell now, of course. It was an irony that the weed she had occasionally smoked herself to lift her mood or anaesthetise her senses after a particularly odious experience was the same drug bought off Martyn and used to excess by her father.

Buying from Martyn, whether cannabis or any other illicit substance he enjoyed, had never been a cash transaction. For Leckie's father, his daughter represented his purchasing power, and Martyn was only too ready to avail himself of the payment.

Martyn was a nasty man—sly, furtive, and a bully. Leckie had made no secret about her fear of him, pleading with her dad not to make her "play" with him. That had earned her a thrashing, and she never asked again. Trembling still at the memory, she wriggled out from behind the bikes, making her way cautiously back to the seat next to Rosie, all the time hoping that Martyn had not seen her and that he was not going to get off at the same stop as them.

Her fears appeared to have been unfounded as there was no sign of Martyn as they reached their destination. At the exit barrier, a repeat performance of struggling vulnerability and an improvised tale of having dropped their tickets in the crush to leave the train earned them a sympathetic response from the official on duty, who obligingly opened the larger gate for them, enabling them to drag their hefty rucksacks away from the platform and onto the wider station concourse. They were free, set to embark upon a new life in a different city.

Leckie wondered now about the wisdom of that last move. Her life here in Chester, so far, had been unremittingly stark. Despite the air of affluence around the distinctly upmarket shopping precinct, the Rows, it had not yielded anything like the rich pickings she had very occasionally enjoyed in London. On the plus side, she acknowledged, there were fewer security guards here, and to date she had seen very little of the local police. If they were around, they seemed disinclined to involve themselves in the sort of petty crime she knew was being committed in the city. Benighted hole, she thought, and wondered yet again just how she was going to survive here. Taking the child had seemed such a good idea at the time. What had Rosie said about the pulling power of the sympathy call?

CHAPTER 13

Pam

Thank goodness her shift was almost over. She was on earlies this week, which meant a ten-hour stint today. Not that this was set to last. She was due for a transfer to night duty next week, where instead of working from 7a.m. to 5 p.m., she would be expected to do a twelve-hour rotation, 8p.m. to 8a.m. At my age, she reflected, ten hours is plenty.

And what a demanding ten hours it had been with all three labour wards fully occupied all day and Mrs McKinnock steadfastly refusing medical intervention up to the moment when the threatened placental abruption meant an emergency C-section. Sarah Cummings had never even made it to the delivery suite, producing her eighth child after her shortest labour ever in the hospital car park. Her husband had known what to do, hammering on the maternity unit door until Pam had heard him and used her pass card to open it. In the next few chaotic minutes, she had managed to summon a small deputation from the ward, and they had all raced down to his car to collect his wife and their new daughter.

Then there was Abigail, troubled Abigail Lamont. She was a strange young woman who, most of the staff agreed, would have been more suited, surely, to a luxurious private suite in one of the leading London hospitals patronised by minor royalty and show business celebrities. But apparently Abigail had had an acrimonious parting of the ways with her wealthy aristocratic family when she had insisted on moving in with her then boyfriend Steve, an aspiring musician (guitar and composition) and sometime partner in a small independent music store, long since defunct, his business partner and the shop's assets having disappeared without a trace several months ago.

To her parents' even greater chagrin, Abigail and Steve had subsequently married. ("A fling is one thing, darling, but did you have to make a commitment out of this thing?" had been her mother's mystified reaction to the whole idea.) But headstrong as ever, Abigail had gone ahead with their plans—a low-key register office ceremony attended by only a few of the couple's more unconventional friends, followed by a wedding "breakfast" consisting of pies and pints at the Golden Orb public house, a rather unprepossessing late Victorian hostelry where Steve and his band held their customary gigs.

Abigail and Steve had had their baby, a little daughter, ten days previously. Had this been an entirely straightforward delivery, they would all have been back in their tiny flat over the abandoned music shop many days ago. The delivery itself *had* been without incident, Abigail having opted for a water birth, with Steve alternately massaging his wife's back or strumming on his guitar, to welcome their child into a world of music, he claimed.

However, Abigail and her new daughter had "failed to bond", a phrase used for several days now in the midwives' record of their patient's progress. At first she had seemed distant and uninterested in her baby, and as the days progressed, the attending midwives were alarmed to see this lack of interest evolving into a distinct dislike. Attempts by them to establish breastfeeding were met with resentment and then marked disgust by Abigail, who withdrew into a quiet lethargy from which no amount of encouragement or cajoling could sway her. Steve seemed baffled by his wife's reaction, his initial concern becoming a growing irritation, which was even more intense when she turned on him as he attempted to cuddle and settle the crying child. He was stung by her acid rebuke and tight-lipped "Leave it alone, can't you?"

Doctors were summoned to the bedside. The obstetric team could find no other reason for Abigail's unhappiness, and a preliminary diagnosis of puerperal depression was recorded. A psychiatrist was consulted, who advised rest and supervision and wrote a prescription for antidepressant medication, whilst awaiting a bed in the psychiatric unit for mothers and their babies. So Abigail remained under the watchful eyes of the midwives, whilst her little daughter spent most of her day in the transition nursery, being brought to her mother at feeding times for a bottle of formula.

Whether or not it was the powerful medication beginning to have a positive effect, over the last forty-eight hours, Abigail's response to her baby had changed, subtly at first, as she appeared to hold the child less rigidly than before, and becoming markedly more relaxed. Now she no longer flinched and averted her eyes when the baby was put into her arms. She had even been seen absently stroking the child's cheek. Today she had amazed the staff by asking to have the baby with her in the ward like the other mothers. Although the staff were only too happy to comply with Abigail's request they were somewhat alarmed by this complete about-face, the more so as she no longer wanted *them* to have any prolonged contact with the child, hugging the infant close to her chest at their approach.

However, in the light of this perceived improvement, and given the number of competing demands on the unit, the staff had relaxed their guard, reassuring Steve that they no longer thought the impending transfer to the specialist psychiatric unit would be necessary. Steve appeared relieved, saying that he hoped he was getting his lovely wife back.

His earlier anxiety, then irritation, with Abigail's strange behaviour forgotten, now he could barely contain his impatience with the staff, brushing aside their sincere expressions of pleasure at this unexpected turn of events and the cautionary advice that he should continue to observe Abigail's progress and ensure that she was taking her medication. Pushing his way through the curtains surrounding his wife's bed, shielding her from the curious eyes of fellow patients, Steve let out a howl of anguish.

It had taken him only a few seconds to register her absence and, beside her empty bed, the equally empty cot that had held their daughter, Geraldine. "Where is she?" he yelled, sending the staff scurrying into the toilets and bathrooms, the ward kitchen, the treatment room, the conference room, and even the walk-in linen store. No sign of the mother and child remained, save for Abigail's discarded nightwear. The capacious soft leather holdall, a legacy from her days at finishing school in Switzerland which had contained the clothing for their eventual discharge home, had also vanished from its storage place under her bed. Shouting that he would find them himself and that "heads would roll" if anything had happened to them, Steve rushed from the ward.

Hospital protocol decreed that any untoward incident should be brought to the attention of the chief executive, the chief nursing officer for the hospital as a whole, and in the case of an incident on the maternity unit, also to the attention of the most senior midwife on duty. Individual members of staff were quizzed and an incident report compiled. Details were given of the staff on duty and any contacts they may have had with Abigail that day. Approximate times were ascribed to each of these recollected contacts, the more accurate ones reflecting routine observations and ward drug rounds. It was widely assumed that Abigail had left the ward unnoticed among a group of visitors and that the hospital security service would find a record of this on their surveillance cameras.

The local police were notified, the desk sergeant assuring them that all units in the area had been given a detailed description and saying they would keep their eyes peeled for her. Given the apparent improvement in her condition, with the likelihood therefore of an impending discharge from hospital care, this report was not immediately deemed top priority. Abigail was not seen as imposing a lethal threat either to herself or to her child, but there was great concern over her need for repeat medication and the smallness and vulnerability of little Geraldine.

All units would be alerted with off-duty officers included in the information in case they were the ones to spot Abigail. Police vehicles were despatched to form a rudimentary cordon immediately surrounding the hospital, while traffic police were instructed to stop and search suspect vehicles leaving the city.

Meanwhile, in the maternity unit, the disruption to their routine and, not least, the implied dereliction of duty involved in Abigail's departure had had a profound effect upon the staff, most of whom sincerely wished that they had never been on duty that day. It was widely acknowledged amongst them that an internal enquiry was inevitable. Not only were they anxious and subdued, but also the distraction of the last few hours meant that everything was running late. There was a backlog of tasks waiting to be completed. The general delay was now compounded by the patients' meal trolley arriving on the unit with the food stone cold.

Everyone was grumbling. It seemed to Pam that any order or protocol had been abandoned. The mothers were loud in their complaints, whilst the visitors were totally ignoring the restriction which was supposed to limit them to two at a time by any bed. Babies were being passed among their relatives like so many parcels; the linen skips were overflowing; and none of the tea time medication had been given.

They would all muscle in and help, of course. Some semblance of order would be restored, and the shift would come to an end. Tackling the immediate tasks with more of an enthusiasm to finish than a desire to do them well, Pam had succeeded in addressing some of the backlog. She glanced at the clock over the midwives' station and saw with relief that it was well past the time to go home. Once in the locker room, she hurriedly changed her duty shoes for her winter boots, and seeing how much later than usual it was, she decided to ignore hospital guidelines for once and go home in her uniform dress. Shrugging on her thick duffle coat, gathering up her bag, and shutting her locker, she made her way to the door of the unit.

Fishing unsuccessfully under her heavy winter coat to retrieve her pass card, Pam was pleased to see that her colleague Lorna, who had worked the same shift pattern this week, was also ready to leave. In contrast to her own increasingly shambolic lifestyle, it seemed to Pam that Lorna was always tidy and organised. True to expectation, she was already swiping her own pass card, then holding the door ajar for her friend. Pam zipped up her shoulder bag and left the unit with Lorna, the two of them comparing notes as to just how awful the day had been.

CHAPTER 14

Leckie

It had all seemed so simple at the time. Too simple, thought Leckie. It had almost beckoned to her, willing her to carry out her plan. A decided plan B she acknowledged, plan A having failed to come to fruition, involving as it had Leckie's ability to "borrow" a child from either a day nursery or health centre.

She had quickly discounted this latter venue. The health centres she had considered seemed too well staffed for her presence to go unnoticed. The couple she had actually enteted during parent and child sessions had proved the point. She had only been in there for a minute or two before being asked the reason for her visit. She had fabricated some story about being new to the area and wondering about registering with a GP there. Daunted by the prospect of continuing the deceit, in one case filling out a form the receptionist had handed to her, and in another being asked to supply the same information which an overly officious woman behind the desk began to enter in to a computer, Leckie remembered something important that she had left unattended outside, and hastily departed from each of these premises.

Leckie's years of living just outside the law had long since furnished her with a ready supply of aliases, and she had developed the habit of *never* revealing her true name. She disliked any contact with officialdom, harbouring a deep suspicion about the real motive underlying even the most innocent request for information. Furthermore, she had no intention of identifying herself in any specific location, preferring the freedom to roam the streets and settle for as long as any particular spot met her immediate needs. The impromptu story about registering with a doctor threatened both her anonymity and her freedom to vanish into the maze of city streets whenever such a move might become necessary. It was an automatic response to confrontation—a plausible tale and a rapid exit.

Throughout her adult life, she had never had a GP. She had never needed one. On the rare occasions when she felt ill, usually no more than a heavy cold or an upset stomach from eating salvaged food past its use-by date, she had merely holed up and, like an animal sleeping itself better, sought seclusion, curling up in her sleeping bag until the symptoms abated.

Day nurseries, too, had proved an absolute no-no. Their security rivalled that of Fort Knox. Entry phones, passwords, and facial recognition by gatekeeper receptionists had prevented Leckie from even getting inside. She had had only one chance, and she had blown it.

For two weeks she had spent her days lurking amongst the cars parked opposite Little Poppets day nursery, which she had selected as having the best opportunity for cover. Arriving each morning after the owners had left their vehicles and gone to work in the nearby shops and businesses, she was able to observe the parents and carers dropping off their charges, noting the times of peak activity. Housed in an impressive Regency mansion, and accessed by a large green front door with the usual entry-protected code, the advantage of Little Poppets nursery was, firstly, the cover provided by the high walls and many mature trees along this road of what would be described as "quality housing stock". Then there was the private parking lot immediately opposite, from where Leckie had an uninterrupted view of the Little Poppets' imposing frontage. But, as far as her plan was concerned, the piece de résistance was the flight of steep stone steps leading up to the front door. They were almost impossible to negotiate with one of today's cumbersome state-of-the-art buggies, meaning that a carer with more than one child to deposit would have to leave the smaller one at the foot of the steps in the buggy whilst helping the older child up to the door.

It presented a brief moment of opportunity. Leckie had watched and waited, ultimately seizing that moment. Reaching the unattended buggy whilst the mother's back was turned as she hurried her three-year-old up the steps, Leckie tried to make a dash with it. Fumbling ineffectively with the brake, she had abandoned that idea and tried instead to undo the child's harness, intending to make a run for it with the baby in her arms.

But that, too, proved more difficult than she had expected. Damn it, she had never had any experience with modern-day child transportation. All she could remember of Gregory's early days was their mother pushing him along the street where they lived in a battered pushchair their father had found dumped at the refuse tip and had brought home for them to use. Its wheels were wonky and unreliable, but at least it conferred some measure of mobility. It had finally collapsed in a tangled heap of twisted metal and vinyl sheeting when Gregory was about two and a half, Leckie remembered. Thereafter, they seldom went out much. She had no recollection at all of them ever going out as a family or of their mother taking the new baby outside the house. That dilapidated pushchair had not boasted the refinement of brakes, nor, she supposed, had there ever been a child's harness.

Struggling unsuccessfully to release the infant, Leckie was startled by a sudden movement, as at that moment the mother had turned. After depositing the three-year-old on the top step, in that brief instant of recognition, she had seen a "scruffy street person" (her later less than helpful description to the attending police officer) crouched over *her* buggy, trying to steal *her* child. She had screamed then at the top of her voice, a penetrating, primal scream. Help had materialised within seconds. The nursery door was flung open, and the bewildered three-year-old, howling his protest at this unexpected turn of events, was grabbed by someone inside and hauled over the threshold. At the same time, the receptionist and two other parents who were just about to leave the premises after dropping off their children came bounding down the steps towards Leckie and the buggy. Compounding her terror, a piercing alarm began to sound from the front of the building.

She had missed her moment. It was only the speed of her reactions that had saved her. Honed to near perfection after a lifetime of watching her back in a situation of almost daily abuse, first at home, then in some of her more unpleasant foster placings (They are only in it for the money, she had thought then, and it was a perfect opportunity for those with a penchant for little kids to subject her to various degrees of cruelty and interference), and latterly during her precarious existence on the streets, Leckie knew how to escape.

Ducking and diving. The phrase could have been coined for her.

Scampering through well-tended back gardens of the adjacent properties, over railings, down narrow gullies, and across rough redevelopment sites, Leckie was conscious only of the receding yells from her would-be pursuers and of a new note which spiked her anxiety to a heightened level: approaching police sirens. Hurling herself unceremoniously into a large concrete waste pipe lying on its side, she huddled close to its rim, listening, ready at any moment to resume flight. God, it will be sniffer dogs next, she thought, brushing herself down. Leaving the sanctuary afforded by the waste pipe, she crossed the site in the opposite direction, moving towards the perimeter fence. Scrambling over rubble and builders' waste, she desperately sought an exit. Finding a gap where the double layer of wire mesh had been secured to a concrete post beside a high stone wall, she was able to squeeze herself through. Not for the first time in her life, she had had cause to be thankful for her slight frame and wiry build, accentuated now by the recent weeks of very poor subsistence.

Taking stock of her surroundings, Leckie tried to orientate herself in this new city. She could just make out the top of the cathedral, and she spotted what she thought surely must be a section of the city wall to her right. She knew now where the shopping streets would lie and where she could lose herself in the anonymity of the crowds.

Later that day, after cleaning herself up as much as she could in the women's lavatories on her way to the city centre, swabbing the many scratches and abrasions she had amassed while evading capture with wads of damp tissue, she had achieved a superficial respectability and was able to mingle unnoticed with the shoppers on Eastgate. She managed to snatch a couple of bread rolls from the display in front of an artisan bakers and had eaten these in the privacy of another toilet block, washing them down with water drunk from her cupped hands. Refreshed and calmer now after her narrow escape, she had made her way back to the rear of the hardware shop where she had stowed her belongings.

Time, she thought, to put plan B into operation.

CHAPTER 15

Sandy

For once, the early tea time traffic was not too bad on the approach to Tower Street underpass. Sensing that the worst of the potential hold-ups were behind her, Sandy switched off the traffic alert on her car radio and hummed along to her favourite music. The irritations of the day fading from mind, she speculated upon her proposed sequence of activity once she arrived home. The flowers would have to go into water; goodness knows how long they had been left in that dry bucket in the supermarket. She had better cut the stems too. That should encourage them to perk up before Helen got home.

She would then kick off her shoes and make herself a mug of good strong coffee. She should even have time for a quick shower before starting their meal preparation. The salad wouldn't take long; she'd been careful to buy most of the ingredients ready-washed. But a couple of hard-boiled eggs would go well in there. Perhaps she should put them on to boil before having her shower.

The insistent notes of "The Laughing Policeman" interrupted her reverie. It was a ringtone that she knew annoyed her colleagues. "Bloody unprofessional" Shorty had called it. Even on his better days, he never saw any reason to humour his much smaller, dumpy young colleague. He effectively looked down on her in more ways than one, reflected Sandy. How she would enjoy pulling off some sort of success which would lead to her acclaim and even possibly to his discomfort. Not naturally a vindictive person, she put this uncharitable thought aside and dwelt instead upon what sort of success she could ever hope to achieve. There was precious little chance of her really being successful, she conceded to herself—not while she had to deal with all the usual shitty stuff. "Mere domestics,"Shorty had said, scornfully describing the incidents which comprised so much of Sandy's working life.

Hoping that it was not Helen trying to contact her, Sandy resisted the urge to look at her phone, over the years having stolidly refused to contemplate the convenience of a hands-free set. Too bloody convenient by half, she had decided. She'd be forever at their beck and call. Wouldn't do to be seen using a mobile while driving, she thought. Word would surely get back to her superiors at the station and land her in more trouble. Not much of a bloody example anyway, she told herself, and turned up the volume of the music being played. It was a compilation of her favourite bands: grunge and heavy metal. Helen had downloaded the music for her, an act of generosity on her behalf as she did not really appreciate either genre, preferring popular classical music and the theme tunes from romantic films.

It was beginning to seem to Sandy that her hopes of getting home well before Helen had been misplaced. Far from the traffic problems being well behind her now, for some inexplicable reason, everything appeared to be slowing down. Drumming her fingers on the steering wheel, Sandy cursed the unexpected delay. The traffic had slowed to a crawl, and she could not see beyond the No.11 bus directly in front of her to judge whether there was any chance of turning off the main road and finding an alternative route home.

CHAPTER 16

Abigail

She had felt as though she were waking from a dream—a bad dream. Everything before seemed fuzzy and blurred. She really had no concept of how long she had been here. Her dream had been interrupted from time to time by Steve, his face somehow distorted and alien to her, bending over her. He had kissed her, she thought, and maybe rubbed her back, but that bit of the dream was more fuzzy than the rest.

They had kept her in bed, pulling the curtains round so that she wasn't able to see much at first, not until she put a chair on her bed and stood on it, stretching up, managing to undo a couple of the hooks securing the corner of the curtain to the overhead rail. That became her peephole, her own little window onto the ward. She kept the curtains pulled tight across the gap when the staff were around, but she could time it so much better now. They came in at regular intervals to give her food or medicine. She supposed that she must have been ill for them to do that—or for her to be here at all. Then there were other predictable times when they would come in and take her temperature and blood pressure, check her pulse, and ask the usual inane questions: Had she been to the toilet? Was she having any difficulties weeing or pooing? How infantile was that? They would press her tummy, and sometimes look at her breasts, asking about any discharge. What an intolerable invasion of privacy that all seemed now. Every two hours some member of staff, never the same one too often, would poke his or her head round the curtain and ask if she was OK, just checking that she was still there, she supposed. Well, they won't be doing that for much longer, that's for sure.

She no longer felt fuzzy and confused. Over the last couple of days she had begun to understand a lot. It was all a ploy—Steve's doing, no doubt. He really didn't want her to come home. She didn't think he even liked her any more. Perhaps all he had ever wanted was the child. Well, that had been a disappointment too. He had had his heart set on a son; she felt sure of it. She hadn't wanted them to be told at the scan. She did not want to have to face him if it was a girl. But it was, of course. The baby they kept bringing to her, that she hadn't even wanted at first because she knew it meant disappointment, was a girl. A daughter. Her daughter. Well, he had not got his precious son, and he was not going to get his hands on her daughter, either. She'd see to that. She would run away and hide both of them from him. She knew she could manage. She had money and, worst-case scenario, could always make her peace with her family, who'd only fallen out with her because of him. She could take Geraldine there.

The staff did not know that she had been watching them for days. As the fog in her mind cleared, she had kept almost constant watch through her curtained peephole, drawing the edges of the curtain together when any of them approached. She was always found sitting quietly on her bed whenever they came in to attend to her. During those first fuzzy days, they had brought the baby to her then taken it away again as though they thought she might even harm it. She hadn't ever wanted to do that; it was just that at first she did not really remember having a baby and couldn't be sure it was hers. Through her spyhole on to the main ward, she saw that the other mothers kept their babies by them in plastic cots on wheels, so she had asked to have Geraldine's cot by her bed. Smiling to herself now, she remembered how pleased the midwife had been. "Really bonding with her now, aren't you, love?"

Still she watched, seeing the staff buzzing visitors into the ward and out again, and how this was achieved. There was a console of some sort by the door and another on their workstation with a little screen showing who was waiting to be allowed through. Either console would do it; all that was needed was one of the pass cards used by the staff. They all seemed to wear them on a sort of lanyard round their necks or fastened to the pockets of their uniforms. Abigail just had to work out how to get one.

Then, providentially, the morning's drama had erupted: a man shouting and hammering on the main door, and the midwives commandeering an empty trolley being returned to the ward by a porter, grabbing him too, and all of them racing for the exit, a tangle of bodies, members of staff jostling to maintain their footing, and for a second, the door left tantalisingly ajar. It was then that she saw it. No doubt it had been ripped off in the upheaval. It was lying on the floor with the broken lanyard still attached. She had approached stealthily, fearful, lest watchful eyes were upon her. There was no one around. Half the staff were on their way to the car park, and the remaining midwives were busy elsewhere on the ward. Aware of the security camera over the door, but not knowing the extent of its range, Abigail had covered the pass card with her foot and, gazing straight at the winking lens, nonchalantly kicked the card into the corner, alongside the medical gas cylinders. Quickly reaching down, she surreptitiously picked it up, putting it in her dressing gown pocket, and returned calmly to her bed. For once the curtains around her bed remained firmly drawn. The staff had instigated this, they said, to protect her from the curiosity of her neighbours, among whom speculation was rife over this long-stay patient in a ward where twenty-four-hour discharges were the norm. Today, she told herself, it was going to protect her from much more than idle gossip.

CHAPTER 17

Ben

Ben could hardly believe his ears. Guiding their narrowboat out of the lock, he had lost sight of Karen. The lock gate remained open, and for a terrifying moment Ben had visions of Karen lying down there in the lock. Perhaps she had fallen and knocked herself unconscious on the unforgiving brickwork of the lock walls, before plunging to her death in the murky water. Perhaps her depression was even more profound than he had realised and she had not actually fallen but had deliberately jumped in, waiting for him to be moving the boat out of the lock so that he would not see her making this last, final attempt upon her life.

And then he heard it—heard Karen. But it was not like the Karen he had grown used to over the last sad few months. It was a Karen, it seemed to him, of aeons ago—Karen in a happier life, Karen as he had first known her and fallen in love with her.

"Ben! ...Ben!" The elated shout rang out across the early evening stillness of the water. "Ben! Ben, look what I have found!"

CHAPTER 18

Abigail

At first she was elated to have got away so easily. She had waited her moment, meticulously planning her escape. When they distributed the bottles to the nonbreastfeeding mothers after lunch, she had made sure that Geraldine took a good feed, burping her as she had been shown how to do and stroking her cheeks gently to encourage the flagging baby to continue sucking and not to fall asleep. Quietly amused to have noticed the midwife's delight in seeing this overt display of bonding with the child, she wondered if she could somehow play on this and think up a convincing story to get the midwife to bring them an additional bottle, one Abigail could stow away for their planned journey. Deciding against this as too much of a gamble, and seeing as the baby was clearly replete and any such request could only attract unwanted attention, Abigail determined that as soon as she was far enough away from the hospital to avoid suspicion, she would embark upon a shopping spree for them both. She would equip the baby with everything she needed and buy herself a few changes of clothing.

Once she was sure that the staff were busy preparing for the lunchtime shift handover, and before there was any chance of Steve coming in to visit, Abigail hurriedly pulled on her outer clothing, and gently lifted the sleeping baby, placing her in the empty leather holdall, thinking that she would zip it up just before leaving the ward where she hoped to be able to mingle with the people on the corridor outside. It was bound to be busy at this time of day with the shift changeover and early afternoon visitors. As she watched from her spyhole between the curtains, the assembled midwives moved away from their workstation, the sister in charge pushing the trolley of medical notes to the first bed, where she took the mother's record charts from the locker top and began the handover.

Abigail made her move. Judging that the distance from the console on the workstation to the exit door was too great to negotiate without being seen once the buzzer sounded, she moved furtively towards the doorway and inserted the pass card. Remembering the surveillance camera situated above the door, she kept her head well down and hoped that no one on the ward had registered her departure yet. A small gaggle of chattering medical students were making their way along the corridor towards the exit sign. She fell in unnoticed immediately behind them, dropping the pass card as she went.

It was that easy. Once out on the main street, Abigail paused in a shop doorway just long enough to undo the zip on her holdall and check on the sleeping baby. All appeared to be well; amazingly, Geraldine was still asleep. But Abigail was aware of the bag's seeming to become heavier with every step she took. Blaming the days of enforced inactivity or else all those drugs they had insisted on giving her, she knew that she could not hope to go much further on foot. What was she to do?

She had money for a taxi, but she had avoided those parked and waiting outside the hospital, thinking that the drivers would be amongst the first people to be questioned once her absence had been detected, so now, of course, there wasn't a single one in sight. She couldn't call one either. She had no mobile phone. They—Or was it Steve? she wondered—had taken hers away from her, muttering something about a suicide watch, whatever that meant. The memory of that whole episode was indistinct, but she had known then that they were all in this together. It was a conspiracy. The midwives, the doctors, and Steve were plotting against her.

Glancing up and down the road, she realised that it was futile to expect a taxi just to materialise when she wanted one. Setting the bag down on the pavement, she checked the baby again, pulling up the little muslin sheet she had brought from the ward to shield her face, and gave a weary sob. All her careful planning had come to nothing. The conspirators would win.

It was then that she saw it. A large white van with some sort of green logo on the side was slowing down, actually stopping beside her. The kindly driver had been sent to help her, she felt sure of that. Forgetting her aching limbs, she climbed in alongside him with alacrity. What a true gentleman he was, going round to her side of the van and lifting her holdall in for her. "You've a lot of luggage in there, young lady," he said, placing it by her feet in the footwell.

CHAPTER 19

The Woman on the Bus

She was thankful to get off the bus tonight. It had not been a particularly good day for her. She had arrived late at Howel and Howardson's, the solicitors' office where she worked as a clerical assistant. Although she had prearranged this with Carol, a solicitor in the family division, she was even later than expected. Her early morning appointment at the hospital antenatal clinic had not run to time. She had had few problems so far with her pregnancy, apart from morning sickness in the first few weeks. This time it was her turn to ponder the inaccuracy of a phrase. *Morning* sickness indeed: it lasted all day, every day, or so it seemed to her then. It was because of this that her midwife had referred her to the hospital, hyperemesis gravidarum appearing for the first time in her patient-held record book.

That was all behind her now. Apart from aching legs by the end of the day and the need to augment her wardrobe with some less tightly fitting items, she was progressing through the pregnancy without any difficulties. But once a hospital referral had been made, that was where any ensuing care would occur. This caused her little concern. As this would be her first child, she had no preconceived ideas of what to expect, and both she and her husband agreed that a hospital delivery sounded reassuringly safe.

If only everyone were as easily persuaded as they had been. This morning's delay at the clinic was the result of the previous patient's resisting advice and arguing first with the midwife and then with the doctor, insisting on her right to a home birth despite all the medical contraindications implicated in her previous obstetric history.

Conscious that her predicted arrival time at the solicitors' office was by now completely unattainable, and not wishing to compound the delay, the woman had avoided the walk into Chester city centre and taken a taxi. Once she got there, her day was unusually stressful as she struggled to catch up on the early morning work, which by now had begun to stack up on her desk. Carol had already left for court, and Tom, one of the senior partners in the firm, had seized the opportunity to offload some of his more routine work onto her, as he was indoctrinating yet another new secretary into the ways of the firm and the particular demands of his department. (I must stop thinking of it like that. Tom was inducting the new trainee, not indoctrinating her!)

By the end of the day, she was unusually late to leave, missing her customary bus home. For the first time since joining Howel and Howardson's, she wondered if her decision to eschew car travel, with the attendant hassle of early morning traffic and the near impossibility of parking anywhere near to the office, had been a wise one. Although the bus route could hardly have been more convenient, passing her door and with the terminus so close to Howel and Howardson's, there were evenings when the bus was so crowded with shoppers leaving the city that she had to stand most of the way—hardly ideal when her legs were already aching. Forty minutes between services was a long time to wait, although a hot chocolate with all the trimmings usually helped.

Not tonight though. She had begun to feel uneasy back in the café. She felt vaguely unsettled, aware of someone's eyes on her. Initially she dismissed this as the product of a tiring day and an overactive imagination. But then she felt it again. There was someone on the bus, she felt sure of it—someone watching her. She was very relieved when no one else had got off the bus with her, but even so, and though her home was only about two hundred yards from the bus stop, along a well-lit road, she was unable to resist the urge to keep looking over her shoulder, glancing round, suspecting that she might have been followed. Fumbling in her bag for her house key, with trembling fingers trying and at first failing to insert the key into the lock, mentally she cursed Alex's reluctance to cut down the spreading myrtle bush outside their front door. Someone could easily hide there, she thought. If he would not dig it up and remove it completely, then some very drastic pruning would have to be on their weekend agenda.

CHAPTER 20

Karen and Ben

"I shall call her Cari. Cari Moses," said Karen ecstatically, cradling the baby in her arms. She had taken off the T-shirt she was wearing and wrapped the little one in it, hoping that it retained something of her own bodily warmth. On top of this she had wrapped a soft cashmere sweater, leaving only the baby's face and hands showing. Gently now, she massaged the tiny fingers, marvelling in their dainty perfection, relieved to see them beginning to lose the bluish tinge as she gradually warmed them.

"You can't. Really, you can't, Karen. We can't keep her here. We have to report finding her. You never really should have brought her on board. We should have left her where you found her and called the police."

Karen's eyes were sparkling, and her skin had a healthy pink glow. Weeks of weariness and the tired grey rings under her haunted eyes seemed to have vanished in an instant. Lightness and vibrancy radiated from her, and in that moment, Ben had never loved her more. But still her decision to bring the child onto the boat worried him, as he sensed a new and powerful intensity in her rebuttal.

"No way, Ben. You know how we struggle for a mobile signal on the canals. We might have waited hours to send a message. She could have died in that time, Ben. She's so very little. And she was already so cold. It was meant to be, Ben. We were meant to find her—to save her."

"Well, we must send a message just as soon as we *can* get a signal," said Ben. "We really have to keep on trying. We can't keep her here, Karen. You know that. It's wrong. She must belong to somebody. We can't keep her."

Ben was tired. Following Karen's find, he had been left to secure the boat alongside the towpath and to walk back to close the lock gate he had just come through. Meanwhile, she had disappeared below deck, protectively cuddling the child, and had stayed down there ever since. In this way, they motored on as dusk was falling, and again it was left to him to find a suitable place to moor and secure their boat for the night. He had hoped they would reach civilisation by nightfall, and then this whole episode could be brought to a close. Help would be summoned. No doubt officialdom in some form would be involved and statements taken, but the baby would be removed from their care and responsibility while the authorities sought to identify her and locate her mother.

That had not happened. Here they were, moored alongside a deserted towpath, somewhere in the middle of …Ben wasn't even sure whether they were in Shropshire here or had crossed the border into Wales. Not that it mattered. There was no sign of any other human life around, no welcoming sight of cottages, their windows lit against the darkening sky; no roads with the jewelled ribbons of headlights from the commuters' cars, returning home at the end of the working day; not even a country lane or the odd agricultural vehicle—and certainly no street lights that he could see. There was no other boat in view either. None had passed them all day. And still no mobile signal.

He was struggling now, under Karen's watchful eye, trying to coax the Morsø Squirrel stove to life, hoping the kindling would catch soon and he could add the coal and close its little glass window for the evening. Then the warmth would quickly circulate around the interior of the boat and they could discard their heavy outdoor clothing, make a meal of some sort, and figure out what to do next.

At his suggestion that he might leave Karen here with the baby while he set out with the torch to walk as far along the towpath as was necessary before finding a canal-side village where he could enlist help, Karen had been furious. "You're not to leave me, Ben. We're in this together. I don't want you going off half-cocked and getting the police and everyone involved tonight, snatching her away from us. She's settling now, see? Let me keep her tonight and look after her. That way I'll know she's all right. Please, Ben, look at her. It's got to be for the best."

CHAPTER 21

Sandy

The traffic was beginning to move again. Not forward though. One by one, the waiting cars and vans began to shunt slowly backwards and forwards, their drivers moving them hard over against the kerb or even, in the case of the larger vehicles, up onto the pavement. Sirens had sounded, distant at first, but growing louder as the shunting traffic made way for a convoy of police cars and ambulances. Must have been an accident, Sandy thought. I wonder if that's why someone tried to get hold of me? Scrolling through her call log, she discovered that both the previous calls were from the station. Both had been some time ago, so it seemed unlikely that they had anything to do with the current incident. No messages had been left: common practice, as it was seldom wise to broadcast any police business over the airwaves.

Better text Helen and let her know I could be late, thought Sandy. Pity it has to be tonight of all nights.

Sandy knew that whatever had occurred, she could hardly improve things by abandoning her car and going to help. That would only complicate things if they managed to get the traffic moving again, only for it all to grind to a halt because of her. If they needed her, they had her number, and whatever it was, if, as she suspected, it had been a serious accident, she would surely get the inevitable outfall to contend with in the morning.

CHAPTER 22

Abigail

The man had seemed so kind at first, asking her name and, once she'd answered with "Cassandra", saying how pretty it was. She hadn't told him her real name, of course, just in case the people involved in the plot against her found out about her Good Samaritan and questioned him about her. She was adept at thinking on her feet—you have to be when people are plotting against you. Cassandra. It was the name of her best friend at school.

She did not know where she really wanted to go, but her quick wits again provided her with an answer: Oswestry. Not that she knew anything about it, but surely it would be easier to remain anonymous in a place where she knew no one and no one knew her, she reasoned. She would find somewhere quiet, hide her tracks, and stay for a while until the hunt she felt sure they were planning had died down.

He had looked at her strangely then, she thought. "Oswestry it shall be then, love." Except, she wasn't his love, was she? Suddenly she didn't think he even liked her anymore.

"You been up at the hospital, then? This your first?" he asked. It confused her. How had he known about Geraldine? She hadn't made a sound. Had he guessed what was in her bag when he lifted it into the van? Perhaps the muslin had blown away from the baby's face. Perhaps the zip had been too far undone. She had left it like that so that the baby could get some air. She didn't want Geraldine to suffocate. There wasn't time to do it up more tightly before she had accepted his lift. He must have seen her then. But perhaps he hadn't realised that it was a baby in there. He might have thought it was a doll. In that case, she had better make sure that he did not find out. Crouching over the bag, she began to zip it up.

It was then that it all went wrong—horribly wrong. Disturbed by the sound of the zip, the child began to whimper. Simultaneously, the man driving the van braked hard, swinging the vehicle round in a half turn and leaving the main road. "What is it? Where are we going?" she shrieked, scared now. He had to be part of the plot after all—one of them. How could she have been so stupid?

"Well, we're not going to bloody Oswestry, that's for sure," he barked back at her. "That's a bloody baby you've got in there, isn't it? Thought you'd trick me. Well, we'll see about that!"

"Please, please." She was pleading, knowing how pathetic she must sound. "Please, just let me get out. I'll pay you. We'll not trouble you any more."

"I won't and you won't. ...*I* won't let you out, and *you* are certainly not going to tell anyone."

She had sat there quietly then as the van bumped down the unmade road. Geraldine's howls were becoming louder and more insistent, but Abigail did not dare to stoop down and comfort the child. Surely he must be stopping now, she thought. The van was slowing down, imperceptibly at first, and Abigail began to hope that this was where he was going to let them out. True enough, the van was braking now, and then the man was leaping out of the driver's seat and coming round to the passenger's door, swinging it open. He was going to set them free.

Abigail's relief lasted only a moment. Pulling an elasticated bungee cord from the parcel shelf, the man dragged her from her seat and swiftly fastened her hands behind her back. She tried to fight back, to kick out at him, but to no avail. He had the back doors of the van open and was unceremoniously bundling her in.

"My baby, my baby." Abigail was distraught now, clawing at the air behind her back with her tethered hands.

"Don't worry, you'll have your bloody baby," he sneered. "You don't think I want the squawking brat, do you?" Flinging the holdall in after her, he slammed the doors shut. Soon she felt the van lurch to life as he reversed over the rocky ground. Abigail tried desperately to undo her wrists but could get no purchase whatsoever on the springy elastic as she struggled to raise herself from the floor of the van where she had fallen, sprawling face down as he had pushed her in. Tottering, unable to stand, she braced herself against the movement of the vehicle and was able to crawl over to where her bag lay. It had fallen over onto its side. She had to wriggle it upright using just her feet, making repeatedly futile attempts to fully undo the zip with her teeth and get the muslin cloth off the baby's face, hoping to be able to soothe its anguished cries. Failing to achieve anything with this approach, she sank down, exhausted, beside the bag and rocked it to and fro with her legs.

Thankfully, the child's howls began to recede, mellowing to a pitiful hiccoughing sob. Abigail was able to take stock of their situation. She studied their prison. It was quite dark inside, but gradually her eyes had become accustomed to the gloom. One entire side of the van was packed with boxes. "Vermaid", she read. She felt she knew that name from somewhere. And then the realisation dawned: she had seen it on boxes around the hospital. She looked at the rest of the cargo, more boxes and crates of packages, making out whatever words she could: sterile dressing packs, syringes, Hollister clips, delivery packs. She'd seen all those things in the hospital. Well, that confirmed it: this was all part of the plot.

She would have to be as devious as them if she was ever going to escape their clutches.

CHAPTER 23

Abigail

The van was moving more slowly now. Abigail could detect a change in the noise of the engine. Fear had heightened her senses, and she was feeling things more acutely. She had become aware of a different sensation as the van had once again left the smooth road. They must have travelled along that road for some way, she concluded: the traffic noise from outside the van had become more distinct. Or was it because she was more highly tuned to it now? Car horns, the rumble of heavy lorries as they passed— was she hearing them, she wondered, or merely sensing the additional vibrations rocking the van from side to side a little? Not only had she been hearing the disparate, disembodied sounds emanating from other vehicles on the road so much more clearly, but also she had sensed a steady increase in volume, barely noticeable at first, then gradually building. Could this be the beginning of the evening rush hour? She had lost all sense of time. With her wrists tightly bound behind her back, she had no way of seeing her watch. She had no mobile either, to give her both an instant time display and perhaps some possibility of summoning help.

But even if she had had her phone and the freedom of her hands to use it, Abigail knew that calling for help was not an option. There was no one to call. They were all in the plot against her. She even doubted her parents' neutrality, if she were to fling herself upon their mercy. If in that moment of recapitulation all her previous misdemeanours were forgiven, how could she be sure that they too were not complicit in the conspiracy?

Yes, they had definitely moved out of the heavy traffic now. The movement of the van was far less smooth. Abigail did not think that they were back on a farm track though, because that was a much rougher ride. This was bumpy at times and far from comfortable, but the main difficulty Abigail experienced was in maintaining her balance and keeping the bag with Geraldine in it from tipping onto its side again as the van swerved round bend after bend. Some godawful country lane, she surmised. Where was he taking her?

Curtailing any further speculation, the van abruptly shuddered to a standstill. She heard the driver's door being opened, and just as abruptly, the rear doors were flung apart. Blinking against the late afternoon sunlight, Abigail was briefly aware of the dark figure standing there. Shuffling on her bottom to the farthest recesses of the van proved so ineffective that she sobbed. All she had achieved was to have put herself farther away from the bag with her baby in it.

The man was inside the van with them now, dragging Abigail towards the door. "Please, please," she implored, "don't do this." The remainder of her impassioned entreaty was silenced by a blow across the mouth from the man's fist. She was choking, swallowing blood now, staggering, almost falling, but then the man was behind her. She could feel his hands on her wrist restraints. The sudden hope that she might be going to be set free, that she had had her punishment now, died almost the same instant it arisen. He was not undoing her bonds; he was using them to strengthen his grip and push her alongside the van. She was dimly aware that they were somewhere near water. She could hear it, and mingled with the sound of the water was another, more insistent sound, one that tore through her heart: the baby, Geraldine, crying.

He had heard it too. Releasing his hold on her wrists, he faced her now. "Bloody brat." Hatefully, vehemently, he almost spat out the words.

"Please, I can calm her. I can stop her crying if it upsets you. Just bring her to me."

"Oh, I'll bring her, all right." With that, he struck Abigail forcefully across the face. With her arms secured behind her back, she was unable to save herself. She stumbled and fell, hitting her head on the stony ground. Her last conscious awareness was of the retreating figure of the man striding back towards the van and of the pitiful sobbing of her little daughter.

CHAPTER 24

Pam

Pam unlocked the front door, thankful that tonight she was home before Ted. The boys, still in bed when she left for work this morning, had, as usual, forgotten to set the burglar alarm. State of the art, it was. Ted's insistence. It would automatically notify the police station in the event of a break-in, or alert the fire service if the linked smoke detector was activated, and it even had a neck-worn push-button alarm anyone old or infirm could carry in the house which would summon medical assistance in the event of a fall or other accident. Not that they had used it yet, of course, but Pam had thought at the time the system was installed that it could prove very useful if either of their elderly parents came to stay.

They really didn't have much time for visitors these days, though, she reflected. But perhaps her father might like to stay for a few days in the spring. A retired university lecturer, her father was a source of anxiety for Pam. Widowed six years previously and living alone, he had developed what she thought were early signs of dementia. Furiously independent, he had opposed any suggestion of domestic help and refused to recognise the need for medical intervention. He had not been to the doctor for years, and he fully intended to keep it that way.

Pam, knowing that Ted would be angry that the boys were failing to set the alarm which protected their property, resolved to have a quiet word with them about it before their father came home. She hoped they would be back before he was, realising, not for the first time, that at that precise moment, she had no idea where they were. Letting them find their independence was part of her mantra as they were growing up. Now she was not so sure that it had turned out to be an entirely good thing. What if they were getting into trouble somewhere, involved with the wrong sort of people? She had seen enough documentaries to know something about teenage boys and gangs, rites of passage, exploitation, and the seductive powers of gaming machines, pornography, and even violence. Surely she would know if either of her sons had got themselves caught up in any of that. But what parent really knows what their children are capable of?

Mentally shaking off such depressing thoughts, Pam consoled herself that her boys had never really been in any trouble. They were untidy, careless, and forgetful, but surely that was because they were teenagers. Putting aside any gloomier premonitions, she went through into the kitchen to make herself a cup of tea. "Untidy, careless, and forgetful," she repeated to herself—well, that just about summed it up—as she scooped up an armful of dirty sports kit discarded in their morning scramble for the school bus, then gathered up their cereal bowls and half-eaten toast.

"God, I need a cigarette." She was trying, and for the most part succeeding, in kicking the habit, but every so often she weakened and reached for the packet of filter tips hidden behind the bread bin on the counter. Ted didn't know that she still smoked. At least she didn't think he knew. He had always hated it—another of her "unpleasant smells" he had carped on about over the years. Well, sod him, she thought. He had no idea of the sort of bad day she had had, and anyway, he had nothing to be quite so shirty about. His criticism of her smoking and his assertion that, as a health worker, she should know better riled her. Of course she knew the health implications of her habit, just as she knew the dangers implicit in his bouts of heavy drinking. That they both elected to ignore these was their own choice alone. They had both made a conscious decision to ignore the repeated warnings on packet and bottle alike. It was a mature choice; they would live with the consequences.

Nevertheless, she would smoke this one outside. That way Ted would have nothing to nag her about—no lingering smell in the kitchen— although he was unlikely to kiss her these days. Going to the door that led from their kitchen to the patio and garden beyond, she was annoyed to find it unlocked. She was going to have to come down hard on the boys over that one. Really, this day was going from bad to worse.

CHAPTER 25

Helen

Arriving home from work before her partner, Helen fished out the anniversary card she had bought for Sandy earlier that day. It was a comic one, rather than the romantic ones that she herself would prefer, bound to put a smile on Sandy's face. She had read Sandy's text and wondered now what she should do in the way of meal preparation for them both. Helen did not usually do much of the cooking. That was Sandy's province. She said it was a perfect wind-down from work, and she was very good at it, Helen had to concede.

She opened the fridge but could find nothing in there beyond a tray of eggs and some rather tired vegetables, and only a little fresh fruit in the bowl. I could rustle up a couple of omelettes, she supposed, but without knowing what time Sandy would be back, there seemed little point in starting them now. Taking off her shoes and pouring herself a glass of orange juice, Helen flopped onto the large, comfortable settee in front of the television. She had missed the national news at six o'clock, but the local programme was on. There was no mention of the accident that had delayed Sandy—too recent, she presumed. Finding little of interest in the report from a food and farming exhibition, Helen turned off the set and opened the paper.

"Is This the Work of a Serial Killer?" clamoured the headline above a brief account of two bodies discovered recently in the Wolverhampton area. Both were of young women, and the sites where they had been found were similar in topography. There was a clear hint that more was known than had been shared with the press so far. An assumption was being made that the modus operandi was disturbingly similar in each case, but again, no details were given. The victims were not being named either, not until their relevant next of kin had been informed. The item concluded with a plea to the general public to exercise caution and to bring any salient information they had to the attention of the police.

It was all a bit vague. With so little to go on, how would one know what was relevant? pondered Helen, before dismissing the article from her mind and turning to the horoscope page. A fervent believer in the veracity of such predictions, much to Sandy's amusement, Helen sought these out on a daily basis, constantly asserting the accuracy of anything they had foretold. Today hers was prophesying a cooling in an important relationship, but fewer concerns over her financial affairs. Hearing Sandy's key in the lock, and not liking the portent of the first part of what she had just read, Helen put the paper to one side and greeted her partner with a great deal of warmth and not a little trepidation.

CHAPTER 26

Leckie

Huddled in the rear shop doorway, her sleeping bag wrapped round her shoulders like a shawl, Leckie had been reliving the events of the day. Having discarded her ill-fated plan A, health centres and day nurseries having proved impenetrable, she had worked hard to come up with an alternative. Then there had been the realisation of what she saw as a viable project. It involved the local hospital, more specifically, the maternity unit at the hospital.

She had spent three days rehearsing this in her mind and visiting the unit. During the hours of daylight, access to the main hospital was unchecked, with a constant flow of support staff, doctors, nurses, clinic attendees, and patients, their friends, and relatives moving about the corridors to the various wards and departments. Leckie had watched people come and go, and knew the procedure well. Posing as a visitor, waiting for her friend to come back down from the special care baby unit, she had lingered in the corridor outside the maternity unit, by the door to the labour and perinatal wards, and scrutinised the scene. She knew now that access would only be gained either by hospital personnel using their pass cards or by members of the wider general public who had to buzz the unit from a console by the door. The latter, having had their identity confirmed as genuine visitors to the wards, usually by providing the name and their relationship to a given patient, would be buzzed in by a member of staff on duty. Leckie had moved close enough to hear a patient's name being given by an excited young man accompanying an older woman—probably his mother, she thought. She had committed this to memory, determining to use it herself to gain access to the ward and, more importantly, to the babies there. She knew from the overheard conversations among visitors waiting to be allowed in that most of these babies would be in cots by their mothers' beds. That might be difficult, she had thought, but surely these new mothers would not be with their babies the whole time. They would have to use the bathroom or go for a shower to make themselves presentable for their visitors, and that could provide her with the opportunity she required. It could give her a few precious moments in which to act.

It might be difficult though, keeping out of sight—and possibly being recognised as someone without a legitimate reason for being there—until such a moment presented itself. What if she was caught, ostensibly waiting to visit a patient she had never seen before in her life? Faced with confrontation, Leckie knew she would not stand a chance. The patient would certainly deny all knowledge of her—and what excuse could Leckie possibly offer?

Then the breakthrough for which she had been hoping came. Outside the unit, two earnest women, grandmothers it seemed, were discussing the babies they hoped to see on this visit. It transpired that these were two infants who had had initial problems, one being small for dates (although its presumed grandmother was somewhat scathing about the midwives' inability to judge the accuracy of these dates correctly). The baby had been assessed as requiring monitoring but was not ill enough to need the full care of SCBU. The other baby, as far as Leckie could gather from the whispered exchange, belonged to a young woman who was ill herself. Leckie, fearful of being observed, had been unable to get any closer and make out the details, but she guessed from their reactions that the mother had some sort of psychological problem being given little credence by these older women, their attitudes redolent of an earlier age and a more critical approach to what they saw as pandering.

But the exchange had provided Leckie with all the information she craved. It was learning that these babies, and possibly others like them, were in a small nursery off the main ward, where, if she was really lucky, Leckie might find them temporarily unattended, that had given her the first real feeling of optimism about her plan. Fortune certainly seemed to be favouring her for once in her life. The second piece of luck was almost too good to be true. Lurking in the corridor, eavesdropping on the grandmothers' conversation, and keeping her head well down lest anyone should spot her there, Leckie chanced upon the one find which would grant her access. Unlimited access, she thought. If I don't carry it off this afternoon, I'll just lie doggo for a few days and then have another go.

Exhilarated by the presentiment of success, Leckie continued to watch as one of the grandmothers pressed the buzzer and the two were admitted. She'd give them a few minutes, she thought, hoping that they would have seen the babies and gone into the main part of the ward to visit the respective mothers by the time she chose to make her move. Fingering the treasure she now had in her pocket, Leckie moved farther along the corridor to a spot where she could maintain her inconspicuous observation, waiting for the moment to act.

Waiting was something that she had become extremely good at. God knows, she had had enough practice in her life. All those years waiting, wanting the unspeakable things to stop. She recalled waiting, listening for her father's return. Would he be on his own, or would any of those other awful men be with him? She thought of her waiting, listening, as the inevitable sounds of his bullying tirade against her mother began. Her mother would be tearful, wheedling, crying that she *had* meant to clean up, she *had* really tried, and he, he would spit out the hated words: "Whore. Dirty slut." Leckie would know then that he had come home alone, and she knew what would happen next. She was just waiting for the horrible things to start.

There were other times of waiting, listening, times when she knew that her father was not alone. There would be no shouting at her mother. Downstairs, there would be the sound of other voices. Dimly recalling the scene now, Leckie wondered if there had been women's voices too. She only remembered the men, hearing them, and waiting for her father to bring them up to her for "playtime" to begin.

The years of waiting hadn't ended there. There were years of foster care, with her always waiting, hoping, that this time the foster family would be a good one, that this time it would work out and she could stay. She had never been good enough, it seemed. She had even failed foster care.

Then came the waiting on the streets, waiting for a stranger's little act of kindness and a coin in her upturned baseball cap, or a cup of tea fetched for her from the nearby coffee bar, the self-conscious commuter assuaging any guilt she might have felt at her own good fortune and the evident plight of others. Hungry, waiting for food, Leckie would be dirty, grimy from the dust and wind blown detritus of the streets, waiting for a chance to get into the nearest public convenience to clean herself up.

She had waited for sleep during the long winter nights in London, shivering in the stained sleeping bag she had helped herself to, taking it from where it had been thrown over a garden seat belonging to one of the better houses—a sleeping bag to keep a wooden seat clean, a sleeping bag to stop her from developing hypothermia!

And there were even worse ways of waiting. Desperate for cash just to stay alive, Lexie recalled waiting on street corners, swallowing both her bitter disgust and any remnants of pride, willing her reluctant body to make itself available to the anonymous groping and joyless sex with a succession of shabby punters. She hadn't been much good at that, either, she thought, having been caught soliciting a few times, with all the attendant waiting that entailed in various police stations. She'd only evaded the threatened magistrates' court by dint of a speedy return to the streets, losing herself in the anonymity they afforded.

God, how she hated prostitution. She never wanted to do that again, with anyone. But if it was either that or starve, she thought after the first depressing weeks in this new city, then she would have to go through with it again. It would be a case of finding a spot not currently worked by the regulars, though. Career prostitutes, she thought of them as, with their own well-defined patches. They brooked no competition from newcomers intruding on their turf.

The front of the hardware shop gave her a good view of the likely contenders. After watching all night, she had decided that it was safe to operate there. She would wait under the street light. That would be a handy place from which to spot any trouble that was likely to occur. Trouble, in Leckie's book, in this context at least, was the police, any thugs bent on aggravation, or another sex worker exercising prior claim to the patch.

At night, the spot she'd chosen had the advantage of being a good place for a car to slow down, even stop. And should she be lucky, there was a vacant parking bay behind the shop where she could take a prospective client. She could leave her meagre belongings in their usual spot, in the rear doorway, and not be too worried that she would find they had disappeared on her return.

With reality seldom being as good as the anticipation, Leckie's first two nights had met with little success. A very drunk builder with cement dust all over his clothes had bunged her a few quid after trying, and failing, to get fully aroused. Not bad takings for a mucky fumble, she thought. At least it would buy her a decent breakfast or two.

But by night three, there was very little money left. Leckie had taken up her stance beneath the street light once again. The pickings were better this time. Two young men on a night out had found her to be an agreeable distraction. They generously plied her with gin and tonic in the local pub before returning to the back of the shop with her for a quickie apiece. She was about to call it a night, but as her luck seemed to be in, she had decided to give it another hour or so, resuming her position beneath the lamp.

It was a flash car, she had noted, as the driver pulled up alongside. Slightly dazzled by the car's interior light, and less cautious than she might have been normally, probably because of rather too much gin on an empty stomach, she had not thought twice about getting into the car and directing the driver to the parking bay at the rear of the ironmongers.

It was only when he had turned off the engine and looked at her that she realised who he was. Sleeker, smarter too, and with the smell of weed much less noticeable now, it was her father's old mate Martyn. The instant this recognition had dawned upon her, she made a futile attempt to escape, clawing desperately at the passenger door of the car before the locks snapped shut, enclosing her in that intimate space with a man who struck absolute terror into her heart. "Not changing your mind, are you, baby? I don't let anyone do that to me, understand." And so she had complied, wearily, mechanically going through with the charade. "Pleasure me, baby. Come on," he croaked, as he grasped her hair and pulled her face into his own, his malodorous breath making her want to retch and vomit. She could only hope that he had not recognised *her*. It was such a long time ago, and she was only a child then. So far away, too, in that shabby little house in Camden. With all the horrors that those recollections revived, Leckie felt all the fight go out of her. She subjected herself to everything he demanded from her. She could only pray that it would soon be over and that this horrible man had not made those same connections and would never seek her out again.

But he had recognised her, of course. "Arthur's lass, aren't you? All grown up and doing well for yourself, I see." He made this last remark with a cruel leer that made her recoil as far away from him as she could within the confines of the car. "Yer dad always said you was a whore."

It was in that moment that Leckie knew instinctively that she *would* see him again, that his hold over her had never gone away. It was no surprise when he tossed her out of the car like so much garbage, refusing to give her any money for what she had just done for him. "For old time's sake, darlin'—payment yer dad still owes me."

For the rest of the night, Leckie had huddled, sore and trembling, in her scruffy sleeping bag. As soon as the toilet block was open the next day, she retreated to one of the cubicles and stripped off her clothes, scouring her skin relentlessly with a pile of paper towels and antibacterial handscrub she had liberated from the handbasin.

CHAPTER 27

Sandy

Despite its inauspicious start, Sandy's evening was going well. Helen, always a considerate lover, seemed even more determined than ever to please her. It was Helen who had seen to the oven chips, sending Sandy upstairs to enjoy a leisurely shower. When Sandy came downstairs, Helen had prepared the salad, adding little touches of her own, the sort of niceties Sandy would never have thought her capable of. Not just the hard-boiled egg they usually included, but also she had raided their rather meagre supplies, adding a few grapes, some pieces of walnut, and delicate slices of orange. In her forage for food before her shift that morning, Sandy had completely overlooked the contents of the fruit bowl. Now that she and Helen were both trying to lose weight, she was remembering to stock this up more frequently. And the walnuts had to have been left over from last Christmas. It was a kind thought and a valiant attempt by her undomesticated partner.

As Sandy cooked their steaks, Helen put the carnations in water and laid the table. They had opened their cards to one another, laughing at the one Helen had chosen, and propped them against the flower vase while they ate. The meal was a success, especially the profiteroles, thought Helen, regarding them as an unexpected treat as she licked the last of the cream off her fingers. There was a time when they would have probably licked the cream from each other's fingers, a nostalgic memory better forgotten. The early passion of any new relationship surely must diminish a little with time.

Now, replete with food and mellow with wine, they relaxed contentedly together on the sofa. Helen could feel the tension draining from her and wondered why she had ever begun to doubt the sincerity of Sandy's feelings for her. They had a future together, she felt sure of that now. Perhaps Sandy had been right all along about not putting too much faith in horoscopes.

They had switched on the news before going to bed, thinking that they would just catch up with the headlines and then have an early night. There was still nothing about the RTA that evening, but Sandy, thinking it was still too recent to be reported, doubted it would make the national news anyway. It was likely to be in Friday's edition of the local rag, but she probably wouldn't have to wait for that. If it was anything serious, she would hear about it at work tomorrow and have to deal with it too, she suspected. Her hand was reaching out for the remote control, about to switch off the set, when there was a breaking news announcement. A third corpse had been discovered, in Tipton, on the outskirts of Wolverhampton. The cause of death was not given, but the body was reportedly found in "suspicious circumstances". The possibility of this being linked to the earlier killings was not being discounted.

The item jogged Helen's memory. She sought out the discarded evening paper to show to Sandy. "Thank God it's not on our patch" was her partner's immediate response. "We could do without that."

CHAPTER 28

Leckie

I very nearly pulled it off without a hitch. Leckie was still thinking about the events of that afternoon and how smoothly it had all happened. Everything had gone to plan. It had been unbelievably easy.

From her vantage point along the corridor, she had seen the grandmothers leave. The tidal wave of visitors had abated. There were very few coming in and out now, most of the early afternoon crowd having already left, hoping to get home before the evening rush hour, she supposed. There were fewer staff movements too, as though the hospital was preparing to close in upon itself for the night. Perhaps it's different in the summer, she thought. People don't really like the dark.

For the last five minutes, the only activity along the corridor was the trundling arrival of a huge stainless steel food trolley towed by what seemed to Leckie to be a sort of little tractor. The elderly porter driving this had dismounted, manoeuvred the trolley into position, and plugged it into a socket set in the wall by the door of the unit. What she would have given for a few moments alone with that. As the little tractor with its remaining cargo of food trolleys disappeared along the corridor, she hoped that the one near her would stay there long enough for her to investigate. She had begun to salivate in anticipation, not caring what contents it held, when the ward buzzer sounded, and a care assistant unplugged the trolley and hauled it through the double doors and into the ward.

All thoughts of the tempting contents vanished from Leckie's mind as she realised the significance of this for her plan. The staff would be busy serving the meals, and the patients would be distracted, eating them. The afternoon visitors had left, so there was likely to be no one in the nursery, only babies.

Deftly, Leckie inserted the pass card that she had found outside the ward, and slipped through the door. Bracing herself tightly against the wall in an effort to make herself as near to invisible as possible, she waited some anxious seconds for the buzzer to stop. No one challenged her. No one even seemed to have noticed. They were bustling about, dispensing medication, pulling bed curtains around those who needed them, pushing trolleys and what she took to be commode chairs, and giving out jugs of water. The food trolley was plugged in here too, and from the cover this provided, she was able to look around and try to get her bearings.

Where is the nursery? she wondered, hesitantly pushing ajar the nearest door. No joy there; it was a bathroom. At least it was unoccupied! Leckie was appalled to think what might have ensued had there been one of the new mothers in there, raising an alarm. The next two doors were equally unrewarding, opening respectively onto a small office, again mercifully unoccupied, and a large linen store. How much longer was her luck going to hold? Surely someone would spot her soon, and then there would be pandemonium, she surmised.

And then she heard it, a faint but unmistakable cry, followed by another, this time in a slightly different range, more of a whimper. Leckie's years on the streets had taught her to listen well. At various times during her precarious existence, her skill at listening had provided the earliest premonition of danger or chance of being caught. Her ears were keenly attuned, able not just to detect the smallest of sounds but also to judge the distance and direction from which they emanated. This time there was no mistake: the muffled cries were coming from a room to her right. Taking a deep breath, and with her heart pounding, she pushed open the door.

Her guess had been right: this was indeed the nursery. Her eyes swept the room: not an adult in sight, just two rows of little Perspex cots, the four lining the nearside wall apparently occupied. Two had blue cellular blankets, and two had pink. Denoting gender, Leckie assumed. What was she to do? Who would be easier to manage, a little girl or a little boy? Tiptoeing to the nearest cot, she studied the infant there. It was covered by a blue blanket, so this one must be a boy. That probably augured well. The only small child she had ever really known was her little brother, Gregory.

The youngest child was only a tiny baby when she had last seen it. All she could remember now was fetching a dummy for her. She had had to stop the crying; their father mustn't hear it.

This was no place for these memories. Time was running out. She had to make her decision—fast—and get out of here before she was caught.

It was in this instant that she realised that the first girl cot was empty. What at first sight she had assumed to be a sleeping infant was merely a bundle of bedding—a crumpled fitted sheet and a pink blanket. The other cot *was* occupied, the little girl sleeping peacefully, her tiny fist in her mouth. She seemed smaller, neater somehow, than either of the boys, and more securely wrapped in her blanket. The boy babies had kicked their covers off and were awake and restless. This baby girl seemed so much more content than the others. More to the point, she was not crying. Leckie's decision was made: she would take this one.

It was only then that the enormity of what she was proposing to do really hit her. She was going to take this baby straight from her warm bed out into the cold autumn evening. She was going to take her with her onto the streets. Leckie, who had no home to go to, no bed of her own, and no way of keeping herself warm at night, was proposing to catapult an innocent baby into her own sordid world. She had nothing to offer this child except privation and quite possibly death. She had no food to give her and nothing for her to wear. And while she knew that she could always go into Boots and steal some clothes and other effects, how could she possibly manage that with a child in her arms? She would have to steal a pushchair—and just how easy was that going to be? The little girl did not deserve any of this. God knows, Leckie could hardly look after herself. How could she have ever thought that she could care for a child?

But she hadn't, had she? Thought, that is. She had never thought beyond the first hurdle, getting a child. What is more, she realised, she had never really thought of that child as an individual in its own right. All a baby had ever been to her was a prop, a prop to sustain her crumbling lifestyle, something to attract the sympathy vote. As the tears began to course their way down Leckie's grimy cheeks and fall upon the baby's head, she bent and kissed the child. It was the first and only time in Leckie's life that she had ever given a kiss and meant it. It had happened so spontaneously that she stepped back from the cot aghast.

She had to get out of here before she was caught. Then she really would have failed again. The wonderful plan would have been a dream, nothing more. And the Leckies of this world were not entitled to dream.

It had all been so easy, but it could so easily have gone awfully, hideously wrong. Angry at herself now, not just for allowing herself to think of failing but also for the unexpected weakness she had shown in the face of failure, Leckie wanted to kick out at someone. It was the only way she knew to respond. The staff *were* careless, weren't they? Not just for dropping a pass card for anyone to pick up, but also for leaving these babies here on their own. Had no one told them what a rotten world this is? Well, she knew better than most that it was rotten. Rotten to the core.

Leckie felt that she should do something, anything, to shake them out of their complacency, to make them think. She, who had spent so much of her life feeling afraid, wanted them to feel fear too. Roused from what she saw as their comfortable middle-class existence and secure working lives, they had to be made to experience what it was like to be really afraid. She must make them fearful about what they had done, let them worry about the consequences, be afraid of losing *their* jobs.

She had to act quickly. She mustn't get caught. Cradling the little girl who had so nearly been hers, she put her in the empty cot. Creeping up to the adjacent cots, Leckie scooped up each infant in turn, putting them back in the wrong little beds, a boy in the cot where "*her*" little girl had been and the other boy in the vacated bed that was left. That should give the staff something to worry about, she thought. She hoped that someone would get into trouble. Surely they would realise that someone had been in the nursery and made the switch deliberately. That should make them afraid; they would be left wondering what else might have been tampered with—the medicines, the patients' food, the babies' bottles? Allowing herself a moment of satisfaction with what she had done, Leckie glanced round the nursery for the last time, picking up the pink blanket she had dumped into the empty cot and, as an afterthought, stuffing it under her clothes.

Desperate now not to be caught, Leckie silently opened the nursery door and, seeing no one in the immediate vicinity, hurried past the deserted workstation and towards the far door. Using her pass card one more time, she made her escape from the unit, walking purposefully down the corridor to the main exit. She knew better than to attract unwanted attention by breaking into a run until she was well clear of the hospital approach road, but once there she did not stop running until she was back in the comparative sanctuary of the shop doorway.

CHAPTER 29

Ben and Karen

They had spent an uncomfortable night. Once he was satisfied that the fire he had lit in the Morsø was well ignited, Ben had made them both a hot drink. In the warmth from the fire, Karen was becoming more relaxed. She was still nursing the baby, gently cradling the child's head and gazing at her little features with rapt attention. How utterly natural and how truly content she looked, Ben realised with a pang. If only the situation were different. Oh, if only this *was* their own child. He knew what he must do. He had to convince Karen that the baby should be handed over to the appropriate authorities just as soon as possible. They must relinquish their care for the child at the very first opportunity. Karen had to let it go.

Dreamily stroking the little one's hair, Karen held her close, whispering into her ear, "Cari Moses. You will be our Cari Moses. It's absolutely right for you, my darling. Ben"—turning to him now—"Ben, that has to be her name. Cari is short for something in Welsh: cariad. I think it means 'sweetheart'. My dad used to call me that. And we're in Wales and we found her by the water, just like that story about Moses in the bulrushes."

"You can call her what you like for now"—Ben's riposte sounded harsher to his own ears than he had intended—"but it *is* only for now Karen. We can't keep her."

And so they had argued, until Ben, realising that he was unlikely to win her round, tonight at least, asked what they were planning to have for their evening meal. Karen's disinterest could hardly have been more palpable. All her concern was for the baby and how they could care for her immediate needs. Tomorrow they would find a shop, she determined.

I shall buy everything she should have. Nothing will be too good for Cari Moses.

It turned out to be rather a scratch meal. Searching the cupboards in the galley, Ben had found some tins of soup, some corned beef, and some boil-in-the-bag rice. He had done his best, but preparing the meal should have been Karen's job if only things were more normal. He was feeling the beginnings of a thumping headache now. Tension probably, he thought, but maybe it was hunger. The last proper meal they had eaten was in the café alongside the staircase lock at Grindley Brook. They had tied up at the head of the locks the previous night and rewarded themselves the next morning with a full English breakfast. Since then they seemed to have subsisted on crisps and biscuits, Karen steadfastly refusing to explore the town of Whitchurch—"too far from the canal in all this drizzle"—or even Ellesmere, where an arm of the canal stretched straight into the little town. No wonder he had a headache.

He had eaten hungrily, washing down a couple of paracetamol with a cup of strong tea. In deference to Karen and her insistence that they needed to keep the boat warm for the baby, he had stoked up the Morsø with fresh coal before retiring to bed—alone.

Karen's meal lay half eaten, congealing on the plate, her tea untouched. Beside her on the bunk seat lay a neat stack of fabric squares which she had sacrificed their bath towels to make. She rifled through her sewing kit for a couple of safety pins. They were quite small but would have to do. At least she had solved the difficulty of nappies for the child. Her improvisation would have to suffice until she could get to the shops and buy a stock of disposables.

Feeding Cari presented more of a problem. The ongoing (and growing) shopping list Karen was compiling started with formula milk, bottles, teats, and steriliser, although Karen had a memory of a work colleague on maternity leave having brought her baby to the salon to show him off to the other girls and who had given the boy a feed from a little disposable bottle filled with milk and ready to be used. Karen would have to try to get some of those. For tonight, though, she would have to use her initiative. Dredging back in her distant memories of GCSE biology lessons, she recalled reading something about cow's milk being twice as rich as that of humans. Having laid the sleeping infant on the bunk seat in front of the

Morsø while searching for the material to make the nappies, she had then gone into the galley to see how much milk they had. Diluting this with an equal quantity of water, she had boiled it and put some into a cup, first having attempted to sterilise this by pouring in boiling water from the kettle. She had put the remainder of the milk mixture into a jug, covered it, and put it in the fridge for later.

Her initial attempt to feed Cari from a teaspoon had not been an unmitigated success, most of the first spoonful drenching the child's chest. Mentally adding bibs to the list, Karen had adopted a different approach, using very tiny amounts of the milk and dropping these straight onto the baby's tongue. Progress had been achingly slow, but eventually either she or Cari got better at this, settling into a sort of primitive rhythm, until to Karen's utter relief, the baby fell asleep in her arms.

Despite being thoroughly exhausted both physically and mentally, Ben had slept fitfully. The heat in the boat was stifling, and he had awakened several times with a start, puzzled at first to find the bed empty beside him. Then he remembered—and the conflicting emotions threatened to overwhelm him. Struggling to reconcile these very different responses, he recalled the joy he had felt in that first brief moment when he heard the lift in Karen's voice: "Ben! Ben, look what I have found." Then came the realisation not only of what she had found but also of the implications of this for both of them. He knew that what she was proposing was wrong, utterly wrong—so wrong, in fact, it was a crime. Yet how could he, who loved her so much and knew how profoundly she had suffered, deny her anything? They had grown up together, grown in maturity as a couple, and grieved together. (Although always he had felt that her grief had been greater than his. It overwhelmed her, totally engulfed her and had stolen her from him.)

He knew that he no longer made her happy. She had not been happy for months—years even. Yet in that moment of discovery, all the old elation was back. She was Karen again. How could he possibly take that away from her?

Pushing aside any chance of an immediate return to sleep, Ben wandered through to the saloon, pausing in the doorway to absorb the scene in front of him. Karen was resting now, not quite asleep, but more relaxed than she had been for as long as he could remember. The child in her arms was sleeping too.

The room was still warm, but the stove had burned low and there was a sweet, slightly sickly scent in the air. It reminded Ben of the rice puddings his great-gran used to make. And then it came to him. It was the smell of boiled milk. More than that: there was something primeval in the smell and the past it evoked. As his subconscious struggled with the thought, Ben recognised it for what it was: the epitome of motherhood. Shaking the disturbing thought aside, he stumbled forward and knelt in front of Karen. Resisting the urge to take both of them in his arms, embarrassed, Ben turned instead to the stove. Sod the heat; he would make it up again. For the time being that was all he could contribute. At least he would keep them warm.

CHAPTER 30

The Woman

It was a crisp October morning when the woman finally awoke. She had been dozing on and off since Alex had left for work half an hour ago, bringing her a cup of tea and a couple of biscuits on his way out. Something of a peace offering, she thought, given her attack on him last night. When asked about his plans for the forthcoming weekend, he had reacted angrily when she ignored his wishes and flatly refused to consider accompanying him in his search for a second-hand car. From his perspective, it was she who was being unreasonable. "Damn it, I can't win!" he had shouted; it was largely for her benefit after all. She was the one to insist that their current car was not going to be big enough when the baby arrived. There was not enough space in the back, apparently, to accommodate a rear-facing car seat, and no way could she hope to get the buggy she had set her heart on into that "pokey little boot".

She had wanted him to spend the day gardening, it seemed. The lawn was a mess, covered in dead leaves now, which made the path dangerous too. What if she were to fall? She couldn't risk that now that there was the baby to think of. And so she had gone on and on, becoming both tearful and petulant in turn. Most of all, she was demanding that he should cut down that bush by the door or dig it out completely. It seemed like a lot of work for nothing to him. After all, the bush did give them a bit of privacy. At the mention of that, she had become quite hysterical, insisting that it was a crime scene waiting to happen; anyone could lurk behind it and pounce on them when they opened the door to come in or out. In the end, he had capitulated: wouldn't do to let her get so upset—not in her condition. It was probably all down to hormones.

Now, recalling the angry scene, she reflected upon the compromise they had achieved. She supposed that she had to be satisfied with it. At least he had agreed to cut the damn thing down at some point over the weekend. If not on Saturday (he was still determined to go to the car auction), then he would *certainly* do it on Sunday. He didn't seem to be taking her fears seriously. Perhaps she should have told him about the way she had felt coming home last night, how she had thought that she was being watched. But he had been so dismissive of her concern over the bush, blaming it on an overactive imagination, that she had decided against it, convinced that he would laugh it off. "Paranoia. Pregnancy hormones," he would have said.

Stretching lazily, she allowed herself a further ten minutes in bed before getting up and taking a shower. She had laid out her work clothes the night before: a smart navy-blue dress, empire line, the little pleats below her bust fanning out over her growing bump; her suede jacket; and a pair of shoes that were a soft shade of beige ("nude" she thought they called it) which she knew flattered her colouring. Just because she was pregnant, it was no reason to be frumpy. She was proud of her good looks and of the fact that she was going to have a baby. Perhaps she should get herself a few new dresses for work. If she left the office early tonight, she could pop into that fashionable maternity store on the Rows *and* still catch her usual bus home. The journey home last night had been horrid.

CHAPTER 31

Pam

If she thought yesterday was bad, then today was shaping up to be even worse. Pam conceded to herself that it had got off to a pretty miserable start. She was still smarting from the aftermath of the previous evening and Ted's sarcastic remark about "Yet another bloody frozen delight" as he had scraped his meal into the waste bin and slammed out of the house to go down to the pub. She had no idea how long he stayed down there; she had gone to bed before he came home. He must have fallen asleep as soon as he got into bed. His side barely looked slept in this morning. He may even have slept downstairs on the sofa. She knew that he sometimes did that when he had had rather a skinful and didn't want her to know how late he had got home. She had not seen him this morning either. He must have left for work before her alarm went off.

It was a horrible mealtime. Her husband's criticism of her cooking was compounded by her youngest son's silent insolence. She had rounded on him as soon as Ted left to go to the pub, thinking that she might encourage him to be more responsible about locking up and setting the alarm if he realised that by not raising this in his father's presence, she had saved him from a far greater punishment: a serious grounding and probably no pocket money for weeks. Instead he had faced her out, defiantly refusing to acknowledge any part in the misdemeanour or to answer her questions as to his brother's current whereabouts. This morning both boys were still in bed when she left for work, neither having had the grace to respond when she had called goodbye to them.

Now, arriving at the door of the maternity department, Pam realised that she did not have her pass card with her. Thinking that she must have left it on the uniform dress she had worn the previous day, she assumed it was in the laundry bin at home. This was going to be a nuisance and get her into a spot of trouble with the senior midwife. Her colleagues would be irritated too, as they would have to buzz her in and out of the unit every time she had to leave the department. It was not helped by today's being a clinic day. That usually entailed a lot of additional coming and going for the staff. Struck by the irony of the situation, Pam cursed her own forgetfulness and wondered, not for the first time, whether she was being too hard on her boys. Pressing the buzzer to gain admission to the unit, she was completely unaware that the day was about to get much worse.

CHAPTER 32

Sandy

Sandy was facing the morning with her customary optimism. Whatever irritations had bedevilled her the previous day, her and Helen's anniversary celebration, once it occurred, had gone well. So it was with some alarm that, on entering the station, Sandy was greeted somewhat tersely by a grim-faced Shorty. "Where the bloody hell were you last night? What the devil were you up to?" She was momentarily stunned by the unexpected attack. It was only when he followed his questions with another "Don't you ever answer your bloody mobile?" that she realised this was not some sort of salacious prying into her and Helen's private life.

"Number flagged up, Shorty, but I was driving. Didn't think it was that important. There wasn't a message. I checked as soon as I could." At this response, Shorty snorted. So, pushing home an advantage when she saw one, Sandy followed this up with, "Well, I was at home all night. You could have messaged me there." He was about to respond when she was called through to the major incident room for the morning briefing. It was here that she learned the reason for the missed calls and about the other worrying developments on their patch over the last few hours. Apparently the calls to her phone had been in the form of a general alert informing off-duty officers, particularly those travelling to and from the city, that a young woman had absconded from the Maternity Unit, taking her new baby with her. While not a criminal act in itself, as patients were free to make their own decisions about care and to discharge themselves from hospital if such was their wish, staff at the hospital had voiced their concerns that the woman was heavily medicated and thought to be unstable. And there were very real anxieties over the safety of both mother and child. Traffic alerts and localised street patrols had yielded no sign of the pair, and the distraught husband was demanding an escalation of activity on their part to locate his missing family. There had been no further developments overnight, and the search was being upgraded from an amber to a red alert.

Among the assembled officers were four other colleagues who, like Sandy, had been unaware of the cause of last night's traffic disruption. They were quickly brought up to speed, learning that a particularly nasty hit-and-run had occurred on the high street. Various onlookers had described seeing the car accelerating as it approached a young woman standing in the lamplight at the side of the road. The vehicle appeared to have been driven straight at her, mounting the pavement, giving a sickening crunch as it collided with the lamp post, smashing into the woman, and injuring three other pedestrians before driving off at speed. It all happened so quickly that none of the bystanders had noted the registration number. Even the details of the car were vague, its being variously described as dark, black, metallic blue coloured, and largish. The one thing that was certain was the severity of the injuries sustained by the victims. Two of the men, commuters returning from work, were in hospital with broken legs and multiple abrasions. Neither was fit enough to have been interviewed as yet, both having spent a large part of the night in theatre and the recovery room. The third person had sustained more of a glancing blow, breaking her arm. Traumatised by what she had witnessed, she had been treated for shock and kept in hospital overnight as a precaution. The only other injury to have occurred at the scene was to a woman who had suffered a nasty fall in her haste to avoid the car, and cracked her head against the kerb. She too had been taken to A & E and admitted for observation.

The individual causing the most concern was the young woman who, it seemed, had been the intended victim of the attack. She had been crushed, her crumpled body left for dead. The police officers at the scene had kept the gathering crowd back as one of the paramedics jumped out of the first ambulance to arrive and began emergency CPR whilst his colleague backed the vehicle into position. They had taken the victim to the City Hospital, where she was admitted immediately to the resuscitation room, then transferred to the intensive care unit. She had not been expected to survive the night, but the news from the hospital this morning was that she was still alive—just. A WPC had been stationed at the unit all night. Although there seemed very little likelihood that the young woman would regain consciousness and be able to furnish them with any relevant information, this was also seen as a necessary precaution against further assault, given that this case was presenting as one of attempted murder. Sandy was detailed to relieve her colleague after the briefing, stopping first to interview the other injured woman whilst she was still in the hospital.

"Any further questions?" Ted Manning asked.

"Well, only the obvious ones. What do we know about this victim?"

Another in the room asked, "Who is she and have her relatives been informed?"

Still another wanted to know, "Are we certain that this was a deliberate act?"

The last question: "How much have the press been told?"

Ted held up his hand for the officers to stop. "Gentlemen ..."

God, how Sandy hated the way he did that, as though he did not realise there were at least five women in the room, WPCs and PCSOs. "Gentlemen," he said again, challengingly, meeting her eye, "all I can tell you at this stage is that this young woman, probably in her early to midtwenties, may be a rough sleeper or working the streets, or may even be a student down on her luck. No ID was found on her person, and none of the officers at the scene, including me, recognised her. That could be due to the severe impact she sustained; her features were not easy to determine. I have had photographs prepared and am detailing Room 16 as a crime-specific incident room. You will find the pictures in there, together with a map showing the exact site of the incident, and an artist's impression of the position at the point of impact and trajectory of the vehicle involved. This was drawn up following the initial report from the scene-of-crime team who gave an approximation of its direction and the speed of both its approach and subsequent getaway.

"DI Barnes, you have already been told that you are to lead this enquiry. As soon as you have selected your team, please let me know. Before you leave, I would like each of you to go to the incident room and study those photographs. It is just possible that one of you will have had dealings with this young lady and will be able to identify her. DS Bostock, you have also already been assigned to the case as you have had experience working with people like the victim. It is quite possible that you might be able to recognise her."

And she's a woman. And there will be relatives to notify once we know who she is. And I spend most of my time doing family liaison and support rather than cutting-edge police work, thought Sandy, wondering briefly what the high and mighty Manning had been doing at an actual crime scene. He seemed to her to spend most of his time prowling round the station, trying to catch the rest of them unawares defying some sort of petty protocol and lording over whatever enquiry a more subordinate officer was supposed to be conducting.

"And, gentlemen." Ted was continuing, the briefing apparently not being over yet. "Before you leave and go about your day's business, I should like to draw your attention to the notice we have received from our counterparts in Wolverhampton. Those of you who have followed the news will be aware that their tally of victims in the recent spate of murders has now reached three. There is the very real possibility that this is the work of a serial attacker. Although they are not at this stage releasing salient details, there appears to be a marked similarity in the MO. There's certainly no wish to provoke any copycat killings. Unfortunately, the press are on to this one, whipping up their usual mass hysteria, headlining a 'Serial Killer in Our Midst?' sort of thing. For that reason, details are available to neighbouring forces only on a need-to-know basis."

How the man enjoys flaunting his superior status, thought Sandy.

"Our black country colleagues would be grateful if you could keep your ears to the ground and pass on anything you might hear on the grapevine which could facilitate their enquiries. Through me, of course. I would expect you to bring any such confidences to my attention immediately."

"Bloody difficult if we don't know what we are supposed to be listening out for," whispered PC Kevin Oldcourt in an aside to Sandy.

"Pompous prick," she responded, before smiling sweetly in Ted's direction and departing for the City Hospital.

CHAPTER 33

Ben and Karen

It was a splendid October morning. The autumn sunrise peppered the sky with flashes of gold, a delicate pink fading to a pale turquoise with vibrant splashes of a deep, almost crimson glow. As the early mist that had gathered over the canal began to lift, the dramatic cloud formation could be seen here too, reflected in the torpid stillness of the water. Rousing from a restless sleep, Ben peered through the porthole over the bunk bed, absent-mindedly rubbing his temples, aware again of the dull ache of an impending migraine. Sod it. He could do without that today. The colours in the sky were hurting his eyes. What was it that they said about red in the morning? Some sort of warning, was it?

With daylight came a renewed clarity, banishing his earlier indecision and strengthening his resolve. Gone were the vacillations of the preceding night. Ben knew what he must do. He had to get the child away from Karen and off the boat. Any other course of action was unthinkable. It could only end in disaster. If he did not do it himself, then surely the authorities would eventually find the child and take it from her anyway. And what would that do to Karen? It would destroy her, them, everything in life that mattered to him. He could only speculate. The prospect terrified him.

Hastily pulling on yesterday's clothes, he made his way through to the galley, rinsing out a mug and swilling down a couple of paracetamol with water from the tap. He knew that he was not supposed to be drinking unfiltered water, but what the hell? That was a pretty trivial concern given what was going on in his life right now. His resolve hardened further when, glancing across to where Karen was cuddling the baby, he saw where the last of their milk supply from the fridge had gone. Damn it, he couldn't even make them a cup of tea. This baby had completely disrupted their lives. It had to go.

CHAPTER 34

The Man on the Bus

Yesterday's debacle had unnerved him. He knew that he had made a terrible mistake. He was a man who prided himself on precision and control. Recognising his own personal demons, he knew that he only made mistakes when he was angry. That's when he lost it. Those were the times when he knew for a certainty that he was not entirely invincible. The knowledge was chastening. With his skill he should be unsusceptible to error. How long had he known that he should never act in anger? It certainly predated those pathetic condescending sessions of so-called "anger management" he had endured at the expense of the taxpayer, courtesy of HMP Wayland. Those were laughable, so far removed from the reality of his life outside that they could have been teaching him nursery rhymes.

He had so much more control these days. Total control. No, *almost* total control, he conceded. He could still react with anger, could lose it sometimes. And the consequences of that were manifestly dangerous. He had to master his anger, have absolute control over it. The potential dangers of not being in complete control over his latent rage were a real threat, a threat that was most potently directed against himself.

Yesterday things had gone disastrously wrong. His first mistake was having given the woman a lift. No, it preceded even that. His first mistake was in not realising that she had a child. Flinching at the naivety of his question, "Is this your first?" he recognised the stupidity of his assumption that she had come from the hospital's antenatal unit. This was clear from the bag she was carrying, containing night clothes, make-up, and child-care books and magazines, all the inevitable clutter these women accumulated for a spell in hospital. He had gone on to compound these misconceptions, believing her still to be in the early stages of her pregnancy. Even as his suspicion grew that he may have jumped to the wrong conclusion about her condition, he had failed to act. Common sense told him that he should have stopped the van right there and insisted that she should get out, but he knew that there were inherent dangers to that. The woman had seen his face. She had seen the van with its stupid green logo. And the knowledge of that made him angry, very angry indeed. Accustomed for so long now to operating under the radar, and fiercely protective of the anonymity this conferred, he was unable to risk any subsequent disclosure. She had to be silenced; the whole episode, eradicated.

Disposing of her had been easy enough. He had lugged her flaccid, senseless body—a gibbering wreck reduced to a bundle of rags—through the gap in the hedge where the lane had widened sufficiently for him to park the van. The lane ran alongside the canal at this point, separated from the towpath only by the hedge. It was worth the drive and the excuse he would have to concoct to account for the extra miles on the clock to get here. He knew this spot well. It was one he had used before. There was seldom any traffic on the little lanes round about—an occasional farm vehicle perhaps, but the roads were too narrow for much modern-day agricultural equipment. Small tractors or four-by-fours were probably about all that ever used the road, and in every previous visit he had never encountered even these sorts of vehicles.

So confident had he been of evading discovery that he had taken his time with the woman. Ugly lump, he decided, revising his immediate impression of her before he made his cardinal error. Post baby fat was a turn-off, for sure. He knew then that he would kill her. But that was all he would do. There was no potential for arousal here, nothing to accommodate his art, no trophy to display.

She had asked for all she got, taking him in like that. She had made it easy for him too, falling down like the fat lazy tart she was and knocking herself out. She hadn't even put up much of a struggle. He had returned to the van and slammed the doors shut on the wailing brat, intending to deal with it later. First he would despatch the lying bitch who had made such a fool of him. The water was deep enough here, just below the bottom gates of the lock, to serve his purpose. It had quite a flow from the bye-wash which would take care of any traces he might inadvertently leave on her body. He had removed the bungee straps from her wrists and, quite dispassionately, had strangled her then, before rolling her unprotesting body deep into the rushes growing alongside the water's edge.

The baby would join her there. Returning to the van, he had retrieved the holdall, avid distaste distorting his features as he registered how it pulsated with every howl from inside. He would not even have to kill it. The canal would do that for him. He could not stand the child's wailing any longer. There was nothing to be gained from carrying it down to join its mother where he had left her, a bit farther back along the canal. He might just as well dispose of the brat here.

Throwing the bag and its unpleasant contents into the bye-wash from the lock, as he had originally intended, was not a sensible option. He had no idea how buoyant the bag might prove to be. Despite the weight of the child, the bag could still take a while to fill with water and sink. The possibility of its floating some way, perhaps remaining visible, the handles an easy target for grasping hands or a retrieving boathook, alarmed him. No, chucking the kid into the lock without the bag was a much better idea.

Even at such a moment, the years of practised caution saw him taking cover wherever and whenever practical. Kneeling in the dense undergrowth, he undid the zip and carried the bag across the neatly mown grass which bounded the lock. Stifling his repugnance, he lifted the screaming child, holding her towards the water, and was about to throw her in. Just then, incredulously, he heard the sound of something which had never occurred to him, not at this time of year and not here, where it was always so quiet. Unmistakable, it was the chug, chug, chug of a narrowboat engine, a sound that firstly paralysed him with fear before catapulting him to his feet and propelling him as fast as he could possibly run back to the safety of the van, dropping the child as he went. He pushed through the gap in the hedge, opened the driver's door, and eased the vehicle out of the parking place. He drove carefully, quietly, not even using the van's sidelights until he had rounded several bends, whereupon he flung caution to the wind and drove back up to the main road as fast as he possibly could.

As the palpitations in his chest subsided and his distance from the scene increased, he realised how close he had come to discovery. He had to remove any possible trace the woman and her brat may have left in the van. Nothing must be left to chance. There had to be nothing to link him to what had happened back there. Most important of all, nothing must be allowed to stand in the way of his all-absorbing hobby.

CHAPTER 35

Sandy

After reviewing the information posted in the incident room, Sandy made her way to the hospital, where she spent an abortive half hour trying to find out what had happened to the traumatised woman with the broken arm. She had apparently recovered sufficiently from shock to discharge herself against medical advice and had left the ward at five o'clock that morning, accompanied by a shifty man claiming to be her brother. Sandy extracted what details she could from the harassed night nurse who was on duty at the time, noting the name and address given by the departed patient while telling herself that they were probably both fabrications anyway. She usually had a nose for these things.

After grabbing a quick coffee in the hospital café, where she had hoped she might have learnt more about the mysterious disappearing patient, she took the lift up to the sixth floor and the ICU. Here she relieved WPC Rudd and settled down for what promised to be a long wait, the ward manager having told her that there was little change in the patient's condition, in her words, "Just hanging in by a thread, poor soul."

Studying the battered features of the young woman, Sandy struggled to place a fleeting impression that this was someone she had previously encountered—and quite recently too. The same thought had occurred to her earlier when she was confronted with the photographs in the incident room, snapped the night before and seemingly rendered even more brutal under the unforgiving flash of the powerful police camera. She should know, Sandy berated herself, acknowledging that her normally excellent memory for faces and the ability to locate these mentally in terms of time and place, along with the associated incident, appeared to have failed her in this instance. It was comparatively recent, she knew that.

The girl had looked different, of course, before becoming the victim of such an appalling act, assuming that they were correct in their assumption that this was a deliberate attack. That was a difficult one to swallow. Who would want to purposely drive a car into a defenceless young woman? What possible motive could there have been for such gratuitous violence? Maybe they were wrong, jumping to conclusions based principally on the account by an eyewitness. It was not good police practice, Sandy conceded. And as she knew, bystanders' interpretations of events were notably unreliable. But, she supposed, she and her colleagues were only human. Preliminary judgements, often unfounded, would be made. The only thing that could be said in their defence was that these judgements invariably would be tempered by the weight of accumulating evidence and that every officer involved would be expected to seek out that evidence.

She was not naive. Sandy had experienced first-hand the insidious, pervading quality of snap judgement. Professionally, too, she knew how bias and preformed ideas could slow down progress towards the solution of a crime and, ultimately, delay justice for its perpetrators.

But if this really was a deliberate act, then the sooner the bastard responsible was apprehended, the better. She wondered what the girl lying in the bed, so terribly injured, could have done to provoke such an attack. She must have been silenced for a reason. What possible motive could there be? Was it revenge, and if so, for what? Just what could this young woman have done that was so dreadful that she had to be killed for it?

Sandy knew she was thinking like a police officer now, the way she had been trained to think. It didn't make her immediate sympathy for the girl or the anger that someone could have done this to another person lessen in any way. If anything, it honed these emotions, channelling the sympathy and the anger in one clear direction. The person who had perpetrated this horrible, despicable act had to be caught. And with so little tangible evidence to go on, they, the investigating team, needed to get inside the mind of the attacker. If only the girl could talk, she could tell them what she knew.

It had to be either revenge for something she had done or an effort to stop her from talking about something she knew. If it was a revenge attack, then it was likely to be personal—and perhaps no one else was involved, just her and the man who had tried to kill her. Again, Sandy thought, I'm making the assumption that it was a man driving the car. None of the witnesses had actually described him. She wondered if they were correct this morning in their assumption that whoever had done this actually had intended to *kill* her. Might it just have been a warning, albeit one that had gone way too far? Perhaps the guy at the wheel had misjudged his speed and had not meant to kill her at all, just to hurt her and scare her into keeping quiet about whatever it was that she knew.

Damn it, Sandy thought, for all we really know, it could be a case of mistaken identity and the girl was never the intended victim at all. What if the man had actually been aiming at one of the other pedestrians caught up in the carnage? The woman who had discharged herself from hospital early that morning, perhaps. Nothing was known about her or her mysterious "brother". There were always so many loose ends at this stage in an enquiry, and this one was promising to have more than most.

But if the young woman *had* been the target all along, what could she possibly have known that was such a threat that she had to be silenced in this way? Perhaps it was something she had seen or even something she had been a party to, but then, for some reason, she had become a liability, dispensable. And if the intention really had been to kill her outright, how long would it be before the attacker learnt that he had failed? Would he have switched on the television news and seen something about it there, or maybe heard it on a car radio? Sandy realised that she did not know whether there *had* been any news coverage of the incident yet, whether it had made the later editions of the national press.

Did he know already that the girl was still alive? And how would that make him feel? Whatever the motive, he might want to distance himself from the whole affair: lie low for a while and hope there would be nothing to link him to the attack. Or if it had been his intention all along to kill her outright, would his failure to have done so have fuelled his determination to try again? He could not know how badly the girl was injured, or whether or not she was conscious and could talk. If she were conscious, then she'd be able to tell them what she knew, implicating him. All these things suggested the distinct possibility that he could strike again. This time he would be sure to succeed.

Sandy knew that was one reason for the continued police presence, one reason why she was here in ICU with the girl. The purpose was not only to be there if and when the victim could speak and possibly give them the information they needed in their search for her attacker, but also for her ultimate protection should she be targeted again. Shivering at the prospect that this evoked, Sandy continued to study the girl's features, searching for a clue, willing herself to remember. Did she know her from somewhere? Where had she seen her, and when? Mentally revisiting the various domestic disputes which had been severe enough to warrant police intervention recently, she wondered if this could have been the result of an escalation, a quarrel brought to a final, horrible end. Surely then she would have recognised the girl. Even with her facial injuries, Sandy was certain that she would have known.

Sandy's thoughts were becoming clearer the more she considered the hit-and-run, the more she analysed it. She wondered about the site where the incident had occurred; was that in itself significant? It certainly didn't seem as though this was a random attack. Did the driver just see the girl there and, on the spur of the moment, drive his car at her with such disastrous results? Sandy did not think so. It seemed to her that this was much more likely to have been planned, that the man knew where to find her. Standing in the street, under a lamp—well, that would have given him a clear view of her. He must have been easily able to identify his victim. And if, as Sandy was surmising, he knew or at least guessed that he would find her there, then this suggested something else: that it was a spot where she had waited previously.

Waited for what? Sandy wondered. Perhaps the young woman was meeting someone. Perhaps she was waiting to meet *him*, not knowing that this time he intended to hurt her, kill her even. Or was she waiting for someone else? A lover perhaps. Someone she had met there before. And was that why the man had driven his car at her, because he knew she was waiting for someone else? Was the motive as simple as that? Jealousy? Did he have some sort of prior claim over the girl, perhaps? Sandy studied the girl's hands; one arm was in plaster, fractured no doubt, and the other was immobilised in a splint, an IV line to a cannula in the back of the girl's hand. Sandy looked at each finger in turn. There was no sign of any rings that she could see, although it was difficult to make out much on the arm in plaster; the fingers here were partially covered and very swollen. If there had been any rings, she felt sure that they would have been removed, probably cut off. She should ask the staff about that; they must have listed the girl's possessions when they admitted her. Not that rings really meant that much these days. The thought flickered across her mind unbidden: should she have given Helen a ring by now?

It was the sort of romantic gesture that would please her partner. Helen herself had preempted it by giving Sandy a gold chain last Christmas: pale Welsh gold, clearly an expensive and no doubt meaningful gift. Sandy had consoled herself with the thought that it was too early in their relationship to exchange the sort of presents which denoted that level of commitment, but in her heart of hearts she knew that the thought simply had never occurred to her. She had accepted the gold chain, allowing Helen to fasten it around her neck, failing to acknowledge the wistful tears welling in her partner's eyes as she opened Sandy's eminently practical present to her: a pair of Norwegian walking poles. Thinking about it, Sandy figured that last night would have been a good occasion to redeem the situation. The thing was, her mind just didn't work in that way.

The girl in the bed did not seem to have been wearing any rings, but that did not mean that someone, somewhere—the car driver—didn't have some sort of hold over her. Maybe he felt he owned her in some way. What if he wasn't the jealous husband or possessive boyfriend Sandy had earlier envisaged and that this was something altogether different, say, a business arrangement? She had been waiting under the lamp. Was she a sexworker and the man her pimp? If so, what could she have done to make him angry enough to want to kill her?

It answered the question of why she had been standing where she was and how the man knew. He had expected her to be there. It also explained why Sandy thought she recognised the girl from somewhere. She looked long and hard at the girl's battered, ravaged face. She did not know her, but still the impression that she may have seen her remained to tantalise and taunt her.

An alarm bell was shrieking now. The monitors over the girl's bed were flashing. She was flatlining.

Sandy was jostled aside then summarily dismissed from the bedside. The crash team had arrived; someone was shouting for paddles; drug names were being called out. Then the young woman's bed was being taken somewhere, porters pushing it through the double doors, out of the unit, and along the corridor, the IV stand attached to the bed swinging crazily.

A staff nurse was holding onto the IV stand now, the girl's notes clutched in her other hand. An anaesthetist was with them, holding a mask over the girl's face, pumping air—or was it oxygen? Sandy's knowledge of such things had been gleaned from her not infrequent trips to A&E following a variety of traffic accidents and domestic casualties, and from the hospital soaps that Helen insisted they watch.

They were taking the girl back to theatre. Not dead yet, thought Sandy. Not this time.

CHAPTER 36

Pam

The day was shaping up to be every bit as bad as Pam had feared. Morning handover was a solemn affair, the departing night staff subdued, almost secretive. There was none of the usual exchange of pleasantries, and they seemed reluctant to enter into any conversation beyond the minimum demanded in relation to the patients' welfare. It was almost as though there was an undercurrent of smouldering anger. Thinking that the cause of this might have something to do with the way the ward had been left the previous evening, one of the midwifery day sisters began to offer her apologies, saying, "If things were not done as well as usual ..." This was immediately cut short by her opposite number on the night duty team, at which point the reason for their reticence became clear.

Shortly after coming on duty, the midwifery ward sisters had been visited by the CEO, who was infuriated by the apparent level of incompetence which had allowed a mother and child to leave the ward unobserved. A "general laxity", she felt, was "rife throughout the unit". Stung by this criticism, which seemingly implicated them all in the disappearance of Abigail and Geraldine, despite its having happened when none of the night staff present were on duty, the sisters were further mortified to learn that all their record-keeping and attention to detail was going to be scrutinised as part of the inevitable internal enquiry into the incident. In the meantime, they were instructed to check every aspect of ward procedure. The drugs had to be accounted for; the bottles of formula and stock in the treatment rooms had to be inspected for their use-by dates; and all areas were to be tidied and cleaned to the highest possible standard. This added enormously to the midwives" usual night-time workload: the mothers and babies still had to be cared for, the treatments had to be administered on time, and the midwives had to be available to staff the delivery suite should anyone be admitted in labour. (In the event, there were two deliveries during the shift, and while neither had required extraordinary intervention, they involved the attending midwives with the usual level of care, effectively removing them from the extra work that had been detailed to occur, placing an additional burden on the remainder of their colleagues.)

Their instructions for the night included gathering together any remaining items belonging to Abigail and bagging these up, ready either for collection by Steve or for possible inspection by the police. The few items of nightwear and toiletries were in a plastic bag in the ward office with clear instructions that they were not to be removed without authorisation. Furthermore, the night staff had been told not to discuss Abigail's disappearance with the oncoming day staff but to make them aware that the CEO would be coming to the unit to address them personally later that morning. No member of staff should talk about the incident outside these meetings, certainly not beyond the confines of the unit, and if they were approached by the press, they were to offer "No comment" as a response and refer the matter to the chief executive's office immediately. No wonder the night staff were subdued, thought Pam. They were probably dog-tired too.

CHAPTER 37

Sandy

She was going to be in the theatre some time. "Massive internal haemorrhage," the ICU sister had told her. Either that, or she would be in theatre for no time at all—"beyond saving". They would let her know either way, and then she could hurry back and resume her vigil at the bedside or not have to hurry at all. She'd come back, collect the girl's pitiful effects, and return with them to the station. Effects—that was what had triggered the faint tantalising memory, a shadowy remembering, barely a half recollection. And yet, suddenly, galvanised into action now, Sandy knew. She knew, in a moment of absolute certainty, where she had encountered the girl before.

Huddled over a pathetic little heap of belongings, a battered rucksack, and a stained sleeping bag far too thin for the oncoming winter, but all the girl had, Sandy had found her crouching in the back doorway of one of the shops on the high street, protectively guarding her things, wary of this uniformed official intruding on her personal space. She was a rough sleeper, fairly new to the town, Sandy had surmised. She had not seen her before then—well, not to recognise. The girl was shifty though, failing to raise her head, avoiding Sandy's eyes.

And then Sandy remembered more clearly now. It was several days ago when they had had the attempted child abduction. Sandy wondered then, recalling the mother's less than adequate description of the would-be kidnapper—"Just a girl really. A sort of scruffy street person. Scruffy. Not the sort you'd want anywhere near children."

Was this young woman the one who had given them such a run for their money and who had lost them all in the futile chase—Sandy's only bit of real action all day?

Sandy was no nearer now than she had been then to knowing the girl's identity. But she knew something, something that just might be important, something which had the potential to earn Sandy the sort of professional acclaim she coveted. She should telephone the station and tell them of her plan, that she was leaving her post at the hospital and pursuing her hunch. Well, *that* wasn't going to happen. She was doing no good waiting here, frittering the time away, while her charge was safely ensconced in the operating theatre. She would go into the city and do a bit of real policing for a change. If she came back with the answer she was hoping for, they were bound to be impressed.

———————————

She had wasted no time in getting here. Careful to avoid the evident police presence along the high street and the cordon around the accident site, marked now with police tape and guarded by a bored PCSO she recognised from this morning's briefing, Sandy made her way through the little side streets to the area behind the shops. The parking bays were deserted, she noticed; presumably, the shop personnel who usually occupied them had been told to stay at home until the stores fronting the cordoned area were allowed to reopen. Glancing around, she was surprised to find herself alone. No need to guard the back then, she thought, and wondered whose decision that had been. They obviously did not know the city's underclass as she did, the winos, the druggies, their dealers, the beggars, and the petty thieves, regulars who were as likely as anyone to have seen something significant and, in the immediate aftermath of an accident, might have been tempted to see if there was anything useful lying about. True, they would have vanished into the darkness as soon as they spotted a police officer, but they would never be too far away, Sandy knew that. And if the young woman had been working the street, it was quite likely that these people would know more about her than had surfaced so far. Sandy would have to tap her sources and do some asking around.

Not now though. She had a more pressing engagement. If she was correct, then she might be able to solve the issue of the girl's identity herself with no need to question the other denizens of the streets. At least not just yet. They could still hold the answer as to why the girl had been targeted so cruelly. But for now, Sandy would play her hunch. Making her way to the rear of the ironmongers, Sandy felt her excitement mounting. She knew where the victim kept her stuff.

She could not see it at first, a wave of disappointment gripping her, but then, suddenly, there it was. Pushed far into the recess to the side of the door, hidden from the prying eyes and possibly thieving intentions of other unfortunates, the girl's miserable possessions were wrapped in a piece of grimy polythene, the entire bundle crushed down as small as she could make it. The lumpy package was tightly bound with a length of frayed string. Fumbling with the knots, Sandy was aware of her own fingers trembling. She was energised with excitement now. Would she find the proof she was looking for, the key to the coma girl's identity? That could provide them with the lead they needed, the first step to finding her attacker and nailing her probable killer.

Spreading the polythene sheet on the abandoned doorstep, Sandy tipped out the contents of the rucksack. Clothing mainly came from the main compartment, and there was nothing by way of identification in the smaller ones, just an empty water bottle and the remains of a packet of biscuits. She would have to go through the clothes and see if there was anything in the pockets. If there were no clues there, she thought sadly, she would just have to bundle it all up again and take it back to the station with her.

She would probably get a bollocking then for going off on her own like this, not the praise she had hoped to attract. Still, however tempted she might be, she could not leave the girl's stuff here. It might yield more when they could scrutinise it more thoroughly. It was her duty after all.

She was turning these thoughts over in her mind as she began to sort through the few items of clothing. The only garments with any pockets were a folded cotton jacket and a pair of skinny sequined jeans. Smart, flashy clothes for soliciting, Sandy thought sadly, no doubt nicked specifically for the purpose. Rummaging through these yielded nothing useful, only a few tissues, a packet of condoms, and a red lipstick. Sandy put them back in the rucksack and studied what was left: underwear, socks, and something else that looked new. It was a little blanket. A pink cellular blanket. Should have stolen something bigger than this if she wanted to be really warm, Sandy thought, returning all the items to the rucksack and heading back to the hospital.

Checking her mobile for messages, she was irrationally irritated to see one from Helen asking about her projected timings later that day. As if she could possibly predict anything with any degree of certainty in her line of work. Helen should really be used to that by now. It did not even warrant a reply. They had not called her from ICU, so she figured the girl must still be in theatre. That must mean that she was holding her own, for the time being at least. Scrolling down, Sandy saw that there was nothing from the station either. She had better go straight back to hospital, she thought, before she was missed. She would take the rucksack back to the station when she had finished her spell of bedside surveillance.

CHAPTER 38

Pam

Chastened and apprehensive, the day staff went about their morning duties, speculating among themselves over the likely form the meeting with the CEO would take. It had been scheduled for eleven o'clock, and it was an anxious wait until then.

The night staff had done a thorough job; the ward had never looked tidier. But as the normal activity of the day resumed, they knew that they had very little chance of keeping it like that. Mothers and babies were not things that could easily be tidied to order. Lynne, Abigail's named midwife from the day before, had phoned in sick, her colleagues showing an uncharacteristic lack of sympathy on hearing this. If she had a premonition of what was about to ensue, she should have been there with them to share the discomfort. Several of those who were on duty were secretly wishing that *they* had found an excuse not to have come into work today.

Sensing the unrest among the staff, the mothers were becoming unsettled. Although at some level the usual care was being given, the customary good humour seemed to be missing. Soon they too were grumbling among themselves. They blamed the pampered woman who had spent most of her days with curtains drawn around her bed, too special, it seemed, to have anything to do with the rest of them. The midwives always spent so much time with her, and there had been such a fuss yesterday when she took herself off home.

The evening meal was awful, and then the night staff had been even busier than usual. Whatever were they thinking, banging around tidying cupboards while *the mothers and babies* were trying to sleep? It was no wonder that people wanted to get out of here and go home just to get a little peace. And so the muttered complaints went on, the mothers' dissatisfaction inevitably rubbing off on their little ones: fractious women and fractious babies. What a morning it was turning out to be!

———◆———

At 10.55a.m., all unit staff not actually involved in the first of that day's deliveries (they would be "brought up to speed as soon as their duties permitted") were summoned to assemble in the ward conference room. At 11a.m. precisely, a stern-faced CEO entered the room. No preliminaries, just, "You know why you have all been asked to be here. Yesterday, a most unfortunate incident occurred, and I hold you, every one of you, complicit in the general laxity and gross negligence which allowed this to happen. How a patient who, I should not have to remind you, had such severe psychological problems that she spent much of her time in your care on active suicide watch was then able to leave the ward unobserved, taking her baby with her, a child with whom, in the words of your own records, she had persistently 'failed to bond', is beyond me.

"As if this dereliction of duty in itself were not bad enough, none of you—not a single one of you—even noticed her disappearance. You, who had the ultimate duty of care for both these vulnerable individuals, were completely unaware of their absence until the moment when the woman's husband discovered that she was missing.

"I do not have to tell you that the adverse publicity attracted by such an omission on your part will do the hospital, and all those who depend upon it for their care, no favours whatsoever. The previously good name of this hospital will be forever linked in the minds of the public with other shameful scandals in care that have occurred over the years. We do not want, and should not deserve, to be viewed in the same light as other, failing hospitals. In the space of a single day, you have undermined the sterling work undertaken year in, year out, by all your colleagues to deliver the service we offer here.

"The matter will not rest here. There will be a full internal enquiry, and any individuals who may be identified as having the greatest responsibility for this appalling lack of due care, this travesty, will be dealt with accordingly. For the time being, all I can tell you is that the hospital legal advisers will be working very closely with the investigating team and the relevant professional organisations.

"However disastrous for the hospital and for some individuals personally, *that*, I should not have to emphasise to you, should not be our primary concern. A young woman and a small baby have gone missing from your care. A young woman with mental health issues and an extremely vulnerable new baby. Until they are found safe and well, none of us should be unaffected by this. As of nine o'clock this morning, the police have reported no sightings of mother or child. The longer they are missing, the greater the cause for alarm. The question being asked is, just how they could have effected their disappearance from your unit with such apparent ease? As I have said, all of you must accept some responsibility for the overall sloppy practices which allowed this to occur.

"However, certain individuals among you may well be identified who have a greater culpability. Footage from the hospital security camera, viewed by me before I left for this meeting, shows no evidence of the missing patient exiting the ward with any of the visitors. A person whom I believe to be the missing patient is seen leaving the ward alone. I must stress at this juncture that the picture is not clear. The woman's face is barely visible, and there appears to be no child in her arms. It is an image of the upper body and shows her raising her hand to the console before the doors open for her. From this—and I repeat, it *is* a grainy image—it seems most probable that she used a staff pass card to get out of the ward.

"I do not have to tell you the severity of such an implication. Until such time when the advanced facial recognition system currently being piloted within the region becomes an affordable option, the entire hospital's security depends upon the responsible use of pass cards. No patient should ever, in anycircumstances, have access to one. Staff members who leave routinely have their passes removed and destroyed. Duplicate passes are only ever issued in extraordinary circumstances. As soon as it is reported, one that has been lost is then immediately remotely deactivated.

"The question, then, is this: how, if it was a pass card that Mrs Lamont used, did this come into her possession? Sister Grenville, I take it that no one has reported a missing pass card to you? Certainly nothing has been brought to the attention of the security services."

Emily Granville, senior midwife on duty, shook her head. And, dreading what was to come, Pam realised that they were all to show their passes to the PA, who would check them off on a long list of staff who would have any reason to have access to the unit. She felt certain that hers was in the laundry basket with her soiled uniform, but how could she be sure? For now, when asked to show her pass, she could only offer her excuses. Embarrassed by the public disclosure, she was further humiliated by being ordered to go home immediately and check, and to report back to the CEO's office on her return.

CHAPTER 39

Sandy

Sandy was disappointed. Stopping at the police station on her way home, she had hoped to deliver the coup de grâce—her recognition of the injured girl and the location of her belongings. She had waited for this moment, anticipating the approbation of her superiors, expecting to have her initiative acknowledged for once.

She had returned to the hospital after discovering the rucksack and, finding the girl still undergoing surgery, had impatiently waited out the remainder of her shift there, eventually being relieved by WPC Parsons. The incoming officer, expecting a long haul until the girl was returned to the ICU, settled down in the chair Sandy had just vacated and opened a paperback. She had come prepared, knowing that this was going to be a tedious shift requiring nothing more than for her to remain at her post until the day relief took over. Provided the victim survived the night, there was no way the officer would be recalled to the station, and there was certainly nothing to engage her interest here. She barely registered the brief exchange with Sandy and had evinced no interest in the grubby rucksack in her colleague's possession.

For her part, Sandy saw no reason to enlighten her, savouring instead the prospect of the praise she felt sure she would receive for contributing valuable additional items to the scanty evidence already assembled in the incident room. She was not in any particular hurry, though, as she realised that in her excitement at recognising the girl and then locating her belongings, she had not stopped for anything to eat all day. Stuffing the rucksack in the boot of the police car she had parked on the hospital forecourt (on official business, so no time restriction here to concern her), she went back into the hospital, going straight to the café in the main concourse, and ordered herself a burger, fries, and a large white. Not the time to be worrying about the diet, she thought.

Feeling much better after her meal, Sandy returned the car to the vehicle yard at Booth Street police station. On entering the building, she was disconcerted to find that no one was behind the desk in the reception area and that the offices directly off the corridor beyond the desk appeared to be deserted. Hearing a mumble of voices as she approached the incident room, she pushed open the door. Immediately the room fell silent. Conscious only of a palpable tension in the air, Sandy set down the rucksack and waited for an explanation.

Ted Manning had been addressing the assembled officers, several of whom, Sandy noted, had started the morning shift with her and should by rights be off duty now. "Ah, Officer Bostock. Good of you to grace us with your presence."

Sarcastic prick, she thought, as the ripple of ill-concealed amusement caused by his comment faded and the tension in the room returned. "*Had* you had your mobile switched on," he continued, "you would have known that you were recalled to the station immediately upon completion of your shift at the hospital."

Bugger, just her rotten luck to have missed out on that particular instruction. She had to have the damn thing switched of in ICU and hadn't thought to switch it on again when she left.

Ted was continuing, his immediate remarks clearly intended as a further dig at her."Your colleagues can bring you up to speed after the briefing. I am not going to repeat myself for your sole benefit."

Sandy squirmed. Go on, make me feel awful. Keep turning the screw. But even as she thought it, Ted's next words were enough to dispel any lingering resentment she felt at her own discomfiture.

"In all my years of experience, I have never known a more cruel, calculated, and revolting crime. The person or persons who committed this vile atrocity must be caught before they strike again. From tonight, all scheduled leave is effectively cancelled. Anyone who has a problem with this, please see me immediately after this briefing. Only the most pressing and urgent of reasons will be acceptable as constituting extenuating circumstances. And finally, gentlemen, I cannot caution this strongly enough: absolute confidentiality is of the utmost importance. The press are already onto this. Any questions related to the case, from whatever source, *must* be directed through me."

CHAPTER 40

Shorty

Shorty also had had a miserable start to the day. He had had a bad night, getting up in the small hours to make himself a cup of tea and to swallow another couple of the stronger painkillers. Following his injuries, he had been referred to the pain consultant at the local hospital, who had prescribed a powerful mixture of opiates and an antispasmodic, gradually weaning him off his developing reliance upon oral morphine, which he had begun to self-administer on an almost hourly basis. He had had other interventions too along the line, including anaesthetic and steroid combinations injected into his spine, and regular physiotherapy, the latter discontinued by him when he realised that it actually appeared to be exacerbating his symptoms.

Long ago disregarding the advice printed on his medicine labels to avoid alcohol, Shorty regularly supplemented his evening drugs with a generous tot or two of good malt whisky. Last night he had repeated this "combination therapy" along with his 3a.m. cup of tea. He had slept soundly then and awakened uncharacteristically late, feeling thick-headed and aware that the pain of the preceding night had barely receded. If it were to continue like this, he might have to reconsider his options. Maybe retirement would be for the best, although how he would fill the days without Margaret, God only knew.

Arriving at his desk, he was irritated to find a backlog of messages, most requiring some sort of action, few of which appeared to have received any attention. There was still no sign of the missing mother and child. One of the messages was from the woman's husband, who was tearful and angry at what he saw as the failure of the police to give the search for them the priority it deserved.

The press were onto it now, with a request for an official statement regarding progress to date. Local television, too, wanted to stage an appeal to the public for information and details of any possible sightings. Steve Lamont has been busy, Shorty thought, somewhat uncharitably. Then, remembering his own devastation in the early days after Margaret's death, he relented. Poor sod. It must be horrible not even knowing what has happened. Just hope they do turn up safe somewhere. But even as he processed these thoughts, Shorty was forced to acknowledge that the longer they were missing, the less likely it seemed that they would be found unharmed. Perhaps a television appeal *would* help. He would talk to Ted Manning about it.

There didn't seem to be any real progress in the hit-and-run enquiries either. True, it was early days yet, but some sort of breakthrough at this stage in the case would greatly enhance their chances of catching the perpetrator. No one had come forward with any identification of the victim. No other missing persons reports had been filed overnight. It was widely agreed among officers at the station that the pictures of Abigail Lamont furnished by her husband bore no resemblance to those of the girl in the hit-and-run. Although the facial features of the latter victim were virtually unrecognisable as a result of the terrible injuries she had sustained, the height, weight, and body mass distribution of the two women was completely different. It was agreed that it would serve no purpose getting Steve Lamont to see the woman in the ICU, even if such would not be a grave infringement of the accident victim's right to personal dignity and protection. Even showing him her photographs had been discounted. It could only serve to distress him further and was unlikely to provide any clues as to the young woman's identity.

At least this woman was still alive—defying all the odds, Shorty thought, unlike his own wife, whose progression from diagnosis to death had been unremittingly, cruelly swift. And while the woman in hospital, "Victim A" they were calling her to distinguish her from the other pedestrians injured in the incident, was still hanging on to life, however precariously, that meant the deployment of a member of the station staff, depleting the human resources at their disposal who could

119

otherwise be occupied following up all these various lines of enquiry. It was increasingly unlikely that Victim A would be in any position to help with those enquiries herself any time soon, if ever, he thought despondently.

The other messages that had come in overnight had largely been dealt with at the time: reports of a break-in at a fireworks factory (three youths apprehended and in custody), noise and nuisance in the city centre (the perpetrators cautioned and moved on), and a crank call about an alien invasion. Even Shorty smiled at that. It was one of their regulars he knew, and usually served to lighten the mood around here. As he was sorting through the residue of paperwork and the computerised information generated by the overnight activity, the desk telephone rang. Was this the possible breakthrough they needed? A burnt-out car was being reported on waste ground beyond the city, apparently dumped and torched the previous evening. Could this be the vehicle involved in the hit-and-run?

CHAPTER 41

Pam

"Good God, Mother, whatever's up?" Robert, the elder of the two Manning boys, lumbered blearily into the bathroom to find his mother sitting on the edge of the bath sobbing, her head in her hands.

On arriving home, Pam had lost no time in going to search for her missing pass, barely registering the fact that the house alarm had not been set. Not even bothering to take off her coat, she made straight for the bathroom, tipping the contents of the laundry basket onto the floor. Rooting through the pile of clothes until she located her discarded uniform dress, she searched through each of the pockets in increasing desperation. Finding nothing, she turned the garment inside out and shook it hard in case the pass had been caught in the layers of fabric. Panicking now, she rummaged through the remainder of the clothes, then tipped up the laundry basket yet again, giving this, too, a vigorous shaking, hoping against hope to find the pass card there, perhaps trapped in the wickerwork.

It was all to no avail. More methodically now, she gathered up the remaining clothes scattered across the floor and shook out each of the items in turn before pushing them back into the basket. The pass card has to be here somewhere! Spurred on by this thought, she searched the bathroom floor again, this time lifting the bathmat in case the pass card somehow had been kicked underneath, then doing the same with the pedestal mats, and shaking out the jumble of damp towels left lying beside the shower. She got down on her hands and knees, hunting behind the washbasin, alongside the toilet, and under the medicine cabinet.

She had taken off her coat by now and dumped it, along with her shoulder bag, on the floor beside the bath. Futilely, she searched the pockets once again and tipped out the contents of her bag, knowing even as she did so that the chances of her having overlooked the card were negligible.

"Nothing. Of course, nothing there." She was keening now, a crushing pain in her chest, her head swimming, as the full force of the realisation could no longer be denied. Unable to pretend even to herself that there could be any other possible explanation, and struggling with the implications of what she now knew to be a fact, she was overwhelmed. It was her card—it had to be—that Abigail had used. Aghast, appalled, Pam sank down on the edge of the bath and began to cry.

She had not heard the shuffling footsteps along the corridor or noticed the young man leaning in the doorway until he spoke, repeating his earlier question. "God, Mother, what is it? What has the bastard done now?"

Dropping onto his knees beside her, Robert clumsily put his arm around her shoulders and held her close against his chest until her shuddering sobs subsided. Embarrassed now, the boy relaxed his hold on her. "Mum, what's the matter? What are you doing at home?"

Pulling herself clear of his grasp, Pam felt it was her turn to ask a question: "And just what are *you* doing here? Shouldn't you be in school?"

Taking in his dishevelled appearance—the clearly slept-in jeans and crumpled sweatshirt, and an all-pervading unwashed smell—she wondered just how late he had come home last night.

"Er, not feeling too good. Must be coming down with something. Got ready for school but felt sick, so went back to bed."

Ignoring the obvious lie—there was no way Robert had been clean and dressed in his school uniform *this* morning—Pam struggled to her feet. It was a lame excuse on his part. She would tackle him about it later, and about the somewhat unflattering reference to his father. Just what did he mean by that? For now, though, she had far more pressing things on her mind.

She knew what she had to do. She had to return to the hospital and report her loss to the CEO. What would happen next, she did not dare to speculate. Right now what she needed was a good strong cup of tea. Then she would face up to her responsibilities, firstly at work. And then, when that was over, it would be time to find out what her boys were really up to.

Was this morning a one-off, as she hoped, or was Robert missing lessons much more frequently? She wondered how much his brother knew. Was he complicit? Did he make up excuses for him at school? Again, she was going to have to tackle them about it.

The nagging doubt Pam had felt for some time crystallised into something approaching fear. She realised that she did not know what her sons got up to after school. Were they really at their friends' houses? And who were these friends? She had known their little companions at primary school, or more accurately, she had known their mothers, sharing moments at school functions or entertaining each other's children on play dates. She had had time for that then as a stay-at-home mother. Resuming a career of her own had curtailed much of that. With a pang, she realised that she no longer knew her boys. She was so busy with her own life that she had no idea what went on in theirs.

———•◆•———

Later That Day

It was worse than Pam thought. She had been sent home in disgrace. Not actually suspended—yet—but told to take the remainder of the week on leave. Paid leave. Is this what is meant by "gardening leave"? she wondered. She had been advised to talk to her union rep about it but had quailed at the thought of doing so immediately. On the few occasions she had encountered Gwyneth Proctor, she had found her loud and domineering. Assertive, she corrected herself. I suppose she has to be in that role. She would probably have to face her later, she conceded, but not now. She needed to go home and think.

Pam wondered what she should tell Ted—even whether she should tell him anything at all. In her last exchange with Robert earlier that morning, in a rare, almost convivial moment, a strange sort of alliance had been reached. They were both dishevelled by now, sitting in her kitchen over a pot of tea. Her face was streaked with tears, and his was still creased from sleep, with his rumpled clothes and spiky just-out-of-bed hair. They tiptoed around in this fragile unaccustomed intimacy.

They were two people with a shared history, two individuals each in their own world, two people each with something to hide, sharing a moment but not really sharing at all, both of them curious about the other's secrets.

Robert was the one to break the uneasy silence. Caught off guard, Pam almost told him the reason for her distress and the entire horrible implication of what she had done. It was too soon for such confidences. She couldn't trust herself to think too deeply about the possible outcome, and she wasn't sure she could trust Robert with that knowledge, so she had told him only a part of it, namely that she had lost something belonging to work.

"Must have been something important for you to cry about it?" Again he was questioning, astute, needling for more.

Well, she had a few questions of her own, left unspoken—for the time being.

And then he was offering her a lifeline, a truce, if that is what it was. "I shan't say anything to Dad about it. Not if you keep quiet about me bunking off school."

For now at least, she had to be satisfied with that. But he can't be the one dictating all the terms. I shall deal with the boys later, in my own way.

CHAPTER 42

The Man on the Bus

He was pleased with himself. This time it had gone well. Waiting at his post earlier than usual, he could feel his excitement mounting but he was not showing it. He knew how to keep a cool exterior. Sipping his tea, apparently immersed in his newspaper, he was fully alert, waiting—watching and waiting.

For three days now he had watched, always in the same seat, at a table three back from the door. And three times it had happened. Three times now it had gone according to plan. He liked the symmetry of it—a succession of threes. It appealed to his sense of order. Three. Three for luck. Lucky for some. Three times now *she* had come past, not stopping for that horrible concoction any more. She was catching the earlier bus now. Trying to get home in daylight, he supposed. Such a sensible precaution. It is always so much safer by daylight.

That's what they had always been told as children. "Get home before dark. Stop playing now. Come inside before it gets dark. You can't go out now; it's getting dark." Well, that was for children surely. He was glad to have left that behind. He wanted nothing to do with childhood any more. Not that life as a young adult had been that much better, he reflected, glad now that this, too, was in the past. But at least he didn't have the silly twilight curfew back then. He was free to come and go in daylight or by night—whatever suited. He had found that he actually liked darkness, the way it could swallow you up, make you disappear, cause you to be invisible, leaving only the things that would be found when the darkness went away—things you *wanted* to be found, things you wanted to be seen, to be appreciated.

CHAPTER 43

Ben

That was when it should have happened, and that was the moment when Ben had wavered.

They had cruised on in the early morning light past the solitary boats moored alongside the deserted towpath, then on past the boats on the private moorings at the other side of the canal. No signs of life here. Many of the boats were already sheeted up for the winter, no plumes of smoke from their chimneys, no lights from the windows, no cheery waves from fellow boaters busy preparing breakfast in their galleys or lounging on the deck, steaming mugs in their hands, lighting that first cigarette of the day. No one seemed to be living aboard any of the narrowboats here. Then Ben piloted past the hire boats, moored and deserted, the matching colours of their paintwork gleaming cleanly in the watery sunshine. These craft had been recently washed down and polished, and were ready for the next wave of eager holidaymakers—a wave not likely to happen now before the spring. Ben had seen no one in the hire boatyard—no signs of activity at all.

They had to be approaching a village now. Ben thought he might see people walking their dogs or joggers out for a morning run, but so far he had not seen a soul. They had passed a caravan site—that too was deserted—and a canal-side pub in darkness, too early even for the cleaners, he supposed.

He knew he had to stop here. There was a lift bridge to operate before they could go on any further. It was down now. He could see the headlights of a car approaching, crossing the bridge, too far away for him to be seen, to attract the driver's attention. Ben made his decision. He would moor here and walk into the village. The Nicholson canal chart showed it to be less than a mile away. He was bound to find someone there to whom he could report their having found the child, someone who would relieve him of this awful, pressing responsibility.

He pulled the boat in alongside the towpath, pleased to find there were mooring rings here, so there was no need for him to struggle, holding the boat into the side while he manoeuvred mooring pins into position and passed bow and stern ropes through these, tying them off securely. As it was, even with the fixed mooring rings, this was not the easiest thing to do on his own. And that is when it happened, so unexpectedly that Ben gasped in astonishment. After all these hours of his managing the boat single-handed, there was Karen! She had emerged from the doors at the front of the boat and jumped onto the bank, and was now busy tying the bow rope to the mooring ring there.

Now, smiling, she came to him. He looked up from tying off the stern, and there she was beside him, working in harmony with him. It seemed to Ben that this was what he had dreamt of. His hopes for the holiday had been just this.

"Darling, you go inside now. Cari is sleeping. I'll nip into the village and get what we need." Cajoling now, coaxing, she said, "Please, darling, I can get everything we need and come back and make us a decent breakfast. Then we can think out what to do."

Unable to resist her pleading, Ben felt his resolve beginning to weaken. He knew that he was being played. He also knew that he should be strong, that it was up to him to take control of the situation. But what harm could another hour or so do? She was right. They would both think more clearly once they had had something to eat. God, he needed a drink too. What he wouldn't do for a cup of coffee right now.

"Well, if you're sure she'll be all right while you are gone. But make it quick, Karen. I don't know my way around babies."

"Fine, love. She shouldn't be any trouble. I got quite a lot of milk into her, and she's sound asleep now. I made her a little bed in the big drawer where all the wet weather stuff was. You won't have to do a thing. I'll be as quick as I can." So saying, Karen skipped off along the towpath and up onto the road towards the village. Yes, that was how Ben would remember this moment: Karen skipping up the road, moving very lightly, very purposefully—joyfully even.

She was as good as her word. It really hadn't seemed many minutes at all. Ben had gone down into the galley and put the kettle on, moving quietly, gingerly opening the cupboard and setting out the mugs in readiness for Karen's return—a teabag in hers and instant coffee in his. He had made up the Morsø with fresh coal, delicately placing each piece in position with the fire tongs, not wanting to wake the sleeping baby by noisily tipping it in from the coal scuttle. Then, stretching out on the bunk in front of the stove, overcome by warmth, tiredness, and emotion, Ben dozed.

Karen was back now, bustling about in the galley, the appetising smell of bacon cooking, Ben with a cup of steaming coffee in front of him, rubbing the sleep from his eyes. He had awakened with a start when he heard the hatch being slid open and Karen struggling down the steps from the deck, her arms full of carrier bags. She had dumped these unceremoniously on their bed before going back onto the deck and retrieving the remainder of the shopping.

He marvelled at the sheer quantity. She must have cleared the shelves, he thought, imagining her doing a sort of supermarket snatch then having to wrestle her way back laden with her spoils. If things had been different, she could have enlisted his assistance. He had always done his share of shopping and never felt it remotely unmanly to be seen carrying home the bags. But that hadn't been an option this time. He glanced guiltily then at the sleeping child, aware that he had paid no attention at all to it in Karen's absence. Thank goodness it seemed to be all right. Karen certainly appeared to know how to look after it, he conceded.

With breakfast over, Karen announced her intention of making the baby comfortable. Ben knew now what had constituted the bulk of that shopping. Deftly unwrapping and stacking her purchases, Karen laid out a supply of disposable nappies, some baby wipes, and a little jar of what looked like ointment. He watched as she retrieved a large plastic food container from under the sink, filled it with water, and added something from a bottle she had bought. Into the mixture went feeding bottles and teats. Then she stacked boxes of formula on the shelf alongside their tea and coffee.

"Karen, what are you doing? We don't need all this stuff for her. We have to hand the baby over."

"All in good time, darling. I know that is what you think. But I have to make sure she is all right and that she looks as though we have taken care of her."

"Karen, it's no good. You have to give this thing up. You can't keep it—her."

Ben was shouting now, aware that Karen seemed oblivious to his mounting concern.

At the sound of raised voices, the baby stirred and began to cry. Instantly, Karen was on her knees, lifting the child from its improvised cot, cuddling and soothing her. "Don't cry, little Cari. We'll take care of you. Let's start by sorting you out a bit." Karen looked up from changing the child, discarding the clumsy square of towelling for one of the disposable nappies she had bought. "We will, Ben. At some point, we will. But we have to show that we have looked after her properly." Then engagingly, disingenuously, she said, "Ben, darling, I don't want us getting into trouble for neglecting her."

CHAPTER 44

The Man

He had checked the paintwork on his van before leaving for work this morning. It had dried well enough to take the vinyl letters he had cut out last night: Logocosts. He was pleased with that one. A combination of Robocop and low-cost logos: how apt was that? It was so easy to make up a logo these days, to decorate his van. New paintwork, a different logo, or maybe no logo at all—keep ringing the changes, keep them guessing. Sometimes it was not even his van at all, but there were inherent dangers in that. What if he should leave some trace of his hobby behind? It was much safer to get the vehicle back to its customary hiding place. That way he could really be sure to remove every possible speck of evidence.

It was tempting to use the work van, of course. Given his policy of using a different-looking vehicle every time, the work van had presented itself as one of those necessary alternatives. The facilities for giving it a thorough cleaning were undeniably good, but even doing that was fraught with a certain amount of tension. The depot transport manager had viewed his assiduous attention to detail with something bordering on suspicion the other night, he thought. But then, it had not been the usual slick performance his hobby warranted. It was wrong, out of kilter. The memory still unsettled him.

He felt sure he *had* got away with it, that his fears were more the product of paranoia than reality, but he had made a gargantuan mistake, and in his experience, error only ever compounded error. There had to be absolute control of a situation. He had learnt that lesson the hard way many years ago. When he was no longer able to have the things that were important to him ordered and precise, when he no longer had control of them, was when he really lost control of everything. He had paid a high price for that then. But his masters had taught him well. He had been an able student, and until the other day he would have said that he had remained in complete control ever since.

That had been such a mistake. Shuddering at the recollection, he knew that there could only really be one chance like that. There was simply no place in his life for errors of that magnitude ever to occur again.

CHAPTER 45

Sandy

Sandy's return to the station and her public humiliation during the postshift briefing had left her feeling somewhat chastened. Her earlier enthusiasm to share the success she had achieved in remembering where she had previously encountered the hit-and-run victim and then retrieving her belongings had vanished. She had duly reported these to DI Barnes, the officer in charge, remarking only that the newish-looking pink blanket seemed as though it could have come from a child's cot, and speculating aloud as to whether this would put the victim anywhere in the vicinity of the maternity unit when the woman Abigail Lamont had gone missing. Deflated by the apparent lack of interest this had aroused, she made her way across the room to the noticeboards on the far wall, where details of the team that had been hastily assembled to spearhead the investigation into the latest murder were posted.

The group of officers standing in front of the board fell silent at her approach, but she was aware of their tangible excitement and of a sort of vicarious horror the most gruesome of incidents so often provoked. Although she felt it herself, the exhilaration of a new case with all the horrible details yet to unfold, along with the imminent challenge to seek out the truth and solve the crime, Sandy was also aware of an element of disgust, a self-loathing this generated: it was almost as though by virtue of their eager anticipation, the gratuitous thrill of the chase, they were somehow complicit in the wickedness which had caused the crime.

Ralph Keating, the duty officer leading the team, lost no time in bringing Sandy up to date with events. The body of a young woman had been found at a nearby caravan site early that morning, although the man who made the gruesome discovery had delayed reporting it until almost midday. He was currently being held in the interview room along the corridor, awaiting further questioning by the team. Apparently the reason for his delay in contacting the police was the illicit nature of his presence in the vicinity that morning. The caravan site was on private land and operated from Easter to the end of September. It was an adult-only site with a coarse fishing lake and a small clubhouse manned throughout the season. The owner lived in a large detached manor house on the upper part of the acreage, hundreds of yards from the lakeside. Access to the site was protected by sturdy metal railings forming a perimeter fence, with an entry barrier immediately adjacent to the owner's house, which was situated on the single approach road entering the amenity.

The unfortunate man who had stumbled across the partially decomposed body had no right to be there. Earlier in the year, he had discovered a missing piece of railing on the edge of the site farthest from the house and had used this on a number of occasions to gain access to the lake and indulge in some unauthorised fishing. Throughout the summer he had successfully avoided any contact with fellow anglers, keeping to the margins of the lake, away from the regular stands, fearing that he might be exposed as having no caravan and no right to be there.

Since the season had ended and all the caravanners had locked up and gone home, he was able to relax and enjoy his angling without the constant fear of discovery. The owner of the manor and accompanying estate was an elderly ex-military man who seldom ventured far around the lake, having no interest himself in fishing and happy to leave the day-to-day running of the site to his much younger wife. She was equally unlikely to go near to the water, and even in season was content for the caravanners to report any problems to the temporary site manager rather than dealing with them herself. Such ground maintenance, as was necessary, occurred throughout the summer and during the short period of concentrated activity immediately prior to the Easter opening. By this time in the year, late October, he was relatively certain of having unchallenged access to his favourite pastime.

Now that he was no longer at work, he was able to come more often, two or three times a week, only too glad of an excuse to get away from the petty irritations of home: a wife who constantly chided him for his idleness and nagged him to get himself another job, and a large, docile daughter whose special educational needs rendered her a less than lively companion. There was seldom any money for him to go to the pub, and he had few friends since becoming redundant eighteen months ago.

No. Fishing was his only outlet, and he did not want to give it up.

So he had reasoned to himself on his hurried return through the broken railing, back to his dismal home life. He was shocked to find her, of course—too shocked, really, to register very much about the scene at all. He was just aware of her body lying there on its back, her clothing all awry, a lot of her naked. And there was something else horrible about that. He had not wanted to get too close to see what it was. The very sight of her and the fright of finding her there had been too much.

He had not wanted to report it at all, knowing full well that it would entail an explanation of what he was doing there without any sort of permission or reasonable justification he could think of. He could pretend to have gone in search of a lost dog, he supposed, but that story would never hold up under scrutiny. They would only have to ask his wife to learn that he had never had a dog. He was retching now, clutching his stomach as he bent over the long grass. Finally, once the spasm had passed, he picked up his rod and ran back the way he had come.

His wife was out shopping when he got home, and the sight of his placid, uncomplaining daughter brought him up with a start. Damn it, he would have to tell somebody. The young woman he had found was someone's daughter too. How would he feel if it had been his Ruby lying out there?

They sent a police car for him then, and he had to show them where he had got through the broken railing, directing them to where they would find the woman. He had been here ever since. All the questions he had faced—it made his head reel to think about it. He had lost track of time and wondered if they were going to let him go home tonight.

To the police officers in the incident room, the man remained something of an enigma. Was he really the illicit angler who just happened to have stumbled across this latest atrocity during his nefarious and ill-fated fishing trip, or was he more seriously implicated? Meanwhile, they must await the result of the forthcoming postmortem before issuing the warning to the general public, which they knew their senior officers were in the process of preparing, before their fears could be confirmed. The Wolverhampton serial killer had moved on to their patch.

Meanwhile, a plastic tent had been erected over the grisly discovery, and arc lights positioned to enable the SOCOs to conduct their in situ examination of both the body and the surrounding terrain. A uniformed police presence had been detailed to guard the scene because, while it was sufficiently distant from the nearest public road to be largely shielded from view, there was always the possibility that the unusual pattern of light in the sky from the powerful arc lamps would attract curious onlookers and the unwelcome intrusion of local media. A detailed fingertip search of the surrounding area was planned for the following day, and while house-to-house enquiries were hardly a feasible option given the rural location, two officers had been despatched to the owner's property, in part to explain the sudden spate of activity, and then to ascertain what, if anything, they knew of the murdered woman or the man who claimed to have found her.

A preliminary visit to the big house revealed only that the owner and his wife appeared to be away. Only a small quantity of mail, visible through the letter box, had fallen onto the floor behind the door, which seemed to indicate that they had not been away long.

On their second visit, the following morning, the post had been moved and could be seen neatly stacked on a small hall table to the left of the door. Hoping this meant that the owners had returned at some point late the previous evening, and curious as to why the officer guarding the road to the house had not reported this fact, Sergeant Heart rang the bell again, this time keeping his finger very firmly on the button until the door was opened by a startled middle-aged woman clutching a handful of dusters. She viewed the two officers with marked suspicion and reluctantly let them into the hall. Confirming her name, Sheila Barker told them that she came from the village a couple of miles away, twice a week, to clean for the owners. No, she hadn't a car; that's why they hadn't seen one out front. She biked it, didn't she? Left it out back, out of sight, same as always. No real need to do that out of season, she supposed. Habit really. Owners didn't like it left out front when the campers were in—said it looked untidy. Any roads, it might get pinched then, she thought. Well, "borrowed" more likely, if any of those lazy buggers didn't want the hassle of moving their cars and just needed to pop out for milk or summat.

Finding it difficult to stop this barrage of seemingly gratuitous information, while at the same time wondering if she would inadvertently let something slip that could give them a bit of a lead in the case, the two policemen smiled at each other and attempted to divert the flow to more relevant aspects of their enquiry. How, they wondered, had she managed to get up to the house without being stopped by the officer with the police car blocking the entrance to the site? Was there another road in, one they didn't know about?

"Oh, I saw him all right. Very helpful young man, I might add. Pointed out my back tyre was flattish-like. I said I'd pump it up when I got up to the house. Told him I always did for them twice a week, and he said to go on up and see to me bike. Didn't say nothing about not coming into work as usual" (this in answer to the question as to what she was doing inside the house). Shaking his head, Sergeant Heart made a mental note to confront the young officer and castigate him for his negligence in allowing unaccompanied access to a possible crime scene. After all, the body had been found on their land. Lord only knows what the garrulous Mrs Barker may have disturbed or contaminated in her spate of domestic activity.

No, she hadn't seen any other policemen. "Where are they?" she wondered aloud. "There only is this one way up to the house, the same road as goes right into the site." She hadn't noticed any lights or anything. She only ever went to the house, never any farther than that. All the years she'd worked here, twenty-five or more, she supposed, she'd never once been down as far as the lake. Why? Had something happened down there? "Always did think that lake was a risky thing. All them campers coming and going. No way of telling if any of them fell in."

And no, she didn't know when the owners were due back. Never told her nowt. Just, "You keep coming in as usual, Mrs. B. We'll settle up with you when we see you. We know we can rely on you to keep an eye on things." They wouldn't take kindly to this, her being hustled out of the house before finishing her hours.

Protesting loudly, "Not even got me upstairs done," Shirley Barker was escorted off the premises and round to the rear yard to collect her bicycle."Can't think why I can't just go through and let meself out the back door. Save all this walking round!" she wailed.

Once they were convinced that the redoubtable Mrs Barker was stolidly pedalling down the road towards the "very helpful young man", the two officers looked at each other. "Just have a quick look round, shall we?" It was Sergeant Heart who had posed the question, not really expecting anything other than acquiescence from his partner. "I know we haven't got a search warrant as such, but a quick butcher's won't do any harm. At least it will let us know if we need to get up here with a search team sooner rather than later." So saying, George Heart pushed open the front door, which he had conveniently left unlatched. Pausing only to briefly peruse the pile of unopened mail, the two officers made their way through the hall and into the rooms beyond.

Their immediate impression was one of stultifying dull normality. Elaborate but thoroughly drab full-length curtains shrouded each window, and equally large drab furniture was somewhat sparsely arranged in the spacious downstairs sitting rooms. The pervading dreariness was alleviated only by the shelves of glasses and decanters and the numerous pictures of shooting scenes. Smaller rooms at the back of the house seemed dedicated to this pastime, the cupboards crammed with tweeds, waterproofs, boots, and brogues. The kitchen and butler's pantry were capacious, but the décor was very old-fashioned, with only the lavishly stocked wine shelves betraying any hint of extravagant enjoyment. In marked contrast was a beautifully proportioned dining room with immaculate furniture and fittings, amid which was the pervading sense that this was a showcase and little used.

Ascending the gracefully curved staircase, the officers found all three floors equally uninspiring. The top two seemed mainly used for storage, filled with unneeded furniture, a large number of suitcases in varying sizes, and a dented old trunk which appeared to have been last used when its owner was away at boarding school. Only the first floor appeared to be in regular use. Here matte grey curtains prevailed, and even the bed coverings were in country colours—tweedy greens and browns—conferring a very masculine feel to the rooms. Little vestige of what could be construed as feminine frivolity could be seen anywhere. The silver-backed hairbrush and comb sets redolent of an earlier age, a few worn cosmetics, and the even fewer bottles of perfume were arrayed on top of the dressing table in the double bedroom obviously shared by the couple. The bathroom, as dated as the kitchen downstairs, was flanked by large painted cupboards, their contents the usual array of linens and towels in complementary dull designs, a depressing array of prescription and over-the-counter medication, and a pile of battered copies of Horse and Hound and the Shooting Times. "Loo-side reading, George," commented Bert Weaver.

The study situated on this floor was fitted out in dark brown leather mirroring the tones of the deep oak shelving and the dull covers of many old books. Nothing much here either to titillate the imagination, George thought. Opening the last door on the corridor, the men were amazed at the contrast with everything that had gone before. This room had substantial wooden shutters closed against the daylight beyond, but it was lit from overhead by a bank of powerful strip lights. Illuminated by these, everything in the room gleamed. Floor-to-ceiling gun cabinets lined one entire wall, with yet more weapons (whether live or deactivated, it was impossible to tell from the doorway where they stood, afraid to venture further now, lest they, in turn, should be guilty of contaminating the scene) mounted on display brackets across the two adjacent walls. Brightly coloured mats covered the floor, with rolls of what appeared to be gun-cleaning equipment. "Quite an arsenal," breathed Bert. "I wonder how much of it is legit?"

"Certainly warrants more of a proper search. We'll have to see about getting that authorised. Meanwhile, until we know bit more about this particular little armoury, we had better get the premises securely guarded." Dropping the Yale lock behind him, George felt for his radio and requested a further deployment of manpower to be stationed at both the front entrance and the rear of the property.

"A very interesting find," Bert responded, "but I don't see what, if anything, it has to do with the body down there."

George was unable to explain the frisson of excitement he felt, nor the acute sense of something not tallying. He had played such hunches before. Indeed, he was renowned for it. And sometimes his hunches met with unexpected success. But it was far too early in this case to put any of those thoughts into words. Instead, he briefed the two PCSO's who had arrived as a result of his radio appeal, instructing them to let *no one*, not even the owners, into the house until further clarification had been sought from the lead investigator. Fingering the bunch of keys in the pocket of his uniform jacket, he led the way back to the scene where the body had been found.

Down at the lakeside, the remainder of the assembled team were having a less than successful morning. The SOCOs, having finished their initial inspection of the body, were now completing their measurements and bagging and labelling all the samples they had removed before the corpse was transferred to the mortuary ambulance, which had made its approach along the site road and across the bumpy terrain beside the shielding protective tent. Members of the team were baffled. They still had no idea how the body had come to be there. They had discovered the break in the railings, but there was no sign of great disturbance from there to the spot where the body had lain. A few footprints could be seen in both directions, but these seemed to have been made by the same pair of boots and were likely to belong to the man who had reported the gruesome discovery, the ones pointing away from the body quite obviously made in much greater haste than the first set, the long grass trampled carelessly aside, spatters of mud filling the imprints there. These had yielded useful casts for comparison with the Wellington boots found at the man's home and brought into the station along with the other items of outer clothing which the officer sent to question the man's wife had acquired earlier that morning.

There was also evidence of vomiting having occurred, although this was less clear-cut, partly because of the activity of some wild animal visiting the area and partly because some of that particular residue could be attributed to the inexperienced young officer who was part of the initial group to have arrived at the crime scene. There were traces of tyre tracks farther from the edge of the lake, but these impressions were faint and mostly indistinguishable from the muddy depressions caused over a season of laden fishing buggies being dragged along from the unsurfaced pathway to the various stands beside the water. The fingertip search had only just got underway, but so far it had revealed nothing other than a piece of discarded fishing line and the broken elastic from someone's pole.

CHAPTER 46

Ben and Karen

It had been three days now, and Ben knew that he had missed his moment. Each cottage they passed, each occupied boat (although there had been few of them),was the home of someone who lived aboard throughout the year and the few individuals he had seen walking along the towpath represented an opportunity lost. The longer he and Karen left it, the more difficult it was becoming. He should have ignored Karen's pleading, her persuasive insistence that they needed to show that they had not neglected the child.

But he just could not bring himself to do it. He knew he was being weak and stupid, and he was afraid too, he admitted to himself. They had left it too long. They would be in serious trouble, he knew it. They might even be sent to prison for what they had done. The thought of that happening to Karen, of what that would do to her, terrified him.

Karen was humming to herself as she prepared their evening meal. They had stopped at the last village, where she had replenished their supplies, buying Ben's favourite food, choosing things she could easily cook in the little oven on the boat. She was making them really good meals now, actually enjoying cooking again. At first she was aware that she was almost bribing Ben by being the perfect housewife, showing him how well she could manage to look after them both and the baby, as well as pulling her weight on this holiday. Busying herself below deck for most of the time, but willing to help with the boat whenever he needed it—working the little lift bridges, securing the mooring ropes, and reading the navigation map aloud to him while he worked the tiller—she knew what she was doing: buying his silence. And for the time being he had accepted it. She no longer cringed each time they passed another human being, scared that this would be the one. That Ben would choose this person, this moment, to bring about their disclosure and shatter the happy little world she was creating for them.

Karen no longer seemed to recognise that hers was a world founded on deception. She was who she had always intended to be: Karen, wife and mother. Mother first and foremost, she acknowledged, as she contentedly chopped the carrots and onions for the stew, glancing every so often at the sleeping baby. They had settled into a comfortable routine: feeding, changing, cuddling, sleeping. The child, too, was contented, still dressed in cut-down T-shirts with a drawer for a bed, but Karen had plans to change all that. They would be in Llangollen soon, and then she would buy everything the baby needed. Cari Moses was here to stay.

CHAPTER 47

Ted Manning

Ted Manning was a worried man. There was something seriously wrong at home, he knew it. And he did not know what to do about it. Here he was, at the peak of his career to date, with every chance that the latest case to come his way would take that career to even dizzier heights. At the same time, he had this awful premonition that things could go horribly wrong, that things were beginning to implode around him. It was contrary to his nature to worry about anything on the domestic front. He had always prided himself on his ability to walk straight out of whatever front door it had been and promptly leave all that behind him. But the niggling doubts that were beginning to build in his mind were following him into work now. He found himself thinking about them at odd times during the day. It was alien to him; he brushed the thoughts aside. Nothing must get in the way of his progress. He couldn't let anything threaten that.

Ted was aware of a growing irritation that this should be happening to him now. He could really do without all these complications at present. In line for promotion, he knew that not only his police record but also any aspect of his personal life which could possibly enter the public domain should be entirely beyond reproach. God only knew, he had been sailing pretty close to the wind for years now. He amended that thought: he had been sailing *dangerously* close to the wind. It was a bloody good thing that Pam was too wrapped up in that silly job of hers to realise just what had been going on, virtually under her nose, for months now.

Pam's "little job". He chuckled at the recollection of how dismissive he had been back then, seeing no reason why any wife of his should demean herself by taking on such a role. He had saved her from all that when he married her, only for her to turn it all about-face and go back to "baby talk and bum wiping". Those were his very words when she first announced her intention of going back to her early career and training as a midwife. He asked himself then what he had done to deserve that. Not only had he the dullest and most unexciting partner of all time—drab in appearance, awkward in company, and totally unexhilarating in bed—but also now she was going to come back to him stinking of hospitals and of other women and their babies.

But it had played out to his advantage in the long run. Often too tired to know or care when he got home, if he even *got* home, Pam was sure to attribute Ted's increasingly random presence in the house they shared to whatever was happening in his life as a senior figure in the police force. Little did she know that he, for one, had compelling interests beyond his place of work, all of which rendered it more crucial than ever that he should be perceived as squeaky clean. He could not risk any of his business ventures being exposed. And he certainly could not take the chance of being seen as anything other than an aspiring and deserving detective chief superintendent—an upright public servant and respectable family man. Which was why it was imperative that Pam should be at his side.

God knows, it shouldn't be much of an ask, he thought. She had not contributed much in the way of happiness in their relationship lately: fairly useless in the kitchen, seemingly incapable of disciplining his unruly sons, and sexually dysfunctional. But then he was even beginning to wonder about that. Having noticed how much more animated she had become on first resuming her career, he wondered then if it was just the work giving her a renewed sense of purpose or whether, in fact, she was seeing another man. Surely it was only in recent weeks that she had seemed too exhausted to function properly any more. But perhaps it was not just the work that was making her tired. That too could be the result of having some sort of illicit affair. He could relate only too well to that, having had a succession of other women over the years.

Then there was that incident the other night. He knew he was being foolhardy even to contemplate a meeting in such a public place—on his own patch, no less. At the time it seemed a calculated risk: it would entail no more than the briefest of exchanges before they went on their separate ways. There was nothing to raise anyone's suspicions. To the most curious of onlookers, it would have appeared to be merely a fleeting encounter.

Suddenly there was this godawful crashing sound as a car collided with the lamp post, leaving the victims scattered in the road as the car sped off down the high street. He had to spring into action then, do what he knew he had to do. There could be no thought of fading into the background, distancing himself from the human disaster before him. He was too well known a figure for that. Someone surely would have recognised him. He might even have been caught on CCTV.

And so Ted Manning had stepped forward and acted out his role as the public would have expected, detailing someone to alert the emergency services as he mentally triaged the casualties. There was no doubt who amongst the was the most severely injured. As he knelt beside the comatose figure of the girl, checking her pulse, looking for obvious signs of haemorrhage, he sought for any form of identification she might be carrying, for a name he could call her.

It was then that he had made the discovery that threatened the very security of the privileged world he enjoyed. He was stunned, shaking now, hastily pushing this proof of identity into his pocket, out of sight—something he would have to contend with later. The full implications were only just beginning to dawn.

As the first police officers arriving at the accident site were variously deployed in keeping back the crowd that was beginning to gather, diverting the traffic flow, and attempting to collect some witness details, Ted handed over his care of the injured girl to the attending ambulance crew. "Victim of hit-and-run. Vital signs very poor. Name as yet unknown. Not carrying any form of identification which could be of assistance." This was the first lie in what was to become a sequence of deception and blame. The item Ted had so hurriedly secreted from view was indeed a form of identity, but that identity belonged to his wife. He immediately recognised the object for what it was: Pam's hospital security pass. What he could not begin to comprehend was how this had happened to be in the possession of the girl now on her way to hospital, apparently barely alive—full blues and twos.

In the moments that followed, Ted fought to marshal his thoughts and maintain his composure in the face of his colleagues. Always appearing the consummate professional, he was relieved to find that this veneer did not desert him now. Internally, though, his mind was in turmoil. Was this what Pam had been keeping from him? Somehow, but he could not guess in what way, his wife seemed to be involved with this despicable street person. Ted could hardly contain his contempt. Was it even possible that she was having some sort of lesbian relationship? How could she have sunk so low? Still, in some ways, it did not really surprise him when he thought about it. Perhaps that was the appeal of midwifery all along. Why the hell else would any normal woman want the sort of job that entailed sticking her fingers up another woman's fanny?

Suddenly recalling the eager-faced student midwife he had courted all those years ago, Ted remembered how the thought of her work actually had added spice to their lovemaking back then. He had assumed, erroneously as it appeared now to have turned out, that someone so intimately acquainted with women's bodies would be liberal and uninhibited in the use of her own. How wrong he had been. He had expected sexual fireworks and achieved something less than a damp squib.

CHAPTER 48

Sandy

Sandy, too, was aware of an increased tension at home. Helen seemed almost overeager to please, and Sandy had begun to find this intensity unsettling, to the extent that the cancellation of all impending leave had come as something of a relief to her. Any talk of a late autumn holiday for the two of them was shelved, and if Helen was disproportionally disappointed by this, then Sandy's additional duty shifts meant that she was not around to notice it.

Sandy had disappointments of her own. Her initial delight at finding the rucksack belonging to the hit-and-run victim had seemingly come to nothing. Forensic examination of the burnt-out car had confirmed that this was indeed the vehicle responsible, but at that point the investigation had stalled. They were no nearer to identifying the culprit, or even possibly *culprits*, involved. Eyewitness accounts were vague, some asserting that there were two people in the vehicle, some only having seen one. Inevitably the descriptions of the driver were equally unspecific. He was a white male; that was about the only consensus so far. The only people who might have been able to give a better account were those who had been injured, and one of them was still deeply unconscious. The two commuters who had sustained fractures to their legs had had their limbs pinned and immobilised and subsequently were discharged to the care of their families. Neither man proved to be an effective witness as, by their own accounts, they were each hurrying through the city centre, barely looking where they were going, such was the ingrained familiarity of the homeward journey. If they noticed anything at all, it was in the immediate aftermath of the collision when, contorted with shock and pain, they registered only that a big dark car was accelerating away from the event.

The woman with the broken arm remained so profoundly traumatised by the event as to be incomprehensible, and the third woman had disappeared from her hospital bed with the man who was her companion at the scene of the incident. This uninjured male had presented as the person most likely to be able to furnish the police with more accurate details, but so far the police had been unable to locate either of them or determine their whereabouts.

Sandy's frustration was compounded by her almost constant deployment at the hospital. Seemingly every shift was at the bedside of the injured woman. With little evidence of any continued threat to her person, this gave Sandy ample opportunity for reflection. Given the very active ongoing murder enquiry and the continued anxiety over the disappearance of Abigail Lamont and her baby, she doubted whether such a sustained level of surveillance could be maintained, expecting every day to be pulled from this task and given something more stimulating to do, disappointed every time that her bedside vigil was repeated.

CHAPTER 49

The Woman

She was pleased that her new routine seemed to be working out well. She had had to be quite firm about it. Not that Carol had been difficult, but the other two legal secretaries were less inclined to be accommodating. She was not oblivious to their rolled eyes and noncommittal shrugs, and was sure she had overheard some muttered grumble about "special allowances". Well, that was their problem. You would think that they, of all people, would be aware of antidiscrimination legislation. Fine, as long as it doesn't impinge on their comfortable little world, she thought. Anyway, she had stood her ground and was leaving the office promptly at 4.30 now. It meant getting there a bit earlier in the morning, but that was not a problem. For the last three days, she had got up at the same time as Alex and he had given her a lift into town, dropping her off as close to the office as he could given the early morning rush hour. It was just a pity that they could not have an equivalent arrangement at the other end of the day, but his working hours were unpredictable and he often had to travel out to see clients in the afternoon, coming home straight from these visits without necessarily going back into town.

This week he had two such appointments in London and would be spending a couple of nights away from home. She had wondered about going to stay with her mother, but that would have entailed a longer journey into work each day. Plus, given her mother's well-intentioned but stifling concern about the progress of her pregnancy, her elderly parents belonging to the era when fewer married women worked and where almost none of them worked once they were in what Mum insisted on calling "the family way", she shuddered at the recollection. "No, much better to be in my own home. I can get a takeaway and pamper myself a bit with Alex away."

She was in a happy mood. Today had gone particularly well. She really was on top of her workload, and with Carol still in court, there was no need for her to stay on at the office. She would make Brown's well before closing time and still be able to catch her earlier bus home. Her luck had held, and she was able to pick out two winter dresses she really liked: one for work and one a more frivolous purchase which she thought would do for Alex's firm's Christmas party. In the end, it was all a bit of a rush, the waiting for an empty cubicle and trying the dresses on, then waiting again in a queue to pay for them. Hurriedly scooping up her carrier bags, she just made it to the bus station in time to board the early bus, unaware of the watchful eyes of the man in the café, who folded his newspaper and followed her out through the departure bays, before getting into a large maroon van.

———————

The bus was crowded with shoppers, schoolchildren, and people leaving work. It was hot and stuffy, and because she was one of the last people to have got on, she was forced to stand for the entire journey. So much for the "privileged seating" notices requesting other passengers to allow elderly, infirm, or pregnant people priority: no one was prepared to give up their seat for her. Her legs were aching now, and she was thankful when the bus finally pulled into her stop. She would be glad to get home tonight and put her feet up for a while before Alex got in. The prospect of the forthcoming period of maternity leave had never seemed more appealing.

She was only dimly aware of the bus pulling away as she set off towards their house. Distracted now, searching in her handbag for her front door key, she hardly noticed the van pulling up a little farther along the road, the driver out of the van and opening its back doors.

And then it happened—so suddenly that she barely realised what had hit her. She was being grabbed from behind. Terrified, dropping her bags, she screamed for help. But there was no one to hear her and no oncoming cars with headlights to illuminate the assault that was taking place. She was struggling against her assailant now, to no avail. Her shoes had come off in the attack as she kicked out ineffectively, her tights brushing uselessly across the man's shins. She was pushed face first into the van, her hands clutched protectively over her abdomen as she crashed to the floor. She heard the noise of the engine as the van pulled away from the kerb. The doors were locked from the outside, impervious to her frantic scrabbling, the darkness inside the van suffocating in its intensity.

CHAPTER 50

Ben

The day had gone better than Ben expected: he found that he could ignore the current crisis in their lives for agreeably long periods of time. He was relaxed at the tiller, no longer furtively seeking any opportunity to unburden himself and reveal the presence of the baby on their boat. He supposed it was because Karen was so obviously happy—for the first time in months, it seemed. It must be rubbing off on him, he thought. And because he was no longer fretting over immediate disclosure of the secret they were harbouring, he was able to dismiss the nagging certainty of the culpability of their behaviour for increasing spells of time.

They had made good progress, leaving the English village of Chirk behind, seventy or eighty feet below, as they entered Wales. Karen had remained below deck tending the child as Ben steered their boat across the Chirk Aqueduct, fascinated by the solid impression of permanence in the mighty supporting columns, themselves overshadowed by the viaduct towering above, carrying the now defunct railway lines which had, in their turn, largely usurped the canals as an industrial transport system.

Emerging from the Chirk Tunnel, they were approaching an even more impressive edifice. As Ben manoeuvred the narrowboat onto the Pontcysyllte Aqueduct, he marvelled at the sheer magnitude of the construction. He had read about it, of course, in the Nicholson guide, and had studied the picture there, counting a span of at least sixteen arches before these disappeared among the trees at the edge of the photograph. He was visualising this now, picturing the tall, slender pillars supporting such a narrow channel, barely wider than the boat, high above the valley, the River Dee a pale ribbon of light so far below. This superb structure, a feat of late eighteenth-century civil engineering, dwarfed the trees below, resplendent in their autumn colours. The tiny clumps of white which, from this distance, appeared to be moving almost imperceptibly were sheep grazing contentedly along the banks of the Dee.

Ben allowed his mind to wander, distracted by the stunning vista and soothed by the age-old pastoral scene. There was something almost immortal in this view of the world and the seasonal changes it portrayed. Somehow this bestowed a fresh sense of perspective, affirming the absolute insignificance of their current dilemma in the grand scheme of things. Roused from his reverie, Ben realised that he was no longer looking over the shallow metal strip between the boat and the sheer drop below. They were leaving the aqueduct behind, well on their way to Llangollen now and whatever resolution that might confer.

CHAPTER 51

Sandy

Surveillance at the hospital was being stepped down. Sandy realised that, more often now, the shift cover provided in the ICU was being effected by PCSOs. She herself had been relieved of bedside duty halfway through the morning, receiving an urgent recall to the station, her replacement being an experienced WPCSO, Daisy Trott. Daisy had been forthright in voicing an opinion that Sandy had already formed but left unspoken, that whoever had perpetrated the hit-and-run, if it really was deliberate, seemed unlikely to attempt to finish the slaughter on hospital premises. Far too much time had elapsed for that. They agreed that the likelihood of learning anything of value by staying here seemed remote, and they wondered just how long any police presence could be maintained given the two very pressing enquiries currently underway.

The first of these involved the prolonged uncertainty over the fate of Abigail Lamont and her daughter. There had been no sightings at all to date, and none of Abigail's relatives or friends had been able to provide any insight into her possible whereabouts. The husband, Steve, had been brought in for questioning on two occasions but remained tearfully adamant that he had had no involvement in her disappearance, also becoming increasingly incensed at what he saw as the implication that he was a suspect.

The second major incident, which threatened to deflect all attention from other ongoing enquiries, was the recent discovery of the murdered woman by the fishing lake. All the big brass from CID and the neighbouring forces had been drafted in to investigate this particularly vile outrage.

Press speculation was rife and certainly *not* unfounded. There seemed no doubt at all that this was the work of the serial killer, currently dubbed by the tabloids as the "Wolf of Wolverhampton". Whoever this depraved individual turned out to be, it was abundantly clear that he had a particular penchant for pregnant women.

Now that the horror had moved onto their own patch, Ted Manning was required to share the hitherto restricted information originally divulged only on a strictly need-to-know basis. The MO was incontrovertibly similar. All four of the victims had been between four and seven months pregnant, three of them in the second trimester, and only one with a gestational record showing her pregnancy to be as far advanced as thirty-four weeks. All the victims had been found beside water, the three Wolverhampton sites along canal towpaths respectively at Tipton, at Autherley, and beside a derelict foundry only minutes away from the city centre. Only in their own case did the pattern deviate slightly with the victim's body having been found beside the lake.

The injuries sustained by the victims were consistent with their having been manually strangled, and forensic tests had failed to find any evidence that they had suffered pre- or postmortem penetrative sex. In all four cases, their lower clothing had been significantly disturbed. Two of the Wolverhampton victims were wearing trousers which had been removed and were found carefully folded and placed under each woman's head. In both of the other cases, their dresses had been cut from neck to hem and opened out to expose their abdomens. And it was here that the horrific similarities of each case were most apparent. Not only was each abdomen exposed, but also, in every single case, it was lacerated, a single clean incision running the entire length from the base of the sternum to the top of the pubic bone. Further horizontal incisions at the apex and base of this primary cut had enabled the perpetrator to open out two large flaps of skin, muscle, and tissue, and remove the principal content of each woman's uterus.

Each small foetus had been placed above the lacerations, on its mother's chest. Two had lived briefly, their undeveloped lungs showing a postdelivery inhalation of air. Two had evidently perished in the attack. Owing to the extent of animal damage that had occurred, the forensic results on the two most decomposed bodies was inconclusive. The two which obviously had been discovered before too much natural damage or more extensive decomposition had developed, chillingly showed that the murderer was a male and that after displaying each body to his own satisfaction, he had ejaculated over the tiny foetus.

None of the more macabre details had so far been leaked, but media interest, already intense, had been further fuelled by the carefully considered decision to provide a moderated warning to pregnant women to be particularly on their guard and report any situation which caused them alarm. Managers of the region's maternity services had overcome their initial reluctance to raise anxiety levels among a group of people already concerned about their own welfare and that of their unborn babies. Local radio and television stations across the West Midlands and North West England were transmitting the assiduously crafted warning, Ted Manning and his Wolverhampton counterpart appearing avuncular and composed as they delivered the well-rehearsed appeal for caution and for any information which might assist in their enquiries.

Back at Booth Street station, the mood was sombre. The initial frenetic activity had been channelled into ordered groups and teams and a sequential prioritisation of tasks. The identification of "Lake Woman" was their first concern, although there seemed little doubt that someone would report her missing soon enough. Once this had been established, Sandy was to be temporarily assigned to DI Waterhall's team, their role being to interview all relatives, colleagues, and contacts of the murdered woman. Sandy's brief would also encompass interviews with the antenatal staff associated with the murdered woman's care.

CHAPTER 52

Sidney Parr

Sidney Parr was feeling pretty hacked off. He'd worked as a labourer on old man Ellacott's farm since leaving school at fifteen—fifty years, near enough—and what did he really have to show for it? True enough, he had lived in a tied cottage for the first forty years, actually on the old man's estate. It was easier in many ways back then, as while the physical work was hard, he was young and fit, and with a growing family to support, he was glad of all the overtime he could get. Agricultural pay was piss-poor—everyone knew that—but there was little else available to a lad like him with no qualifications and no expectation of anything any better.

Joey, his mate from school, *had* bucked the trend by getting himself apprenticed to a firm of agricultural engineers. He'd be rolling in it by now, Sidney thought with envy. Meanwhile, all *he* had achieved was getting older in the same job and becoming worse, not better, off. His lads had left home now, married with their own children, and there was just himself and Marie to think about.

Old man Ellacott had fairly pulled the rug out from under his feet. Even though Sidney had always known that the tied house offered little in the way of security, despite the much-vaunted "everything found, no rent, the rates and electricity paid" the reality was that because of this, the wages were so poor that there was no chance of them ever moving into a home of their own. But he certainly never had expected this latest turn of events. Old man Ellacott, perhaps a better businessman than he was a farmer, had seized upon the opportunity presented by the proposed canal-side regeneration and summarily evicted Sidney and Marie, preferring the lucrative alternative of offering "their" cottage, along with others on the estate, for private rental.

The trades union had been fairly useless in upholding any claim Sidney felt he had upon the property, so it was that for the last ten years he and Marie had been renting a postwar council house bought as a buy-to-let in the next village. It was better than nothing, but the rent took up a hefty proportion of his monthly pay. There was certainly no money left for any of life's luxuries. Damn it, he couldn't even afford to run a car—this much to Marie's disgust, as she lost no opportunity to remind him every time she had to use the infrequent bus service to buy their groceries or go to the doctor or dentist in town. She "would have been much better off married to that Joey". That was the latest of her barbs, not a comparison that Sidney relished.

Here he was, a man in his sixties, unable to even contemplate retirement despite the work's getting harder and more demanding the older he became. He was feeling the cold so much more these days too, and that was a dismal prospect with winter just around the corner. No two ways about it, Sidney was discontented with his lot. And his general gloom was all the more pervasive as he trundled his ancient bicycle along the towpath between Ellacott's farm and the village where he and Marie now lived. That blasted thing was cracking up too, he thought. He had picked up a puncture immediately upon leaving the farm. Bloody thorns—all down to the ritual of autumn hedge cutting and the mess that it always left in its wake.

He would have to walk all the way home now, pushing the damn thing, and hope to get back with enough daylight left to mend his puncture before morning. What normally took him about half an hour on his bike would take at least three times that long, even if he eschewed his usual route along the country lanes and took the path alongside the canal. It wouldn't be as smooth as the road way, but it should shave off at least half an hour from the journey time.

———◆———

It was while on this path that he saw her. Not that he registered at first just what it was that he had seen. He had glimpsed something pale, almost pink in the setting sun. Quite a large shape, he thought, deep down among

the rushes at the side of the canal. He had a vague impression of clothing—
well, fabric of some sort—and wondered if it was perhaps a raincoat or
jacket dropped by a walker. Whatever it was, it would probably wash up
all right and be of some use to Marie. There might even be a pound or two
in the pockets. Dumping his bike against the hedge, he went down to the
water's edge and pushed aside the densely massed sedge and bulrushes.

What he saw then made him gasp in horror. Racing now (who would
have guessed that he could still muster such a turn of speed?), he reclaimed
his bicycle and set off as fast as he could towards the village. It was a
woman's body, that much he had ascertained, but in his shock upon
making the dreadful discovery, he had noticed very little else. He knew
without doubt that she was dead. She seemed to be horribly bloated, and
not pink at all when he got close to her, but sort of mottled and blotchy:
pink, purple, and black. He knew what he had to do. He must get to the
village and report what he had seen. There was definitely no way he could
have dragged her clear of the reeds and out onto the towpath, even if he
had not been appalled and sickened by her appearance.

Sidney did not possess a mobile phone—had never seen the need for
one. All he had was his decrepit old bicycle and the urgent need to get as
far away as possible from the horrible thing he had stumbled upon.

CHAPTER 53

Ted

Contrary to his usual practices, Ted had hurried home on the evening of the hit-and-run. Once he was sure that the attending officer had noted his presence and, more importantly, had observed him acting calmly and capably in the situation that had occurred, he felt able to leave the scene and return to the little back alley where he had parked his car. His mind was in turmoil. He could not shake the thought of Pam and whatever she might have been getting up to with that girl. His own impetuosity appalled him now, in retrospect. He had been such a fool even to contemplate making any business arrangements in such an obvious place. Whatever must have possessed him to throw his customary caution to the wind? He could so easily have been uncovered, with all the political implications that prospect held.

Fingering again the incriminating pass card, Ted was tempted to dispose of it immediately down the nearest drain. Pulling it out of his pocket and standing over the kerbside grid, he almost let the thing go, to fall into inevitable oblivion below. But the thought of Pam, and the barely constrained anger at whatever she might have been doing behind his back, stayed his hand at the very moment he was about to let the thing go. Damn it, it wasn't just any old pass card. To Ted it had become the *trump* card. He would bide his time, and just when she was least expecting it, he would confront Pam with what was rapidly becoming the certainty of his suspicions.

Let her wriggle out of that one, he thought. She would never be able to criticise him again. More than that—and he licked his lips at the realisation—it conferred upon him the power to make her comply with his every wish. She would have to give up her job; he would see to that. And there would have to be a return to the sort of domestic order he craved. Decent home cooking would be a start. And he thought with relish of the punishment he could exert in the bedroom. No more Little Miss Frigid, she would have to accommodate him, whatever he desired. And she could include her lesbian girlfriends in all of that. He would show them just what a real man could do.

CHAPTER 54

The Man on the Bus

He had been keeping a watching brief on this particular spot for some time. That was the beauty of the sort of job he was in: he could very easily make a little detour and spend a few minutes assessing a location to ensure it met with his increasingly stringent requirements. One such visit would seldom suffice. It would take several, in some cases frequent, visits to satisfy him. He had always been one to pay meticulous attention to detail. It did not pay to rush things. His art was in the planning.

Undeniably, the execution of each project also depended on accuracy and skill, but without his scrupulous concentration upon every aspect of the endeavour at the planning stage, he could not hope to achieve a satisfactory result. Impetuous action on his behalf threatened the ultimate fulfilment of his mission. His hobby demanded total immersion in the preparation and setting for each episode. The longer this could be maintained, the greater his gratification.

He had not always acknowledged this, he thought ruefully. It had not come naturally to him at first and had been a hard lesson to learn. His youthful impetuosity had led to nothing but disappointment. Disillusionment dogged the early years of his marriage. God, how he hated his ex-wife for that. A brush or two with the law had earned him a stretch at Her Majesty's pleasure which, while being something of a respite from the continuing domestic grind, had also provided him with this one valuable skill. He had to concede that now, although at the time the mandatory anger management course had been accepted with a great deal of scepticism on his behalf. Dismissed sarcastically by him and his fellow

161

inmates as "the brainchild of some namby-pamby, sandal-wearing do-gooder", it was a requirement for his eventual parole. And he had complied.

He had returned home not so much a changed man, but a man in charge of his own change. The anger and smouldering resentment remained, but he was able to disguise it now. His acts of aggression were more rigidly controlled, and while he was still inclined on occasion to be a little too handy with his fists, for the most part he was able to contain such an urge to fight. Driven to violence less frequently now, he, when it did erupt, was generally able to mete out whatever punishment he felt was due in a coldly, calculating fashion.

Well, this spot he had selected certainly appeared to meet the necessary criteria: it was a secluded location and, now that the campers had left, was pretty in its own way. Beside the sculptured contour of the lake, the trees at its margin, resplendent in the glowing colours of their autumn foliage, cast a dappled reflection along the water's edge. It was well hidden from the road, and this end of the lake would not be visible from the owner's house.

It was not completely deserted, a factor that he had observed and which was to play an important part in his plan. He had seen the solitary fisherman squeezing through the broken railings and furtively making his way through the undergrowth to the vacant peg at the foot of the lake. He had watched this man at different times throughout the preceding weeks and calculated the duration and frequency of these visits. It was always the same man—and what a creature of habit he turned out to be. Always the same stand, and never more than two or three days between each appearance. That could not be better. It was almost too perfect to be true.

If the narrow gap between the railings did not immediately serve his purpose, he now had recourse to a more fitting method of fulfilling his plan. After all, this is what attention to detail really meant: absolute efficiency. No plan of his was going to founder because of inadequate preparation. He prided himself on that.

His reconnaissance had included several visits to the owner's house and garden, usually observing these from his position parked in the layby opposite the entrance to the caravan site, until he was sure that the owner and his wife were not at home. Once he saw that both their cars had left the premises, he had moved swiftly up the unmade road and tested the security system. The CCTV camera was above the reception area and could be easily disabled. He would have to come here at night to do that under the cover of darkness, but he was no stranger to the task. The most rewarding discovery of all was that the security barrier had been left in the raised position ever since the site had closed for the winter months, presumably to make it easier for the owner, his family, and any occasional guests to come and go at their leisure.

That was a find indeed. It was predestined.

CHAPTER 55

Ben and Karen

The time in Llangollen had passed without incident. Ben moored their boat in the basin and obtained the necessary authority to stay. If he had been tempted to reveal the presence of the baby on their boat, the casual demand for the overnight mooring fee dispelled any such intention. Besides, he was tired now and really could not face the upheaval he felt sure his and Karen's disclosure would provoke.

The last few miles had been difficult. The canal had narrowed to a single boat width, although he had not encountered any oncoming craft, which would have necessitated using the designated passing places. He had to moor up and walk on ahead to check that they had the opportunity for unimpeded progress along this stretch, as Karen was busy feeding the little one and had been no help at all. Moreover, the water level seemed unnaturally low and the boat laboured along increasingly slowly, to such an extent that it was almost dark by the time they reached the basin. The shop selling mooring permits was about to close, and the man in charge, who seemed to be the only person there, was preparing to lock up for the night. His obvious irritation certainly gave Ben no reason to believe that he would be sympathetic to their plight.

It was with consummate relief that Ben detached the tiller arm, stowing it in the boatman's cabin, and went below deck into the warmth, where the remainder of the evening passed pleasantly enough. The baby had fed well and was sleeping soundly in her makeshift bed while Karen busied herself cooking supper. Ben stretched out luxuriously in front of the Morsø stove and dozed contentedly until their meal was ready. After this, they made desultory conversation before deciding that they were both tired and should turn in for the night, Ben swallowing his disappointment that, despite the more recent harmony between them, Karen still refused to join him in bed, maintaining the need to remain close to the child. Despite this, they both enjoyed a quiet night, the baby waking a couple of times to be fed but, now that she was getting a decent quantity of formula, soon falling asleep again.

After breakfast they went into the little town, Karen carrying the baby snugly wrapped in one of her own jackets, until they made their first purchase: a small, foldable pushchair that could be converted into a car safety seat. If Ben realised where this was going, he did not intervene, accepting Karen's justification that they needed something to enable them to get about for just as long as they had her and that the pushchair would double up as a safer cot bed for her than the drawer.

Once or twice he looked around as though seeking someone in whom he could confide, but Karen's pressure on his arm deterred him, a pressure that she increased almost imperceptibly on passing signs to the police station and on encountering a uniformed traffic warden. And when the shop assistant who sold them the buggy admired the sleeping child, asking her age and complimenting them on having the sense to bring her along to try the pushchair for size, Ben was unable to bring himself to confess their deception. Only when the shopping tray at the base of the buggy was completely filled with tiny items of clothing, bedding, and a fluffy white teddy bear did he acknowledge the full portent of these actions. At that moment Ben knew. Karen had won the day. Cari Moses was staying.

CHAPTER 56

Sandy

Activity levels at the Booth Street police station were at an all-time high. Not only did they still have a serious hit-and-run to investigate—a total of six people hurt, one of whom was still in ICU—but now it appeared that a serial killer was at large, having moved onto their patch only that week. The officers there were becoming increasingly frustrated. To say that progress in both these cases was painfully slow would be to flatter them on their combined efforts to date. There had been no leads in the hit-and-run. Of those injured who might have been able to supply some relevant information, the one key witness remained deeply unconscious, another was too traumatised to talk, and a third had disappeared without trace. The two injured commuters had seen nothing of note, the accident having happened too quickly for them to have registered anything significant. Even the burnt-out car had yielded nothing more tangible in the way of evidence beyond confirming that it was responsible for causing the damage to the lamp post at the scene of the incident. It bore no number plates, and there was nothing left of the interior to provide any clues as to its ownership.

The serial killing had attracted massive attention from the neighbouring force where the first victims had been found, but neither the staff there nor the officers at Booth Street investigating the sole victim in their area had come anywhere close to identifying the perpetrator. As yet, they did not even have an identification of his latest victim. Compounding the accumulating lines of enquiry was an unsolved attempted abduction in the city centre and a missing mother and child. Efforts either to isolate these events or determine some link between them had failed to draw any results, and although speculation was rife, the police were no nearer to nailing the motive or the outcome in any of these cases.

Separate teams had been drawn up and a joint incident room established. All police leave across two forces had been cancelled, and following the discovery of the most recent body, members of the local press were being held at arm's length for fear of engendering widespread panic across the region. It was doubtful how long this stance could be maintained, as news of the killer's spree in nearby Wolverhampton had certainly attained the front pages of the tabloids. Until such a time that their commanding officers determined that a press release would have a value-added effect upon their investigations, they had been cautioned to keep as low a profile as possible while conducting their enquiries.

It was an impossible brief given the insatiable insistence of the journalists, hungry to add as much salacious detail to their accounts as possible in an attempt to boost readership figures above those of their rivals and to earn career approbation for themselves. The assembled officers knew that it would only be a matter of time before information and misinformation went viral. There was little they could do to stop it happening.

Resources were stretched to capacity, and until sufficient further reinforcements could be drafted in from other forces, the officers assembled at Booth Street were carrying this unconscionable load. They were exhausted and staff morale certainly could have been better. Into this maelstrom of frustrated endeavour was suddenly catapulted a further crisis, the impending magnitude of which threatened their collective sanity and all hopes of a return to normal duties anytime soon. As by five o'clock that evening, the body of another young woman had been discovered.

CHAPTER 57

Helen

Helen was on her way home from work, wondering dully what the evening held in store. She had hardly seen anything of Sandy all week, and while she had experienced periods like this before when her partner was involved in some particularly demanding aspect of her work, she had never known one to be so protracted. When they did actually coincide, Sandy seemed abstracted, often lost in her own thoughts and uncommunicative. Either that, or she was so tired that she wolfed down a hastily prepared meal and almost immediately fell asleep. One time, she actually dozed off completely in the midst of eating and, instead of responding to Helen's gentle prodding reminder to eat with a chuckle of amusement, had rounded on her quite savagely, retorting, "You just don't get it, do you? Safe in your comfortable little world and ever so safe and boring job." Helen was stung by that, struggling not to let Sandy see how close to tears she was. And even when Sandy made a clumsy attempt to apologise at bedtime, Helen lay awake for a long time pondering the future of their relationship together.

Now, as she made her way along the street where they lived, she debated with herself whether to tell Sandy the latest snippet of office gossip. She wondered if it might be more than that, even if she might be telling Sandy something that would potentially be of use to her and make her a bit happier and easier to live with, at least for a while.

What she saw next cemented her resolve. The evening edition of the local paper was out, and the poster on the A frame outside the newsagents shrieked an attention-grabbing headline: Pregnant women warned of a stalker at large. She knew of one pregnant woman who had failed to make it into work that day, and while it might not mean anything, Helen had an uneasy feeling that it just could be significant.

She had spent her lunch hour with a friend from a nearby rival company of solicitors. Polly had arrived late for their prearranged meeting, blaming it on a colleague who had not come into work that morning, berating the fact that the woman had not even had the consideration to let them know that she was going to be absent. Probably forgot to tell them about an antenatal appointment or something and then decided to give herself the rest of the day off. Yet another example of the pandering afforded to mothers both before and after birth, they agreed, ignoring the equal opportunities and antidiscrimination mantra propounded (overtly, at any rate) by their respective employers.

A phone call to the woman's home by Helen's friend (not to be construed as harassment, just an example of a colleague's concern, she hastened to assure her) had failed to elicit any response. In fact, her actual motive was far less altruistic, as she had been eager to establish whether the growing resentment and undisguised envy evoked by this unofficial holiday (and probably a shopping spree and coffee in town!) was justified. She had tried the number again, just before leaving for their lunch date, with the same result: just a dialling tone followed by a prerecorded message on the answerphone.

CHAPTER 58

The Man

He was angry, very angry indeed—angry with himself. This was *not* how it was supposed to happen. It never was intended as a showcase for his art. By his own recognition, it was clumsy and inept, falling hundreds of points below the very high standards he always set himself. Its execution was hurried. It had not started out that way, but he was cruelly forestalled. He should never have deviated from the project manual. That was his first grave mistake. He had acted on impulse, had misread the signs for sure. There had been none of his customary research and preparation. He acknowledged that now. And what was more distressing, it caused him to redraw his plans. Prior to this, he thought that he had perfected every detail in all his recent project work and did not want to alter any aspect of the approach which had served him so well. But this horrible incident had forced his hand. He had to revise the formula, revisit the criteria, and ensure that they would be met to his satisfaction despite the changes that were now imperative to his methodology.

It was all the more disappointing because the last time had been so beautiful, everything playing out exactly as he had intended it. His meticulous planning had paid dividends. He was delighted with the outcome. It only temporarily satiated his lust for perfection, however. As always, once a project had been accomplished to his absolute satisfaction, the urge to continue remained undiminished. He already was devising his next piece of work, researching the background and compiling the list of potential recruits, when this latest, unprecedented disaster had occurred.

He never intended the woman's body to be found like that. He had not been able to push her as far out into the canal as he had hoped. The tangle of rushes at the water's edge had prevented him from shifting her weight into the centre of the cut. At the time, he was struck by the irony of the situation. The very reeds and rushes which he had thought would provide such an effective camouflage had actually led to her untimely discovery. He had hoped that as the dying foliage began to collapse under the unaccustomed weight, she would sink out of sight below the surface of the water. If anything of her body was ultimately to be discovered, he had hoped that it would not be before the warm weather and the next holiday season. By then, the damage precipitated by her prolonged immersion in the water and the scavenging activity of fish, insects, and animals would be complete. He knew that this section of the canal was little frequented during the winter months, even the most zealous of anglers preferring the stretch of water beyond the reed beds, for while the occasional large predatory fish could be found lurking there, tempting capture, the almost inevitable tangle of lines which resulted proved too much of a deterrent.

He certainly had not anticipated the late holiday hire boat making its irrevocable progress towards his killing field. He had given the disgusting flaccid form one last push, thinking he could return to finish the job, and was just about to despatch the wailing brat to its watery grave when he heard it. It was the closest shave he had had in a long time. He should never have courted disaster like that.

CHAPTER 59

Pam

Pam didn't know how to occupy herself. Robert had left for school cleaner and more presentable now, with a marked swagger that simultaneously sickened and angered his mother. He was the image of his father, she thought: the same swagger, the same air of studied disinterest and arrogance. And Pam was angry with herself for letting him get away with it. She felt such a failure, fearing her career was in ruins and acknowledging her family's almost total disregard for her, as evidenced by the boys' lack of consideration and Ted's barely concealed contempt.

Since her summary dismissal from the ward earlier that afternoon, she had returned home as though on autopilot, not really registering anything about her surroundings. She had let herself in and made the customary cup of coffee. Sitting at the kitchen table with her head in her hands, the reminder of the coffee congealing in the cup before her, her view of her world seemed very bleak indeed. She was startled to realise that it had already begun to go dark. Mentally shaking off the profound torpor to which she had succumbed, Pam struggled to her feet and began to make a desultory attempt at tackling some of the domestic chores.

Mindlessly sorting the laundry which had spilled onto the bathroom floor, she took each pile into the kitchen and put the first load into the washing machine. She turned out her uniform pockets once again, aware all the time of the utter futility of the exercise, before transferring her attention to the post breakfast chaos of spilled cornflakes, remnants of toast, and a sticky, glutinous mess she presumed was the remains of the butter and jam which had fallen from it. Well, at least Richard (the younger boy) had had some breakfast *and* made it to school, she reflected. She would cook them a proper meal tonight. It would give her something to occupy her thoughts, to distract them from endlessly replaying the sequence of this morning's events, the realisation of her culpability, her panic and shame. If only Abigail and her baby were to turn up soon, happy and unharmed, then perhaps things would return to normal and Pam's involvement would seem to be no more than constituting part of an unfortunate chain of events. Security would be tightened, of course, and Pam herself might have to work under supervision for a while, but she could live with that. It didn't have to spell the end of her cherished career.

Even as she allowed these conciliatory thoughts to occupy her mind, Pam knew that the outcome of any presumed negligence was seldom as optimistic and straightforward as that. For now, she did not know when—or if—she would be allowed back to work or if anyone would even think to keep her informed about the Abigail situation. It would be as though in her single act of carelessness she had forfeited any right to be acknowledged. What if she were at home for weeks until something was resolved? Whatever would she tell Ted?

CHAPTER 60

Sandy

Sandy was disappointed to find that despite the air of purposeful activity within the station as a whole, the team to which she had been assigned under the direction of DI Waterhall had yet to hone in upon the focus of their remit. Lake Woman was, as yet, a Jane Doe: no identification was possible. No young pregnant woman had been reported missing, and the garish scene-of-crime photographs had only just been processed, with a certain amount of discretionary editing having been imposed to produce a reasonable facial image with which to confront the staff in the various maternity units and clinics across the region. Sandy's role was to visit each of these departments in their area to see if any of the staff recognised the woman in the photograph. Pleased to have a definite purpose to pursue, she assiduously compiled a comprehensive list of all possible units, prioritising these in the most efficient order in which she should visit them. She had initially thought to commence her enquiries in the immediate vicinity of Booth Street station and work her way outwards in an ever-increasing radius, possibly taking in the nearest branches of Mothercare and other stockists of maternity wear. With all the competing demands engendered by the concurrent investigations, available personnel were at a premium. For the time being, she would have to conduct these preliminary enquiries on her own. It was a good job; she knew her patch so very well. Even so, the enormity of the task was daunting.

Wondering if there was any other way she could rationalise the search, Sandy realised with a start that the obvious place to start and from which to begin her outgoing radius was the City Hospital—surely the place with the greatest footfall of antenatal patients. And while she was there, she could pop up to ICU to check on the progress of Victim A from the hit-and-run.

She knew, even as she formulated the beginnings of these plans, that such a visit was not strictly necessary. The girl was still being guarded round the clock by a succession of WCPOs, but something about the case continued to haunt her, prompting this feeling that somehow she had a prior claim upon any developments there. It was only natural, she convinced herself. After all, she was the one to have recognised the girl and reunite her with her belongings. That these now resided, unappreciated, in the Booth Street incident room rankled more than a little.

And so it was that Sandy, armed with a stack of photo reprints, set out ostensibly to pursue enquiries into the identity of Lake Woman. She parked the car in the usual priority bay, resisting the temptation to stop for a coffee and cake, and made her way into the hospital foyer, going straight up to the sixth floor and the ICU. There she was surprised to be greeted quite animatedly by the officer on duty, the same one who had relieved her the other night. WPC Parsons seemed to be markedly less bored now than she had been on that occasion. Not a paperback in sight, but rather a studied concentration as she focused all her attention upon the girl in the bed.

Victim A was holding her own, the sister informed Sandy. Indeed, there had been some gradual improvement and a tantalising hint of returning awareness. Ever such slight movement of her head and limbs had been detected, and a hesitant mumbling sound had come from her lips. The WPC excitedly reported this latest development: "It was almost as though she was trying to speak," she told Sandy.

Damn, it was just her bad luck to miss out on surveillance duty now that there was actually a chance that the girl could help with their enquiries. I wonder what she *does* know? mused Sandy. Were they on the brink of some momentous discovery here? Could what was seeming increasingly likely to be an attempted murder or, at the very least, deliberate grievous harm be one step nearer to being solved? Knowing that it was imperative for her to get on with the job in hand, Sandy pressed her colleague to keep her informed as to the girl's progress, then made her way down to the maternity department, firmly resolving that she would make time to continue visiting the girl, albeit in her own off-duty periods.

The photograph of the lakeside victim failed to draw any positive response from the midwives on duty, several of them citing their own impossible workload, stressing that with such a large clientele, it was often difficult to recognise any of the new mothers until after they had spent some time as an inpatient. Unless there were complications, this tended only to occur once they were in labour. Sandy left a picture with them to be displayed on the internal noticeboard. No superfluous details given, just a request that should any member of staff recognise the woman, they were to contact Booth Street station on the following telephone number.

The remainder of Sandy's shift was spent equally unproductively, her carefully sequenced round of maternity units, clinics, and shops drawing a decisive blank.

CHAPTER 61

The Man

He was in a quandary now, a range of conflicting emotions chasing through his mind as he drove. It was a very good thing that he had drawn his usual work van from the transport bay that morning. He felt he could manage that anywhere, almost on autopilot, he thought. Time spent on the road between deliveries gave him ample opportunity to reflect. It was at times like these that he revelled in the clean, clinical beauty of his hobby, reliving every moment of the most recent episode.

He always felt like this afterwards: a huge sense of satisfaction in a job well done. This was his realisation that all the planning, the gradual build-up of a confidence based on the thoroughness of his research and his meticulous attention, down to the last detail, had resulted in something as near to perfection as any a man could hope to achieve, a perfection that reached its ultimate conclusion in the execution of that plan. Execution. He liked the sound of that. For once that was an apt use of words. He savoured the double meaning here: execution of the plan and execution of the victims. He smiled to himself as a further duality occurred to him then, namely that in the choice of victims each time there was this pairing of mother and child, host and parasite.

This was the culmination of all his planning, days and days of planning—days when he felt his lust rising, until the very moment of its conclusion and the final arrangement of his subjects. He was the consummate artist arranging his still life. Yes, that was what it was every time, life stilled, a still life—and his own life affirmed in that final moment of sexual release.

At first that had been enough. His hobby was to locate his intended victim, devise the perfect individualised plan, perpetrate it, and display his handiwork for maximum impact. Masturbating over the display not only provided relief from the sexual tension which had been mounting throughout the entire planning cycle, reaching an unlikely peak in the performance of what he dubbed the elective surgery element of the project, but also demonstrated his utter contempt for his victims. Now, far from diminishing his desire, the relief he obtained was temporary at best. In the early days of pursuing his hobby, it had sustained him for several weeks, but while he still achieved the same satisfaction from a mission completed to his own exceptionally high standards, it was becoming increasingly short-lived. The time between projects was decreasing. Already his bloodlust was rising. It was imperative that he should identify the next potential candidate for his art.

CHAPTER 62

Alex

"For God's sake, man, just tell me. Was she hurt in any other way? I mean, I know you say he strangled her, but for Christ's sake, man, she was almost five months gone. Just tell me he didn't interfere with her in any other way. Please, she can't have been raped, not in her condition?"

Alex was pleading now, beseeching the grim-faced officers who had appeared at his door within seconds, or so it seemed to him, of his having made that call. In truth, he had been fretting about Roseanne all day, anxious to get home and have all his fears quashed. Irrational fears surely, he had told himself then. But watching the breaking news at 8a.m. in his hotel bedroom, he had been gripped by unspeakable alarm What if …what if it was *his* wife who had been found like that? Some poor devil would be waking up like him, or perhaps he hadn't slept all night, hoping against hope, only to have his worst fears confirmed: that his wife wasn't just missing but had been found murdered. It was the stuff of nightmares, something that threatened his comfortable existence.

But throughout the day, his sense of foreboding had increased. He had tried phoning home, hoping to catch Roseanne before she left for work, cursing the heavy drinking with his business colleagues the night before for his not waking in time to speak to her before she left to catch the bus. Of course, she would have to be that much earlier without him there to give her a lift. His call had gone to answerphone, and for some unaccountable reason she seemed to have her mobile switched off. Could be that she had a clinic appointment. He knew that they weren't supposed to have their mobiles on inside the hospital. He didn't think that she was due for an antenatal appointment this week, but he was ashamed to admit that he had not really followed the intricacies of this pregnancy with as much fervour as she would have liked. The thing was, while it was all new and very exciting for her, he had done this bit before. In a brief, earlier relationship, his then girlfriend had carried their child, a little boy that he never saw any more.

They had done all the proud prospective parents thing then, only for it to go tits up at the end. She had blamed him for the pregnancy, blamed him for everything really, and had gone back to live with her mother before the baby was even born. He had only seen her a couple of times since the birth, hoping that they could smooth things over, that her reaction was hormone-driven and that now the child was here, she would want them to settle down and be a family. But she had made it abundantly clear that she wanted nothing more to do with him and that she and his son were out of his life.

In fairness, she had never asked him for a penny for the child. He had paid no maintenance then or since. His only contribution was to stuff her a cheque for £500 to buy the baby some of the things he would need. She was even reluctant to take this, but finally she had the grace to accept it. "I'll put it into a savings account for him," she told him. "He's got everything he needs for now."

He had Roseanne on the rebound, he conceded, charmed by the absolute contrast between her and his hippyish girlfriend. They had quickly become an item. As the months went by, he was proud to have this smart, intelligent woman as his wife. The gloss had faded a little of late. She always seemed to be nagging him to get something done. But he did love her. It was just that things were not as much fun anymore.

She had been desperate to start a family. How much of that was driven by an unacknowledged jealousy of his previous girlfriend, he never knew. He wished now that he had never told her about it, but he was fearful back then of any possible repercussions further down the line. What if the girlfriend's independence faltered and she came after him for financial support? Or maybe the son he had last seen as a tiny baby was to seek him out, anxious to know his father and discover why he had never been a part of his life. And so he had told Roseanne. At first she seemed very accepting about it. How much of that was really a facade? he wondered.

But all that was behind him now. As of this moment, Roseanne was his only concern. He had tried unsuccessfully to reach her by telephone throughout the day and had even put a call through to Howel and Howardson's, strictly against their company policy, only to be told by some jumped-up little secretary, a bit aggressively, he thought, that Roseanne had not come into work that morning. The thought of her lying ill, unable to get to the phone, haunted him. She must be at home, he concluded. Surely if she had been admitted to hospital, someone would have let him know. He wondered then if he should call her parents, but hesitated. Until he was certain that she was not at home, there seemed no sense in alarming them. If truth be told, he had a somewhat uneasy relationship with them. The old man was friendly enough, but Alex felt his mother-in-law's unspoken criticism and censure of him: Not really good enough for our daughter, a man with a past. He wished that he had never told them about that.

Still, there was no denying their delight at the prospect of becoming grandparents, his father-in-law toasting the couple, and his mother-in-law insisting that they should buy the cot and equip the little nursery at their expense. It would serve no useful purpose worrying them right now.

The day had dragged. There was a seemingly interminable meeting, Alex with his mind elsewhere, barely focusing upon the tedious Power Point presentation (just how old school was that?) and the detailed analysis of company statistics. He had tried ringing again at lunchtime and just before he left, an involuntary sob of despair greeting the third set of roadworks and a two-mile tailback of traffic on the M6. He was aware that he was driving on his brakes. Stop, start, first gear, second gear, stop, groping in the glove compartment, furious to find that he was out of cigarettes, remembering now how Roseanne had pleaded with him *never* to smoke in the car, the irreparable harm it could do to their unborn child. All a bit OTT, he had thought, recalling the reefers he had smoked with his ex-girlfriend throughout her pregnancy, but as he was trying to kick the habit anyway, he had agreed to go along with it. Anything for a quiet life. Now he was missing smoking like mad. What he wouldn't give for a cigarette right now.

So the tedious journey progressed until finally he had arrived home, tired, jaded, and emotionally drained. He let himself into the house, glancing as he did so at the myrtle bush, visible only as a dark, brooding shadow in the light from the porch. "You'll have to go, mate." He spoke this aloud, after the unremitting noise of the traffic, startled by the sound of his own voice, the thought coming unbidden, not for the first time that day, that perhaps this was all a deliberate ploy by Roseanne to shame him into taking her fears seriously. Goddammit, why did women have to be quite so bloody complicated?

Going from room to room in the house, finding no trace of her, Alex felt his own fear mounting. Hurriedly checking the garage, hardly daring to entertain thoughts of possibly finding her there hanging from the beams, he pushed aside the unlikely notion of her suicide. True, her behaviour had not been all that rational of late, but he knew how desperately she wanted this baby. Surely she would never take her own life.

Wearily sinking onto the settee, a can of lukewarm beer in his hand, Alex began to scroll through his phone. He had her parents' number and the numbers of one or two of her friends. He had better make a start with those. Far from conferring the relief he sought, these calls served only to amplify his fear. None of Roseanne's girlfriends had heard from her for several days. She had even been inactive on social media, her last posting only berating men's obsession with cars—a dig at him, he presumed.

The reaction from her parents was predictable, her father ineffectually attempting to console him with the picture of her relaxing somewhere with a friend they didn't know about, having completely overlooked the time. In contrast to this, his mother-in-law's evident anxiety rendered her attack on him for not doing something sooner the most acerbic and cutting he had ever known. She was beside herself with grief and anger, her frightful screeching sending reverberating shock waves through Alex's head. There was nothing for it. He had to telephone the police and report Roseanne missing.

They responded immediately. He had barely had time to open a second can of beer before two uniformed policemen arrived. After listening intently as he told them the story of his day and the repeated unsuccessful attempts he had made trying to reach his wife by phone, he was alarmed to find that he was being ushered to the waiting police car and taken to Booth Street station. His protestations that he needed to be at home in case she came back unexpectedly were to no avail. Now, seated in the stark interview room, having recounted the day's events for a second time, and having answered all the seemingly irrelevant questions about his relationship with his wife, he realised that he no longer knew whether they believed him or not. Am I a suspect? he wondered. There had been no hint of that surely. He had not been cautioned, only told that his statement was being processed and that he would get to read it through before signing it.

The WPC had seemed the most approachable and had even brought him a cup of tea. It was lying on the table before him now, untouched, as the older of the two uniformed policemen showed him the photograph of the woman's face—her face, Roseanne's face.

He knew then, for sure, that it was his wife's body that had been found beside the lake. He could barely grasp the reality of that, as yes, he could identify her, but for God's sake, why could they not tell him what had happened to her? They were going to take him to a mortuary somewhere to make a formal, definite identification. Was there anyone he wanted with him?

Yes! he felt like shouting. Yes, yes, yes. I want my wife. I want Roseanne.

CHAPTER 63

The Man

The press had got on to it. They were having a field day. 'The Lady of the Lake' they had dubbed her. Ignorant fools. Did they know nothing? That was just so unoriginal. The title had been used before. He remembered that. Some woman drowned or killed by her husband, he had forgotten which, but he remembered the body turning up months later, what was left of it, and the husband, an airman, he thought, being charged with her murder.

Well, this Lady of the Lake was not going to provide any information leading to her killer, he had made sure of that. It had been perfectly executed. Such a successful project. Sublime.

She had been found, just as he knew she would be found, by the solitary fisherman he had earmarked for the role. The police had arrived in force after that, inspecting the body and combing the area for clues. He had seen that for himself and knew without a shadow of doubt that they were no nearer to discovering anything about him. They would have seen his display just as he had intended them to, and admired his art in situ, snapping endless pictures to satiate their appetite for detail—salacious detail with which to regale their colleagues back at base. There would be some who knew enough to be able to appreciate his consummate skill. They would marvel at it and wonder. And just how unproductive all their speculation would be. They would see links where none existed and patterns which had nothing to do with the patterns in his head, the patterns in his life. They would ponder and question, turning the facts as they saw them over and over in their minds. It would be like turning over every dead leaf in a wood in winter. They were not going to get even close to the truth. He was confident of that.

He had been scrupulous in his attention to detail. Every stage of the project had been planned. There was even a manual for it, from first selecting his subjects to studying their lifestyles and movements, then determining the venue for each stage of the plot, never appearing to use the same vehicle twice.

It was a pity he had ever veered from the plan. That was an absolute catastrophe, a total disgrace. He had compromised his own high standards and paid the price accordingly. It meant that he had had to instigate certain changes, and he was not entirely happy with that. He would have moved on to another area soon enough without that having happened, which had always been his pattern, but it forced his hand. He would have to go back to the manual to make the next selection earlier than he had intended. It was with considerable regret that he would be abandoning his recent choice of display sites. He loved the canal-side scenes, the drama of discovery never far away.

The man drove on mechanically, conscientiously observing traffic regulations, not wanting to attract any unwarranted attention, making his specified drops and exchanging desultory remarks as he handed over the goods in return for the signatures that marked his daily progress. It was a boring job, one that befitted an unambitious man, one that gave him ample thinking time. Over the years it had served his purpose well as he had acquired an encyclopaedic knowledge of each area he had worked, often deviating from the main routes to explore interesting byroads and the tiny villages beyond the seething cities. London born and bred, he had long since decided against working there—too many memories, too close to home. It was in the sprawling conurbations of the West Midlands and North West of England that he forged his metier. He had had a number of jobs, each one providing greater insight into a particular area, this last one conferring even greater assets: no tachometer, no insistence upon using satellite navigation to plot the shortest route between points, and the undeniable advantage in the type of goods he carried.

He had only returned to work that morning, having taken a couple of days' leave to make one of his rare visits to his old home. There were certain things he had to do there—people to see, arrangements to make.

He had travelled by rail, taking a single ticket to London and then a Tube ride to the suburbs, and made the remainder of the journey on a bus out to the countryside beyond, his only luggage a small suitcase on wheels and a bundle of banknotes in his pocket.

He needed time to study his project manual, his bible, and to bring his plans up to date. Besides which, certain items of a potentially incriminating nature had begun to accumulate. He couldn't risk their discovery. That would jeopardise his entire existence and the hobby which brought him so much satisfaction. He needed somewhere to dispose of them unobtrusively.

Arriving at his old house, he opened up the lean-to and checked the state of his own van. The paintwork had dried well. It was as he had hoped, so he could use the van to return to his lodgings. Confident that the cottage was sufficiently isolated and that the scrubby neglected garden was not overlooked, he lit a bonfire and burnt the contents of the suitcase— carrier bags and the woman's new clothes—before returning indoors to formulate his next set of plans.

The interior of the premises was dank and smelled musty. He was glad that he had only taken two days' holiday. He could manage to survive long enough to do what he needed to here, living on the food in the rusting cans in the tiny pantry and wrapping himself in a worn duvet for warmth. Tomorrow he would take the van and go up to town, where he'd get a decent meal and settle his outstanding business, being careful, before he left, to obliterate any remaining traces of this recent visit to the cottage, which would include kicking a pile of leaves over the floor of the lean-to where the van had stood and locking the premises behind him.

CHAPTER 64

Sandy

Sandy knew she should go home to Helen. Things had not been too good between them over the last few days. She had been working long hours and had vented some of her frustration and impatience upon her long-suffering partner. But there was one thing she still needed to do. She would stop by the hospital and make a quick visit to ICU. WPC Parsons had not been in contact with her since the other day, and Sandy wanted to see for herself what progress, if any, the hit-and-run girl was making.

Once Sandy was in ICU, the reason behind Judy Parson's silence became immediately apparent. Her role at the bedside had been withdrawn. The girl was alone in the ward. Drawing up to the bedside, Sandy was aware of two things. The first was the young woman's obvious vulnerability after having been so closely guarded for so long. Not only was she the only patient in the unit at present, but also Sandy's own entry and approach had been neither noted nor challenged. The second was a distinct impression of something's having changed. Peering more closely at the girl now, Sandy was sure that she could detect a flicker, if not of recognition, then of something approaching awareness. Her eyes were open, undeniably focused. But focusing on what? Not on Sandy, whose studied scrutiny she seemed to be avoiding. No, the girl's attention appeared persistently drawn to the large double doors at the entrance to the ward. It was as though she was expecting someone.

Uncertain whether the girl might be capable of responding to her, and keen to establish her own justification for being there, Sandy made her way to the ward office, where she found Sister Mackie busy on the telephone. Sister Mackie gestured to Sandy to take a seat. On finishing her call, she greeted the officer with evident warmth. The ward sister was able to confirm what Sandy herself had surmised. The police presence had been gradually diminished over the preceding few days (the priority no doubt having been downgraded as a result of the number of concurrent enquiries and the escalating workload). Over the last forty-eight hours, there had been no police officer on duty here for an entire shift, although they had visited at changeover times and instructed Sister Mackie to report any significant improvement in her charge's condition.

It was not just the police who were suffering staff shortages, Sister Mackie was quick to assert; the NHS, too, was strapped for cash. She had fewer trained nurses now upon whom she could rely, necessitating a greater dependence upon auxiliary and agency staff, while she herself spent much of every duty desperately trying to arrange sufficient cover for the unit. Indeed, that is what she was doing when Sandy had called.

Sensing an opportunity here in the other woman's disappointment, Sandy sought to reassure her of her own continuing commitment to the case, whilst establishing whether the hospital staff had come any closer to identifying the girl. Had she had any visitors, or had anyone enquired about her? Expecting that the answer would be negative, Sandy was surprised to learn that one of the night staff had mentioned that there had been a telephone enquiry. As the caller had failed to identify themselves or their relationship with the girl, this had been dismissed as a probable crank call following the publicity surrounding the hit-and-run accident. No information was given, and no further importance had been attached to the incident.

As for the patient herself, well, most the staff had noticed some slight improvement in her condition. She appeared to be awake for much of the time now but remained stoically unresponsive. And yes, Sandy was more than welcome to visit her, any time she liked. Sister Mackie could see no harm in allowing her to try to elicit some reaction from the girl.

Buoyed by the hint of promise this conferred, Sandy returned to the bedside then, only to find the girl evidently sleeping deeply now—or was she once again lapsing into unconsciousness? Sandy could not be sure. Disappointed, she took her leave of the sister and returned to her car. She was going to have to make a point of calling in and spending time with the girl as often as possible if she was ever going to solve the apparent mystery surrounding her. There was no more she could do at the moment. At least tonight she was not going to be too late home after all. Perhaps she could begin to make her peace with Helen.

CHAPTER 65

Robert

God, what was that all about? He couldn't ever remember seeing his mother this upset, not even when his father's cruel jibes had caught her completely off guard. Usually they all anticipated them and were able to shrug them off at the time without giving the bullying sadistic bastard the satisfaction of knowing he had got to them. No, something had gone seriously wrong for his mum. He couldn't begin to think what. Surely losing something belonging to work was not such a big deal.

Well, he couldn't start thinking about that now. He had worries enough of his own. Thank God his mother had been too preoccupied with her own problems this morning to have obsessed over his. He knew his story was a bit lame, but he thought she had swallowed it. And they'd made a bit of a pact, hadn't they? He smiled at the thought of that. Really, *he* was the one who had called the shots. His mother normally never would have been quite so gullible. He would certainly play that advantage for all it was worth.

But in the meantime, he needed to do some serious thinking. As he saw it, all his current difficulties boiled down to two things: his appalling lack of available cash and the knowledge that his brother could drop him in the shit at any time. He couldn't do much about the money at present, wondering briefly if he could bring some pressure to bear on his mother to resolve that particular problem. He doubted that it would work though. She was unlikely to advance him the sort of sums he needed without going far too deep into the reason for his demand. As for Richard, well, if he only knew where the little fucker had got to over the last two days, he would be in with a head start. He had a vague recollection of his being there earlier that day, but his memory of anything preceding his mother's unheralded return from work was anything but clear. Now she was going to be at home indefinitely—well, at least for the foreseeable future and just where did that leave him? It was going to be hard enough to keep up the pretence of going to school every morning, assiduously dirtying his sports kit and leaving textbooks open beside his bed. Lord knows how he was going to manage the various assignations later in the day.

He had managed to keep his suspension from Peel Street Academy secret up till now, intercepting and destroying the letters to his parents and forging their responses apologising for Robert's misdemeanours and assuring the school that he was currently waiting to resume his studies elsewhere in the city. "They" felt sure that the staff at Peel Street would be relieved that he was going to be transferred beyond their remit as, despite their sterling efforts on his behalf, he seemed unable to respond satisfactorily. "They" hoped that this fresh start would mark the beginning of a new chapter in his life and once again thanked the staff for all they had tried to accomplish with him. (That letter was a work of sheer genius, he thought. Should keep them off his case for weeks.)

What he did not know was whether Richard would uphold this story on his behalf. He hoped so. The little wanker at least owed him that. It was Robert who had put him in the way of earning megabucks for himself. That Richard had subsequently outstripped his brother both in earnings and in demand was causing him to reevaluate his concept of brotherly love and loyalty. If only he could get his hands on half what Richard earned, his problems would be over.

CHAPTER 66

Ben and Karen

Ben thought she had never looked more beautiful. She was radiant, her movements light and purposeful, her eyes dancing, bright, and focused.

Their journey back had been largely uneventful, marred only by the persistent rain. He was handling the boat so much more confidently now, managing the locks single-handed should Karen be busy below deck with the little one. Earlier that day they had passed the point where the baby had been found. Ben had marvelled at how completely unremarkable it seemed. There was nothing to see there now, only the greens and browns of autumn vegetation and a couple of mallards pecking at an upturned bag. He didn't know what he had expected as, with some apprehension, he eased the boat through the lock, attending to both sets of paddles himself, mildly cursing the rain, which was falling heavily now, rendering everything that much more difficult to grasp. It was wet and deserted, with nothing there at all to mark the momentous change the baby had brought to their lives.

The wind had changed direction slightly, and the rain was driving into his face. Visibility was poor, but just a little further along from the lock, Ben thought he glimpsed something, little more than a vague shape, lumpy and pale, practically submerged amongst the dense reeds. He guessed it must be a dead sheep, one that had wandered onto the towpath and fallen into the canal. He wondered briefly about telling a farmer but had no idea where the nearest farm lay or even if that was where the sheep had come from. He was just glad that Karen was not on the deck with him. It would only have upset her. She was almost too tender-hearted.

They had shopped for provisions en route, Ben realising that he no longer scanned every passing face wanting, or perhaps fearing, disclosure. He had accepted the new order, content that Karen was happy again. For her part, Karen maintained her role as dutiful wife and mother, cheerfully cooking, cleaning, and caring for them all, enjoying every moment spent with her baby, and helping Ben with the boat on the odd occasions when he needed it. They had negotiated the staircase lock without incident; Karen, having settled the baby to sleep, was able to jump off the boat and assist the lock-keeper as before. If *he* noticed a change in the cheerful young woman, he never mentioned it, relieved that theirs was the only craft moving on the cut on such a dismal day.

Despite the deterioration in the weather, their progress was steady. They made a number of stops, once to refuel and a couple of times to refill the water tank and drop off their rubbish. Descending the final four locks of the Hurlston flight, they left the Llangollen Canal behind, turning right onto the Shropshire Union Canal towards Autherley Junction and the outskirts of Wolverhampton. Not that Ben and Karen were travelling that far; they had picked up their hire boat this side of the Audlem flight, fifteen locks in all. Even with his newfound confidence, Ben would have found that a challenge to manage, in all probability, on his own. No, the marina which was home to their boat was only a short distance and two relatively shallow locks away.

Already Karen had planned their manoeuvre. Ben would drop her off, with the baby in her pushchair, on the towpath approaching the boatyard. The rain had finally stopped; it would be no burden for Karen to walk on into the village. Meanwhile, Ben would return the boat and deal with any necessary paperwork involved. He would load all their belongings (so many more now that they had the child) into the car and meet Karen in Audlem. There were three decent pubs and a couple of tea rooms in the village, so whoever got there first would have somewhere comfortable to wait.

It had all gone according to plan—almost *too* smoothly, he thought. Now that the holiday was over, a honeymoon period in which they had played out their fantasy life, the reality of the situation began to assert itself. He had almost expected to be challenged, loading the car with all the luggage they had taken on board at the start of their trip, plus all the extra packages of baby clothes, bottles, and disposable nappies. On reaching the village, he was equally surprised to find Karen sitting at one of the little tables under the shelter of the awning outside the Lord Combermere pub, evincing no interest at all from the few locals going about their business. If Cari Moses had been missed, word of it certainly had not reached this stretch of the canal network.

CHAPTER 67

Pam

Her husband had been angry with her; Pam was aware of that. Although their paths seemed to cross less and less frequently these days, when he was in the house, it seemed to Pam that he was more than usually uncommunicative and abrupt with her. Their meals were seldom taken together now, most of his plated helpings scraped into the waste bin or remaining completely untouched beside the microwave oven where she had left his food for him. When he did come home, it was often to shower, change, and go out again. Pam had stopped asking him anything at all about his movements, all too often recently having borne the brunt of his impatient response: "Pressure of work. You of all people should know. We've got a lot going on."

Tonight was different though. Ted's demeanour was beyond surly, his customary impatience becoming an ill-concealed anger. He slammed the bathroom door so hard that the sound waves reverberated through the house, followed by the tinkling sound of shattered porcelain as the last of the ceramic fish, souvenirs from a long-distant holiday in Sicily, fell from the wall opposite the shower, splintering into a myriad of tiny fragments as it hit the tile surround.

Later, as she swept up the pieces and consigned them to the rubbish bin, Pam was overcome by an overwhelming sadness, so entirely out of proportion to the damage done to her bathroom décor, or the loss of this last remaining memento of happier times and their first holiday abroad, that even as she wept, Pam knew that she was mourning something far more profound: the death of her marriage, shattered dreams, and the disintegration of family life.

The tears had started earlier that day with the discovery that Robert had not been home all night. Normally she would have kept such a revelation quiet, promising herself that she would try to tackle him about it later that day. But today of all days, Ted had made one of his rare forays into his elder son's bedroom, probably to harangue him about some perceived misdemeanour. It had to have been something particularly gross for Ted to become aware of it. If he only knew the half of it, Pam thought, so accustomed she was to maintaining her own counsel about their sons' shortcomings. Anything to preserve a vestige of peace, a veneer of harmony in their household.

Ted had rampaged through the usual heaps of detritus on Robert's bedroom floor, kicking aside the scattered clothing, trampling underfoot the plate of half-eaten food and the crumpled remains of a roll-up. "Where the bloody hell is the dirty, idle little bastard?" he thundered at Pam, giving her no time to reply, before seizing her by the shoulders and shaking her.

"You know what he's up to, don't you? Why are you protecting him? Think you can make it up to him, do you, all the times you weren't there for him? Weren't there for any of us. Too caught up in your precious job. Well, you've only yourself to blame. Not only a lousy wife, but also a pretty useless mother you've turned out to be."

Now, as she absent-mindedly stroked the developing bruise at the top of her arm, Pam realised that it was not just the physical pain of Ted's assault which caused her to weep, but also the cruelty of his words. Had she really sacrificed her family for the sake of her work—for the sake of a job from which she was temporarily suspended, whose future was uncertain? What if she was left with nothing? No sort of life at home, no longer the satisfaction of the work she so enjoyed, no longer the lynchpin of their nuclear family, no longer even a midwife.

CHAPTER 68

The Owner

The major general and his wife had flown in from Malta earlier that day, having spent a few days, mixing business and pleasure, on the island of Gozo. By now he was very tired and increasingly irritable. The plane, having been delayed on the tarmac while someone's credentials were authorised, had missed the scheduled time slot for its departure. By the time they had touched down, cleared customs, and were on their way, both the M25 and the M11 were horribly congested. The A14 was not much better, and the M6 was at a virtual standstill in places. The major general had endured his wife's whining complaint about his chosen route until he could stand it no longer. "Damn it all, woman, you know I always go this way." Years of service in the Midlands and East Anglia meant that he knew these roads quite well. He had tolerated her complaints long enough. She knew that his business affairs meant flying from London rather than an airfield nearer to their home. She benefited from these deals, so she would just have to put up with it.

Then, having got so close to the end of their journey only to be confronted with this was all too much. "Good God Almighty. Whatever sort of country is this that a man is refused access to his own home? Don't you know who I am?" Puce in the face now, his eyeballs protruding and the veins in his neck visibly pulsating, Major General Greenslade accosted the luckless police constable whose patrol car was blocking the entrance to the approach road. "Just what in God's name is this all about? I shall take this to the highest authority. You mark my words. Heads will roll."

Despite the major general's blustering, the young PC remained implacable. He certainly was not going to get *another* reprimand for letting someone through. The epitome of courtesy, he attempted to placate the belligerent ex-army man by referring to "an unfortunate incident" and saying he was operating upon his superiors' instructions.

To be met with such intransigence from such a very junior personage was, in the major general's opinion, absolutely the last straw. Here was a man who, for the last sixty years of his life, had enjoyed a succession of leadership roles: head boy at his public school, then on to Oxford, where he was a rugby blue, then Sandhurst, followed by an impressive career in the army. On his father's death, he had inherited the land, a sizeable estate with established fishing lakes and shooting rights, and the Elizabethan manor house, one of several homes which he owned outright, the one where he had been content to spend most of his time and from which, now, he was effectively barred.

Had he been on his own, he would have turned tail and headed back to town to spend the night at his club the In & Out naval and military club in St James's Square, but that was hardly an option as he had Leonie with him. He would have to book them into a hotel, he supposed. He would most certainly talk to Ted Manning about this just as soon as he saw Leonie suitably accommodated out of earshot.

CHAPTER 69

Leckie

The shadows were shifting. Everything was hazy and muddled. She was assaulted by images, fuzzy, merging—flashes of absolute clarity—before they, too, were sucked into the melting pot of her dreams, changing, blurring, gone. At first she had willed herself to hang on to these moments of lucidity, forcing herself to concentrate, to keep them in the forefront of her mind, trying to stop them from becoming engulfed in a sea of confusion. It was exhausting, and she really was so terribly, crushingly tired. She had not wanted them to come, content in her brief moments of wakefulness to lie there in her hard hospital bed, idly staring out of the window, watching the treetops swaying and the clouds scudding by. But they *had* come, unbidden, unstoppable. The harder she had tried to retain her tenuous grasp on them, the more fleeting and elusive they seemed. It was like trying to hold on to jelly with her bare hands. One minute they were there, and in the very instant once she became aware of them, they were already slipping away, dissolving, to be reabsorbed into the mind-muddled soup of her dreams.

It was only then that she became aware of the person sitting by her, not sure whether she, too, was part of the fabric of her imaginings, shifting and changing like the rest of them. She—yes, it was almost certainly always a she, but sometimes she was tall, a willowy blonde slouched in the chair, stooping over her book, barely glancing at the bed. At other times she seemed to have metamorphosed into a short, stocky person, one who was staring intently in her direction now, whose gaze never faltered. She felt more drawn to her in this manifestation. She was beginning to dislike the disinterested version, sensing no rapport or empathy there.

Recently the images had been occurring much more frequently, and the cameos of clarity lasted moments longer before they too faded into the pea-soup muddle of her brain. She did not like them then, no longer seeking to hold onto them but wishing them to go away, to leave her in peace. She clenched her eyes shut as if this in itself would have the power to disperse them.

She thought there were times when the she-shape disappeared completely. The trees and the sky were still there—in the same place, where they had been all along—but the chair was empty now. There was no one, tall and bored, short and intense—no one, a void. She felt strangely alone then. There always had been someone there before, surely. Her eyes were heavy from trying to force the image to form again, to summon the woman, whoever she was. She must have slept because next time she was aware of the shifting world again, the she-shape was there.

Her head was pounding now. I have to tell her. There was a baby, and then there wasn't one anymore. She didn't know what had happened to it. She ought to tell someone. Someone ought to know. She hoped it would be the little dumpy shape, because in that form she seemed to be interested, almost as though she was waiting to be told.

She was changing shape again. This time, a man? It had to be. Vaguely familiar. No. It couldn't be him, surely. Shaking now, trying not to hang on but to erase the thought, delete the image—forget, forget, forget—she wanted the comforting she-shape to come back. She would even settle for the thin, bored version—anything—as long as it was not the man. That shape terrified her. So real. So very real, there in the foreground, the background images accompanying him fast and furious. Nasty, invasive. Half remembered and best forgotten.

She was shuddering uncontrollably now, her limbs, which had lain inactive for so long, twitching and jerking. She thought she must try to run, to hide, but the man shape had disappeared and she was only aware of heightened activity happening all around her. Not shadows any more, these were truly real people in real time, and something was happening to her. They were putting something into her arm. Her eyes were so heavy now that she couldn't fight it any longer. Her world returned to black—a blank black canvas.

———•———

She did not know how long she had slept. Her head felt fuzzy, and she was still so very tired. She was finding it difficult to stay awake. Must have dozed fitfully, she thought. Had they taken her somewhere? She had been only vaguely aware of people, more people and machines—and questions, even though she knew that she could not answer them. "Did it hurt?" or was it "This won't hurt"? She couldn't remember.

The darkness in her head was beginning to recede. She was back in her room again—the same window with the same view. And the shifting shapes were returning, distant, faint at first, but clearer now. She was actually quite glad about that; she didn't want to be alone, hoping the kindly she-shape would be there again.

CHAPTER 70

The Man

Long gone were the days when he sought to buy the runt's favours with the currency of flesh. Now he had money to spend and the real bargaining power that it conferred. He felt that he had left his erstwhile companion behind years ago, seeing him now for the loser he was. He hadn't known it then, downtrodden by circumstance and indoctrinated with a pervading sense of his own worthlessness, any ambition he may have harboured in his youth long since consigned to memory and the crushing defeat of what might have been.

He could afford to pay for the man's services now. Years of living frugally had achieved this for him. It was all down to planning, divesting himself of the trappings associated with unnecessary spending, trappings that could have sucked him dry, evaporating his meagre earnings. Dependents, fancy clothes, lavish meals, drink or drugs, he had had no need of them for years. Time spent variously at HM Prisons, subsequently on the road, then in a series of ill-paid jobs, had taught him the value of doing without, the value of having very little. An interesting juxtaposition; he liked the sound of that.

Now it was his turn to call the tune. He would use the man again, he knew that now. He'd call in a favour, and if that went well, he'd call in another, until his own position was as strong as cast iron, bombproof. He still had to settle with him for the earlier job. Indeed he would have done so before now had everything gone according to plan. But the execution was only a partial success. He was not so naive that he accepted the half-truths he had been told. No, the stakes were even higher now, and he had the wherewithal to dictate the terms. Anything short of absolute achievement would not be tolerated. Imperfection made him nervous. He had to maintain nerves of steel to accomplish his mission.

He knew that the time was right. He had to start watching again. The comfortable satisfaction that his own most recent mission had been well accomplished was lasting for shorter periods of time these days. It did not mean that he had to compromise any element of his planning. He would never accept that. But it did mean that he would have to move on apace, from the first stage of the planning process through to its eventual execution.

Before he could move on with the plan, he had to give some serious thought to a couple of issues that had arisen. First there was the vexed question of location. While he was more than happy with the city centre as the base for his investigations, the canal network had lost its greatest appeal ever since his last bungled episode with the woman there. The lake was a stroke of genius, but he made a point of never using the same site twice. That would be to court disaster: someone recognising him or his vehicle from an earlier visit, putting two and two together, and hitting the magic four.

Then it came to him. Why had he not thought of it before? He did not have to abandon his love of the waterways, but instead of merely using them to display his art, he would use his knowledge of them to identify the next location. While the city itself was one of the farthest points on the Shropshire Union Canal, it did not have everything he needed. But the canal probably did, meandering its way across the Staffordshire, Cheshire, and Shropshire countryside. Particularly Shropshire, he thought fondly, a county of meres and mosses, with lakes varying in size and seclusion, so many of them accessible from the canal network.

As for the other issue that was giving him cause for concern, he had to acknowledge that his recent home visit had failed to bring one particular item of outstanding business to a satisfactory conclusion. He had left instructions, of course, and hoped it would only be a matter of time before the matter was safely resolved, but for the moment there was a shadowy feeling of misgiving. He had hoped it would have been over before this. He hated loose ends. They were anathema to his love of ordered precision. And he really did not want to have to go up to town again.

CHAPTER 71

Ted Manning

Ted did not appreciate being awakened from sleep. As he had risen through the ranks, that was one aspect of police work he was happy to leave behind: being dragged out of bed and back on duty because of some element of breaking crime. Now it was only when there was an investigation of such magnitude that such a thing would ever happen, and even then it would be at his own choosing.

Earlier that day he had sought to demonstrate solidarity with his colleagues and, he was shrewd enough to acknowledge, increase the sway of his authority over them by announcing his intention of working on well into the night shift in an attempt to draw together the disparate strands of information pertaining to each of the major enquiries underway. He had hovered over the officers in the incident room, holding spontaneous brainstorming sessions with them, before retiring to his own office and comparing notes with senior officers in the neighbouring forces tasked with the job of assisting them with their enquiries. It had turned midnight before he left the station, causing a collective sigh of relief among his colleagues, who had been labouring under an unnatural sense of restraint the whole time he was eavesdropping on their discussions and commandeering any snippets of progress they felt they were making.

Too tired and too wired to seek solace elsewhere that night, Ted had returned home and poured himself a couple of extremely generous measures of malt whisky. Lifting the cover off a plate of food Pam had left for him by the microwave, he was revolted by the appearance. Whatever it *had* been, he could not attempt to guess. Even though her cooking had improved of late, this particular offering was unidentifiable, an indistinguishable mess of dark green and brown sludge with what may have been potato croquettes perched upon a sea of congealed gravy. Shuddering with disgust, he scraped the contents into the pedal bin, downed his second whisky, and turned in for the night.

It was only a matter of minutes, or so he thought, before his stertorous breathing was ratcheted up to a new level and his dreamless, untroubled slumber was shattered by the persistent ringing of the landline phone beside the bed. Partly dreading what else of such significance could have disturbed the officers on his patch to the extent that they would summon him from home, and partly exhilarated by the possible prospect of a result, he struggled into a sitting position, eased out of bed, and took the cordless handset into the bathroom. No point in waking the whole damned household.

"Ah, Manning. Perhaps you can tell me what is going on?" He was less than enthused to recognise the blustering, bullying tones of the major general. Now *that* was a complication he could do well without.

"See here, Manning, it's just beyond the pale, denying a chap access to his own home. Whatever your lot may or may not have found down by the lake, there is no way on earth that my home can have anything to do with it. As for that upstart telling me that it is a potential crime scene, I'm sorry, I just don't buy it. My home was locked and alarmed in my absence. My woman comes in from the village while I'm away just the same way she does when we are here. She would have been the first to know if something wasn't right in the house. I don't need to tell you, Manning: we need to keep a sense of perspective in all this.

"Meanwhile, after a tiring journey back from Gozo, Leonie and I are holed up for the night in a less than desirable country house hotel six miles down the road from our own front door. And that caused a bit of a stir, I can tell you. Coming in at that time of day without any prior booking and with our home only a matter of a mile or two away.

"Can I have your assurance that there will be no more of this nonsense? Tomorrow we shall have breakfast here and will fully expect to be back in our own home by lunchtime at the latest. Do I make myself clear?"

Not normally lost for words, Ted Manning had been holding the handset away from his ear throughout the increasing volume of this tirade.

Now, before he could begin to formulate a placatory answer, he heard the caller's phone being returned noisily to its stand. Thoroughly wide awake now and convinced that he was not going to get any more sleep that night, Ted flung his own handset onto the bed and went back downstairs. God, what a muddle this was turning out to be.

CHAPTER 72

Pam

She had heard the phone—of course she had—and was aware of the cumbersome form of her husband hauling himself into a sitting position, then disappearing into the bathroom with the handset. Lying awake as she had been doing night after night since her suspension from work, Pam had heard Ted's homecoming, including the slam of the pedal bin and his heavy footsteps on the stairs. It was at this point she began her nightly charade, feigning slumber and hoping that soon he would be beside her in a deep and absolutely authentic sleep. It obviated any necessity to speak, to make small talk about her day or his, in her case a fabrication of events, as she had as yet failed to tell Ted that she was no longer at work. Having put it off initially in the hope that the situation might resolve itself, she no longer knew how she could even begin to broach the subject.

She was glad of the nights when Ted failed to return home, no longer wondering or even caring where he had been. A night without Ted in bed with her was a night when she could play out her nocturnal insomnia unnoticed and unremarked. The nights he did make it to the marital bed were more of a strain. True, she no longer cringed as he rolled towards her, fearing a drunken pawing and his aimless groping. She knew she had little to fear from a return to any sort of sustained intimacy. Their life together had gone way beyond that. It was quite clear that he no longer wanted her. And for her part, she had begun to find him physically repulsive. He was a bully, and she was fearful of that. Emotionally crippled from his constant undermining criticism, she had begun to dread having to confront him with anything approaching an explanation.

During the long wakeful nights, she fretted about her sons, listening for any sounds emanating from their rooms which would reassure her of their presence. Some nights she knew that neither boy was at home before she went to bed, and she lay awake anticipating the telltale sound of their keys in the lock, illuminating the time display on her watch, noting when they came in and how they sounded. There were nights when she never heard them come in at all, hoping that she had dozed intermittently and missed the unmistakable sounds, worrying that she hadn't dozed at all and that they had been out all night. Challenged about their movements, both boys were sullen and uncommunicative, Robert adopting a sneering "I've got one over on you" pose so reminiscent of their father.

During the long, quiet days at home, Pam had taken to tidying their rooms, imperceptibly at first, fearing the inevitable backlash and accusations about invading their privacy. But the boys seemed not to have noticed, so as the days passed, her forays into their rooms took on a longer, more searching approach. As she tidied the clothing strewn across floors and chairs, she automatically felt in the pockets just as she did when the worn items found their way into the wash. She did not know what she was looking for. Clues? Answers? She was just certain that she would know when she had found it.

To date, Robert's room had yielded few surprises. It was dirty and disorganised: plates of congealed food, half-eaten snacks and soiled clothing under the bed, a residue of broken sports equipment and childhood toys spilling off the shelves. In his wardrobe there was a stack of pornography—catalogues, magazines, and videos. She found a bong and twists of weed pushed deep into the penholder on his desk, and everywhere were sheets of paper covered with some sort of calculations—old maths homework that had never been finished or submitted, she surmised.

She had ventured to raise the issue with him one morning as he moodily chomped his way through a bowl of breakfast cereal, before leaving for school. Richard had already left. and Pam wondered how Robert managed to leave so late every morning. He must be at the very last minute catching the school bus, she thought. He had shrugged off her concerns and shuffled into his outdoor shoes, slamming the back door behind him as he left the house. Never mind, there would be other mornings. As for today, well, it was Richard's turn to have his belongings searched through while he was gone.

It was here in Richard's room that Pam received her biggest shock. Sitting on the rug beside his bed, she rocked back and forth in disbelief. She had been tidying up the clothes that were lying about, putting them away in drawers and the wardrobe, when she made the first discovery. Amongst the jeans, hoodies, and assorted tops she recognised as his, she was startled to find a selection of clothing that she had never seen before: tight designer trousers, beautiful shirts, and well-cut jackets, slim-fitting and ornate. And the shoes. There were more shoes at the back of his wardrobe than she had ever possessed in her lifetime. Again, these were of beautiful quality: fine Italian leather, top-of-the-range trainers, ankle boots. She had no idea where any of these had come from and had never seen Richard wearing them. Had Ted, perhaps, been treating him? But as soon as she formulated the thought, she dismissed it. They were seldom around together, and as far as she could tell, her husband had no particular fondness for either of his sons. Had Richard been shoplifting? She would have to tackle him about that. Oh God, could her life get even worse than this—disgraced, suspended, and her son a thief, a criminal? Ted was going to have a field day with that.

Sitting on the floor now, Pam could see under Richard's bed. In contrast to the earlier chaos, the area underneath the bed was filled with lidded plastic containers, each one neatly packed with brown cardboard boxes. He had his stash of porn magazines here too, but they seemed to be of a different quality, a different genre even, from those in his brother's room. They were sophisticated, glossy publications. Pam found the contents highly disturbing. Lord knows, she wasn't a prude. As a nurse and midwife, she had seen most things and didn't think she could be easily shocked. But these magazines, with the graphic depiction of extreme sadomasochism, both appalled and fascinated her in equal measure. She could not put them down; each page was a revelation, a new and more horrific illustration.

What was her son Richard doing harbouring such a collection of filth? So engrossed was she that Pam never heard the outer door open and the soft footsteps on the stairs. Suddenly aware of a presence behind her, she turned, startled, dropping the magazine, in time to see Richard bearing down on her with what looked like a baseball bat. Screaming, she scrambled to her feet, knocking over the pile of boxes she had lifted out of the nearest container. Lids flew open. It was like a scene from a bizarre carnival as the contents spilled out across the floor.

Tumbling piles of condoms, all sorts of colours, shapes, and sizes; tubes of lubricant; sex toys—and all the time Richard bearing down upon her, a smile of rictus on his thin young lips and a cold, sullen fury in his eyes.

CHAPTER 73

Sandy

Sandy was aware that she was skating on thin ice. With all leave cancelled and the pressure mounting in both the recent murder investigations, the priority in terms of enquiries had a clear focus. The hit-and-run had been downgraded and no longer demanded a constant police presence. Instead of this, the investigating team was reliant upon the hospital staff to let them know should Victim A ever regain consciousness and be able to answer their questions.

But Sandy couldn't keep away. It was as though the injured girl evinced some sort of magnetism which she, Sandy, was incapable of ignoring. She felt drawn to the bedside, a commanding physical pull which she could neither rationalise and understand nor resist. At first she had thought it was because of her early involvement in the case, her recognition of the girl as a street person and the gratification of knowing exactly where she could be found. Sandy had played a hunch before and acknowledged that this was much more than just the satisfaction of having gauged something correctly. It was the sense of power, of ownership, and the invincibility that this bestowed. This time it had gone way beyond that. It was no longer about being the one to solve a mystery or even about the acclaim that would necessarily follow. At a primal level it was about knowing—sorting the half-truths from the speculation and celebrating the completeness of discovery. It no longer mattered who else knew. Sandy just needed the knowledge for herself. In some sort of bizarre twist, she owed it to the girl in the bed.

And so, after shifts and between shifts, wherever her assigned duties had taken her, Sandy would make her way up to the unit to study the girl lying there. She had listened intently to muffled mumbled sounds emanating from the slight figure, unsure whether or not they were an attempt at speech. She had held the girl's gaze as she held her hand, willing her to keep her eyes open, to share whatever it was that increasingly seemed to be disturbing her rest. And when the dreams had come, so powerful that they wracked the frail body, she had held the girl's hands more firmly, assuring her over and over again that she had nothing to fear.

At first the ward staff were relieved to have been able to delegate their surveillance of the girl, but as the days went by, a certain unease settled over the department, Sister Mackie voicing her concern at shift handover that perhaps there was something unhealthy in the intensity with which the young policewoman was monitoring their charge. But they were perpetually busy and almost permanently short-staffed, so it seemed churlish to reject the help that Sandy offered. And so the visits continued unchecked, until the fateful day when Victim A suffered some sort of terrifying relapse. Returning to the bedside after handover, the day staff had been alarmed to find the patient apparently suffering a seizure, writhing uncontrollably, eyes wide open, staring sightlessly, her pulse racing and her breath coming in short, shallow gasps. The medics had been alerted and the patient sedated. She was resting quietly now in the semidarkness, the blinds half drawn and the powerful treatment lamps turned off.

Sitting beside the recumbent form, so peaceful now after the drama of the last couple of hours, Sandy could only marvel at the barely contained violence she had witnessed. She could not dispel the feeling that there was something evil in what she had seen; the girl had seemed possessed. And just what, wondered Sandy, had she meant by the half-formed words tumbling, muted and hesitant, tantalisingly indistinct, from her lips: "Baby. ...I have to take the baby"?

CHAPTER 74

The Man

"Well, you look after yourself." Mandy smiled. "Can't be too careful with this nutter about," she said, before reluctantly turning her back on the delivery bay and making her way back into the store. Ideally she would have liked to stay there longer talking to the kindly delivery man and enjoying the weak autumn sunshine, wishing she could have her customary fag break. That was one of the worst parts of being pregnant, being urged—no, *pressured*—every time she had seen the midwife. "Not smoking now, are we, Mummy? We know what's best for baby, don't we, Mummy?" God, how she hated the way they talked down to her, all the "we" this and "we" that, and calling her "Mummy". Time enough for that when she had the kid in her arms. For now, she just wanted to forget the whole damn mess. Mummy indeed. Dummy, more like.

She was pregnant at thirty-seven, no man in her life, now or ever, it seemed, just a drunken one-night stand and, hey, bingo, there it was, this bloody little alien, unwanted, unasked for—not to mention all the clucking that ensued, the tut-tutting from her mother, who had long felt that her only daughter was wasting her life in a dead-end shop job, only to be confronted by this latest disaster. There was concerned clucking *and* ill-concealed irritation from her father. Of course he would do his best for his little girl, for both of them. "These things happen, love. You'll cope with it. We'll all cope." This to his wife's chagrin, as she did not want to cope. She wanted a grandchild, yes, but all in the right sequence—a textbook romance, a lavish white wedding, and then, as Mandy was already in her late thirties, perhaps a honeymoon baby. But not this, an unknown father and no sign of there being any sort of happy family played out here.

No, Mandy conceded, she could have done better. Why hadn't she got rid of the foetus the moment she realised that she was pregnant? Fear, she supposed—and then inactivity compounded inactivity. Perhaps she would be lucky enough to miscarry anyway.

And so it was that Mandy Wheeler had cruised through the first three months of her pregnancy in total denial that it was happening to her, and once she had acknowledged the inevitability, telling her parents and the girls at work, it had set the whole damn caravanserai in motion. Questions, always questions. Where would she like to have the baby? (In a far off-land, preferably among cannibals who eat children, she thought moodily.) What sort of birth would she like? How the hell did she know? The only sort of birth she would want was one that was totally pain-free, preferably occurring in her sleep, and then she would wake up and discover, joy of joys, no baby—it had all been a nightmare, nothing more. "And who would Mummy like as her birthing partner?" Well, if George Clooney were to be available, or perhaps that nice young Zane from One Direction …

She was just a container, Mandy saw it now. From the moment her pregnancy became public knowledge, she had ceased to be a person in her own right. She still dressed smartly—the more so, if anything—not wishing to have everything about her lifestyle dictated by her pregnancy, the little interloper within. But it was as though she had become invisible; the focus of any attention and any interest at all seemed to be the baby.

That was why she had enjoyed chatting with the delivery man when she went outside to sign off his load. He seemed different from the others, asking about her. Did she live around here? He hoped she didn't have far to travel into work each day. And what time did she finish? "They are long days, aren't they?" Mandy had been immeasurably cheered by this interest in her, rather than in the course of her pregnancy, and found she was telling the man quite a bit about herself.

No, she didn't have a partner—was still living with her parents, would you believe? One of the old semis down Brinksway Road. Hoping to be able to move out soon though. Get a place of her own. Usually walked into work. Not really any sense trying to get a bus in from there. If it was teeming down, her dad would drop her off on his way to pick up the morning papers. Same at night. Walked home, cutting through the estate—only took her about quarter of an hour.

She wished she could have stayed there all afternoon talking to him. It was good to have a sympathetic listener, but she knew that she would be in trouble if she wasted any more time. There were already mutterings among the other girls about the number of times she had to leave the shop floor to go to the ladies'. Not as though she could help that—the kid seemed to be pressing on her bladder—but she knew her line supervisor had her eye on her, and she didn't want to push her luck. Reluctantly, Mandy shut the outer door behind her and rejoined the workers inside. It had been a pleasant interlude in an otherwise dull day, and she really hoped that she would talk to the delivery man again. It was just so refreshing to be treated as an adult again.

As he slammed shut the rear doors of the van, the delivery driver smiled. He would see Mandy again. He knew that.

CHAPTER 75

Steve

Steve had been having a horrible time. Ever since the discovery of his wife's body, he'd fielded the endless questions, which were tentative at first, trying to establish whether it could be the missing patient they had found. And then, once they were surer of their facts, they had taken him to that awful place, the city mortuary, and asked him to identify her, Abigail, his beautiful, talented wife, looked like nothing he had ever seen before. To give them their due, he conceded that they had tried to warn him. All that time half in, half out of the water, she wouldn't be looking like he remembered, but he would have to do this. He would have to look and try to see beyond the bloating and the horrible livid discolouration, and try not to notice the bits they had covered up with dressing pads. The tissue there was too badly damaged, they had said. A euphemism, he suspected. The tissue was probably gone—ravaged, rotted away, or eaten by some animal. He couldn't bring himself to think about that.

And still the questions. Was there anyone else who could identify her? Did he want someone else with him? What about her parents, perhaps? "No, no, no." He realised that he was shouting now. No, there was no one else he wanted there, no one else he wanted to see what he had to see. It was because of him that she was there. If he hadn't taken her away from her comfortable upper-class existence, if he had not married her and got her pregnant, if he hadn't agreed with them that her mind was unsettled by the birth. If only he hadn't agreed to their keeping her in hospital. If only. If only.

The identification was every bit as horrendous as he had feared. He had broken down, sobbing like a baby, and still the questions came. Had he known that she wanted to leave the hospital? Had he ever suspected that she might have wanted to run away? Had she ever talked of taking her own life (not that this appeared to be a suicide, but they had to ask)? Did he know why she would have gone to the place where her body had been found? Had she friends or family in that area? Finally, cruelly, what did he think she did with the baby?

Questions. They asked him questions till his head pounded. They suspected him, he was sure of that. He thought he had detected a change in their tone as, in his anguish, he had berated himself for all the ills that had befallen her. They hadn't actually said as much. They certainly hadn't arrested him—yet—but they had told him not to go away from home, adding that they would need to be able to contact him "should there be any developments".

And so he had gone home, back to the little flat over the music shop. He had shut himself away, not answering his phone, living on tea and toast, avoiding everyone.

CHAPTER 76

Booth Street Station

Speculation was rife. Had the murderer taken the child with him as some sort of macabre trophy? Had she been taken by a fox, or had she perhaps floated away down the canal to the next set of locks?

Police frogmen had been called in. Clad in wetsuits, they waded up to their necks in muddy water, encountering the miscellaneous detritus that had found its way into the canal beds, which were not so gross here as in the more urban stretches of water they had explored on previous occasions, but still, amazingly, they found a couple of bicycles and a supermarket shopping trolley. No sign of the baby, though, nor any potential clues as to the murderer.

There was a brief moment of excitement when the leather holdall had been spotted floating upside down beyond the reeds. They could only guess that it had been thrown there, or possibly blown into the canal by a sudden strong gust of wind. Their exhilaration was short-lived. It was empty, of course, just a wet muslin square caught round the handles.

Forensic tests had yielded little of note, although the man, Steve, who had been brought in for further questioning had positively identified the bag as having belonged to his wife. That they were no nearer to discovering what had happened to little Geraldine was tearing him apart. He could think about nothing else. There was nothing more he was able to do for Abigail. The baby was the only thing he had left.

Until Steve had had the foresight to turn off his mobile phone, Abigail's mother was bombarding him with calls and, when these remained unanswered, leaving increasingly vitriolic messages for him. *She* clearly held him personally responsible for what had befallen her daughter, almost accusing him of complicity in the disappearance of his baby girl. She was incensed at not having been the one to identify Abigail's body, steadfastly refuting her husband's assurance that it was probably for the best, that they should remember their daughter as she was, not as what she had become.

"Heartless men." She tarred them all with that—her husband, her son-in-law, officers of the law—masking her own profound grief by the ferocity of her verbal attacks on all and sundry involved in the case. Even the dumpy little policewoman who had been detailed to contact them following the gruesome discovery of Abigail's body was not spared from this criticism. She had taken an instant dislike to her. Something about her attitude offended her. She was not sure why, but she thought the woman might be gay. What could a woman like that possibly know of how a mother felt on hearing that her only child was dead?

Meanwhile, urged on by his wife, Abigail's father was seeking some sort of redress from the hospital authorities, calling in support and favours from his many influential friends, concealing his own despair with an outpouring of frenetic activity. Someone had to be at blame for her being able to disappear from the ward like that. He was determined to leave no stone unturned in his pursuit of the likely culprit.

CHAPTER 77

Ben and Karen

Back in Norfolk, Ben had concerns enough of his own. Buoyed by the success of their deception so far, Karen had assumed a seemingly unassailable stance, telling anyone who enquired that she had gone into labour unexpectedly while they were away on holiday. In her eager enthusiasm, old animosities were forgiven, and both her parents and ex-colleagues unwittingly were drawn into the fabrication, Karen proudly displaying little Cari ("Just for now Moses has to be our secret name for her," she had insisted to Ben) and basking in their congratulations.

"Darling, we still have to deal with the formalities." Karen was wheedling, coaxing again. "Come on, Ben, it can't be so difficult. All we have to do is register her birth, then she really is ours forever. No one can take her away. But we need to do it as soon as possible. We mustn't leave it too long, or they might start asking awkward questions."

Ben had no doubt at all just what those awkward questions would entail. He could only remember so much from the very few parent craft sessions he and Karen had attended, but he was sure that they needed some sort of documentation from a hospital or midwife to say that they had delivered their baby. But Karen, as certain of this as she had been in her determination to keep the child, had searched extensively online and assured Ben that, whilst midwives would normally issue such a certificate, there was no requirement in law for that to be produced when the parents went to the registrar.

"We say we had her on holiday, that there was no warning and no midwife around. And seeing as I felt very well afterwards and the baby was

220

clearly fine, we didn't think we needed to try to find one before we came home. After all, we were mobile on holiday, weren't we? It wasn't as though we were just staying in the one place. *And* we hadn't got transport or much of a phone signal, so the thought of trying to track down a midwife from a narrowboat was never really feasible."

She had told them the same story at the GP surgery and had been gratified to receive a clean bill of health for little Cari from the health visitor there, despite the noting of something in her records about the inauspicious nature of her delivery. To avert any further suspicion, Karen had agreed to a postnatal check, mentally planning to defer this for as long as possible with a sequence of trumped-up excuses—minor ailments or pressing domestic issues. She was on a mission, unstoppable. Cari was theirs, and Karen was determinedly setting about to establish that incontrovertibly.

CHAPTER 78

Robert Manning

Robert was floundering. He did not know how much longer he could keep up his pretence of attending school or for how much longer he could hold his creditors at bay. What had started out as a bit of a flutter had rapidly become a gambling habit. It made no difference whichever way he did the sums, he still owed a lot of money. He couldn't even sneak back home during the day and keep a low profile that way, not with his mother there all the time now. On the rare occasions when his path crossed with that of his father, he had found him to be even more distant and domineering than usual—no chance of a rapprochement there then. And Richard was worse than useless. He had made it abundantly clear that all he intended to do for his brother was to go along with the lies circulating at school. No way was he going to drop him in it, but equally there was no way he was going to risk his own neck by putting his brother in touch with his own current sources of finance. He worked hard for his cash, and there was no way that tosser was going to get a share of it.

Robert knew that he still had something of a hold over his mother, but he had begun to realise that this was becoming increasingly tenuous. He couldn't see how he could blackmail her into giving him the money he needed without the necessity of divulging why he owed it and just how much was involved. An inventory of his saleable assets was depressingly unpromising; the sale of his school laptop and a few computer games was hardly likely to make even the smallest dent in his mounting debts. Dealing on the streets was increasingly difficult. He had nothing in the way of funds to outlay, and he had already called in any favours he had from boys to whom he had supplied in the past. He hated the thought, but there seemed only one possibility open to him. He would have to steal some things to sell.

And where better to start than in his own home? His mother was notoriously careless about where she left her handbag. Rifling through this, he had found only her mobile phone. That might be good for a few quid, he had thought, pocketing it and turning his attention to her purse. A couple of bank cards; they could be useful. Not that he knew her PIN, but it was bound to be something amazingly obvious like her date of birth. He could only give it a try and hope to strike lucky before the account locked out. Tipping out the remainder of the contents, he found another thirty pounds in notes, not a fortune, perhaps just enough to buy him a little time to come up with a better solution.

He had already lifted her engagement ring from its resting place on the tail of the little silver-plated cat which served as a ring holder, useful when she was cooking, standing as it did on the windowsill over the kitchen sink. There was nothing for it; he would have to see what else she kept in her jewellery box. He couldn't hear her in the house. She must have popped out to the shops, but he was taking no chances, so he crept upstairs to her bedroom in his stocking feet.

It was then that he heard it, a low moaning sound, a strangulated sob, coming from—he was confused now, but it certainly seemed to be coming from Richard's room. Then he saw her, his mother, Mum, lying on the carpet, her eyes wild and staring, her hands clutched protectively over her head. Of his brother there was no sign. Nor was there any indication that he had recently been there. Just a few cardboard boxes pushed under the bed, alongside the recumbent form of their mother. Nothing else about the room seemed at all out of the ordinary.

Kneeling beside her, Robert felt for her pulse and wondered, for the second time in as many days, just what was happening to their family. She was still making the little whimpering noises, but he couldn't see anything immediately wrong. Why wasn't she speaking to him though? Was she really unconscious? Robert wondered if she might have had a stroke. He tried splashing water on her face, but nothing changed. He was getting scared now. He didn't know what he ought to do. Should he call his father? send for an ambulance?

Remembering the latest terse rejoinder from his father, Robert decided that the ambulance was a safer bet. Pulling his mum's cell phone from his pocket, he dialled and waited. "Emergency. Which service do you require?" And so the wheels swung inexorably into motion, the patient operator telling him what to do and what not to do. "Don't try to move her. Is she responding, answering you? You will need to go downstairs and unlock the front door for the paramedics. Whatever you do, stay on the phone."

Suddenly they were there, the ambulance outside, its blue flashing light coursing across the bedroom ceiling, the paramedics calmly assessing the situation, reassuring him, and checking his mother's vital signs, all the while talking to her, telling her what they were doing. Then they lifted her onto a stretcher and carried her out to the waiting ambulance. Did he want to go with her? Was there someone else they should tell?

Robert shook his head. He would talk to Dad later, once he knew what was going on. In the meantime, he was going with his mum to the hospital, riding in the ambulance, comforted by the unflappable paramedics. He never gave a thought as to where Richard might have been and hadn't even begun to wonder what his mother was doing in his brother's bedroom. For once, even his own dire situation had receded from the forefront of his brain. He was genuinely surprised when, overwhelmed with conflicting emotions, he had reached into his pocket for a tissue and had felt the hard circular shape of his mother's engagement ring.

CHAPTER 79

Richard

Richard was terrified. He really didn't know what had happened back there. He didn't know what to do. Tidy the evidence away and then leg it as far as possible from the scene? That was all he could think of achieving.

Now, huddled in a doorway off the main boulevard, he pondered his next move. He could go home as though nothing had happened and face whatever was waiting for him there. Or, given that he had money, he could hole up somewhere in town, get a cheap room for the night and consider his options. Alternatively, he could get away as far as possible—catch a train to London and lose himself in the big city. They'd be looking out for him; soon, he had to decide. On balance, putting the greatest distance between himself and the scene back at home seemed like the most intelligent choice.

It was a simple enough thing to get on a train away from here. He bought his ticket from a machine on the station forecourt. He didn't want some beady-eyed employee in the ticket office remembering him. There were to be no memories, no identification. Nervously glancing over his shoulder as the station concourse filled with early evening commuters, Richard was profoundly relieved when the London train was announced over the tannoy, and even more relieved when it eventually pulled out of the station and he was on his way.

He hadn't any clear idea of what he might do, but he was used to thinking on his feet and was no stranger to making his own fortune. He would wait until things had settled down—make a new identity for himself and see what else life had to offer. He had been increasingly disillusioned with life as knew it. The writing was on the wall. It was high time for a change.

CHAPTER 80

Alex

Alex hadn't slept a wink since reporting Roseanne missing. Ringing round her friends, then facing her family, he had drawn a complete blank. Then there were all the inevitable questions and the attempted reassurance: "I'm sure your wife will turn up soon, well and happy. Probably met up with friends and not realised the time."

When had that changed? He had sensed it altering, imperceptibly at first, from benign caring to something altogether more aggressive and accusatory. He had been taken to the police station, kept down there for hours, and questioned endlessly. How could he account for his movements over the last forty-eight hours? What sort of relationship did he have with his wife? Was it possible that she had left him to be with someone else? What was she wearing on the day she had disappeared? He didn't know. Why didn't he know? Because he had not been there, had he? Could he supply them with a list of all her friends—family too, of course?

That was the one that really did it. Choking back the tears as he went through their Christmas card address book, impeccably set out in his wife's super neat, childlike script, had really got to him. She was always so thorough, so careful, and he did not deserve her. He didn't even go out of his way to please her any more.

Pray God she's safe, he mouthed. "I'll make it up to you, darling. So help me, I will."

CHAPTER 81

Helen

She had awakened with a start, surprised at first to find herself alone in her and Sandy's king-size bed, sunlight streaming through the gap in the curtains, falling in oscillating golden bands across her pillows. Why aren't the curtains drawn? she wondered. Not like this, neither open nor closed. If she could just summon up the energy, she would pull them right back, allowing the sunshine to fill the bedroom. For the moment, though, she was happy just to lie there, luxuriating in the knowledge that she did not *have* to get up, not yet anyway. It was Saturday and she had the whole day to do what she pleased, a day that stretched out tantalisingly in front of her. The warmth of the bed and the cheery, flickering sunlight was contagious. She felt a corresponding lifting of her mood, a dancing light-heartedness that had evaded her of late. If only she could hang onto it. If only there was someway she could make it last.

She realised what must have happened. Sandy would have opened the curtains just enough to be able to see to get dressed before leaving for work that morning. A considerate move, trying not to disturb her sleeping partner. Somehow, though, that thought sat uneasily with Helen. She really wasn't sure about Sandy's intentions any more. Was it an act of kindness, of consideration, or was it something altogether more sinister, a betrayal of their intimacy, an act of secrecy? Helen's happiness of only a few moments before was beginning to dissipate as she mentally tallied the number of times recently that she had awakened alone, Sandy having left for work without so much as an early morning cuddle.

Helen was beginning to ask herself when it had all started to go wrong.

She knew that Sandy had an exacting job, that her hours were at best irregular, and that in the event of any major occurrence, she could be called into work at a moment's notice. It had hardly mattered when first they were an item. They would make the most of any time they could spend together, joke about the times apart, and text each other at intervals throughout their working day—loving texts, mundane texts—"Missing you"; "What do you fancy for supper?" Intrinsically, though, they were *caring* texts.

With a jolt, Helen realised that their early, easy messaging no longer occurred. They seldom sent each other a text these days, except for possible reminders that the central heating boiler was due a service and one of them needed to be at home for that, or some other similar contingency. When she was there, Sandy was so preoccupied that she barely seemed to register Helen's presence. Helen had never known her to be so abstracted before, even when the pressures of a case were at their most extreme, Sandy had always managed to shrug her concerns aside for an hour or two and participate in their life together.

Determined not to let herself dwell upon such negative thoughts, Helen pushed aside the duvet and got out of bed. She had no idea when Sandy would be home and wasn't going to waste her day off fretting about that. She had wondered about going to the gym, but that seemed such a dull thing to do on her own. She just couldn't muster the necessary enthusiasm. Their joint attempt at a weight loss programme had foundered with her partner's increasingly limited leisure time and with their membership at the sports club having almost lapsed. Helen did not think that this was the moment to revive it.

A day round the shops held similarly little appeal. It was Saturday, so everywhere would be crowded. Besides, there really wasn't anything she needed. She would just be spending money unnecessarily. Family visits were not an option either. She knew that her parents were away. They had a holiday home in the South of France and would be enjoying the last of the year's golf at the club there. Of her only brother's movements, she knew even less. He worked in London and lived there with his long-term girlfriend. The siblings had never really been close and were certainly not on the sort of terms that involved dropping in on one another.

No, she would enjoy this day on her own. She would have a ride out into the countryside and have a leisurely pub lunch somewhere and

possibly even a walk, making the most of what promised to be a lovely autumn day.

Spurred on by the thought, Helen had a quick shower and breakfasted on cereal and coffee before packing her walking boots, a bottle of water, and an anorak in the boot of her car and setting off. She had no idea how long she would be out, and she really didn't care.

CHAPTER 82

The Major General

The major general was incensed to learn that he was still not at liberty to return home because of its proximity to the crime scene beside the lake. He and Leonie would have to spend yet another night at the country club, playing havoc with her social life and threatening him with something he had not experienced for a very long time: fear—a creeping, all-pervading disquiet.

He wasn't even sure what it was that he feared. He just knew that the longer he was effectively banished from his own home, the tighter the knot in his stomach became. It was untenable, keeping him at arm's length from his possessions like this. And with the very real threat that he would not be allowed to enter his home unaccompanied, that he would have to be escorted onto the premises by a uniformed police officer, he was troubled.

It was not merely the degradation this implied; he was beginning to experience genuine alarm. What if they insisted on accompanying him on a thorough search of the house? Even worse, what if that search was to be conducted without his being present? He felt sure that, in law, no such search could be undertaken without either his permission or a warrant to that effect. But the last thing he wanted to do was to draw undue attention to the house. The need to protect it from prying eyes and from probing, searching fingers was paramount.

He could only imagine the gasps of surprise at the magnificent contents of his gunroom. And while he could produce valid firearms certificates for most of the exhibits, he knew that there were others there which he would have to pass off as being harmless replicas, hoping against hope

that his assurances would not be put to the test. These were items of such astounding provenance that they would never have seen the inside of a specialist auction house, nor could they ever have been offered for sale on the open market. Their value was incalculable. Not only was their provenance unique and profoundly significant historically, but also their true value to an aficionado such as he was in their ultimate destructive capabilities.

He had taken a calculated gamble over the years that the firing mechanisms would appear to have been disabled. Only he knew that several of his most prized possessions were completely capable of discharging a lethal load, their apparent disablement merely a cosmetic ruse. Long ago he had decided to maintain as many of his key exhibits as possible, not just with full but, wherever it was feasible, *enhanced* working capacity. It was not so much an act of bravado but more a matter of pride, initially at least. There was no place in his armoury for emasculated weapons. He needed to know that they were capable of absolute destruction. He needed to experience that power and guard that revelation.

His wife and Mrs Barker had never evinced the slightest curiosity about his collection, accepting at total face value his assurance that most of the guns were merely scale models incapable of inflicting any harm. To the few associates with whom he had shared a somewhat sanitised version of his interest and to whom he had shown the gunroom, he maintained a similar stance. There were those, he was sure, among the ex-military who might have harboured their suspicions, but he had been at pains to impress upon them the legality of his pursuit, citing his associate Ted Manning as someone who knew the full extent of the collection and the thoroughness with which it had been researched and legitimately displayed.

In truth, Ted had never appeared to be particularly concerned about the old soldier's arsenal, and he either did not know or did not care that the nondeactivated weapons were kept out of sight for the five-year inspection and reissue of licences by the regional firearms officer, a retired copper based locally. All the remaining guns were duly accounted for and the necessary firearms certificates available for perusal should anyone be interested. Not that many people were, although in fairness, not that many people knew about his passion for collecting current and antique weaponry. Even the referee he had persuaded to act in that capacity for the

last fifteen years, Colin Rix, the chairman of the golf club, had been happy to sign the necessary forms without ever requesting to see the numerous items described.

The last thing he needed now was an uninitiated plod looking too closely at his stock. He had wondered briefly if he could get a message to Mrs Barker to lock the gunroom and possibly push a wardrobe in front of the door to conceal the entrance. Then the crass stupidity of that idea struck him. It was not just the risible concept of little Mrs Barker hefting a man-sized wardrobe into position across the doorway but was also the certainty that, as he and Leonie had been denied access to the house, surely the same prohibition would apply to their cleaning lady.

There was nothing for it. He was going to have to face it out. He had to speak to Ted Manning as a matter of urgency and get him to give him the all-clear to enter his home. There was more than his collection of guns at stake here. Their value on the black market represented only a portion of his business interests.

CHAPTER 83

The Man

Congratulations were in order. He felt sure of that. He could congratulate himself on a job well done, on the thoroughness of his preparation. The girl had been incredibly stupid. She was pretty, true, but stupid, vacuous, a waste of space. Fancy her telling him all that stuff about herself. If they were all that silly, there would be no need for him to do very much research at all. Not only had she told him her name, not that he needed or even wanted to know it, although sometimes it helped if his victims required a bit of persuasion, but also she had virtually told him her address. He had hardly needed to prompt her to learn that she lived with her parents, so there was no anxious boyfriend likely to sour his pitch. And she had been equally forthcoming about her journeys to and from work—not only the route she took, but also the time she actually got away.

What could be easier? It was almost too good to be true. All he needed to do was to watch her for a day or two to verify the information she had given him and to prepare the vehicle he would use. Then, once he had finally determined his optimum site for the display, he was free to make his move.

That was what had preoccupied him all day. He had driven his round abstractedly, dropping off each load, considering his options. He hadn't wanted to engage in any sort of exchanges today, making only perfunctory comments and getting the necessary signatures then pressing on with his deliveries. The timing had worked out well and he had been able to make a couple of detours along familiar country lanes close by the canal network, to bring him out by two of the local meres.

Early in the day he had made a drop at a chemist's shop in Nantwich and had driven alongside the mere there, only to discount it, as he had suspected he would, for being too open and too public an arena. There were tarmac paths around the circumference where mothers wheeled young children in buggies, stopping to feed the ducks and geese; seats where older people sat, idly passing the time; and everywhere people walking their dogs. There was a constant flow of traffic on the road alongside, and the lake itself was overlooked by a row of houses. No, that was never going to be a possibility.

Later in the day, his delivery schedule had taken him to Ellesmere. He had parked the van and walked back along the towpath to an area dubbed the Shropshire Lake District. Stupid that, he thought, convinced that Ellesmere was actually in Cheshire. The lake from which Ellesmere took its name was once again too central, its surroundings too urbanised to fit his criteria. Another large lake appeared to have a number of small sailing boats anchored in a bay farthest from the canal and a couple of log cabins overlooking both the canal and the lake. An ideal venue for a holiday perhaps, but not one that would suit his purposes at all.

And then he saw it.

The private fishing lake was something else. It was bordered at one side by the towpath, three solitary anglers' bivouacs standing deep among the undergrowth at the very edge of the water. Only one of these showed any evidence of recent activity: a stand with three rods and an elaborate bite alarm system set up outside the tent, which appeared to be zipped shut. He did not know if the owner was inside or not, but it mattered very little, because the area which drew his attention was way beyond here, on the distant side of the lake. He had a memory that this was accessible from a single track road. He would have to investigate further, but now was not the time to do it. He would get the work van back to the depot for an early cleaning tonight. There were things he had to do.

CHAPTER 84

Shorty

Tempers were becoming very short. Pent-up emotions, and periods of frenetic activity alternating with sessions of intense reflection, concentrated introspection, and obsessive poring over computer screens and printouts, could hardly fail to impinge upon the studied calm of the outer office and the desk sergeant on duty there.

Shorty was envious. At earlier times in his career he would have been in the thick of all that, contributing, leading, seeing where it was all going. His current role was so much more constrained. Even the assurance from senior officers that the front desk would be where any breaking news or crucial items of information would be received failed to lift his spirits. Since the start of this enquiry, the messages received on his watch—indeed, the messages in total received at the front desk—had contributed little of any value. There was the usual plethora of enquiries from unaffected members of the general public, overly concerned about their immediate safety, the equivalent of the "worried well" plaguing medical personnel with their anxieties. Despite the scepticism greeting most of these calls, all possible sightings of interest had to be logged and collated, with all the additional work that this generated.

Then there were the crank calls—disturbed individuals claiming to know about the crimes, even to have perpetrated them. A semisophisticated filtering system had been devised in an attempt to separate out the really bizarre calls claiming an entirely fabricated knowledge from those messages which just might contain a sliver of real evidence, a contribution to the actual facts of any of the cases under review. People purporting to be the murderer needed to be identified and able to be investigated further should the assembled facts begin to point in their direction. They needed to be located, interviewed, and cautioned. Wasting police time was not something this or any enquiry needed. Above all, their stories needed to be scrutinised in case they were found to conceal any shred of truth.

Pertinent aspects relating to each of the cases had not been released to the press, the officers of all forces involved having access to key items of information which, should they be proffered by any caller, would immediately raise the alarm that this individual could be their suspect. There was still no real consensus that they were looking for one perpetrator in relation to all five of the murdered women. Whilst the MO for each of the pregnant victims certainly suggested that this was the work of a single serial killer, there was no proof that he had acted alone. An accomplice or accomplices could not be entirely ruled out. The discovery of the body of Abigail Lamont had further clouded the picture. Had she fallen prey to the same perverted killer? Opinions were fairly equally divided between those who thought that this was the only likely explanation and those who believed that there were sufficient differences to suggest the likelihood of there being another predator at large.

Shorty was fully aware of this and was professional as ever in his dealings with the public, knowing that it often took only one piece of salient information for the threads of a case to begin to weave together, but he had little faith that any such developments would be his to receive and pass on to the investigating teams. God, how he missed being at the cutting edge of an enquiry.

Whether it was the effects of suppressed tension or the hours of concentration checking and cross-checking the messages, Shorty's back was aching more than usual. His customary analgesics hardly seemed to take the edge off his discomfort. He felt tired and irritable; the station seemed in chaos; and his desk was becoming a shambles. His suggestion that a junior officer might be deployed alongside him for a while, just to tackle the backlog of information and downright fantasies that was steadily accumulating, was met with barely suppressed ridicule by his peers. "God, Shorty, what do you think we have, a bottomless pit of PCs just waiting to help you out? Don't you know there's a murder investigation going on?"

Chastened, Shorty retreated to his post and began the thankless task, between answering telephone queries, of finalising the next duty roster. The computer software was good, but only as good as the information it was given. There had been so many changes of late, and with all annual leave cancelled and the accumulation of additional hours overtime, it was difficult to see how he could be expected to produce a fair copy that was in any way a true reflection of their working situation. He felt that he was merely going through the motions, but he knew that it had to be done. The officers on the ground needed it; health and safety would demand it; and the finance department would rely upon it.

When the telephone enquiry came in, he was ill-disposed to deal with the caller sympathetically. No, the officer concerned was *not* currently on duty. Personally, he had no knowledge of the officer's whereabouts. And no, it would not be possible for him to get a message to the officer. Protocol. Protecting confidentiality and all that.

CHAPTER 85

Karen

Karen was planning the christening. They were not a churchgoing family, but this was to be her way of showcasing her, *their* beautiful new daughter. She had been dreaming of this day for years, ever since the faint blue line of that first failed pregnancy. It was going to be the most perfect day ever. She was planning everything, down to the very last detail.

It wasn't going to happen just yet, but when it did, it was going to be wonderful. She would wait until the baby was about four or five months old—holding her head up really well, taking notice, and having grown and filled out—so that she would best display the elaborate christening robe Karen had chosen for her. Belgian lace. It was beautiful, sumptuous. Handmade in Bruges. She had bought it over the net, paying for it by credit card, not daring to tell Ben just how expensive it was. Karen felt the deception was warranted. After all she had been through, she deserved her day in the clouds. After all little Cari had been through, she too deserved the most elaborate party possible.

The baby was sleeping beside her now, in a pretty cradle with a fine lawn drape suspended over the head end. This wasn't her real cot. That one was much more substantial, a robust construction that could be converted to a cabin bed as the child grew. That was her night-time cot, the one in the nursery that Ben and Karen had decorated for her, or rather, for her succession of unrealised predecessors. No, this was her "display cot", a lightweight dainty arrangement covered in frills of flocked muslin. It was where Karen kept her during the day, in order to show her off to the greatest advantage when anyone called—the girls from the salon (Karen had barely waited a week before letting them know she was home with her baby) or either of the two grandmothers, with whom she had forged an instant rapprochement in order to gloat over her little girl. Ben's mother was delighted and convinced herself that little Cari looked just like Ben had at the same age. Karen's own mother had been more difficult to read, rightly suspicious of her daughter's motive in making such friendly advances after all this time and irritated beyond measure with Karen's refusal to discuss anything about the birth. After all, wasn't that what mothers and daughters did, shared experiences, even to the point of horror stories about the delivery, anything that proved them stronger and more resilient than their partners, a coming together that excluded those who could not identify with their tales of personal trauma? Karen's mother knew as little about her granddaughter's birth as she had when Karen first broke the news. The child was born on holiday, and Karen and Ben had waited until they got home to share the good news with their families? Whatever sort of first-time parents would do things like that?

Glancing adoringly at the little girl sleeping in her fairy princess bassinette, Karen smoothed the fronds of silky brown hair away from the child's eyes and resumed her search of the internet. She was pleased with her trawl today, having sourced silver-trimmed plates and matching napkins for the christening cake and having located a beautiful pair of little satin shoes. Unsure whether or not these would be visible under the christening robe, she had ordered them anyway, together with a pair of tiny frilly socks. She had just discovered, on a neighbouring website, a gorgeous angora shawl (convincing herself that Cari might need this should the weather in early spring still be unseasonably cold) when the doorbell rang. Quickly checking that the sleeping child had not spoilt the effects of her beautiful cradle and pastel Babygro by bringing up any of her last feed, Karen went to answer the door. Before she could get there, the bell sounded again, imperious in its persistence, waking the baby and startling their elderly cat.

The two police officers from the East Anglian force, more used to conducting house-to-house enquiries, were detailed to follow up the address they had been given by the narrowboat hire firm on the Anglo-Welsh border. Incongruous as it seemed to them, there being a well-established boat hire business operating throughout the fens, the couple at this address had chosen to go on a narrowboat holiday somewhere in the vicinity where the body of the murdered hospital patient had been found. According to the details with which the police had been furnished, the hirers were a young couple, Ben and Karen Aldiss. No mention had been made of a child, but perhaps the parents had left the baby in the care of its grandparents while they were on holiday.

Once she had calmed the crying infant, the woman, Karen, was most helpful. Yes, they certainly had been out on the canal system during the time in question, but they had not seen anything untoward. The weather was pretty foul, and they had only cruised for part of each day before tying up for the evening and settling down beside the fire. Yes, her husband would certainly bear that out, and yes, they were welcome to come back and talk to him at another time if they needed to. About the baby, she said nothing, and the officers never asked.

CHAPTER 86

Leckie

The terror never really went away. During the day she could force herself to stay awake, watching the staff going about the usual routines, or looking through the window and seeing the trees almost devoid of leaves now, their branches latticed against the sky. It was much more difficult at night. Her eyes were heavy with tiredness; her whole body, dull and lethargic because of the drugs. All she wanted to do was to sleep, but she knew that she had to fight it. No good came from sleep. She dimly remembered learning this at one of the schools she had sporadically attended. Something about "in that sleep, what dreams may come?" She knew only too well what forms those dreams were likely to adopt.

There was the horrible, frightening man, the one who chased her endlessly through the chambers of her sleep, room after room. Or sometimes it was carriages in the train, coach after coach after coach. Hiding was never an option. He would always find her. And the smell, one she recognised, was something she remembered from way back when. It was the smell of something she used herself in an effort to forget. It was all horribly mixed up in her mind now: the remembering, the forgetting, having to remember, trying to forget.

Why was no one with her any more? She felt sure that once there had been. She could remember shapes—shifting shapes at that—sometimes male, but usually not. They were good shapes, protecting her. Surely they had protected her at first. But then they changed. Sometimes the good shapes couldn't stay and the bad one took their place. She had to stop that happening. She had to stay awake.

———•————

She wondered if wishing had made it happen. Tired, so tired of being alone, of having to keep her eyes open to stop the bad shape returning, she still must have dozed a little. Now, forcing herself to open her eyes, she was aware once again that the good shape had come back. Not the supercilious one, but the kindly, dumpy shape in whose presence she felt so much more content. And the shape was talking to her. She couldn't really hear what it was saying, but she was aware of sounds, far-off sounds like waves gently lapping on a distant shore. She knew that if only she could get closer, she might know what the sounds were saying.

There. She had managed it, had wriggled: any movement she achieved, oh so slow and heavy, the progress almost imperceptible. But she had made it. She was inches nearer now to the guardian shape. Uncanny. It was almost as though the shape was mirroring her own struggle to get closer, her dragging the metal hospital chair with her feet so that the shape actually touched the side of her bed, leaning in, bending over her. And she could make out some of the sounds now. Something to do with a baby? Finding her? Leckie wasn't sure what that meant: finding her, or finding a baby? It all seemed to be mixed up with another sort of question, this time to do with a car, a car coming for her—or at her? And the mention of a blanket, a little pink blanket.

It was there again, somewhere in the muddle of her mind: a baby, a blanket, a car. Was it only one baby? She couldn't be sure. It felt as though there might have been other babies, lined up. A row of plastic cots. It was coming back to her now.

She had taken one—had chosen it because it was quiet—but when she got back to her shop doorway, there was only the blanket. However hard she tried, she couldn't remember what had happened to the baby. Had she put it down somewhere and lost it? Was it with her when the other thing happened? She was beginning to remember that now, fragments of memory, her feeling cold, hoping someone would give her the price of a cup of tea. Then *bang*, a black shape bearing down on her, blocking out the lamplight. Bang. Then nothing more.

It all seemed so long ago. She must have been asleep, because that was when she started to notice the shapes. And today the shape was back, here, beside her. It was the kindly one, speaking to her, words at first very indistinct, but much clearer now. Leckie could almost make out the shape of the words—a *baby* and a *car*? Well, she certainly hadn't got a car when she took the baby. Never had a car, not even a licence to drive one, but she could remember cars with which she had been familiar long ago, cars whose engine noises were trapped forever in her memory, sounds she recognised, striking fear into her after all this time, a recollected fear, waiting for the bad things to happen.

She thought there were cars more recently too. Getting into cars. Hitching a tight little skirt even higher to climb up into one big car. A black car. *The* car.

Suddenly she knew. The black shape cutting out the lamplight—it was a black car, a big black car she had been in before. She should tell the shape beside her about the car. If only she could make the words.

Things were clearer now. Her head did not seem so dull and heavy. It was as though the fog was beginning to lift, with half-formed pictures no longer shifting before her eyes, disassembling, then disappearing into the miasma. Floating together now, the pictures started merging, becoming something else, something that Leckie, even in her drug-induced state, could recognise, could identify. Images were forming, fast and furious now, and she began to think that her head would explode with the magnitude of it all.

It was reassuring that the friendly shape was still there. Perhaps if she tried hard to focus, the barrage of shifting shapes and half-held memories would begin to recede and she would know what they meant and what was being said to her. Fixing her gaze on the form by her bed, she was startled to find that this, too, was beginning to disintegrate, blurring and mingling and blurring again, before settling as a shape she recognised. It was a person, a woman, someone she may even know. Had they some sort of shared history, she wondered?

The woman was bending close to her, whispering words again, fixing her eyes on Leckie's and holding the latter's flickering stare. And in that moment, Leckie knew: this was her guardian. She must have been there all along, a dark shape most of the time because she had been wearing dark clothes, a uniform of some description. Not today though. She seemed to be casually dressed in jeans and a chequered shirt, the top button undone, revealing the mere glimpse of a pale gold chain.

There was nothing to be afraid of. This person had been sent to help, to confer some reasoning, some rationality, upon the muddle in Leckie's brain, to help her to live again.

CHAPTER 87

Mandy

She felt as though her bladder was about to burst. She had to find some way of relieving herself, but that was never going to be as simple as it sounded. Her hands were tied behind her back and her ankles bound together with what appeared to be bungee straps. She had managed to wriggle her chin free of the scarf he had tied across her mouth to stop her from screaming out, but it made no difference. She had screamed until her chest ached with the effort, causing her to change her tactics and drum her heels on the floor of the van where she was lying. Now, utterly weary with all the pointless energy she had expended, her throat so sore with the shouting that she felt as though she had swallowed sandpaper, she was experiencing a new and excruciating discomfort. She desperately needed to wee. Unsure how much longer she could hold it in, she squirmed and twisted until, with a supreme effort, she managed to manoeuvre herself into a sitting position with her back resting upon the side wall of the van.

In the hours that had passed since the van finally slowed and trundled to a halt and she heard the driver's door slamming shut, she had gone from blind panic to a total paralysing fear. Now she needed to make some sense of her surroundings and fathom out what her next move might entail. But first she needed to get comfortable. There was no way on earth that she could free her hands and remove any of her clothing, nor, for that matter, loosen the bonds that secured her ankles and prevented her from moving her legs apart. By now the pain was intolerable. There was nothing for it, she simply couldn't hold it in any longer; she would have to relieve herself where she sat. As the warm rush of urine pooled beneath her buttocks, staining her jeans and rapidly cooling into an uncomfortable icy puddle where she sat, Mandy felt the despair brought on by this ultimate humiliation. She would be better off dead than enduring this. He was going to kill her, she felt certain of that. Her only hope now was that it would all be over soon.

CHAPTER 88

The Man

He had done his homework well, following up the clues that the stupid girl had unwittingly revealed. He had watched her for three days now, finishing his shift on time and returning the work van for cleaning before resuming his observation.

She was as good as her word, totally predictable, leaving the shop at the same time each night and walking through the estate towards her parents' house. He was using his own van for this surveillance but had already thought out how he would "decorate" it this time. He had the logo ready to apply:

Charles Fell

Tree Surgeon

In addition, he had a bogus mobile number and website address. He liked the sound when he read the words of his logo, appreciating the irony of a tree surgeon called Fell. Not much good at his job if he had to resort to felling all the trees he had been contracted to trim!

On Thursday night he had given the van a thorough cleaning before securing the logo and using electricians' tape to alter the format of his registration plate: U became O, I became D, and the last number, 1, was transformed to 4. It wouldn't pass muster on very close inspection, but he was satisfied that the camouflage was sufficient to fool anyone who might later remember seeing the vehicle in the vicinity of his intended abduction. Not that he had seen many people about on the estate at that time of day. They were either in their cars on their way home from work or already indoors, feet up in front of the telly. That suited his purpose very well. Tomorrow he and Mandy would meet again.

———◆———

Friday, and according to plan, Mandy left work and was walking home. His van was idling on the corner of a deserted cul-de-sac, the houses in darkness, and even the street lights here seeming to cast little illumination in his direction. Either they were too widely spaced, he thought, or the council was on an economy drive and was only letting alternate ones be lit. Not that he was complaining. He hardly needed arc lighting for what he was about to do.

He heard the tapping of her heels before she came fully into sight, wearing stupid fashion boots with heels too high and certainly too loud for his comfort. Gently slipping the van into gear, he made to follow Mandy for a short stretch of the road before overtaking her and pulling into the parking area in front of the shops. All bar two of these were closed and shuttered for the night, the only exceptions being the Eastern European food store and the fish and chip shop. His confidence, already peaking with the realisation of the accuracy of his plans, received a further boost when he realised that his was the sole vehicle in the parking bay. How much better could it get?

He had slipped out of the driver's door and was standing by his van, ostensibly checking his near side tyre, when Mandy rounded the corner. "Well, I never!" he exclaimed. "We get to meet again. You *are* the girl from Fenwick's, aren't you? Mandy, isn't it?"

Startled, then agreeably surprised when she recognised the man as being the delivery driver she had encountered earlier that week, Mandy felt a surge of gratification that he had remembered her name. She hadn't recognised the van, but supposed he must do a number of different driving jobs, realising that, while she had told him quite a bit about herself, she really knew very little about him. Still, he seemed kind and genuinely interested in her, and she felt no pangs of anxiety at all when he suggested that they might go for a drink. She felt flattered that he had noticed her. Perhaps he fancied her, even in her present state. And so what? Even if he was a bit old for her, it was nice to be appreciated for once.

"We don't have to do it tonight if you've something else planned," he said, hoping like hell that this would be met with a flat denial on her part, making it even easier for him to persuade her into the van.

He was thoughtful, too—and no, she had nothing especially planned. Mum wouldn't be cooking till later. "A drink would be very nice, thank you."

The man smiled to himself at this, opening the passenger door for her to climb up into the van and sit in the seat next to his.

It was at that moment that the doors of the fish and chip shop opened and three youths spilled out onto the pavement, loud in the lamplight, jostling each other, clutching their bags of food, lifting the cans of lager to their lips, jeering and swearing. "Hi, Mandy. That yer baby's daddy, is it? Where you find 'im? Down the day centre? E's old enough ter be yer granddad!"

Humiliated by their catcalls, Mandy turned to the driver. "Let's just get going, shall we?" she said, completely failing to notice the look of clenched determination and the pent-up anger behind his steely-blue eyes.

———————

There could be no backing down now. The girl was in the van, but he could not go ahead with his plan. It was way too dangerous. The chip shop louts had seen too much. What's more, they knew Mandy by name. They had become a force to be reckoned with.

In the meantime, he had the girl, wittering now about how the boys on the estate had been rude to her before, how they were no better than her. He had to shut her up. He had to be able to think.

They were leaving the outer environs of the sprawling estate now, Mandy still jabbering on about how the boys always went to the chippy on a Friday night (Pity she hadn't told me that before, he thought wryly) and how they had started calling out after her, asking, "Who's the daddy then?" generally making her life unpleasant. Well, it was just about to become a whole lot more unpleasant, he was certain of that.

Pulling into a lay-by, he strode round to Mandy's side of the van and dragged her from the seat, silencing her protestations with a sharp blow across her mouth. She was cowering now, alternately covering her face with her hands then clutching them across her abdomen. Satisfied that none of the passing vehicles were slowing down to see or even interfere with the drama being enacted in the anonymous darkness of the lay-by, the man hauled the whimpering girl round to the back of the van, opening the doors and flinging her inside. Her ordeal did not end there as he clambered in alongside her and pulled her hands away from her face, firmly tying them behind her back. The feet came next. Two bungees soon stopped her attempts to kick him away, as he tightened them mercilessly around her ankles. She was lying on the floor now, any thoughts of escape long gone, as he smacked her again across her jaw, pulling the scarf from her neck and securing it across the lower part of her face. Only her eyes and nostrils remained uncovered, and all she could taste was the blood in her mouth.

⎯⎯⎯◆⎯⎯⎯

It was no answer. He knew that. But at least it would give him valuable thinking space. He had baulked at the thought of killing her there and then. The road was too public. Any time at all, a lorry could pull in behind him, or a family car, the driver or one of his passengers needing to get out for a pee. The chances of discovery were too great, and he would still have to dispose of the body. It was a bit too close to the area where he had picked up the girl and where those thugs at the chip shop hung out. They had seen him drive off with Mandy in the van, and what was worse, they knew who she was. There could be no body dump here. It was just not feasible. This was one body which was never going to be displayed, was never to become an example of what he thought of as his particular art and science. She would have to be taken care of in another way. This was one body he had to be prepared to lose.

He had driven on then into the night, a cold blast of air from the open window clearing his head, the crimson mist of his earlier rage dissipating. He knew now what he had to do. He would take her to his house in the woods and deal with her there. Distracted by the thoughts of what he was about to do, he almost failed to notice the vehicles ahead beginning to slow down. Then he saw it, blue flashing lights, way ahead on this road with its central reservation and so few turning opportunities. Were his worst fears about to become reality, a roadblock ahead and the girl in the back of his van trussed up like the proverbial Christmas turkey? He hoped against hope that it was too soon for there to have been word of the girl failing to arrive home after being seen getting into his van, the van with the clever distinctive logo, so immediately recognisable—the van he was driving now.

It was with a profound sense of relief that he caught sight in the rear-view mirror of the first of several ambulances overtaking the vehicles behind him. After that it was stop, start, stop, and wait …

A bored young WPC, resentful at being deployed away from the centre of activity occasioned by the three-vehicle pile-up, redirected traffic away from the accident scene, which meant that each of the vehicles ahead of him had to effect a tortuous many-point turn, avoiding the debris in the carriageway, and slowly return past the waiting cars and lorries—and the man's van—back the way they had already travelled. Already the traffic behind the man had backed up as far as he could see, the dipped headlights a ribbon of colour against the night sky. There was no telling how far they stretched, besides which, the last roundabout he had encountered was miles back. There was no alternative. He had to follow the retreating vehicles through a series of twisting minor roads, some little better than lanes, to find a different route, as yet undesignated by temporary diversion signs, always hoping that they would lead towards his intended destination.

It was going to be a very long night.

CHAPTER 89

Ted Manning and the Major General

Ted Manning had problems enough of his own. He could do without the constant barrage of attack from the major general, by now incandescent with rage at the prolonged banishment from his home and its surrounding estate. Leonie had been giving the old man hell, progressing from an initial lofty disparagement of his concerns, through a painstaking rendition of her own inconvenience at having to withdraw from her planned social engagements whilst "roughing it" in this expensive country house hotel, to an icy refusal even to speak to him, let alone consider any suggestion he may make as to how she could retrieve something from the difficult situation in which they now found themselves. She refused point-blank to concede that there could be any possibility of her regaining a semblance of normality in her life by attending some of the functions from which she had so arbitrarily withdrawn. She had clothes enough in her luggage, he knew that. In all the years they had been together, Leonie was never known to travel light. And there was no reason why she couldn't shop for anything else she might need. Whilst he felt that he had to be on hand here at the hotel, ready to return home immediately should the eventuality arise, she could always take a taxi. The hotel might even supply their own transport, and she could both shop to her heart's content *and* honour her arrangements with her circle of associates. She had summarily dismissed his offer of hiring a car for her to use. There was no way he would let her drive his BMW; the concealed compartments were his secret, and he fully intended them to remain so.

He was a man accustomed to getting what he wanted, to giving orders

252

and expecting—no, *demanding*—instant obedience. It was a natural trait, born of generations of privilege, honed to perfection by his years in the army, and helped not inconsiderably by the influence generated from his increasing wealth. He was a man other men looked up to, a man used to ordering and dominating other men. It was a skill he had practised all his life. The only person he had never been able to bend to his wishes was Leonie. In her he had met his match; he found himself at as great a loss now as to how to exercise any control over her as he had done throughout their marriage.

Theirs had been a society wedding, following a carefully regulated courtship which, despite the discrepancies in their ages, he being ten years her senior, had been instigated and approved by both sets of parents. The ceremony was held in the prestigious Henry VIII Chapel in Westminster Abbey, followed by a dignified and elaborate reception at the Naval and Military Club, St James's Square. Leonie looked stunning in a Givenchy gown which was rumoured to have cost almost six times his monthly salary. He had worn his dress uniform, and they had left the abbey under a guard of honour formed from the ranks of his own regiment. Their entourage was no less impressive as befitted both the occasion and the subsequent photo shoot for Hello magazine: ten bridesmaids, his own two sisters and eight cousins of Leonie's, dressed in a rainbow of delicate pastel gowns with garlands of fresh flowers in their hair, and two sullen, disgruntled pageboys, silently and very evidently resentful in their satin suits, carrying the cushions that had borne the twin rings that were now firmly, irrevocably round the ring fingers of his and Leonie's left hands.

He had felt stiff and uncomfortable throughout the proceedings and had returned thankfully to his regiment after the statutory (in Leonie's family's eyes) honeymoon as guests upon an extremely well-appointed yacht. He had not enjoyed that experience either, never having been a good sailor and seeing little of value in the enforced inactivity of days aboard the vessel. From the start, Leonie had made it abundantly clear that while he was expected to perform his matrimonial duties as and when she wished, she harboured no desire then, or for the future, for there ever to be any children from the marriage. It was not what he had expected to hear, certainly seeming to run counter to the wishes of both their families and the usual expectations amongst his friends and associates: "Be starting your own little corps any time soon then? Better get your boy's name down for Sandhurst now, old man."

Leonie was adamant. She had quite enough in her life with her horses and the social life she had forged for herself among her many contemporaries and acquaintances. The marriage was desirable: it conferred a status of its own. She had warmed to the idea of being an officer's wife, an officer who looked to be going far and for whom promotion seemed inevitable. More than that, it had got her parents off her back—well, her mother anyway, who had dreamt of and planned for this day since her only daughter was born and who had worked tirelessly throughout Leonie's late teens showcasing her to a succession of potential suitors drawn from "the best families around". It was an anachronistic ritual, one that Leonie had despised and from which she had sought to extricate herself in the only way she knew. She would go along with the charade, marrying well, and continue with her life free from parental pressure to conform. John, now Major General John Greenslade, had presented as something of a saviour. Here was a man who clearly wished to pursue his own ambitions. She liked him well enough and had seen in their potential union the chance for them both to live the lives they wished. What was more, he had proved to her in the early days of their knowing each other that he was a man capable of being moulded by her. She would make of their marriage what *she* wanted it to be.

It was a pattern that had served them well over the years. John had gone on to establish a successful career, and she had played the part of trophy wife when required, while continuing to enjoy a largely separate existence from her husband. They had few mutual friends and almost no shared interests. John didn't ride (didn't really trust the beasts) and had been particularly accommodating when she had announced her intention of keeping her mounts at a convenient livery stables nearby, where they could be cared for and exercised whenever their mistress was away. The major general moved awkwardly in the pseudo-cultural world frequented by his wife, finding little enjoyment in theatre and even less in the poetry readings which she had latterly espoused. He did like art, and had derived some pleasure from accompanying her to various galleries, but he was a man of strong opinions who favoured all that was old school and gave little attention or credence to anything more modern or challenging. His was a tempered enjoyment. He liked paintings with a realistic, photographic quality, and he liked the thought of possessing them, of putting them on display and seeing them as another prized collection.

There were similarities, he thought, in the level of workmanship evident in both: the craftsmanship that went into a pair of perfectly balanced guns and that which went into a detailed depiction of a recognisable landscape. There were similarities, too, in the extent he was prepared to go to acquire the best examples for himself. Not all trading was the carefully regulated province of the renowned auction houses.

CHAPTER 90

Sandy

What was she really doing here? Sandy pondered the question which, unspoken and unbidden, had returned to haunt her over the last few days. She should be at home planning a day out with Helen, happy that for once their leisure time coincided. Since the start of the multiple murder enquiries, there had been an embargo on extended leave and she had had very few entire days away from work. This was the first Saturday she had had off since then, and although it was late October, the early morning sun held the promise of a beautiful day to come. Helen would have wanted them to make the most of it, only too aware that there could be months of dreary winter weather ahead. But instead of sharing the anticipation of a day to do as they pleased, once again Sandy was making her way through the hospital concourse, no question here of duty or orders with which she had no choice but to comply. This was entirely her decision: an action neither known about nor sanctioned by her superiors in the force. Sandy knew only too well the folly of this. She was playing a hunch, following her intuition, all the while aware, oh so aware, that the answer to part of the conundrum surrounding this case was tantalisingly close.

Why had no one else seen it? At an early stage in the enquiry, they had dismissed her speculations as just that, fevered speculation fuelled by an overactive imagination and the desire to impress. Well, she was going to show them. Certain now that she was on the cusp of discovering the key to the unfolding investigation, Sandy had dismissed any thought of protocol and expected procedure from her mind and, with it, the hovering discontentment with her domestic situation.

Helen had been behaving oddly. Sandy saw that now. Always the more demonstratively romantic one of the partnership, Helen, it seemed, had withdrawn into a shell. Conversation between them, when it occurred, was stilted, seemingly forced, and unnatural. Intimacy was a thing of the past. They shared a home and a bed, but that was the extent of it. They no longer shared anything of themselves.

Sandy was not sure when she had first become aware of this. It seemed to her to have begun around the time of their anniversary. The changes were subtle, imperceptible at first, but like the gradual movement of two adjoining tectonic plates, the hidden momentum began to increase until there was no farther they could go before an unmitigated catastrophe occurred. She sincerely hoped that they were not about to reach that point, hoped that disaster could be averted, and yet, ever the pragmatist, if she could no longer give Helen the care and security she craved, then perhaps it was time for them to go their separate ways. But these were decisions for the future. As for today, Sandy knew where her priorities lay. Smiling an acknowledgement towards the staff around the nurses' station, she approached the injured girl, pulling up a chair beside her bed and settling herself comfortably for yet another vigil.

CHAPTER 91

Third Time Lucky

Twice now he had been thwarted, so close to achieving his goal, only to fail yet again. The first time was sheer bad luck. By rights she should have died right there, on the spot. Nothing equivocal about that. But somehow the little bitch had managed to survive.

He had hoped that he had got away with it, that she was going to die anyway and he would get his just rewards. What could it matter that it took an hour or two longer for her to succumb? He had done the deed, hadn't he? He had put his own safety, his freedom even, on the line.

He had planned to lie about it anyway, to say that it had all gone according to plan and that the girl was dead. But he hadn't reckoned on the publicity. Somehow the press had got hold of the story, and now the whole wide world knew the score. No corpse, no glory, no reward.

And then the second time, all that waiting in the wings, watching, biding his time until the moment to strike. He stood lurking in the shadows, merging with the background, inconspicuous, unnoticed, unremarked.

That in itself had not been easy. The place was like Fort Knox, staff always on duty, gatekeepers alert to any potential invasion of their premises. There were so many people coming and going, all scrutinised, all with distinct roles, recognised and permitted. And he was an alien, incognito, a trespasser on their territory, about to execute the most profound sacrilege on their turf.

At first there was a constant police presence. He backed off then, resolving to finish the business later. But his was a hard taskmaster. The job had to be completed—and *immediately*. He allowed himself a wry smile then, remembering his father's insistence that the children's chores should be tackled "immediately, if not sooner!"

That the second attempt should also fail was again down to incredibly bad fortune. He had picked his moment and had marked his prey, unattended and vulnerable. He had got close to her then, close enough to detect the foetid stench of body odours, stale breath, perspiration, and something else: blood. He was no stranger to that smell. As a young boy, he had trapped and gutted rabbits, and wrung the necks of poached gamebirds or chickens stolen from a neighbour's coop. But in a woman, *no*. The disgusting creature was menstruating. How he hated that word, and all the words associated with it, not just period, but also silly, girly euphemistic words and phrases: monthlies, visitor, the curse. That just about summed it up for him: a curse, devised to frustrate and punish men like him, men who liked their women clean—perfume, make-up, the full works. And if he was really lucky, stockings and suspenders. Yeah, that was his sort of woman.

Not that a man in his position could always afford to be choosey. The few real relationships he had known never lasted, always the women wanting more than he could give and him getting tired of their perpetual demands when what had once been their winning ways became more of a whining way. On the streets, too, they were a disappointment. Little girls, the runaways, were young enough to be his granddaughters. Get caught with one of them and they'd have you pegged as a paedophile or worse. Or ditzy blondes nearer fifty than thirty under the light. Raddled old hags, some of them, if you were to scrape off their warpaint. Saggy breasts you wouldn't want to touch, let alone get a turn-on sucking them.

This one had looked OK to him back then. She was young, but not dangerously, illegally so. She was clean as far as he could tell. Willing too, until she realised. Had he known who she was all along? After all, he knew she had come up here to work. Or was it only when he was close to her, his fingers teasing their way under her tight little skirt, feeling, hoping for suspenders but finding only a tiny thong, that he really knew. He hadn't found her repugnant then. Not only had she satisfied his basic primal urge, but also it had amused him to have her at his mercy once again, this time on his own terms. Life was like that sometimes: circular.

And it was then that he had realised the bargaining power that this conferred. No longer was he the supplicant waiting on his master's pleasure before he could get his own. No, this discovery gave him the upper hand. He could use it to his advantage to put the frighteners on, to dictate the terms and procure his just reward. What was more, should he play his cards right, it would turn out to be an ongoing cash cow. He had licked his lips in anticipation back then, relishing the prospect of repeated gratification. He figured that if he were to play his hand right, he could up the ante, promising himself to find out how much she knew, offering to take care of her, to keep her in his sights, to buy her silence.

He should have known. That was never going to be enough. There was to be no continuing payout. *He* would want her silenced permanently, before she could do him any lasting damage. It was then that he realised the limitations of his bargaining tool. It was time limited. He would have to ensure that he got maximum payoff, first for revealing what he knew and then for any subsequent action on his part to silence the girl forever. His was a dangerous game, so the payoff for it needed to be suitably extravagant.

If only he had known back then just how protracted this next step was going to be, he might not have taken the job on at all. True, he needed the money. He had dealers on his back, always wanting more for the goods they supplied. His profit margins were shrinking all the time. So many transactions now were conducted over the internet that it left people like him, the middlemen, negotiating a fickle marketplace.

He had to make this one stick, to screw it for all it was worth, and to stress how much she knew, her readiness to spill the beans. He had to exaggerate the danger, fabricate what he didn't know, pile on the pressure, play on the other man's fears.

He had dressed carefully that morning: a pair of navy trousers, well worn but pressed and clean; a sky-blue shirt; and a navy clip-on tie, this a charity shop find he had surreptitiously pocketed whilst ostensibly examining the Boys' Brigade and St John's Ambulance clothing on display. Mimicking the uniforms worn by the hospital porters, he could merge with his surroundings, unremarkable, unchallenged.

He had made his way up to the sixth floor and the corridor leading to the ICU, using the stairs rather than the lift. It was easier to remain inconspicuous that way. No one passing him on the stairs would give him a second glance, whereas the enforced proximity within a shared lift space could subject him to unwelcome scrutiny. There were comparatively few people about at that time in the morning, most of the staff already ensconced in their respective wards and departments. The day shift was well underway, the night workers long since having left for home. All the activity would be centred on the outpatient department and the café in the concourse at the other end of the hospital. It was too early for general visitors, and the few who were permitted, because their loved ones were seriously ill, would be too preoccupied with their own concerns to give him more than a cursory glance. Worst-case scenario, he might be mistaken for one of the porters he sought to emulate and be asked for directions. Well, he had been in and around the hospital long enough to answer the most obvious enquiries with authority, and if he was really stumped, he could always recourse to his practised excuse, a mumbled "Sorry, I'm new here—only started on Monday."

As it was, he had only encountered one potential catastrophe, the full significance of which did not impinge until a little later. Just as he had opened the doors at the head of the stairs, suddenly there was the unmistakable sound of approaching wheels as two genuine porters came into view, one at each end of the long enclosed trolley they were pushing towards him. Realising that they would almost certainly recognise him as an impostor, and fearful of discovery now, he silently closed the doors and shrank back against the wall, just in time to hear the younger of the two men address his companion. "Just where is the morgue, then? This is my first. Only started here on Monday." The irony of that appealed to him, hearing the very words of his own well-honed excuse and, with it, coming to realise what he had just witnessed. They were pushing a mortuary trolley, the adjunct to a clinical anonymous hospital death. Inching the door open just a fraction, he listened to the retreating sounds of the trolley wheels, then the lift gates at the end of the corridor opening and closing. Satisfied that the two porters were out of sight and that he had the corridor to himself, he took a deep breath and resumed his interrupted progress towards the ICU.

Still, it was with considerable relief that he approached the unit, his eyes darting this way and that, picking his moment. When the two nurses by the station were engrossed in an animated discussion and those out in the ward attending to patients had their backs to him, he crept silently towards the bay where he would find the girl, propped up on her pillows, not moving, an IV line in her arm, her flickering, sightless gaze always directed towards the window, that patch of sky over the vista of distant roofs and trees that he knew so well. Today the curtains were drawn around her bed. Blast. Did that mean someone was in there attending to her?

What was he to do? He dare not risk his cover being blown, but by the same token, he could hardly linger here without drawing unwelcome attention to himself. It was then that he made up his mind. He would have to take a chance. He had to know if there was anyone with the girl. If his luck was in and she was on her own, what better time could there be for him to strike? A few seconds would be all that was needed, and then the job would be done and he would be on his way, no one any the wiser and he a good step nearer to claiming his bounty.

Sidling now to the side of the bed, out of sight of the nurses busy in the ward, he tentatively prized open the curtains just enough to peep within. The sight that met his eyes was not what he had expected. He was appalled, and then exhilarated as the significance dawned upon him. The girl was not there. The bed was not just empty, it was bare, the waterproof mattress shiny blue on the unforgiving frame, no sheets, no pillows, and no drip stand. There was nothing on the locker or the table over the bed. No charts, no possessions. Nothing. It was as though she had never been there.

It had been her on the mortuary trolley. His job had been done for him. He could claim his prize and no one would be any the wiser. Hastily closing the curtains and picking his moment, he left the ward as unobtrusively as he had arrived. Resisting the impulse to run from the scene, he retraced his steps along the corridor, down the stairs, and out into the welcoming anonymity of the main hospital concourse, unaware of someone's curious glance cast in his direction. Job done. Payback time.

CHAPTER 92

Shorty and Mandy's Mum

Her mum had not been unduly worried at first. Sure, she had been irritated, then annoyed at Mandy's lack of consideration. If the wretched girl wasn't going to be home in time for tea, then surely she could have called or sent a text. It was the least she could do. After all, they had let her come back and live at home again, just as soon as they found out about the baby, and because they knew that she was barely able to look after herself, or so it seemed, let alone another little soul. Still, perhaps she had gone out for a few drinks with friends from work and just forgot the time. She was entitled to a bit of social life. She didn't get out much these days and probably would have even fewer chances once the baby arrived. Despite all that Mandy's mum had said when her daughter had first told her that she was pregnant, and despite both of Mandy's parents being prepared for her to carry on living at home for as long as she needed, it did not mean that she could just leave the child with her mum all the time. *She* was not prepared to be an unpaid childminder. Secretly she had known even then that she would help out and would actually enjoy having a little one to care for again, but she resented being taken for granted. If the girl had made impromptu plans for the evening, then she could at least have let her know.

When there was still no sign of her daughter later that night, Mandy's mum became steadily more annoyed. It really was too bad. By 11p.m. her annoyance turned to anger. Mandy still had not had the decency to text, and her own messages had gone straight to Mandy's mobile answer service. Well, she wasn't going to wait up for her any longer. She knew how much it irritated her husband. "Treats the place like a bloody hotel. More fool you for letting her." His usual refrain. And she knew Mandy had her housekeys with her, so there really was no point in prolonging the situation.

Next morning, on discovering that her daughter's bed had not been slept in, Mandy's mum was more than usually inclined to agree with her husband. She had made the girl a cup of tea as she did every morning before leaving for work—an early shift at the processed-food factory, the same job she had done since leaving school, with just a couple of years at home after Mandy was born. She had always been a conscientious employee. They'd instilled that into them in those days, she mused, not like the flighty girls nowadays. Heads in the clouds, all of them, seemingly more interested in the unattainable lifestyle of the various celebrities than in the work they were supposed to be doing. And then there was the way they got themselves up to go out: false eyelashes like centipedes, clothes that barely covered anything, heels the size of stilts—so clumpy and unattractive too. Make-up you could scrape off with a trowel. Either that or a permanent orange tan and a plethora of tattoos. Tattoos! How she hated to see those on a woman. They covered all their arms and goodness only knows where else, some of them: chains, names, faces. Unbelievably common, she thought. More suited to sailors. *Her* mum would turn in her grave!

Still, she supposed Mandy was no worse than any of them. True, she'd got pregnant and wouldn't—couldn't?—tell them anything about the father. Perhaps that was where she was now—had been all night—with the child's father. They could be planning a proper future together, even at this minute. Maybe they were right now thinking of names for the baby, talking of getting married even, or at least settling down together like a real little family. With that reassuring thought uppermost in her mind, Mandy's mum locked the door behind her and set off for Cresta Foods.

Truth to tell, she'd felt cheered by that envisaged scenario throughout the day, the routine shift work passing quickly enough, and even the young women alongside her seeming happier than usual. In this state of pleasant anticipation, even the rain which had begun to fall on her walk home failed to dampen her spirits.

Letting herself in through the back of the house and divesting herself of her raincoat and outdoor shoes, she was aware of the telephone ringing and, failing to reach it in time, the insistent bleep denoting a message. As she pressed the button for playback, she was surprised to find that eight messages had been left for them over the course of the day. Bless her, Mandy must have been desperate to share her happy news with them. It was so unlike her to ring more than once.

Gradually, her elation fading as she reached the sixth message, Mandy's mum began to feel something like rising panic. So far, there were no messages from Mandy. There were three from her work, a couple of friends there wondering where she was, and an older, starchy-sounding female requesting an instant return of her call. The following three messages were more of the same: workmates speculating about Mandy's nightlife, and the starchy woman again, this time *demanding* a response. But it was the final two messages which provoked an instant crushing fear. No words were spoken—none necessary—as Mandy's mum heard only the sound of a strangulated sob and then silence. And the final call: only that, absolute silence, but the number displayed—Mandy's mobile number—telling her all she needed to know.

CHAPTER 93

Sandy

The girl was more restless today. Sandy sensed a change in her almost immediately. It was as though she were more focused somehow, her gaze no longer vacantly fixed upon the patch of sky, rose and gold now with the breaking sunrise, only fleetingly glancing there, and then pivoting towards the door of the ward and returning, piercing Sandy with a look of sheer intensity before veering off and around, then coming back to her again. There were sounds too. You couldn't really ascribe them to words, but they held a certain form, a rudimentary pattern. Not speech exactly, but communication of a sort surely.

Sandy felt her own excitement mounting. *If only you could tell me what you know.* She bent closer to the emaciated form in the bed, desperate now to catch some gist of what the girl was trying to convey.

This was how Sister Mackie found them minutes later, not for the first time concerned that the young WPC appeared to be becoming somewhat unprofessionally involved with the accident victim, as yet unnamed. Well, that was not going to be *her* worry for much longer. The girl was clearly improving, although it promised to be a long haul yet, but they could no longer justify using a critical care bed for her. Her vital signs were stable and she was breathing unaided now. Furthermore, recent CT scans and an EEG had shown clear evidence of returning brain activity. It was time to move her to another ward.

Only that morning had a bed become available on the female neurosurgical ward downstairs. It was an irony really. With critical care beds always at such a premium, especially at weekends, "bed blocking" was seen as a constant problem here. After weeks of maximum occupancy, today there would be two vacant places. The middle-aged scaffolder who had sustained dreadful internal injuries after falling and becoming impaled on security fencing had lost his fight for life in the early hours of the morning. It had taken until now to contact his relatives, but as soon as they had had the chance to come to the unit and pay their respects, his body would be leaving the ward.

As for Victim A, Sister Mackie had just been told that the staff from neuro were ready for her now. The ward clerk was currently assembling the paperwork, and the senior nurse on duty would supervise the girl's transfer, accompanying the porters moving her bed.

Sandy was particularly pleased with this revelation. Not only did it offer the promise of more effective communication with the girl, who was now established on the road to recovery, but also there was always the chance that the change of surroundings might prompt some sort of reaction, which might even supply a clue as to her identity. Sandy had seen that before: suspects and the victims of crime, removed from their comfort zones, inadvertently revealing a salient fact or suddenly able to recall something of relevance to the enquiry. Cheered by these musings, Sandy's thoughts reverted to a more pressing concern, as she realised with a pang that, in her haste to leave home without waking Helen, she had missed her breakfast. She would see what the café in the hospital concourse had to offer before following her charge onto the neuro ward.

CHAPTER 94

Shorty

The woman was incoherent. Fear did that to people. Shorty knew that. In his long experience of police work, Shorty also knew that it was in those moments of immediate aftermath when panic was at its zenith, that people unwittingly gave out the clues which upon later, more sober reckoning they would strive so hard to conceal. As he tried to make sense through the wracking sobs, he managed to piece together the woman's rambling account of her daughter's disappearance. Not for the first time Shorty cursed his inactivity, resenting the curtailment of his duties, confined as he was to being permanently on the front desk. How he wished that he could be with her in that room, watching her face to face as she gave her account, searching, seeking the signs which would lead to a fruitful outcome. As it was, it would be left to him to convey what he could of this jumbled telephone conversation and any impressions he had formed as a result, whilst conceding the excitement of the subsequent interrogation to other (and in his view, less intuitive) colleagues.

From what he could make out, the woman's daughter had been missing for about twenty-four hours. Given that she was an adult, and possibly especially one who still lived at home with her parents, it would not normally be a case to evince a great deal of interest. Grown people go missing all the time, often for very good reasons. Sometimes they return almost immediately, and sometimes they are never heard from again. And it does not necessarily follow that any crime has been committed. People have their own reasons, their own lives to lead.

But just occasionally, an instance of a missing person implies something more significant. Obviously, sometimes it concerns a minor or a vulnerable adult, or there is a reason to suspect that foul play could be involved. In this case, the woman sobbing on the other end of the telephone revealed just such a concern. The girl who was missing had never done this before, and most crucially of all, she was six months pregnant.

CHAPTER 95

Helen

Helen had enjoyed her morning, exploring the countryside by car, stopping off at one of the small market towns en route for a coffee and to buy a newspaper. Something of an afterthought, she also bought an OS map of the area, thinking that she could use it to plan her walk later in the afternoon. Her lunchtime stop had been less successful. The pub she had chosen looked attractive from the outside: little wrought-iron tables with pale blue sun canopies advertising some Belgian beer she had never heard of, with hanging baskets filled with trailing fuchsia and troughs of gaudy dahlias completing the picture. The menu looked interesting, if slightly pretentious, and the waiter who took her order seemed less than interested when she ventured to ask him to explain some of the more obscure culinary terminology—"restaurantese" as Sandy would have called it. Helen would have loved to order a bottle of wine, to hear it chinking in the ice bucket as it was brought to her table, but she did not dare risk it as she would have to drive home—along unfamiliar roads too. So she had satisfied herself with a modest glass of Pinot Grigio, spinning it out to last through her pâté starter and main course, a dressed crab with some unpronounceable, and to her knowledge unrecognisable, salad items. Not that the food was intrinsically bad—although it was overpriced and ungraciously served— but it was the loneliness of it all. Helen, normally content in her own company, was suddenly acutely aware that she was the only single diner there, all the tables but hers having multiple occupancy—not just couples but also entire families or groups of young people, eating and drinking, talking and laughing together.

Even her newspaper offered little respite from the unremitting solitude of it all, the pages moving with the breeze, so that managing to keep it flat on the table had become too much of a challenge. She fared little better with the OS map, putting it away and resolving to study it later in the shelter of her car. She supposed that she could have gone inside the pub, but it seemed too nice a day to do that. Besides, she was indoors all through the week and relished the opportunity of spending some time in the sunshine. She would just have coffee, settle her bill, and then go back to her car and plan her walk.

It was while she was waiting for her coffee to cool down that Helen's thoughts returned to the week just passed. She and Sandy had seen so little of each other. She could barely recollect when they had last spent any quality time together. She knew that they no longer shared their thoughts. Why, only the other day Helen had remembered something that she felt she should convey to Sandy. What was it now?

Yes, she recalled the memory that had arisen, unbidden, a couple of times during the last few days—never when Sandy was around to share it though. It had something to do with the missing girls and the ones who had been murdered, the pregnant ones. Helen knew now what it was that had been a tantalising half memory, something she had thought at the time could be salient, but until now she had kept that fleeting, transitory thought to herself. It was when she and her friend from the rival firm of solicitors had had lunch that day. Polly had been so aggrieved about the woman from their firm who seemed to be using her pregnancy as an ideal excuse to come in late, leave early, or even not turn up at all, inventing some story about being afraid of a stalker, as though that gave her the right to come and go as she pleased.

That was it. That day she had neither come into work nor had the decency to proffer any sort of explanation. According to Polly, they had tried ringing her on both her mobile and her landline, but no joy. She hadn't answered them all day. And then Helen had heard it on the news: the girl's body had been found and her husband taken in for questioning. She remembered thinking at the time that it just went to show that you could never really tell what a person might be capable of. Polly had met the guy, Alex, a couple of times at the firm's Christmas do and had told Helen that he seemed quite a catch—a bit of a ladies' man, but good-looking and

271

a real charmer with it. But it was the recollection of what Polly said next as they sat together in the sunshine outside Nero's that had come back to haunt Helen.

It was something Helen realised that she should have shared with Sandy at the time, but somehow the time had never seemed right. Sandy was out all hours as the intensity of the investigations grew, and when they did have some time together, the recollection of what Polly had said was furthest from Helen's thoughts as she struggled to make sense of the insidious changes in the relationship she had with Sandy.

What if her protracted silence had really impeded progress with the hunt for the killer? Had it, heaven forbid, allowed him to strike again with impunity, safe in the knowledge that the police still knew nothing about him? Horrified by this prospect, Helen knew what she must do. She had to tell Sandy about the possible stalker straight away.

Flipping open her mobile phone, Helen was surprised to find that she had a message from Sandy:

Won't be back until late. Don't wait the meal for me. Sorry.

—S

When she tried to return the call, the message went straight to voicemail. No surprise there; Sandy often had her phone switched off when she was at work. There was nothing for it, she would have to ring the station. Helen hated having to do this, only too aware that Sandy kept a discreet distance between her work and her private life. But this was important. Surely that warranted the call.

It was answered immediately. Shorty was on desk duty and made it a point of honour never to let the phone ring more than twice before he picked up the receiver. Helen was relieved to recognise his voice. She had met very few of Sandy's colleagues but had spoken to Shorty before and knew that he was less likely to be offhand with her or, worse, demand to know what the call was about than some of the more officious ones. Civilian support workers, she supposed. It was funny how people lower down in any particular hierarchy seemed to be the ones who were inclined to throw their weight about. She saw it all the time in her own line of work with lowly court officials. Then there were the self-important doctors' receptionists … Here Helen's musings were cut short, as Shorty asked what he could do to help.

She explained that Sandy had left for work early that morning before she, Helen, had had the chance to tell her something that just might be very important to her. No, it was not a domestic issue. In answer to Shorty's gentle probing, she said that it had to do with work, with the enquiries. Shorty had stopped her there, Helen wondering if she had already said too much. She knew that Sandy was not supposed to talk about the cases they were working on. It went without saying, implicit really, just as Helen was bound to respect the confidentiality of the lawyers' clients.

But no, Shorty's tone was gentler than ever now as he explained that Sandy was not in work today. He had the duty roster on the screen in front of him now, and she was not even marked as being on overtime duties. He was trying to break it to her kindly, telling her that perhaps there had been an extraordinary meeting of the staff that he didn't know about and Sandy may have been deployed as a result of that, but Helen could tell from his voice that he was only saying it to reassure her. Even as he was wondering aloud whether it would be of any help if she could tell him, Helen switched off her phone.

CHAPTER 96

Karen

The girl was being evasive. As an experienced midwife, Connie Swales recognised the signs. First there was the story of how she had given birth unexpectedly while they were on holiday. "On your own? Just with your husband, sorry, partner there?" Connie questioned gently, trying to picture the unlikely scenario. A first-time mother, one already deeply psychologically traumatised from her repeated miscarriages, she surely would have wanted all the assurances of medical intervention to guard against anything going wrong this time. Then there were all those missed antenatal appointments, seeing them only (here Connie consulted her records) when the pregnancy had been confirmed and then at the twelve-week scan. Why had she evaded contact with them throughout the remainder of her pregnancy?

Sensing the older woman's growing incredulity, Karen had admitted then to having had help: an elderly woman, a retired midwife, fortuitously found living aboard the only neighbouring narrowboat on this remote stretch of canal. No, there had been no other help, and she had not been told to go to the nearest hospital. There was no mobile signal anyway, and the midwife had reassured her that there was no need for that, saying that everything was perfectly normal.

Connie could not shake off the feeling that there was something here that just did not gel. Karen had been incredibly vague about just where the birth occurred, and stating "no, she never did get the elderly midwife's name or even the name of the narrowboat she was living on. Everything had happened so quickly. She had been shocked, going into labour like that, and then so delighted that their baby was all right that she hadn't thought to ask. From the start she had been such a good baby. You only had to look at her now to see how well she was doing, so forward for her age, and a really healthy weight too."

The only reason the midwife had called today was that Karen had taken the child to the local health centre to register her with their doctor, to get her weighed (only they had told her they'd stopped doing that routinely), and to find out about her immunisations and so forth.

The midwife was entering all these details now in the little red book which would chart Cari's progress for the remainder of her early childhood, a little red book which announced to the world the legitimacy of Karen and Ben's possession. It was held tantalisingly close now as the midwife explained the meaning of the centile chart, but Karen was barely listening, transfixed, her eyes never leaving the little book, the book that marked Cari as their own and Karen as a bona fide member of that great band of mothers, a rank to which she had aspired for a very long time.

It was the last piece of the jigsaw. Registering the birth had been easy compared with this. (Karen remembered just how screwed up Ben had been about that, anticipating all sorts of terrible denouements, a major showdown, and years in prison for them both.) It was a good thing that she was handling *this* situation on her own. She could just imagine him breaking down entirely and confessing everything to this inquisitive health professional. But now they had everything within their grasp. She just had to keep a cool head for a minute or two longer, resist the urge to snatch the red book from the woman's hand, and maintain her side of the story.

Sobbing with relief now, all pretence over, Karen closed the door after the midwife left and then collapsed onto the sofa, cradling little Cari in her arms, rocking backwards and forwards, giving vent to all the pent-up emotion which had been building up ever since their discovery of their, *her*, Cari Moses.

CHAPTER 97

Richard

Richard had spent a horrible night. His initial relief at having got away was gradually giving way to the realisation that he had absolutely no idea what to do next and that he had hardly any accessible cash left after paying for his train ticket south. He was tired too, having tried to sleep in the station waiting room only to be moved on by an officious railway employee. Not knowing what to do, he had wandered towards the town, hoping he would find a park bench where he could doss down for the night. He rolled a joint and smoked it as he walked along. God, he was hungry now, the Golden Arches of the nearby McDonald's beckoning him. Mentally counting out the pennies, wondering whether he ought to be spending any of it yet, he was taunted by the thought of all the money he had stashed away, squirreled away, in a separate account he had opened for himself, not the one his father had condescendingly "allowed" him to open on his sixteenth birthday and which he felt sure was only too easy for the old man to supervise, monitoring all the petty little transactions expected of him: depositing his birthday money and withdrawing the meagre pittance of an allowance they gave him (a pathetic amount really, with the two of them working and getting good money). He was sure his father kept an eye on that. After all, it was he who had stood over him when he set up the online banking, chivvying him about the need for a secure password. A joke really. Richard was sure he knew a damned sight more about the internet than any of his father's fossilised generation did! Still, it paid to be careful. And so he had kept the pretence going that the account his father had opened with him (and, he was sure, still scrutinised from time to time) represented all he had in the way of financial assets.

He had his bank cards for both accounts with him, of course, but he couldn't risk using them. It would be only too easy for them to trace him like that. He had a few quid on him. He always made sure he carried some cash; you just never knew when you were going to need it. But there was no way that the money he'd brought was going to be enough for what he needed to do: really escape this time. Not just disappear for the odd day like he and his brother had often done, but vanish completely, set up a new life for himself somewhere, put all this behind him. Oh the horrible memories. His mother lying there, where she should never have been, looking at his secrets. And the blind panic. Then the frenzy that ensued, hitting her over and over, the blood spilling out onto his bedroom carpet.

No, there was no way he could go back now. She was dead, he was sure of that. He had left her lying very still, but her eyes were wide open and seemed to be brimming over with tears. With that powerful recollection seared upon his mind, Richard found his own eyes welling up. For the first time in years, he broke down, sobbing uncontrollably.

CHAPTER 98

Confrontation

The earlier jubilation he felt had all but receded now. As he confronted the man—cornered at last, holed up here in his lair—he felt nothing but repugnance, castigating himself for having been in his clutches all this time. He was angry and tired, his nerves taut to breaking point.

His earlier visit to the man's lodgings had proved abortive. No sign of him there, and the only other person in the house, a young Vietnamese with a vacant appearance and little grasp of English, had been unable to help him. In recent years they had nearly always met at a prearranged place, usually the Clock Café on the outskirts of town, a long prefabricated building, very much a roadhouse. "Your typical greasy spoon," the man had sneered, but it served their purpose well. With such a throughput of customers, no one was ever likely to notice the individual comings and goings. On rare occasions after work, they would meet at the man's lodgings. It was here that he had thought to find him. He had no phone number for him. "Safer that way," he had been told, the man contacting *him* whenever he needed to.

Cheated of his original purpose, furious now, he trawled his memory for where the man might be. As far as he knew, there was no woman in the frame. He knew the man wasn't queer but had no idea what he did for pleasure nowadays in that respect. The memories of their early years were clear enough. They had both moved on, but even now he could recall the squalid cottage where latterly they had had their fun. Could he possibly be there? he wondered. And what was even more salient, could *he* even find the place again?

So began what felt like the longest night of his life. Setting out into the countryside with only the haziest recollection of the area and certainly no address that he could recall, he brought the moped to a stuttering start for the uncomfortable journey along twisting unfamiliar lanes. The road surfaces were treacherous with the mud and fallen leaves; the street lighting, nonexistent. Entering the darkly wooded valley with only glimpses of moonlight between the trees to guide him, he miraculously began to recognise his whereabouts. With a profound sense of déjà vu, he pulled up some little distance from the cottage, not wanting to advertise his arrival there, witnessing the second miracle evident in the slight column of smoke from the single chimney: someone was at home. Making his way silently on foot now, he felt all the old anger returning. The man had used him, taken him for granted, repeatedly avoiding paying out what he was worth to him, only giving him half the information he needed. Tonight was a case in point, a wild goose chase that never would have been necessary had the man been where he had expected to find him. Trembling with compressed rage, he reached the front door without attracting any attention from the person within and knocked on it as hard as he could.

Even now, with his reward within reach at last, the old man had somehow managed to sideline him, refusing to let him over the threshold, telling him, "This is not the time," pushing him away, the sweaty palms hard across his chest so that he stumbled and fell backwards, down the worn stone steps of the cottage and onto the unforgiving gravel beneath. The man was standing over him now, eyes glazed, distant, inhuman, as he plunged the kitchen knife into his chest again and again. Then, as he faded from consciousness, he heard the cottage door being firmly shut as the man retreated inside.

CHAPTER 99

The Man

On the other side of the door the man was standing, rocking, keening to himself. Hell, is this never going to end? How? How, he asked himself, has it come to this? He had prided himself upon perfection, meticulous planning, the obsessive implementation of every detail, scrupulous pre-research, utter compliance with his book of procedures, and the rehearsing of every aspect, orchestrating it to his ultimate satisfaction. When, he wondered, had it all started to go so hideously wrong? But he knew. Of course he knew even as he questioned himself. He could trace it all back to that first horrible mistake, the time when he had wittingly forsaken his binding protocol, the time when, acting on impulse, he had completely misjudged the situation, when nothing had gone to plan.

He was being punished for that, he knew this now, that one lapse, the precursor to all his subsequent mistakes. As if that one huge error of judgement not only had tarnished his record of perfection (all those times he had evaded discovery, when he had played with them, his would-be persecutors, setting out his showcase art, his calling card clear for them all to see, laughing at their ineptitude, their evident bafflement) but also had reduced him in his own eyes, and the eyes of the world, to the burgeoning ranks of the other, ordinary killers. Error begetting error, the phrase whispered in his subconscious, thundering now in his ears, his brain bursting with the harsh poetry of it all, something half remembered, recollected from only goodness knows when:

Evil begetting evil, imperfection begetting imperfection again,
Sins of the fathers, always the fathers,

Visited upon the children of men.

But it wasn't ever the children of men that had driven his passion. He had never once in the entire pursuit of his art considered them children of men. No, it was the women, always the women who had evoked this overwhelming instinct: a primal stirring of something approaching attraction. Or was it excitement at the potential they offered which caused his erection, spontaneous and unchecked, only to be followed in every instance by a profound and increasing repugnance? No, the sin was entirely theirs—it always had been—in calculating, scheming, and trapping the hapless male. How many lives had been ruined? How many noble aspirations had been squashed? How many promising careers had been thwarted and binned, as his had been, by that one act of folly, letting the woman lead him on—and the inevitable entrapment that ensued.

First the woman: "You have to stay with me now. It's your baby too." And the stern endorsement from her damned family: "Marry her. Do the decent thing ... marry her ...marry her." That was how it was in his day, as a raw youth growing up in the stultifying clutches of extended families, housed in neglected properties on sprawling run-down estates."Close-knit communities" the pundits described them as, closer than they, in their distant ivory towers of privilege and affluence, could ever know—so close that the kids in several families shared the same dads. Fathers fucked their daughters; brothers groped their little sisters. And yet, when inevitable teenage fumbling led to unwanted pregnancies, the whole might of morality bore down upon the luckless youth. Whereas those among his peers lucky enough to grow up in nominally Protestant or, more rare in those days, actual atheist families might get the liberating option of a sordid backstreet abortion, those like him with mothers (seldom fathers, he noted) who were both ground down by their burgeoning family responsibilities and devotedly and pathetically committed to the Catholic tradition that ensured the perpetuation of their enslavement would bring the whole weight of their blinkered faith to bear upon their wayward sons and daughters and insist upon hastily contrived shotgun weddings. Sins of the fathers. Whoever is responsible for those words in the Good Book got that wrong, didn't they? Sins of the mothers, more like. ... Sins of the mothers ...sins of the mothers. As the phrase repeated again and again in his subconscious, uncharacteristically for him, the man let his guard slip as, for the first time in days, he himself slipped into a deep, untroubled sleep.

How long he had actually slept, he had no idea. Pale shafts of watery autumn sunshine fell across his face where he lay sprawled in the tattered reclining chair, speckles of dust moving lazily in the slight draught from the grimy ill-fitting window above his head. Opening his eyes and reluctantly focusing upon the familiar scene, he gave an involuntary shudder of repugnance at the sordid surroundings, marvelling again at the profound dichotomy pervading his life, the creative thrust of his art, the perfection of it all, and the filthy hovel that had once been his home and was now no more than an occasional bolthole, a fox's lair in the countryside. He liked the sound of that, himself a cunning fox, a victorious predator returning to his den in the woods, always living close to the edge. He was cleverer than them, trapping his victims, evading discovery—the ultimate predator.

Shaking off the remains of sleep and the pleasant thoughts he had been indulging in, the man threw aside the old blanket and staggered to his feet, his limbs cramping momentarily as they were released from the restricted confines of the recliner. Clumsily locating the kettle among the debris on the drainboard and filling it from the single cold water tap, he fumbled with the damp matches and, at the third attempt, managed to light the gas ring. The bottled gas must be getting low, he thought, applauding his discretion years ago in refusing to consider a property on mains supply. Even then he had not wanted the traceability of regular bills with periodic meter readings, an invasion of his precious privacy.

The granules of instant coffee were a little damp too, sticking to the teaspoon as he decanted some into a large, stained enamel mug. All he needed was cigarette, he thought, half wishing he hadn't kicked the habit years ago. That would be the perfect English breakfast: coffee and a fag. Still only half awake, he stumbled to the cottage door, intent upon relieving himself outside in the garden. The cottage boasted no internal bathroom, and the toilet in the lean-to was in a filthy condition; the basin had been cracked for decades, with limescale deposits to challenge the stalagmites in a Derbyshire cave. (He had seen those once on a rare school trip and remembered the glistening otherworldly protrusions, cold and austere, with a menace of things alien and remote from his everyday life.) Moreover, the toilet was covered with several autumns' worth of dead leaves, and heaven only knew what various wildlife made their home there now.

As he went to go outside, cursing with the momentary pain as his bare feet kicked the base of the door, the wood sticking, swollen from years of damp weather, never really drying out, sheltered as it was by the tall trees in the adjoining woodland, the man gave a sudden gasp. But it was neither the instant stabbing pain nor the chill of the autumn breeze on his face which had roused him from his reverie, alerting him to a terrible impending danger. It was the sight of the darkening blood pooled on the worn steps, the discarded knife, and the trail of bloodstains, heavy at first, but gradually becoming fewer as they wove along the weedy gravel out into the woodland beyond. Moving automatically, whether propelled by a morbid fascination or growing sense of disbelief, his steps assumed a momentum all their own. Christ, what happened here?

And just as suddenly, a terrible realisation dawned that somehow he was implicated in this, so far removed from his usual meticulous modus operandi—not part of the plan at all, but nevertheless his doing. Then unbidden, unchecked, the recollection flooded back in an awful fraught crescendo, the waves breaking over him, overwhelming him. He was furiously paddling now, at first swimming against the tide, then rising and rolling with it, crashing headlong into the rocks along the way, his head pounding, bursting with thoughts, as the jumbled memories began to clear.

It was then that he heard it. Somewhere close at hand was the sound of a muffled explosion, followed by an ominous crackling. Startled, he turned around in time to see a pillar of smoke rising through the trees back in the direction from which he had come. My God, it has to be the cottage! Rapidly retracing his steps then frantically breaking into a run, he had almost reached the front door when it appeared to implode, flames leaping out of the blackened cavity, sizzling along the ivy and up the walls to the tiny bedroom above.

He thought to retrieve the knife from where it lay beneath the step but was beaten back by the intensity of the heat and the myriad sparks from the falling timbers. There was certainly no way he could rescue his precious manual. All he could hope to do was to put as many miles as possible between himself and the conflagration, and to do it as quickly as he could. Panting from the exertion now, he raced round to the rear of the cottage, feeling in his pocket as he ran, fumbling for the keys to his van. Shit, shit, shit. Where were they? Then he remembered coming in late last night, driving round to the back of the house (out of sight, out of mind), parking by the lean-to, locking the van, and putting the keys down on the draining board just before he filled the kettle.

It had been his intention to take out his manual of procedures. Perusing the carefully scripted columns of data always had a soothing effect upon him: the restoration of order to a chaotic world. But he had been altogether too dog-tired to bother. He had left his key ring where it was and had been about to hunt out a can of beans for his supper when the unprecedented knock at his door had surprised him.

CHAPTER 100

Leonie, the Major General, and Ted Manning

Meanwhile, in the Clarendon Country House Hotel, Leonie was silently fuming. Her self-imposed incarceration was beginning to pall. While the food was consistently excellent, produced to Michelin-star quality, it was overfussy for her taste. She found the text of the menu pretentious and longed to be back in her own home, confronted with nothing more challenging for breakfast than buttered toast and a couple of eggs poached exactly as she liked them, cooked in the poaching pan so that they were perfectly circular, with their whites completely set and the yolks still runny. Mrs Barker had been doing them for her like that for years, and Leonie never failed to enjoy them.

Leonie was sullenly perusing the breakfast menu and recalling the disaster of the previous morning, when she felt that her request for poached eggs had been met with something approaching disdain. And the actual meal, when it had appeared, resembled, to her eyes anyway, a couple of pale, rather rubbery testicles perched precariously on an unforgiving chunk of griddled ciabatta, tastefully decorated with chopped chives and sprigs of some feathery herb that looked like a bit of early bracken. So much for Michelin stars, she thought. For all their fancy ideas, Mrs B could teach them a thing or two about breakfasts.

Her husband had been more easily satisfied, settling for a full English every time, before hastening back to their room and making the telephone contacts he felt compelled to undertake. After a brief and somewhat acrimonious exchange with some upstart desk officer, he had demanded to speak to Chief Inspector Manning and to be put through to his private line immediately.

Ted Manning had been expecting just such a call. Few people apart from his fellow professionals knew that he had a private extension in his office, and even fewer of them dared to use it! The major general was an exception. Their acquaintance went back a long way, their shared business interests predating Ted's rise to his current eminence. As an aspiring young beat copper, Ted had encountered the major general, only recently retired, and a fellow member of the City Golf Club. They had formed a tenuous connection in those early days. Ted was an unashamed social climber consciously attempting to widen his circle of potentially useful contacts in the furtherance of his career. The major general recognised this, and more than that, he recognised the younger man's susceptibility to influence. It was just what he needed in an ally, a man with a ruthless ambition, with contacts in the right places and unparalleled access to the existing legal framework about which the major general knew comparatively little. He had not known then how bribable the aspiring young police officer would turn out to be, but his years of assessing and managing men in the theatre of war had given the major general a shrewd insight into the strengths and weaknesses of his fellows. As he cultivated this early relationship with Ted Manning, he formed the distinct impression that here was someone who might know how to skirt around the law and who, given sufficient incentive, would not be afraid to put that knowledge to good effect.

Their relationship had flourished over the years, the major general gradually introducing the impressionable young policeman to a number of powerful individuals—fellow golfers and people in the wider community. For his part, Ted Manning had been able to certify the documents needed for firearms certificates, providing the authorisation required for the legal acquisition of further items for the major general's collection. And while this was not totally necessary, as the major general knew many individuals with the requisite professional standing to do this for him, it gave him an insight into the other man's willingness to be involved. As time passed, things progressed seamlessly from this to more dubious statements of authentication.

CHAPTER 101

Sandy

The girl lay still, motionless, peaceful now, the only indication that she was still alive being the incessant regular beeping of the monitor and the oscillating bands of colour on the screen. Permitting herself at last to look away, to give herself a break from endlessly peering at the girl, hoping in vain for some flicker of movement, a recognition of the wider world beyond the sightless limits of her near vegetative state, Sandy glanced around the unit. Six beds, separate bays when the dividing curtains were drawn, each capacious enough to accommodate the battery of medical equipment which might be required for any patient there. It was a unit specifically designed and dedicated to sustain existence and to return as many of the temporary residents as possible, however physiologically impaired, to a meaningful life beyond these walls. The dividing curtains were seldom closed, individual beds being screened only when the patients there were receiving intimate care. For the remainder of the time, all the curtains were pulled back to allow the staff an unhindered view of their charges. Such was the suddenness of any change in someone's condition that the ICU staff were constantly alert for the telltale signs, their hearing attuned to the mechanical sounds of the respirators in use, their eyes sweeping the unit, resting briefly on each unfortunate inmate before settling again upon the specific patients for whom they were allocated as named nurse for that shift.

Sandy realised that she, too, had adopted this response, concentrating upon the girl, Victim A, for perhaps 98 per cent of the time, but allowing herself the occasional glance away, taking in the activity around her,

287

mentally clocking the arrival of any new incumbent and the relatives accompanying them. Not that there had been much in the way of change during her periods of observation. For much of the time, two of the beds remained empty, the staff duly checking the equipment there at the start of each morning shift and affixing fresh "I'm clean" labels to the suction tubing and the various flasks and containers. Of the three other patients, Sandy noted little, not wanting to stare. Despite her police training, this seemed an unacceptable invasion of their privacy, a further assault upon their vulnerability. But that had not stopped her from observing their visitors, feeling a sense of unspoken almost camaraderie as they and she maintained their separate vigils beside someone who, for whatever reason, was important to them.

It was then that she first noticed the man, hovering uncertainly by the door. She thought he looked haggard, haunted even—beset by anxiety and perhaps confronting a grief almost too great to bear. She was unsure who it was he was visiting and sensed that same uncertainty in him. He seemed to briefly scrutinise each bay as though searching for some element of recognition, edging forward for a better view, then fading back into the shadows, disappearing from the unit as silently as he had arrived. She wondered why he had not approached the staff for help, but perhaps he had satisfied himself that the person he was seeking was not to be found in the beds here. Maybe, his hopes rising, the person was somewhere else in the hospital—not so acutely ill as he had feared, but in a general ward somewhere. Or could it be that the person had never got as far as ICU? A desperate scenario, this: the patient he sought already dead, the body in another place, perhaps already in the hospital mortuary.

Shaking off the dismal speculation, Sandy was surprised when, on a subsequent visit, she again saw the man in the corridor outside the ICU. Happily for him that must mean the person he sought was still alive and in a ward here. He must have got out of the lift on the wrong floor. There were no other wards on this level.

Whatever the reason, he seemed to be in a great hurry to leave, and there was no escaping the sense of elation he bore. It was in complete and absolute contrast to his prior demeanour. Whatever the situation, his personal tragedy appeared to have been averted.

CHAPTER 102

Leckie

She could no longer see her familiar square of sky, the trees, almost skeletal now without their leaves, bending and swaying in the wind, and the distant rooftops damp with dew, glistening in the watery early sunrise. The curtains were closed around her bed, she realised now, but even they seemed different. Not the pretty pale blue pleats she had become used to, but somehow a more glaring, strident blue, the blue of holiday brochures in the travel agents' windows, a hard, uncompromising blue. As she stared at the curtains, the pleats began to swim and dance before her eyes, but no matter how hard she tried, she was incapable of holding them motionless. Her eyes were heavy still as though she had only just awakened, but they had been like this for a long time. She remembered all those occasions when, no matter how desperate for sleep, she had forced her eyes to stare and stare, trying to make sense of the things around her. She had a recollection of the staff shining a light into her eyes, seeming not to know or even care that she was awake, her pupils aching from the pressure, aware only of black spots—things like tiny creatures, some like monstrous caterpillars, others no more than cells really, unbidden, floating across her line of vision. Her tired eyes would close, but the spots and cells would persist, purple and green, transformed, energised.

And voices too, distant, indistinct. What had they been saying all along? That she couldn't really see, that her eyes were open, meant nothing. Lights on and nobody home.

She remembered staring, forcing her eyes to stay focused, watching the shapes that came and went beside her bed, the shifting shapes friendly at first, until somehow they became different. She felt sure there was another shape, a sinister alien shape, menacing in its sudden proximity, the memory stronger than ever now as she fought back the fear, tears coursing down her cheeks as she gripped the bedclothes, her whole frame contorted in an involuntary shudder. "He was here," she managed to say, the words sounding strange to her ears—a faraway sound like tiny waves rippling over distant sands. Had she really said that aloud? She tried it again, stronger this time. "The man …" But no, that image was fading, gone. Yet the whispering remained. She repeated the words in her head, pulsating, saying them out loud, except she knew that it was not loud really, more of an echo heard from afar—words which were fervid in their insistence. And now a different image, different words. "The baby. There was a baby …"

Mesmerised, Sandy bent nearer to the girl, desperate to catch the mumbled sounds, wanting more, willing the girl to go on, to articulate clearly, to tell her what she knew. Her face close to the girl's face, intent upon the scarcely moving lips, she could feel the girl's foetid breath warm upon her own cheeks. "Go on, darling, tell me all about the baby."

That revelation was not about to happen. The magic was broken and the moment lost as the bedside curtains were drawn back to reveal a short angular man with heavy spectacles and disproportionally large hands. He was accompanied by another white-coated figure: a slender Japanese woman pushing a small stainless steel trolley bearing an assortment of instruments, the ward sister, proprietary, hovering protectively over the patient as the entourage approached the bedside, motioning to Sandy that she should leave while the neurologists examined the girl. In the hubbub that ensued there was only time for Sandy to blurt out the momentous information: "She's speaking! Spoke actual words, recognisable."

As all eyes fell upon the supine figure of the girl, Victim A, she gave a languorous sigh. Her eyes fluttered before opening fully. Fixing her eyes upon the assembled group, she announced, "Leckie. I'm Leckie."

CHAPTER 103

Robert

"What's happened here, lad? Your mum's had a nasty fall, you say? You found her like this on the floor?" Questions, always questions. That was what authorities did best. But these guys were different somehow, their questions seemingly no more than an affirmation of events.

He watched capable hands lifting her onto a stretcher as he heard radio or walkie-talkie sets crackling. Last century's technology, he thought, but, heh, information *is* being relayed. Then came his sudden panic, knuckles clenching. God, what if they are getting the police involved? Too late to make a break for it now. Not that he could anyway, however tempted he was to resort to this, his familiar coping mechanism, by avoiding confrontation at all cost. Something much more powerful was kicking in. For all her nagging, scolding, and tears of despair, this was his mum. There was no way on earth he could leave her now.

But no, he was relieved to see that all their concentration was on her again, checking her pulse, attaching her to some sort of monitor, putting an oxygen mask over her mouth, then fixing the restraining straps before carrying the stretcher out to the open doors of the ambulance, beckoning the boy to follow.

After that it was blues and twos all the way, his mother slipping in and out of consciousness, Robert straining against the seat belt, leaning forward on the little collapsible chair in the main body of the ambulance, watching intently as the paramedics tended her, wondering what the hell he should do next. Should he accompany his mum, making sure she was OK and that he knew where she was and what they were doing with her?

He knew he had to tell his father. Uncertain now, he wondered if someone from the hospital would have to do that anyway. He would have to try to forestall them, think up some watertight reason why they shouldn't do that, at least not immediately.

He had to get back to the house and see for himself what had happened there. Why Richard's room? He needed to know. What dirty little secrets had his brother been keeping from him? Not that he really saw that much of Richard these days. He knew that they covered for one another—an unspoken agreement that—skipping school and keeping the authorities at arm's length. But he knew little beyond that, except that his brother always seemed to have money on him. He had some flash gear too, designer stuff, he said. Not that he flaunted it in front of their parents, but Robert had seen it when the oldies were out at work, Richard going out dressed to the nines, picked up by taxi at the door, telling his brother to keep shtum or else!

CHAPTER 104

The Man

The man had made sure no bills could be traced back to him. He had "inherited" the property years back in part as payment for a drug deal gone sour—not that he had ever told her that, instead inventing some story about a long-lost relative. The important thing being that this little house had never been in his name; he possessed no deeds or proof of the transaction, paid no council tax, and didn't suppose they even knew of its existence, tucked half into the forest at the end of what was little more than a deer track. There was no mains supply, so he used oil lamps for illumination and an open fire for warmth. There was a single cold water tap in the kitchen from a well outside somewhere, a tin bath on a hook on the back door, and a cesspit out behind the cottage. He'd had to have that emptied a couple of times over the years, but he knew a mate whose day job it was to do such a thing, and he always paid cash in hand, so there were no records of any transactions there.

In the early days he had harboured the idea of moving the family here, doing the place up, and settling down. Exasperated by his mother-in-law's constant drip, drip, drip of complaint, he'd loaded his wife and baby into the van one Saturday afternoon and taken them out to see the cottage, telling his wife to not take too much notice of how it looked now. He would do it up, modernise, get everything they needed to make it a real home.

She had taken one look and dug her heels in. "No place, this, for a family. Whatever were you thinking of? Not a house this; it's a hovel, a rathole."

Throughout their marriage, the little cottage in the woods was never mentioned again. He didn't know if she ever thought about it again after that one abortive trip, if she knew that he still visited his bolthole, his refuge, the workshop for his craft.

She had moaned, of course, although she never really wanted to leave the city, content, as far as she was ever content with anything, to carry on living as they were, the three of them, him, her, and the baby, still with nowhere to call their own, one room in her parents' place, a three-bedroom council house on a sprawling postwar estate. She had insisted on hanging in there, on waiting their turn on the council housing list, delighted when they finally got one of their own on the same poxy estate as her parents. That was where all his bills had gone, where the woman, pregnant again, had had the next kid, and the next. Always another mouth to feed, keeping them in poverty, stifling whatever ambition he may once have held.

CHAPTER 105

Professional Negligence

In a cramped office on the third floor of Mancroft House, a meeting had been hastily convened. Such short notice had been given that this seldom-used room was the only one available. Banker's boxes full of dusty files were stacked on every shelf, where a perfunctory stab at date-ordering them had been attempted. The boxes were unlidded, with rough cardboard dividers thrust between the contents, each one bearing an alphabetical range and year identifier, the earliest of these showing the legend "A–C, 1959", and almost all of them predating the computerised records with which she had become familiar. She wondered how many had even been copied to microfiche, made it into the database. How many were ever consulted now?

Nervously glancing round at the dingy furniture and redundant archives, Sister Mackie pondered again the wisdom of what she was about to do. It was a conscience call, a difficult one to make, risking alienating a vulnerable service user and possibly bringing the entire force of professional legislation upon someone who, however miscalculatedly, had been placed in an invidious situation and had probably only acted out of kindness. Should she have said nothing, thereby compromising her own professional standing, running counter to her sense of integrity? That was the dilemma which had kept her awake at night as, tossing and turning amid the tangled bed sheets, she watched moonlight come and go and the pale shafts of too many early daybreaks.

It was after one particularly restless night that she had reached her decision. She would have to take this one further and alert her supervisor to her anxieties. Which is why she was waiting now, closeted in the stuffy storeroom, summoned away from her familiar patch, her comfort zone, to the imposing health authority building, only to find herself possibly facing one of the most crucial issues in her whole professional life, relegated to the level of stores and perched upon an upturned box. She anticipated not only her own fate but also that of all the other players in this particular melodrama.

At least the interview was not to happen here, as Sister Mackie was called through to an adjoining room where the interview panel had assembled, the secretary who had fetched her exuding an air of efficiency but little in the way of empathy. The CEO was unavailable at such short notice, chairing a meeting of sector heads, before leaving at midday to catch a flight to Zurich to attend a conference there, but her acting deputy, a ruthless and ambitious man, was leading the enquiry. The head of the HR department was present, accompanied by Justine Leggart, Sister Mackie's line manager. And entering the room at precisely the time given for the start of the proceedings, flustered, red-faced, and out of breath, was Maggie Silcox, the Unison union rep.

There had been little attempt to put her at her ease before the barrage of questions began. "Can I ask why you thought fit to bring this matter to our attention? And why now?

"What was it that you noticed particularly, and why was this a cause for concern?

"Does the patient have any other visitors, family members maybe, with whom you could have raised this concern?"

Christ, she thought, they hadn't even read the girl's notes to know that she was only known as Victim A and that despite the publicity surrounding the case, no relatives or friends had come forward to identify her.

"What was it about the woman's demeanour that made you think her interest in the girl had gone beyond a mere professional interest?"

And still the questions came: How often did she come to visit? How long did she stay?

When was Sister Mackie aware that official surveillance of the girl had been withdrawn? Who had told her? Had the suspect made her aware? offered any explanation for her continued interest in the girl? Had there been any instances of particular intimacy?

She must be very careful how she answered this last one. The girl in her present state was a vulnerable adult, with everything that implied.

"Sister Mackie, were you aware that this is a safeguarding issue? Had you at any time challenged the woman? Duty of care. Shouldn't have to remind you. Failure to act in a timely manner to bring to your superiors' attention. Unsafe practice is a dereliction of duty."

Unsafe practice. Unsafe practice. Her head was swimming, the phrases like individual gunshot, relentlessly peppering her with the spray, urgent, demanding, incessant. She was floundering, sinking in mud, swallowed in the mire of bureaucracy, her career in tatters, sunk without a trace.

Maggie, the union rep, had remained silent, tight-lipped, throughout the exchange, but she was speaking now, interrupting the barrage with an arsenal of her own, short staccato phrases, as alien to Sister Mackie as the interrogation had been: "a break-in procedure"; "due process"; "before these things gain a momentum of their own"; "time to enlist expert advice"; "willing to reconvene at a later date"; "no question of suspension from duty"; "report to appropriate authorities"; "alert senior staff as appropriate, those on the neuro ward"; "there may be a problem here"; and "meanwhile, strict supervision of visits".

But Sister Mackie wasn't really listening any more, the phrase "safeguarding issue" echoing in her head, her professional judgement held to account and found wanting. What had she left?

CHAPTER 106

Ben

Ben was aware of the man's scrutiny. As he bent over the bench where he had been dismantling a broken component, he realised that the man had approached closer and that the other two mechanics had stopped working and were looking in his direction. The man was directly in front of him now, fishing some sort of ID out of his pocket. There was a younger person with him; Ben hadn't noticed her before. More ID, introducing themselves. "Police …your local branch. Just making some routine enquiries, sir. Your cooperation would be appreciated." Then they paused, watching him, draping their coats over the end of the bench.

It was the holiday. That was the focus of their interest. "Where had you been? Which hire boat company? Had you done that sort of holiday before, at that time of year? How long were you away? How far did you get? Just the two of you, you say? …Didn't meet up with any friends then? Managed all right then, just the two of you?"

Lord, Ben's tongue was tripping him up. "No, no," he spluttered, aware now of their scrutiny. He was also dimly aware of the others, watching him, waiting for him to trip, to fall into their trap. "No, we had the baby. Karen, my, er, wife, had the baby with her most of the time really, so we didn't get as far as I had hoped. As well as steering the boat, I had to hop off and see to the locks if she was busy with the child, feeding her or whatever.

"No, we didn't really see anyone else to help. I think we were the only people on holiday then. It was way out of season. The waterways were really quiet. But we'd always said we would do it. Karen needed the break, and it was good to get away."

Ben was sweating now, his fists clenched beneath the bench, his pulse racing, his breath coming out in short, spasmodic bursts. He was acutely aware of their scrutiny. The distance between himself and his questioners seemed to have shrunk, and he felt in their proximity a sense of foreboding, a threat hanging in the air, waiting to be fulfilled. One false move on his part and the whole weight of the law was set to bear down on him.

If only he knew what they really wanted. They hadn't actually asked him anything about the child, but surely they couldn't have missed his mumbling, incoherent answer to their early question and the almost throw away comment, repeated, deliberately innocent: "Just the two of you then?" They were looking at him strangely now, he thought—not quite menacing, but these were the stares of those in possession of some hidden truth, a secret waiting to be disclosed. But then, just as suddenly, they were gathering up their coats, preparing to go, bidding him "good afternoon", thanking him for his help, and nodding to his supervisor, who was hovering now within earshot of their comments. His colleagues, shamefaced, averting their gazes, returning to their tasks. A gesture to them all: "No, we'll see ourselves out, thank you. We don't need to speak to anyone else today." Ominous words, clearly meaning that it was only Ben in whom they had any interest. Just a few words really, but enough to set him apart from his fellows, from normality, the routine of the workshop disintegrating before him.

Ben was shaking now, his hands trembling as he resumed his work on the damaged assembly. Fumbling, he dropped a tiny washer. Cursing, tracing its erratic trajectory along the bench and down into the dust below, nervously glancing at his watch as he retrieved the renegade washer from the particles of metal shavings and numerous little screws and O-rings, Ben had only one thought: how long to go before he could make his escape. He had to get home to Karen and warn her about his encounter.

CHAPTER 107

Victim Six?

Another day, another dog walker, and another grisly find. Notification of this flashed across the secure intranet. Kidsgrove this time. Not their patch, thank God, but across the county boundary in Staffordshire.

There were scant details so far, but the body was well decomposed, apparently. It was too early to say if the MO was the same. Body parts had been found in woodland, courtesy of the young woman's overenthusiastic sighthound, a juvenile saluki. Tiring of the unrewarding chase, the dog had watched as his uncooperative rabbit disappeared down one of the many holes Julia had stumbled across—this time quite literally stumbled into—on her walk. The dog, bored with running now, it seemed, began digging, furiously at first, the light loamy soil flying out behind his flailing paws. And then came the bits, initially unrecognisable as human, until the pup unearthed an arm, frayed folds of fabric enclosing long bones, the wrist still held in the tightly ribbed cuff, the hand virtually complete. It was then that Julia had fainted, coming round to find Wrangler standing over her, gnawing a length of something, bone or stick, she didn't want to determine. As she dragged him, protesting, away from his trophy, clamping his lead to his harness, stifling the retching coming from the depths of her gut, she reached for her mobile and dialled 999.

Unable to give an accurate description of her location (carefree, she had wandered off the usual paths to let Wrangler enjoy the freedom of the woods), she reluctantly obeyed the instruction to stay where she was until the police arrived, their having been able to track the coordinates from her phone.

A cursory examination of the scene had revealed what appeared to be further remains scattered across the little glade. Whether these had lain there previously undisturbed and been covered by falling leaves or were buried in a shallow grave before being unceremoniously flung from their resting place by Wrangler or some natural predator, it was impossible to say at this stage. The bits the dog had not interfered with were undeniably human. The area was clearly to be treated as a crime scene and was cordoned off accordingly. After furnishing the more senior police officer in immediate attendance with as many salient details as she could recall, a very shaken Julia was allowed to leave, accompanied by a sympathetic young WPC and Wrangler, pulling urgently on his lead, hyperactive now after the period of enforced inactivity whilst waiting for the police to arrive.

Speculation was rife, both by the duty officer at the station and his contemporaries elsewhere across the county and beyond, and among the hastily assembled team: PCs, detectives, and the scene-of-crime officers studying the tangible remains, exposed to the dying light of a late autumn afternoon. Blue tape snaked amongst the trees, encircling the glade and its immediate environs, proclaiming this patch of woodland a no-go area: police property. Tents were being erected, where officers screened the surface findings from invasive perusal and the vagaries of an early November night. Arc lamps were being assembled then carefully wheeled into place without disturbing the recently scattered subsoil. The photographer was angling his lenses, directing the powerful camera at the pieces of bone and flesh visible among the leaves. It was a slow and meticulous process, frustrating even to the most seasoned detectives there, who were anxious to bag the obvious remains and conduct a thorough search of the area, hunting for clues before turning over the soil to search for whatever else the woodland resting place had to reveal.

And all the time the questions, verbalised and unspoken: just who was this, and why had they ended up here? How long had the body lain here? Was this a recent killing or something from the past? Could this be a further victim of the serial killer they had dubbed the Wolf of Wolverhampton? Just what were they dealing with here? Had the Wolf returned to their patch, or maybe never left it at all? Were they contending with one killer or two? There was always the possibility that the murders which had occurred beyond their patch were the work of a copycat killer. Was this the work of their man or not?

True, the remains had been found in woodland and not beside water, but the Trent and Mersey Canal ran close by, and there was always the possibility that the killing had occurred there and that the body had been moved for some reason. Even their surmise that these were the remains of one body, a female victim of murder, could be flawed. What if the corpse was not that of a young woman but of a man? What if he or she had died of natural causes? What if the remains were not just of one person?

Across the Midlands and the North West, databases were being interrogated and missing persons records scoured. Reporters drawn to this latest development, hungry for details, demanded an update, some information they could feed to an anxious, often gratuitously fascinated public. Meanwhile, the Chester police had another, seemingly more pressing and possibly related, concern on their hands.

Returning to a level of consciousness, potentially as fleeting as the memories it evoked, after all these weeks, the girl, Victim A, had begun to speak. Identifying herself only with some mumbled name sounding to the assembled ward staff and now to one of their WPCs like "Vicki", she had repeatedly uttered the single word baby. There were other words among the incoherent mutterings which seemed to suggest that this was a baby that Vicki at some time had had in her possession, possibly her own baby, taken into care maybe. Liaising here with tight-lipped social workers, overly concerned it seemed to them, with the service user's rights to confidentiality, and anonymity had the adoption process been involved, the officers investigating the hit-and-run occurrence had drawn a blank. They were no nearer to discovering if this baby, if indeed there had ever *been* a baby, could be the one they sought in relation to Murder Victim 2, the woman found half submerged in the Llangollen Canal, Abigail Lamont. If only they could unlock the girl's mind further and find out what she really meant.

The lead investigating officer had toyed with the idea of reestablishing round-the-clock surveillance on the girl but had had to reject the possibility. Their resources were already stretched to capacity. He was only too aware of the pressure upon the officers concerned with the competing demands of the various crime scenes and streams of enquiry, the multiple sites and number of victims, the trail of leads and potential interconnections, hard facts and tenuous recollections, possible sightings and vivid conjecture.

Already they had amassed an extraordinary number of witness statements of varying relevance and coherence. Liaising with the neighbouring police forces involved had so far served only to multiply the avenues of enquiry. They were inundated with data, bogged down with facts, statistics, and surmises, exhausted by the sheer volume of material as each event which may or may not be related emerged. Meanwhile, the normal demands of their job continued unabated: burglaries and petty crimes, vandalism and violence, and the ever-present threat of terror-related incidents.

No, he could not justify spending any further time with the girl. The medical and nursing personnel were aware of their concern and would be detailed to contact the investigating team should there be any further developments in her care, most specifically if she should begin to talk about her situation, tell them her full name, or say what she remembered about the accident and the baby she had mentioned.

Satisfied that he had covered all eventualities as well as was possible given the circumstances, DI Hammond turned his attention to the incoming data stream conveying the news of a small forest fire, a burnt-out cottage, and a severely injured man being airlifted from the scene.

CHAPTER 108

Ted and Robert

The boy was a gibbering idiot. OK, he was obviously in shock, having found his mum like that, but his account clearly didn't hold water. "Must have fallen and hit her head," he'd said, when all the doctor in A & E had told *him* was that she was suffering from multiple contusions requiring an emergency brain scan and his consent for any surgical intervention which could be indicated.

It was Robert's disingenuous "Perhaps she disturbed a burglar" that had sealed the conviction in his father's mind. This was no accident, and it was most unlikely that Pam had been accosted by an intruder in the house. He had no doubt that by now the uniformed oiks, alerted by the emergency call centre to the likelihood that this was no accident, had sealed off his home, declaring it a crime scene, and that the SCOs were combing the premises for evidence of the alleged culprit. He was equally sure that they would find nothing there to support the theory. Given that he was cynical and jaded after decades of experience in the force, to Ted Manning this bore all the hallmarksof a domestic assault, and for once, not one that could be laid at his door.

The voice of the casualty officer at the other end of the phone had been both soothing and unflinchingly insistent. As a method of gaining maximum compliance from the listener, it was a ploy that he recognised and one which had always served *him* well. Reluctant at first to give any details other than that Ted's wife had "sustained severe head injuries", the casualty officer's measured response to his insistent probing revealed what Ted had suspected from the start, that this was no domestic accident caused by something as trite as a fall on the stairs. Gradually his irritation at being summoned from his desk had dissipated, turning to anger, as all he could picture was Pam, poor dowdy Pam, being attacked in the privacy of their own home. And as quickly as his anger towards the perpetrator of what he felt must have been a ferocious beating flared, it turned towards Pam herself. What had she been doing to provoke it? Had she taken a lover behind Ted's back, wiling away the long boring days since her suspension? Thought she'd kept that from him, did she? It was one of the first things about the case that had registered with him, the list obtained of staff members from the unit where Abigail Lamont had gone missing, with recent leavers (always the potential there for some sort of grudge revenge) highlighted and, jumping off the page at him, his wife's name: "Pamela Manning", followed by "Staff midwife: current suspension". Well, if she had been entertaining another man and somehow succeeded in pissing off the bloke, then she had it coming to her. Stupid cow.

Funny, because he'd had her pegged as swinging the other way these days, ever since finding her hospital ID on that hit-and-run girl. Had to have been quite a burly, butch lass to have inflicted head wounds like that. On second thoughts, it must have been a bloke.

Whatever. Once again Pam's stupidity had jeopardised Ted's situation. While he was fairly sure that he had covered his tracks pretty well, the last thing he needed was some overly ambitious young detective going through his effects. He had no illusions. He knew that he was not popular within the force and that many of his contemporaries would be delighted to find and exploit any chink in the armour of success with which he had surrounded himself. He was not so naive as to be unaware that some, at least, of those alongside whom he had risen through the ranks might have had occasion to speculate about the methods by which he had gained that success. Damn it, the last thing he needed was for any of them to go poking about in his private affairs.

For the moment, he could think of no way to curb their enquiries without drawing unwelcome attention to himself. He must be seen to be beyond reproach. He had to allow them access and could not be seen as impeding progress or disturbing what they saw as a crime scene. There was nothing for it, he had to play the cooperative approach. As much as it terrified him, and for once in his life, Ted Manning was truly frightened, he had to stay well away from the family home. Better not flaunt his comparative wealth. Nothing too flash. He would book himself and the boys into a Travelodge for a night or two. And he had better make that one near to the hospital. He would play the part of the anxious husband, devastated beyond belief that this could have happened to his wife.

—————

Robert hadn't made his getaway in time—couldn't leave his mum there on her own. Amid the bustle of an overstretched A&E, no one was answering his question, the only question that mattered: "She will be all right, won't she?" Then came sudden orchestrated activity, his mum stretchered out of the first cubicle into a forbidding area designated as a resuscitation room, him pushed to one side and the double doors swinging shut behind them. A man in a green smock with a surgical mask hanging below his chin was coming out of the doors now, approaching him with sympathetic smile. "Not to worry, son," he said, as he ushered him to a waiting area consisting of just a couple of chairs in the corridor beyond the double doors. "Your mum, isn't it? They have taken her in there, somewhere quieter, so that a thorough examination can be made."

But Robert had seen through the practised professionalism of the man, his aura of purposeful calm. He knew what he had witnessed in the ambulance. The monitor didn't lie. His mum was in a really bad way.

He was in a quandary now, desperately wishing he were anywhere else at all, but at the same time utterly unable to go, to turn his back on the double doors, walk away, and abandon his mum. Alone in the waiting area, he was only aware of the time dragging by, only able to picture in his wild imaginingswhat was happening behind those closed doors, his heart thumping and his every sense attuned to the muffled noises emanating from the resuscitation room. He knew that the longer he was here, the less likely his possible escape would become. He wanted to put the hours and miles behind him, to disappear, become "unavailable for questioning", a phrase of his father's, overheard on the telephone, uttered scathingly as only his father could do. He knew now that he would never make it home in time to see for himself whatever it was that his mum had discovered in Richard's bedroom. His father would be home any time now, albeit for one of his rapid "shower, change, and go out again" routines. His father, a man he both despised and hated, a man he profoundly feared—the man who would have to be told of his wife's accident, who possibly even now had been alerted to her condition by the medical staff and summoned to her bedside.

Robert knew what his father would do, of course; it was utterly predictable. He would make a grand entrance, dressed to impress, oozing phoney concern, playing the part of the devoted husband. Robert really didn't think he could countenance such sickening deception. Strengthening his resolve, he cast a lingering and totally unrewarded glance towards the double doors of the resuscitation room, still resolutely closed against him, and prepared to leave.

Turning to collect his parka from the back of the chair where he had been sitting, he failed to notice the doors at the end of the corridor opening or the darkening shape of the approaching figure. A firm hand clasped his shoulder as Robert gave an involuntary shudder at the sound of the familiar overbearing voice:"Suppose you tell me just what the hell has been going on?" Robert was going nowhere. His father had arrived.

CHAPTER 109

Ben and Karen

The christening had gone really well. The carefully orchestrated components had come together just as Karen had planned, the entire performance running like clockwork. Cari, the star of the show, had behaved impeccably. Gorgeous in her sumptuous christening robe, she had barely flinched when the vicar splashed the water on her head, smiling angelically as he made the sign of the cross and cooing with delight at the sight of the candle lit in her honour. Photographs had been taken. and relaxed now that the main event had taken place without a hitch, Karen allowed her precious child to be passed around among the assembled relatives.

True, there had been some mutterings when the priest said her name— "Cari Moses, I baptise you in the name of the Lord"—but Karen stood defiant, challenging them with a look which bordered on self-satisfaction.

"Cari Moses. Can't think where they dredged that one from," her mother-in-law was heard to say.

"Shush, dear." Ben's father was as placating as ever. "It could be so much worse. At least it's not Chardonnay"—this last an oblique reference to her sister's children, Tarquin, Estella, and Mignonette.

Karen's mother, dressed for the occasion somewhere between society wedding, Royal Ascot, and may be a rather classy pantomime dame, basked in reflected glory, content now that some sort of rapprochement had been reached with her daughter, parading as only she could, the epitome of a successful mother and grandmother.

The only person who did not seem to be enjoying the occasion was Ben, who was clearly ill at ease and reluctant to engage in conversation with any of their guests, even avoiding the child's godparents: his brother Andrew; Sophie, wife of his friend Carl (Ben and Karen had been witnesses at their wedding); and a delighted Amy, who seemed to have visibly grown in maturity as she morphed from tiresome little sister to proud godmother and aunt. He had taken his place beside Karen at the font, a reluctant participant in the group photographs, and had retired to the back of the church hall clutching a small glass of sherry. Such an unfamiliar drink, he thought, at least to his generation, but that had been his mother's doing, her having been determined to contribute to the celebration and make *her* mark as the supportive grandparent.

Throughout the afternoon he had been unable to shake off the sensation that they were all colluding in an elaborate charade. At any moment, he felt, the bubble might burst, leaving them exposed in their deception. It was the police visit to his place of work that had unnerved him. He was unable to shake off the premonition that this was merely the precursor to something much worse.

CHAPTER 110

Leonie and the Major General

Elsewhere in the county, another dressy charade played out as Leonie, resigned now to further temporary residence in the country house hotel, had regained some of her fighting spirit. Casting aside her former apathy, she had taken a taxi into town and spent a fruitful morning shopping for clothes—her choice, as always, favouring an uncluttered elegance. Leonie had always felt that she needed little in the way of make-up, relying on her aristocratic good looks and the deceptively simple but inordinately expensive contents of her wardrobe. On returning to the hotel, she had availed herself of the proffered amenities in the spa and beauty department and enjoyed a relaxing massage and facial, the sort of luxuries in which she indulged whenever she was away from home, having long since realised that her husband had little patience with such feminine fripperies and relished the stark masculinity of his chosen surroundings. Unable to make an immediate appointment with her stylist Xavier, Leonie had reluctantly allowed the resident hairdresser to shampoo and set her hair. No way would she permit someone she privately dubbed as a provincial amateur anywhere near her with the scissors! The overall result was passable, she thought, at least until she could make the necessary appointment with Xavier. With that, she rebooked the taxi and returned to town, launching herself with as much dramatic effect as she could muster into the familiar coterie gathered at Micha's bistro for the inevitable precursor to an upcoming society wedding to which they were all invited.

As much as this resumption of normal service had cheered Leonie, it was nothing compared to the relief felt by the major general. Without his wife's clucking discontentment, he felt better able to appraise his present situation. The conclusion he had reached was not a happy one. For the time being, he had been informed, his house and grounds were to remain forbidden territory. Well, he would have to see about that!

If only he could get hold of Ted Manning. Over the years, their friendship, forged on the golf course, had become more and more of a business arrangement, a repeated transaction of reciprocal benefits. Recently, however, the major general had had the distinct impression that he was procuring more in the way of benefits for his friend than he himself was receiving in return. If ever there was a time to redress that balance, surely this was it. He was not an unreasonable man. He was quite prepared to compromise. They could retain their occupation of the grounds; he didn't give a damn about that. After all, that was where the body had been found. But he had to get back into the house—and not with some snotty young constable fresh out of school yapping at his heels.

Ted could arrange that. The major general had to get hold of Ted.

CHAPTER III

Karen

Humming quietly to herself, Karen carefully shook out the lavish christening gown, minutely inspecting it for any spots or stains which might mar its pristine magnificence. Finding none, she placed the elaborate garment on a satin-covered hanger, which she suspended from the bathroom shower rail. Safer to try to get out any creases that way than risk damaging the opulent fabric with an iron, she thought. Freshly bathed and dressed in her night-time Babygro, the child was propped against the pillows on her parents' bed, watching her mother at work. Karen had switched on the little television opposite the bed, as much for company as anything else. Ben was so gloomy of late that he and Karen had barely spoken since getting back from the christening. She had left him downstairs in the sitting room morosely clutching a beer, half watching football on TV. In the kitchen beyond, the regular hum of the washing machine and the noisier revolutions of the tumble dryer's drum formed a fairly constant backdrop to their activities these days, Karen having developed the routine of putting in a load of laundry every evening: any clothes the little girl had worn that day, and the used bath towels and cot sheets from the night before.

Busying herself clearing up the toys with which she had been attempting to distract Cari in her bath, certainly not a routine the child appeared to enjoy, Karen had been paying scant attention to the news, vaguely registering something about a body, another possible murder, before turning up the sound to catch the local weather forecast. If it was going to be sunny tomorrow, she had plans to take Cari across to her mother's. She would walk her there in the buggy rather than troubling Ben to take them by car. In truth, she wanted an excuse to be without him for a while and to be able to talk freely with her mother, now that their peace had been established. Karen wanted her mum's advice. For once in her life, she didn't know what to do.

Suddenly, inexplicably, the comfortingly familiar domestic sounds were drowned out by a shattering, ear-piecing scream. Dropping the toys and rushing over to where Cari lay across the pillows on the bed, where she had left her, Karen found the child totally transfixed by the image on the television screen, her little body rigid and unyielding. As Karen gathered the unresponsive infant to her, Cari's tiny frame suddenly convulsed in a series of juddering, shaking movements, her limbs flailing, her eyes wide open, starting sightlessly towards the television, her mouth formed into a ghastly protracted scream.

CHAPTER 112

The Aftermath of the Fire

Fire crews had battled through the night to bring the forest fire under control. Thankfully, the wind which had swept the flames beyond and away from the cottage, igniting ancient woodland and modern plantation firs alike, by daybreak had dropped to a whispering breeze and as surely as it lost its terrifying momentum, the fire crew succeeded in damping down the last of the conflagration. As soon as it was deemed safe to do so, four of the firefighters entered the skeletal remains of the little house where they ascertained that the fire had started. None of the second storey remained, a few charred timbers and rubble from the walls having fallen to the floor beneath. It was impossible to make out the contours of the individual rooms, all the dividing walls having been devoured by the flames. Floorboards, furniture, and fittings had been destroyed, leaving twists of molten fabric and naked springs, their provenance unrecognisable amongst the ash and fallen debris. At one point when the firefighters had first arrived at the scene, they had attempted to enter the building but had been beaten back by the flames and the intensity of the heat. As far as they could to tell, the premises were unoccupied at the time the blaze had started, but still they searched meticulously through the fallen rubble, relieved to find their earlier conjecture correct: there were no signs of any human loss of life.

They were surprised to find that the framework of the dense stone outer walls remained, for the most part, mainly intact, certainly up to the height of the ground-floor windows, where wooden frames and architraves had perished in the fire and the surrounding stonework along the length of its courses had crumbled and fallen away.

All vestige of the lean-to had gone, leaving a tangled mass of twisted ironwork (the struts of its construction) and the burnt-out remains of what appeared to be a number of vehicles and garden implements—a hideous web of contorted metal amid which it was just possible to discern what was left of a motorcycle and sidecar, a garden rotovator, a lawnmower, and an old-fashioned mangle.

Beyond this stretched an area of scorched earth and the skeletal remnants of garden shrubs and trees. Clearly the fire had not extended much beyond the house in this direction. Even the wooden gate at the far end of the garden was unscathed. This was where that they found another more substantial vehicle, its paintwork bubbled and peeled, the blistered colours barely recognisable, its tyres scorched and flattened, and its windows cracked and crazed from the heat. It was here that the weary firefighters and attending police officers made their startling discovery. Satisfied that the van was unoccupied, having found no one in the front two seats, they went round to the back of the vehicle and forced open the doors, which were warped and sticking as a result of the fire. Whatever contents they had expected to find among the heat-damaged plastic wrapping and the collapsing stacks of boxes, they had not anticipated finding the badly burnt body of a young woman, a tightened bungee still binding the slender ankles above her blistered feet. She had a cloth of some sort across the lower part of her face—whether as a gag or something she had contrived in a desperate attempt to avoid smoke inhalation, it was impossible to tell. Some of her clothing appeared to have almost melted into her body, emphasising the unmistakable bulge of her advanced pregnancy. Aghast, the nearest crewman climbed into the back of the van alongside her, the heat, retained in what was little more than a metal box, permeating the layers of his protective clothing and searing his bare hands as he fought to find any signs of remaining life in the still, silent body before him.

"By Christ, she's still alive! …I swear I can feel a pulse."

CHAPTER 113

Accident & Emergency,
Contingency, and Chance

Indira Sayeed did not take kindly to being patronised. She had reacted badly, she realised that now. No doubt the man was in shock, although there was precious little about his attitude to indicate this. Still, she shouldn't have snapped. Long hours, combined with the unremitting weight of responsibility, the constant demands, and the need to switch from one patient to another, one life-threatening emergency after the next, being always on the alert, not risking anything other than absolute attention, was bound to take its toll, to spill over sometimes. She was only human after all.

Sure, it was what she had trained for—fought for the right to train for even, defying the parents and the uncles with their dated concept of a girl's future, namely an arranged marriage and lifelong domestic servitude. Even her older brother was on their side. She was surprised and hurt by that. Surely he, who had gone straight from head boy at the grammar school to Cambridge undergraduate, completing his Master's in four years and studying now for his PhD, would have sensed the urgency in her plea to be treated the same, to be able to leave school and take up the coveted place at medical school?

There were times when she felt as though she had been fighting all her life. Rebelling against the rigid discipline of her parents, she had been delighted to shed the trappings of her family's culture. Embracing the comparative freedom of the local comprehensive school (no grammar school for her), she had been an avid participant in the drama group and in all the sports. She was little and feisty, and what she lacked in stature she made up for with her enthusiasm. She was a ferocious opponent on the hockey field, a fearless gymnast and footballer, and a member of the rugby second fifteen.

Finally she had got her own way. After hours of her wrangling, weeping, and bargaining, the elders of the family had succumbed. Indira had taken her place in medical school and felt as though her life was just beginning. But even there her fight had continued. Not academically—she excelled in every area of study, working long hours alone in her room, in the medical school laboratories, and in the university library.

Her aptitude and determination delighted her tutors, but still Indira felt that she had to fight to be taken seriously by her contemporaries. Determined not to be seen as a bluestocking, Indira had, belatedly, in her third year at university, entered the social scene. Striving for acceptance, she had all but renounced the teachings of her family and her faith to become Indira the party girl—a hard drinker and even harder to date! Boyfriends came and went, few staying the course beyond a week or two, some barely lasting the night. Here she experimented with her sexuality, as often as not welcoming a woman into her bed. Her appetite was voracious, and inevitably her grades began to suffer. The wake-up call came in the form of the end-of-year examinations which, to her utter chagrin, the former A-grader was forced to resit. This time she scraped through and avoided the ignominy of having to repeat the year. Thereafter, her appetite for the social life abated and she resumed her studies with an even fiercer determination to succeed.

It was at this point in her training that lengthy clinical placements occurred, with the young Indira competing with her colleagues on the course for recognition and acceptance. In each area, she found favour with the senior physicians and consultants in charge, most of whom would have gladly effected her joining their team. But it was her placement in A&E in her final year that really fired her enthusiasm and cemented her resolve.

Indira Sayeed would become a specialist in trauma. She loved the unpredictability of the admissions and the heightened drama surrounding the various life-threatening events, seemingly thriving on the frequent tension this incurred. She knew that this was the sort of doctor she wanted to be and that this was the team to which she must belong. Competition for the junior doctor post was intense, so it was not without resentment from some of her peers that Indira had clinched the appointment.

All of which made her response today the more regrettable. She, Indira Sayeed, who had smilingly beaten off all the opposition to get to where she was, had totally lost her cool and allowed herself to be riled by that officious policeman, the husband of the injured woman they had all been fighting so hard to save. Flinching beneath his supercilious gaze, she had become Indira the child again, scolded by the uncles so utterly omnipotent in their judgemental masculinity.

Casting aside the oppressive weight of exhaustion, straightening her stance, and visibly growing in stature as she did so, Indira's hard-earned professionalism kicked in as she calmly faced the policeman and gestured for him to follow her into an unoccupied treatment room, where she explained something of his wife's condition and the procedures she had undergone so far, carefully omitting any mention of the other, older bruising that she had seen on the woman's arms and chest. That could be pertinent in their management of the patient; she was not going to broach the subject until she had had the chance to discuss it with her colleagues. For now, one thing was certain: Ted Manning was not going to be left alone with his wife.

Robert had been dimly aware of the changing dynamics of the situation, as he witnessed his bullying, exhibitionist father rendered impotent by the little Asian casualty officer, meekly following her down the corridor. He didn't waste a moment longer speculating as to the nature of the discussion happening between them. Another glance in the direction of the resuscitation room saw no change there. The doors remained firmly shut, but his mum was still alive—the doctor had said as much.

There was no point hanging about. This was his opportunity to escape, and he took it, pushing through the double doors at the end of the corridor, going out through the A&E waiting area, and walking quickly to the car park beyond. He had no plans at all. He just knew that he had to get away from here to give himself time to think.

What happened next was purely serendipitous. As Robert pushed his way between the solid phalanxes of closely parked cars, he almost collided with a child's buggy. It was being propelled at speed along the roadway behind the cars by a tiny boy, no more than three years old. Catching the buggy with one hand to prevent damage either to himself or any of the cars, Robert confronted the petulant toddler, instinctively grabbing his arm and pulling him close as car after car cruised along the roadway in the search for a parking space.

Looking anxiously around to trace someone responsible for the child, Robert saw a young woman strapping a baby into the back of an SUV. When she saw the toddler, she gave a shriek, whether of recognition or relief, Robert could not be sure. She was effusive in her thanks, strapping the recalcitrant youngster into his seat alongside his baby sister as Robert, wrestling with the unfamiliar technology, succeeded in folding the buggy and stowing it in the back of the car.

Shaking now at the realisation of the possible tragedy that had been averted by the young man's intervention, the woman sought to thank him again, offering him money and a lift to wherever he needed to go.

CHAPTER 114

Helen

The tenancy on the little house was drawing to a close. Leafing through the terms of their agreement, Helen felt an overwhelming sadness. They had started out with such hope in their hearts, each convinced that she had found her ultimate soulmate. The future held such promise then.

How had it come to this? Her partner was at work (or not—she barely registered the ongoing deceit any more) whilst she, Helen, sat alone at their breakfast table, the plastic crate of letters and documents on the floor beside her. Early on in their relationship, it had been decided that as she was the more organised of the two, she would deal with all the domestic concerns, keeping their insurance up to date, filing guarantees and operating instructions, and paying the bills. True, Sandy contributed her calculated share with a regular direct debit into Helen's account, but beyond that she had shown little interest in any of the arrangements. At first, Helen had been only too pleased to accept this caretaker role, seeing it as recognition of her value as someone who is methodical and reliable. Now she merely found it irksome, another job to be done for which there would be no acknowledgement and certainly no gratitude.

Lifting the crate onto the table, Helen began the onerous task of sorting the contents which had accumulated over the past few weeks: recent receipts in one pile, to be tallied with the bank statement she had downloaded from the PC; reminder letters of renewal dates for various items of household insurance; and invoices for work done on both their cars. All that remained in the crate was a stack of holiday brochures. No point in hanging onto those, she thought. Sandy had never shown any enthusiasm for travel, always citing the unpredictability of her work as an excuse. Early on in their relationship, Helen had found Sandy's insistence that there was still so much to see in England and that just being at home together was holiday enough childishly touching. But while Helen may have been successful in subjugating her own desire to explore more-distant places, the allure of the brochures never left her. She spent many a quiet evening going through them when Sandy was working, imagining what some of the places were really like and mentally forming a clear list of preferences, always the thought that perhaps one day Sandy might change her mind.

To the left of Helen on the table was a stack of folders she had taken from the filing cabinet, along with a neat pile of new folders, pristine and inviting. She had it in mind to completely rejig the system. Instead of using the existing ones labelled "car", "insurance", and so forth, she would divide the contents. Taking two of the new folders, in her neat handwriting she labelled one "Helen's car" and the other "Sandy's car". It proved comparatively easy to distribute the contents accordingly; after all, the older items were each in their own places within the existing folder. She merely transferred these appropriately, together with the new receipts.

It was when she attempted to apply similar logic to the allocation of items in the household folder that the system, and Helen, broke down.

Was this what the end of a relationship was, the calculated apportioning of possession rights, the division of assets? The sterility of the exercise defeated her. Where was the passion in this arbitrary dispersal of goods? How had something which had begun with such explosive impact on both their lives been reduced to this pathetic whimper?

Shoving aside the crate, not caring as the neat little piles of documents and folders teetered and toppled onto the floor, Helen, normally so self-contained and composed, let her head fall forward onto the tabletop, her entire body cowed, wracked by shuddering, convulsive sobbing.

CHAPTER 115

The Man

Another bungled enterprise, and this one had gone catastrophically wrong. Common sense told him that he was lucky to have got away, that there was nothing—nothing at all—to link him with the fire. He had left no traces there. The cottage wasn't even in his name. As far as he knew, it was still in the name of his predecessor, that is if it had ever in living memory been registered in anyone's name. Judging by the state it was in, it had probably ceased to figure on anyone's radar about two centuries ago. In all his visits there over the course of the years, he had never seen the slightest evidence of any interest from officialdom—no unwelcome visits or any letters, not even any junk mail.

As far as he could be sure, there was nothing in what must by now be only the shell of the house that could possibly be traced back to him. He had stayed around just long enough to see that the conflagration had really caught hold. He'd heard the windows cracking and popping with the heat, and from his vantage point beyond the gate, where he waited, poised for flight, already seated on his newer, powerful motorbike, he had seen the flames leaping out of the empty frames. No, there would be nothing left on the ground floor, just ash and debris. Not a single fingerprint could have survived such an inferno. As for the floor above, he hadn't been up there in years. In all his tenure, he had never so much as pulled back the rotting curtains or slept in the bed. It had always seemed too cold and damp for that.

He had kept the tools of his trade, his hobbyist paraphernalia, in a box downstairs: cutting boards, plastic lettering, and sheets of vinyl.

They would have been amongst the first things to burn, by their very nature fuelling the blaze. His precious surgical instruments—scalpels and retractors, individually wrapped in oilskin—were stored separately in a small wooden box, now safely stowed in one of the panniers on his motorbike. The bag on the other side was poignantly empty. It was here he had planned to transport his "bible", the manual of planning and procedures, the meticulous details of his crimes.

It was a pity about the van. He had had to leave it there. It would have attracted far too much attention driving away from the scene. He knew that the emergency services would have been alerted as soon as someone spotted the blaze, and the last thing he wanted was to be seen fleeing from the scene.

This had been his bolthole for years. He knew the area like the proverbial back of his hand—better even than that. He had used his motorcycle to explore the network of paths and roadways around here, negotiating obstacles and familiarising himself with all the navigable tracks and detours. He felt certain that he could evade discovery now, and that as soon as he reached more major roads he could open up the engine and effect his getaway.

The van and its contents hardly worried him, so certain was he that they too would be completely destroyed by the fire raging within and beyond the little house. Should the van's earlier presence in the vicinity have been noticed at all, the authorities would be searching for Andrew Fell. Even if the woman's remains were to be discovered and eventually identified, the last people to see her alive were the boys from the estate, and they too would probably recall the logo of the mythical woodman. He doubted they would have had a sufficiently good look at him to be able to recognise him again: "Old enough to be your father," they had chanted. Well, there were lots of old blokes around, if that was all they had to go on!

Confident that no one had seen him anywhere near the cottage, he pulled into a passing place where the track widened just before meeting the tarmac road. He did not want to be observed emerging from the woodland path; that might seem too suspicious. He would wait for his moment, when there was no oncoming traffic in either direction, before pulling out of the shadow of the trees and continuing his journey along the B road ahead.

The unfamiliar noise had caught him by surprise, so much so that he stopped the bike, killing the engine, and waited, heart thumping. It was the sound of a helicopter circling above the trees. At first he could only make out its lights, then, as the night sky became illuminated by the reddening glow of the forest fire, he was able to distinguish the unmistakable shape, dark against the rising pall of smoke. Unable to move, like a startled rabbit caught in the headlights of a car, he stood transfixed, straddling the motorbike, certain of impending disaster. As the helicopter circled again, surely a sign that he was clearly in their sights, the full moon emerged from behind the blanket of clouds and smoke, allowing him the ability to distinguish the colour: it was not the ominous black of a police helicopter but the reassuring yellow of the local air ambulance. Apparently someone was having an even worse day than he was!

Trembling with relief, he waited until the helicopter had circled beyond the trees where he was sheltering before restarting the engine and edging the powerful bike out onto the road, which was mercifully clear of traffic, although he could hear the sounds of sirens in the distance and could picture the fire appliances and police cars racing along the motorway towards the blaze. It was just as well that he had chosen the B road for his escape.

CHAPTER 116

Robert

At that moment, Robert knew exactly where he wanted to be. He wanted to go home, to clear up the mess before his father saw it. She had bled so much from that fall that he knew his father would be angry, no doubt blaming her for being clumsy. Poor woman, she was in enough trouble about something that had happened at work without having to deal with this. Besides, he was curious. He wanted to know what his mother had been doing in Richard's room. And to be honest, he wanted the opportunity to look in there himself, hoping that his little brother might have left some cash lying around, or something he could flog to pay off some of his debts. Failing that, perhaps he would at least find some weed. He could certainly use some right now.

Jumping in beside the children's mother, he gave her directions to his house.

CHAPTER 117

Twin Suspects

Police stations across the Midlands and the North West of England had been placed on high alert and were being urged to share whatever information they could which might lead to the identification and arrest of the serial killer (if indeed all the attacks on young, predominantly pregnant women were the work of one individual). Team loyalties were being challenged, along with the understandable desire among many of the officers concerned to be able to solve crime which had occurred on their patch, without the help of their contemporaries in other police districts. Individual kudos and ambitions were at stake, and not everyone welcomed what some among them had dubbed this latest "care and share" approach. Nor had they been best pleased when specialist officers from the Met were drafted in to assist with their enquiries. The staff at Booth Street station were not immune to these heightened pressures. In a renewed attempt to be seen capable of solving their own incidents, they had brought in for questioning two of the earlier suspects they had released without charge.

Neither Alex nor Steve had been able to furnish them with any greater insight, although it was telling just how differently the passage of time had affected the two men. Alex, as belligerent as before, continued alternately to bluster or to threaten the officers interviewing him. He left them in no doubt that he was a very angry man. He was angry at their perceived incompetence and about the fact that, to date, no progress seemed to have been made and no one had been arrested and charged with Roseanne's murder. He was also angry that apparently he was still a suspect; angry about the inconvenience and speculation this caused; and angry that his home had been treated as a crime scene, "torn apart"—his words—by the officers looking for, and failing to find, any clues.

Was he angry enough to have killed his wife or at least arranged to have her killed? This they wondered.

It seemed unlikely that the man before them, trembling with pent-up fury, hands clasped tightly together, occasionally unclenching them to thump the table to emphasise a point, could have been capable of the precise mutilation of the body found beside the lake. But perhaps he was one of those people whose unchecked anger was channelled into action the longer it festered. Unlikely as this seemed, they could not dismiss him from their enquiries—not yet, at least. Repeating the caution that he was to remain at the address he had given them and not leave the country, they had no alternative but to let him go.

Steve, on the other hand, seemed to have shrunk in stature since their earlier questioning. The interviewing officers were shocked by his appearance. He looked dishevelled and neglected as though he had not shaved for several days; his clothes, none too clean either, seemed to be hanging off his almost skeletal frame, his hair wild and uncombed. His eyes, sunken and lifeless, never left the officer sitting across the table from him in the interviewing room.

"You haven't found him yet then?" It was more of a statement than a question. And then, in a voice so quiet and tightly controlled that the officer had to strain to listen to him, he asked, "And our baby? Do you know what happened to our baby?"

However hard they pressed, it seemed he could add nothing further to his earlier statement. His answers, dull and repetitive, were entirely consistent with what he had told them before. There seemed no way he could have been capable of murder or had had the initiative to arrange it. The man before them was totally consumed by his grief. Either that, they thought, or else he was a consummate, practised liar.

CHAPTER 118

Leckie

It was almost better, she thought, when she had been cocooned in a tight little world, restricted to what little she could observe from her ICU bed: the pale blue curtains that denoted the confines of her existence; her own window and the patch of sky, sometimes blue, often grey; the scudding clouds; and the distant rooftops. Back then, there had always been the comforting hum of machinery, quiet and contained, a rhythmic, soothing monotony. And there was the chair. That was where her recollection clouded, unsure now after the passage of time whether the chair had contributed to her remembered sense of security or not. The image blurred and faded then, reforming almost immediately: another chair by another bed, she sitting on the chair, her mother in the bed. What was she doing in bed? Why was Leckie there, watching her, hearing again the rasping, laboured breathing? Then came the realisation that her mum had come here to die and that she, Leckie, was powerless to help her, just as she'd been all those years before when she had stood by, wretched in her juvenile frailty, her impotence, her inability to make things any better.

She knew now that the last time she had seen her mother, it was in a hospital bed. As certainly as she recognised this, she realised the truth about her own situation. She too was in a hospital bed. The earlier memory of the tight little world behind the pale blue curtains, and now this, the bustle of a busy ward, people in beds to either side of her, the constant noise, chatter, groans, and laughter, it was just different beds in different times perhaps.

She had a sense of returning clarity, of emerging from a thick mist, of rising to the surface in some lost, lonely lagoon, of pushing aside drape after drape, the heavy curtains that had been clouding her mind giving way to lighter and lighter fabric, now only a transparent voile between her and certainty—and with that certainty, the knowledge that she was in a hospital ward. How she came to be here, she didn't yet know, but the details no longer bothered her. She had ceased straining to catch hold and hang onto any fragment of reality. It would all become clear eventually. Meanwhile, she was only thankful to be rid of the shifting shapes, to be back in control of her own thoughts and feelings. There were things she still needed to sort out in her own mind, things to keep secret and things to tell. For now she was content to lie back against the pillows and idly watch the activity around her. There were things she still had to make sense of, but, as with someone resting after an arduous journey, this was her time to let go of the tension inside her, to re-form and recollect. She was not ready to answer any questions yet.

———————◦———————

Later

She did not know how long she had slept. She had been dimly aware of people coming and going, having barely responded when the nurses were at her bedside doing their regular observations, not wanting to endure the barrage of questioning she felt sure she would face once they recognised the full extent of her returning faculties. Knowing that they were excited by her earlier abortive attempts to speak, she wondered if her new wakefulness meant a return to fully coherent speech. Very, very quietly she tried it out for herself, whispering the first words that came into her head. "Hello, I'm Leckie. I think someone is trying to kill me. I've done some bad things, but I don't deserve this. I didn't take the baby—just gave her a cuddle and put her back in her cot. He drove straight at me. He's been here too. I think he was looking for me."

These last words surprised her: they seem to have arrived unbidden, but even as she breathed them to herself in the tiniest voice she could muster, she knew that they were true. Suddenly she didn't feel so safe any more. She should tell someone. But then the recognition hit home: they probably wouldn't believe her, Leckie the dropout, down and out, down on her luck and sleeping rough. A rough sleeper, street beggar, and petty thief.

A no-hoper, a nobody who, in order to eat, had resorted to prostitution. No good arguing that she'd only done it because she had to, that she had hated every minute of it.

She never wanted to harm a child. She'd waited so long, plotting and scheming, and then finally, when she had her chance, she hadn't been able to go through with it. She felt certain they would never believe that, any more than they would believe that someone wanted her dead. There was only one hope, one slender chance. If only she could summon up the kindly shape again, she felt sure that she was able to trust just this one person.

CHAPTER 119

Scene of Crime

Despite all their best efforts, the man had died on the way to hospital. The crew of the air ambulance had battled to maintain an airway before resorting to an emergency tracheostomy, hardly the easiest of procedures to perform in transit. The strong wind which had fanned the flames below them was causing significant turbulence in the air above as the medics aboard the helicopter made the incision and inserted the tracheostomy tube, connecting it to the available oxygen supply.

Such an intervention would normally have resulted in an almost immediate improvement in the patient's colour, but in this case the man was so badly burned that his face was virtually unrecognisable, the skin having blistered and peeled away, leaving an expanse of open flesh where half of his features should have been. "Poor devil, probably better for him if he doesn't make it," said the young doctor, securing the tapes holding the tube in place, articulating what his companions in the struggle to save the man's life had probably all been thinking, but that didn't stop the sinking feeling of utter failure as he observed the man's vital signs dropping, soon becoming unrecordable. All their attempts at resuscitation had come to nothing. The urgency of the crew's mission was replaced by an overwhelming exhaustion as they made their scheduled return to the helipad. There the waiting ambulance standing by to transfer their patient either to A&E or the county burns unit was redirected to the hospital mortuary, where later that day, the duty pathologist would unequivocally confirm what they, in their more cursory examination, had suspected, that the man had suffered life-threatening wounds apparently unrelated to the extreme trauma caused by the fire.

———◆———

The fire in the forest had gradually been brought under control, but the fire crews were reluctant to leave. In winds such as these, there was always the possibility of some small spark reigniting the blackened brushwood and any remaining bracken still standing, even at a considerable distance from the locus of the original fire. They had damped down as much of the surrounding area as possible, but until they were able to source the original cause of the fire, they couldn't yet discount the likelihood of a further flashpoint, so they chose to remain on standby for as long as was necessary.

An extensive area around the cottage had been cordoned off with scene-of-crime tape, an area extending now to include both the front garden, the access road where the girl in the van had been found, and the wooded area behind the house, right down to the end of the more established road where the fire appliances and police vehicles were parked, just beyond the copse where the injured man had been discovered.

The scene-of-crime officers were fretting. They had been waiting since first light, wanting access to what remained of the house before any further evidence might be destroyed. But the safety officers from the fire department were adamant; they had to carry out their risk assessment first. There must be no further casualties—certainly not ones which could be laid at their door. No further unlicensed access would be permitted until chief fire officer on duty was convinced that the area had been rendered safe, even if the integrity of the site had to be compromised in the attempt.

A low-loader was parked in the narrow lane beyond the cordon, waiting to transport the fire-damaged van to police headquarters for detailed forensic examination as soon as the SOCOs had completed their on-site observations and the police photographer had taken all the footage he needed of the vehicle and of any remaining tyre tracks which could help to establish the vehicle's movements prior to the fire. As a crime scene, this area had already been enormously compromised. Of necessity, the ambulance called to transport the badly injured woman to hospital had to get as close to the van as possible. The county's only air ambulance was already out on a call, ironically to the other victim of the fire, and it was imperative that this woman should be moved and handled as little as possible to prevent any exacerbation of her injuries. The ground around the van was now a confused network of criss-crossing tracks—the tyres of the van and the ambulance, wheeled stretcher tracks, and countless footprints left by police, fire officers, and paramedics—leaving little chance of distinguishing any that might be attributable to the perpetrator of whatever crime or crimes had been committed here. There was a great deal of work for the photographer to do before the van could be removed from the scene. Given the enormous complexity of the crime scene, encompassing the extensive area covered by the fire, the burnt-out house, the van which had held such shocking contents, and the copse where the injured man had been found, extra officers had been drafted in to help. With the number of organisations involved and the enormity of the task confronting them, it was probably fair to say that no one knew exactly what they were looking at here. Was this case of arson, a fire deliberately started to destroy incriminating evidence of some other unlawful activity? Who was the woman in the van, and who was the man airlifted from the scene? At this stage they could not discount his involvement in the crime. Had he tied her up and left her in the van, and then started the fire, leaving her there to die, or were they looking for someone else, the person who had wounded him, perhaps? Was that why he had been running away from the scene, to escape the fire or to avoid capture? And if another person was involved, who was it, and more importantly, where was that person now?

CHAPTER 120

Ted Manning

Silently fuming at the patronising tone adopted by the young casualty officer explaining to him in exaggeratedly simplistic laymen's terms the severity of his wife's condition, as though he was an ignoramus, Ted Manning weighed up his options. He could stay here, doing no good at all, waiting outside closed doors while his wife was in theatre—"in for the long haul", he had been warned; he could pace the floor, wringing his hands, accepting proffered cups of lukewarm tea, waiting for some nugget of information, to all appearances the devastated, devoted husband; or he could turn his back on the place and the pathetic little drama being enacted in there (it was all her own doing, he had no doubt, silly bitch) at least until morning, or earlier if he was summoned back because of some great change in her condition. At least that way he could get on with his life. Desperate to find out what was happening at his house, he also thought he could go back to the nick and sound out his colleagues. Then he could book himself and the boys into the Travelodge and sort out a few basics for them all: toiletries, toothbrushes, a change of clothing, that sort of thing. Even as he thought it, he knew that it was not going to happen. There were way more pressing concerns he had to contend with. His mind made up, he strode out of the waiting area without so much as a backward glance in the direction of the resuscitation room. Had he done so, he would have been aware of the doors' silently parting and of the speculative gaze of Dr Indira Sayed.

CHAPTER 121

Karen

The child was sobbing now, great juddering sobs, her little body convulsing in a paroxysm of distress. Karen, holding her close, folding her into her breast, stroking her hair, could feel the intensity of the emotion gripping the child. She didn't know what was happening to her. Was she ill, in pain? She should take her temperature, find a glass, and check for signs of the dreaded meningitis. God, what if she should lose her now, after everything they had gone through? Frantic with worry, she was surprised to realise that it was Ben whom she needed now. Possibly more than ever before, she craved his calm reassurances. Ben, the steadying influence—implacable, unflappable Ben. At least that was how he had always seemed to Karen, until now so completely absorbed in her role as mother that she had failed to register her husband's palpable anxiety and distress, dismissing his black moods and failure to engage with her enthusiasm over the christening as puerile resentment of the fuss and family involvement, and his anxiety over the police visit merely an overreaction.

"Ben! Ben!" she called, desperate for his attention now as she ran to the head of the stairs, hugging the crying child. As Ben, blearily rubbing his eyes, came up the stairs towards her, she sank to her knees on the landing, cradling the baby to her, tangible relief flooding through her as the violent spasms subsided and the child lay quivering in her arms, the awful cries becoming a mere whimper before one last shuddering sob wracked her tiny frame, then little Cari slept.

CHAPTER 122

The Man

At the end of the day, it was all down to planning. No one could fault him on that. He prided himself on the thoroughness of his preparation. Meticulous attention to detail that was what counted every time. That was how he had got away with it for so long. And that was how he had got away this time. Only someone with a detailed knowledge of every pathway, track, and turning could have made their way undiscovered through the dense woodland and out onto the minor road beyond. He had a mind map of the area just as he had of all his exhibition sites. It was only when he failed to stick to the plan that his missions foundered.

Looking back over the years, he realised there had been many more successes than there had been failures. There were a couple of times early on in his career when his calculations had proved less than perfect. Twice he had diced with almost certain discovery, abandoning the task before completion. The first time this occurred, he had clearly misread the signs. Oh, the woman was pregnant certainly, and he had no difficulty in persuading her to accept a lift, but she had succumbed to bouts of sickness, retching and vomiting in the passenger seat next to him, pleading to be set down somewhere quickly, to get into the fresh air. And he was only too happy to comply, disgusted by her presence, hating the stinking residue in the footwell of his van. Having let her out at the next set of traffic lights, he had spent a third of his week's wages on cleaning materials and most of the weekend trying to rid the van of the smell, only to be confronted late the following Sunday afternoon by the woman's husband who, driving through the neighbourhood, had recognised the van from her description and determined to have it out with him for not treating her with more care and consideration. It was then that the man had resolved never to pick up a potential "model" for his art so near to his home again.

The second occasion, he had almost succeeded in subduing the victim, only for her to rouse sufficiently to put up a spirited fight, lashing out, calling out, and drawing attention to herself, until he managed to silence her with a sharp blow to the head, before dragging her body away from the track where he had taken her and out into the bushes beyond. Once there, he had bound and gagged her before taking the scalpel from his top pocket and making the first and final devastating incision into her jugular vein. Stepping back as the blood flowed from her neck, he had wiped his blade clean and, gently parting her clothes, lifted the flimsy cotton dress to expose her abdomen, firm as he liked them and gently rounded now in the second trimester of her pregnancy.

It was then that he had heard the hikers, only yards away on the track he had just left. Surely they would go past, unaware of the drama he intended to enact in his makeshift woodland theatre. But no, the bushes were being parted as one of them left the path. "Just going for a pee," he had called to his companion.

Hearing this, the man waited no longer, pocketing his scalpel and quietly slinking away through the scrubland and up over the hillside beyond. He could collect the van later; the imperative now was to avoid discovery. And as always when a mission had to be aborted (he liked the sound of that—after all, all his missions resulted in an abortion of sorts), before it had really got underway, he knew that with his lust unsated, he must strike again soon—and that this time there must be no mistake.

CHAPTER 123

The Major General

Impervious to his demands, their insistence prevailed and the house remained sealed. Furious, an impotent fury which sought retribution, the major general lashed out at the only person available to take his venom. But the man before him remained stoically implacable, hardly even seeming to register the urgency of the situation. Resisting the powerful urge to seize the other man by the shoulders and shake him, the major general clenched his fists, his knuckles whitening with the restraining force, and took a step away from the man. Understandably, the man had worries enough of his own, what with his wife in such critical condition and his not knowing what had happened to his boys. He mustn't be too hard on him.

Yet, however much he tried, the major general found it difficult to empathise. Years of hearing the feeble excuses made by men under his command had rendered him incapable of a truly sympathetic concern. It was an aspect of management he had been only too glad to delegate to his immediate subordinates. As far as familial concern went, he and Leonie led such a mutually independent existence (there was little real affection in their marriage) that he found it difficult to put himself in the other man's position. He had always thought Ted Manning was more like him in that respect: the chief inspector had complained often enough about his tedious domestic life. As for the boys, well, the major general could put him right about them—one of them, anyway.

Suddenly, the other man straightened up, and for the first time in this encounter squarely met the major general's eyes. He announced flatly, "I really can't help you there. You see, I've been shut out of my home too."

CHAPTER 124

The Man

The wily fox, fleeing his pursuers, returns to the lair to lick his wounds. Scathed and scarred, but unrepentant, he will attack again. The man liked this mental picture: imagining himself firstly as a fox, then surely the wolf, his tabloid pseudonym. He liked that better, but *he* was no pack animal—a lone wolf surely, with all that that implied. Gradually the image faded. With his anger dissipating now, and with the thick red mist that clouded his eyes more a product of this than of the burning wreckage of his cottage in the woods, the man began to take stock.

He had escaped. For the time being, at least, he was free, and as far as he knew, there was nothing in his past to link him to the cottage now. He had not only retained his liberty but also had in his possession the basic tools of his trade and, in the powerful Honda, the mobility to put himself well away from the scene of his latest crimes before some blundering plod could stumble upon any clues he may have inadvertently left behind. He would have to get rid of the bike, of course. It could too easily be traced to him. And while he would be sad to part with it, he was sure he could replace it with something more anonymous—forged plates, a colour change, engine numbers effaced, all quite within his remit.

Here he floundered, his mental list of positives overtaken by the dawning reality of his situation. What of the devastation he had left behind? The burnt-out shell of his former home was unlikely to yield much in the way of evidence, but there was still the man being airlifted to hospital, the man he thought he had killed, the man with links to both his present and his past. Just how badly injured was he? He had left him for

339

dead. Was it too much to hope that he might still die, taking their dirty secrets with him to the grave?

Then there was the van and its incriminating cargo. How much of that remained? Enough to link him to the place, or had the later massive explosion been proof of its ultimate destruction in the fire which he assumed had engulfed it? How satisfactory that would be, annihilating once and for all every trace of his latest bungled abduction, nothing surviving but a burnt-out carcass. Yes! He liked the sound of that: a carcass concealing forever another carcass, the carcass of the witless Mandy and within it, like a gruesome series of Russian dolls, the carcass of her unborn child.

He would have to check, of course, leaving nothing to chance, but that would come later. For now, he guessed, and for the immediately foreseeable future, the place would be crawling with cops, like maggots on a decomposing corpse. No, he would lie low for a day or two, keep an eye on the media, and see what was being reported, always guessing what more might be known and which was being deliberately withheld in an attempt to draw him from his cover. How well he knew their ploys and how they had persistently underestimated his intelligence. It was how he had managed to evade detection for so long, always one jump ahead of them, toying with them, playing out his sadistic game.

He would return to work, act as though nothing untoward had happened. Best not to draw unwarranted attention to himself. He had contemplated disappearing for a week or two, not returning to work or his crumby lodgings, but that could only serve to attract the sort of unwelcome interest he would not wish to court. No, he would act as normally as possible, all the while assessing developments, employing whatever damage limitation he might require to avoid discovery He would take stock of the situation and reassemble his hobby kit. It should be easy enough to pick up another van. Then could be the time to move from his current lodgings, to disappear into the anonymous underbelly of a different city. He would have to fabricate a plausible enough excuse to leave his present job and then lie low for a week or two. He had sufficient funds for that, before finding another driving job which would suit his ultimate purpose. First he must return to his lodgings and assemble his sparse possessions: clothing, toiletries, and his stash of stationery, including A4 paper lined and unlined, pens, and a hole punch. All he needed to purchase was a large loose-leaf ring binder, and then, as soon as the vexed question as to where he would establish his next home was settled, he could embark upon the daunting prospect of rewriting his procedure manual. In a strange way, he was almost relishing the task. It would be good to go back and rethink his experiences, to order his thoughts once more and set it all out afresh with his usual meticulous attention to detail in the beautiful delicate script he had perfected for the purpose.

Powered by the thought, he throttled hard, pushing the bike almost to its limits, enjoying the freedom of the open road before common sense prevailed and he released the throttle to decelerate sharply and join the traffic ahead, stringently obeying the speed limit now. This was no time to be courting confrontation with the law!

CHAPTER 125

Futures

As Sister Mackie contemplated her future—not stripped of her qualification, her right to practice, but severely reprimanded, cautioned against ever allowing her standards to slip again—she cringed at the thought of the ignominy involved in being reduced to working under supervision for the next twelve months, followed by a detailed reappraisal of her performance targets. This after a working lifetime devoted to her job, facing the daily challenges entailed in the constant struggle to manage diminishing resources yet still provide the level of patient care she had always striven to attain, as well as facing the relentless changes in the NHS, its management and structure, its lines of authority, and the extent of personal accountability. For the first time in her adult life, she found herself dreading the return to work, wishing herself anywhere but here, doing anything other than following a career in nursing. God, how she hated what the job had become. She fancied a complete break, a long holiday abroad, somewhere warm, she didn't care where. Perhaps she could cash in her pension plan, open a little shop—a sweet shop maybe, although people were probably buying fewer sweets these days, courtesy of government health warnings about the impending obesity crisis. She would find it hard, even in the face of her profession's rejection, to espouse a cause so in contradiction of all that she had practised and upheld for years. No, it would have to be a little wool shop. Haberdashery, yarns, ribbons, knitting wool, sewing thread, fabric, scissors, pins, and patterns, she could see it all in her mind's eye now.

———◆———

Elsewhere in the country, other futures were being considered. As Helen bagged and labelled the last bunch of receipts, consigning them to the crate earmarked for those items belonging to Sandy, she glanced across at the clock on the mantelshelf, their hearth space, the scene of so many evenings past where, content in each other's company, she and Sandy had relaxed and unwound at the end of the day, sharing experiences and exchanging intimacies.

It was time to move on. She was no longer able or even wanting to rekindle the past. Her train would leave in an hour's time; her taxi was booked; and her luggage was stacked beside the door. She was only taking what was essential for now. She would collect the rest later—get Sandy to send it on even. For now, she really did not care. Her sister was expecting her. She could stay there as long as she needed to, her sister's two boys, eleven and seven years old now, apparently delighted that Auntie Helen was coming to live with them.

———◆———

Sitting in McDonald's, his hoodie pulled forward, mostly obscuring his face, Robert relished the warmth and anonymity it bestowed. He was making this burger last. He didn't know when he would next be able to eat. Not for the first time recently, he had absolutely no idea how he was going to manage.

Earlier that evening, hanging back in the shadows, he had surveyed the scene surrounding his family home. He was grateful to the young woman for getting him there, jumping out of the car with alacrity at the end of the road. "Just set me down here, thanks. That's great. I only live around the corner." But beyond the bend in the road, his steps faltered. Police cars, their blue lights flashing, were parked diagonally, bonnet to bonnet, across both carriageways, while two of the officers had been despatched, one to each end of that section of road, effectively closing it to any further traffic.

Thinking at first that there must have been an accident, Robert edged forward in time to see blue scene-of-crime tape stretched across the driveway of his home and all the lights in the house suddenly switched on. Hastily withdrawing into the shadows cast by the mature trees of the adjoining properties, he spotted a neighbouring house in darkness. Picking his way silently through the garden, he heaved a sigh of relief as he reached the road running parallel behind their own.

Now, as he gloomily surveyed the last of his fries, he wondered just what his next move should be.

<hr />

Coincidentally, in another McDonald's miles away, his brother, Richard, was facing a similar quandary. With little money left in his pocket and no clear agenda, Richard considered the options open to him, sadly realising the stark truth that actually he had few, if any, real choices left. Returning home to face his bullying father and whatever retribution lay in store was never going to be an option. Throwing himself on the mercy of the police here was equally unlikely to work. He could just imagine it, turning up at the police station, saying, "I think I may have killed my mum."

Recollecting the scene brought tears, stinging his eyes, dripping onto the soggy remains of his meal. He didn't know why he was crying. Was it for his mum and the knowledge of what he had done to her? How much of it was for himself, for the loss of a familiar, if nefarious, lifestyle? He just couldn't be sure, but thinking about that lifestyle prompted him to consider his remaining options.

There was no way he could pick up where he had left off. For one thing, all his contacts were in and around his home town. And so was all his expensive gear: useful on the pull, and a necessity, he had found, when impressing other boys at least the younger, naive, and disenfranchised ones he had introduced to the game. No, starting afresh in this new location may have presented as an option, but it was way down the list of his preferred actions. There remained the vexed question of his sponsors and benefactors. It was not going to be feasible to approach them individually, as this would involve returning to his home territory. He would do what he had once, very forcefully, been told that he must *never* do. He would go straight to the top. There was one man who could sort out this muddle for him. He would start there, confront him once and for all, not to throw himself upon the man's mercy but to demand repayment, a return upon the many favours he had executed upon the man's behalf.

As for tonight, he was sure he could wheedle his way into someone's warm bed. The team manager overseeing the youngsters working here could be quite promising.

CHAPTER 26

Ben and Karen

After the trauma of the police visit to his place of work and the difficult time over the christening, life for Ben had settled into a regular, if slightly uneasy, routine. He went to work, where he socialised reluctantly with his colleagues during the day, studiously avoiding the Friday evening recourse to the pub, and saw little of his extended family, always pleading pressures of work when his mother suggested that they might like to come over for Sunday lunch. While those who knew him might have thought this incredibly dull, it was hardly a personality change. Ben had been withdrawn and solitary for much of his adult life, coping with the repeated tragedies of their miscarriages and the inevitable strain upon their marriage.

Karen was concerned. Since the incident in the bedroom when the child had apparently had some sort of "turn" (she refused to believe that it could have been a seizure; her perfect child could have no such defect), Karen had observed little Cari more carefully than ever. She had resisted the urge to take the child to the doctor less from a desire to avoid being seen as an over anxious mother and more from the nagging suspicion that something actually could be wrong with the little girl. Karen needed help, the sort of reassurance that only another, more experienced mother could give. Karen needed her mum.

On the surface, little Cari seemed no different. She ate and slept well, snuggling up to Karen for cuddles and hugs. And propped in her baby

346

gym, she made purposeful grabs for the toys suspended there. She had begun to babble to herself, and according to the health visitor, with whom Karen had no wish to share her concerns, the child was achieving all her developmental milestones. But the nagging fears remained. To be honest, Karen had noticed a subtle but distinct change in the little girl's behaviour. Whereas previously she had always quite enjoyed her bath time, graduating from the pink baby bath to the full-sized family tub, lying on her back, kicking and being swooshed up and down by Karen and occasionally, at the weekends, by Ben, she showed a marked difference now. Just a phase she's going through popped up, unbidden, intruding into her thoughts. But was it just a phase? Karen was not so sure. One thing of which she *was* certain, the laughing, happy baby barely tolerated bath time, and then only if she didn't see the taps turned on and the bath being filled. It was as though the mere sight or sound of the running water was enough to terrify the child. Not for the first time in recent weeks Karen found herself wondering just how much a baby could be capable of remembering.

A Google search of "babies' memory formation" had yielded little actual help. Thrown back on her own resources, Karen thought of her own mother and wished she knew how to broach the subject without arousing suspicion.

CHAPTER 127

Shorty

During his long years in the force, Shorty had gained something of a reputation. He was the ideas man, capable of studying all the available evidence and reaching a conclusion which had otherwise evaded detection. It was a peculiar and valuable skill. Shorty was one of those rare individuals who combined the meticulous mental assemblage and ordering of all the known facts in a given case, however tenuous and apparently insignificant, with outstanding perspicuity and a gift for extraordinary lateral thinking. It was what had marked his time as a detective and earned him unstinting respect from even the most cynical of his colleagues.

Grateful, at first, for the proffered light duties and the opportunity such would afford him to remain in the force he loved, he had soon begun to feel unsuited for the role. He found it mentally stultifying, mostly repetitive, and very dull. He was also painfully aware that the job he had been given was one which normally these days would be undertaken by a civilian or police trainee gaining prequalification experience. He longed for the cut and thrust of active service and the chance to pit his wits against those of the cleverest crooks they encountered. He was understimulated, depressed, and in pain, as yet unable to accept the enormity of the decision he had taken at 5a.m. after another restless night, pitching and turning in the empty void of the king-size bed.

Shorty had composed his letter of resignation.

CHAPTER 128

Closing In

The press release had been guarded. A forest fire, cause as yet unconfirmed, had destroyed a small property in the locality. Two people had been recovered from the scene and were being treated in hospital. Their names would not be released until the next of kin had been notified.

This noncommittal statement concealed a maelstrom of activity. Scene-of-crime officers at the site, who had waited impatiently for the area to cool down sufficiently for a thorough investigation to start, endured the added irritation of having to wait for clearance by the health and safety inspectors before their painstaking search could begin.

Inevitably so, the integrity of the area as crime scene had already been compromised by the passage of recovery vehicles and the firefighters' and rescuers' boots and equipment. To make matters worse, the officers beginning their intricate fingertip search of the area had little idea what, if anything, they were searching for or might even find amongst the settling dust and still warm ashes.

The remainder of the investigating teams assembled in the major incident room at the hub of the enquiries and in provincial police stations and incident rooms across the Midlands and the North West were equally perplexed. The sheer complexity of the case (cases?) was overwhelming. They had progressed from single identified crimes to more than a dozen separate occurrences. To what extent these were related remained unclear. They had gone from one horrific situation to another, from few actual leads to a plethora of possible connections, from no clear suspects to a growing shortlist of people who just might be involved.

Public interest, once aroused, hadn't dissipated, from those with a genuine desire to assist to those whose only contributions could be described as no more than a vicarious fascination with the macabre elements of the case. At this point in the multiplicity of the ongoing investigations, these elements remained largely the subject of conjecture and wild imagining as little had been released to the press beyond the killer's apparent predilection for pregnant women. The untold horrors of the case remained protected information, not only to spare the victims' relatives from the more gruesome aspects of the killings, but also because it might assist the police in discriminating between true suspects and the cranks and attention-seekers laying false claim to the atrocities.

They had already been inundated with calls offering clues, nonclues, possible sightings, and frenzied speculation, all of which information was assiduously filtered and fed into the data-processing system. The latest spate of calls included one which had aroused their interest, not least because of the unlikely and, some felt, dubious nature of the informants, a group of teenage boys not noted for their compliance with authority, some of whom were already known to the police for a variety of petty incidents—minor offences involving noise, graffiti, truancy, and suspected shoplifting (the odd bar of chocolate and can of drink).

Whilst possibly not the most reliable of witnesses, these individuals' self-importance at helping with the enquiries was tempered by an instinctual, feral distrust of the police. However the scene they described resonated with the investigating officers variously deployed to obtain the boys' statements. It was providential that the youngsters knew and could positively identify the missing woman, Mandy, as being the passenger in a van driven by a man they did not recognise (and here the boys' descriptions faltered, all agreeing that he was certainly older than Mandy, ancient, old fossil, and granddad being the least pejorative terms used), but their actual physical descriptions were less conclusive. He was wearing dark clothes and a big jacket; either his hair was dark and slicked down or he was wearing a beanie hat pulled down over his ears. "Only a glimpse, mind you"—it was definitely not someone they knew. About the van used, they were in more agreement: a transit, probably a Ford, white with some sort of logo on the side advertising something, but not one with which they were familiar. Tellingly, none of the boys could recall the actual logo, but one of them thought it had something to do with the countryside. Most importantly, they were able to furnish the police with an accurate timeframe, confirmed by the owner of the chip shop. It was their regular Friday night takeout on their way home from kick-boxing, which would place the last confirmed sighting of the missing woman at between 8.45 and 9p.m. on Friday, 18 November, in the shopping parade on Earlham estate.

———◆———

Heightened police activity had yet to produce any solutions to the by now extensive range of possibly related incidents: the missing women, the recent horrific murders, and a number of cold cases where the modus operandi suggested something of a similarity. With pressure on to solve the current cases, not to mention the overt competition across the various district forces most immediately involved, attention was focused on the leads so far. No new suspects having emerged despite the repeated appeals for public cooperation, previous persons of interest were being scrutinised afresh.

Today's team briefing at Booth Street station had placed both grieving husbands, Alex and Steve, back in the frame. Of the two, Steve seemed the more unlikely suspect, although the probable assets of an heiress could never be entirely discounted. He hardly fitted the boys' description of the "old geezer" implicated in Mandy's disappearance, although at their ages, they probably regarded anyone over twenty-five as well over the hill. Furthermore, Steve's grief appeared immediate, tangible, a devastating, crushing, all-encompassing desolation. And on each occasion subsequently when any of the police officers had encountered Steve, arriving unannounced at the tiny flat, searching for any evidence of Abigail's intention or of his possible involvement in her disappearance, they were shocked both by the recent neglect of the premises—used dishes stacked precariously on the draining board, with dirty water and a film of congealed grease in the sink—and by the appearance of Steve himself, who was haggard and pitifully thin, with his clothes, obviously unwashed and worn for days, probably even slept in, hanging off his emaciated frame. He was unshaven, his complexion grey, and his pale eyes watery and lacklustre. His reticence in responding to their questions, along with the answers, when they came, mumbled and semicoherent, spoke of a man in deep mental distress.

Alex was proving to be more of an enigma. His earlier anger towards the police had dissipated, to be replaced by a sullen arrogance and barely concealed resentment at their intrusion into his private life. None of the officers who had encountered him liked the man, although a few grudgingly admired the way he had kept his cool, refusing to buckle even slightly under the most aggressive interrogation allowed. The interviewing officers made no secret of their distaste. Whilst openly pondering the possibility that he could be the killer they sought, they fervently wished it would prove to be so. Whatever else there was about Alex, he certainly appeared to have something to hide.

With no other leads to go on, isn't it time to bring him in again for questioning? Signalling their intention to Shorty, the detectives detailed for the task left the station, but not before the older of the two, a colleague of Shorty's since way back, who saw past the grumpy man on the reception desk to the perceptive, meticulous detective who had been his mentor, had given him one last task: "Just get up his details and anything we have on him, Shorty, will you, and have it ready for when we get back?"

He conceded that they had point: Alex, at fifty, fit the description given by the boys of an older man (positively *ancient* to lads of their age), and he had no previous form. That was how he had kept beneath the radar; there was nothing in his recorded past to link him to any of the crimes. And that was why their job was proving to be so difficult.

Shorty sighed. He couldn't even put his notice in uninterrupted. Grudgingly accessing the information on-screen, he noted the man's employment details. Ever the consummate detective, his senses alerted now, Shorty studied the patterns of absences described by their suspect as "working outside the area". Playing a hunch now, he dialled the man's place of work and was put through to someone in human resources who, after much prevarication and citing data protection legislation, confirmed what Shorty had begun to suspect. While some, but by no means all, of the two- and three-day absences coincided with specific work commitments, many of these were single-day meetings with clients, only some of which necessitated overnight accommodation correctly claimed through company expenses, often followed by one or two days taken as annual leave. Others appeared entirely random: single days taken as holidays. None of these was a Monday or Friday, Shorty noted, pleased now to have something tangible—real police work—to get his teeth into. In his experience, single days of leave often abridged a weekend for those with regular Monday-to-Friday jobs or were taken either side of other days off for those with irregular shift patterns, thereby increasing the periods of leisure time and effectively creating useful minibreaks from work.

Thoughtfully splitting the screen display before him, Shorty correlated the two sets of data, namely Alex's periods away from home and the dates, actual and conjectured, in their current enquiries. He was pleased when some of these corresponded and was fearful when they did not. How many more crimes in this spate of atrocities were yet to be discovered?

CHAPTER 129

Sandy

Since the end of her relationship with Helen, Sandy had flung herself wholeheartedly into her work, arriving early, leaving late, sleeping little. Unable to bear the empty silence at home, she had the radio on 24/7 and kept the television on, mute but flickering, providing an illusion of this being a lived-in space. Glad of the near-permanent overtime, the occasional day off stretched before her, long and lacking structure, a day of utter boredom and purposeless activity, her mind constantly elsewhere, registering little of the familiar surroundings or the repetitive mundane tasks at home. Loading the dishwasher, little more than a week's supply of the mugs she used for coffee and a few cereal bowls and side plates (she no longer cooked for herself, existing on canteen lunches and takeaways), she felt a sudden wave of desolation and loneliness. Realising afresh how few real friends she had ever made, Sandy was beginning to regret having kept her work colleagues at arm's length for so long. Sure, her chosen lifestyle had contributed to that: an openly gay cop was still sufficiently unusual, at least in the local force, for her to feel reluctant to be the butt of their jokes and even overt hostility. But she and Helen hadn't needed anyone else. They had been so totally absorbed in each other that, until recently, their relationship had provided all the companionship she craved. Work and Helen had been her life, and without Helen, it seemed that all she had to live for was her work. Well, *that* was about to change. Switching on the dishwasher and taking a last look round her kitchen, Sandy took her jacket and shoulder bag from the back of the dining chair, locked up the house, and left.

It was early yet, too early even for her first call, but the café in the concourse would be open. As Sandy nudged her car into the first available parking space, then ferreted in her glove compartment for her police parking permit, she was mentally savouring the prospect of a cooked breakfast here before making her first momentous move in her new state of singledom.

———◆———

Humming softly to herself, Sandy was jubilant upon returning to her car, the first part of her plan concluded. It was all so much easier than she had expected. Although she was not to know it, she was also extremely fortunate in that Sister Mackie's disclosures had somehow failed to be related to the junior relief sister on duty that day. Even so, Sandy had been anticipating all sorts of severe reservations, even downright refusal, and had come prepared with as much proof as she could muster as to the appropriateness of her offer. She had photographs on her mobile showing details of her house and the amenities it provided: the little en-suite guest room downstairs with its views across the garden, the cosy kitchen, and the sitting room with its comfortable furniture and open fireplace.

She had covered the care angles too, recognising that the girl might need sustained support, certainly in the early days following her discharge from hospital. A carer would be found, someone with the necessary skills who could come in on a daily basis as required. Sandy herself would be there during the night, she had assured them of that, her hands thrust deep in her pockets, fingers crossed. There remained the vexed question of who could be there at short notice on those occasions, hopefully rare once the current crisis was resolved, when all available officers were required to work a night shift. A lot depended on the carer: the right person would be able to step up to the mark and provide the necessary fallback cover. For the moment, Sandy was not prepared to own this particular scenario; it had to be work in progress. A quick glance at her recent payslips had convinced her of the affordability (just) of what she was proposing. And if it were to become more protracted and expensive than she envisaged? Well, she told herself, that's what plastic's for.

Invigorated by this renewed sense of purpose, Sandy was set to tackle the next part of her plan. She had a contact from a case some years ago which had resulted in the conviction of a couple running an illegal puppy farming business. Debs, who had reported the atrocious conditions under which the animals were kept, was a young woman who had turned her back on the teaching career which had been her life, and which threatened to break her, to set up in business running a doggy day care and overnight boarding facility from the rambling old rectory which was home to her and her family. Sandy was about to pay her a visit.

Later

The catch-up with Debs had proved rewarding, the two women hugging in greeting and settling down companionably on either side of the large scrubbed pine table with coffee and freshly baked cookies. The usual pleasantries having been exchanged, Sandy outlined her plan, Debbie nodding assent. Not only had this given Sandy the approval she had sought, but also Debs was able to furnish her with a couple of useful addresses: that of a local breeder (cocker spaniels, potential gun dogs) and that of a small independent rehoming centre.

After a hasty lunch of a pasty and a chocolate bar, Sandy prepared to visit the rescue centre, having had time to consider and reluctantly reject the immediate appeal of a new puppy. The probable cost was one factor as this whole venture was likely to prove more expensive than she could realistically afford to dismiss, but also she had begun to recognise the sheer impracticality of introducing a very young dog into the mix. With her varied shifts and the unpredictability of her actual working hours, feeding, toileting, and training the animal would be chaotic. Even with Debs's help, it would be nigh on impossible to establish any sort of routine.

No, a rescue dog, older and steadier, was the answer: company for her, something that Sandy theorised might be easier than other people for the girl to relate to, perhaps even something which could help to restore her trust and sense of purpose. The possibility that the girl might not even like dogs never entered her mind: Sandy was on a mission and a suitable dog would be found.

CHAPTER 130

Ground Force

The van had been wrapped and sealed to preserve any residual evidence following the massive contamination incurred in the first desperate attempts to resuscitate the wretched victim found bound and trussed like a chicken smouldering in her own body fat. As it was removed from the site on a low-loader, the SOCOs extended their fingertip search into the area to the rear of the house. The distorted metallic frames of old bicycles and a moped, a lawnmower and a mangle were photographed from all angles before the delicate task of removing them enabled the officers to continue the search of what remained of the ramshackle lean-to—little more than twisted girders and a paved floor.

Even the most hardened of the officers deployed to the task were unprepared for the next startling discovery. Surprised by the quality of the flooring in what was an otherwise dilapidated construction, they had tentatively lifted a few of the heavy-duty paving slabs only to discover that these had been laid over a concrete floor. Why would someone have gone to the trouble of such elaborate reinforcement were it not to support some sort of massive machinery or permanent installation, rather than this burnt-out collection of cheap and obsolete equipment? Intrigued, the officers removed the remaining slabs, revealing the rest of the concrete floor beneath and the blackened cylindrical outline of an old well shaft.

Weary, their lungs aching from the pervasive acrid stench of burning, the fine dust which had settled on everything, even permeating the breathing masks they wore, the first team of SOCOs were replaced by a fresh cohort equipped with crowbars and sledgehammers.

CHAPTER 131

The Major General

For now, restrictions had been relaxed. The major general was to be allowed to enter his home—but he alone. That liberty had not been extended to Leonie. It was providential that she was out and about socialising with her friends, he thought. He could just imagine what she would have made of *that*; there was no way she would have accepted it without a scene. Not that he was relishing his own return, its having been made abundantly clear that he was only to be allowed access to his home accompanied by one of the senior investigating officers. Still, he supposed it was progress of a sort. At least he would get an idea of what had been touched, of what had be seen, moved, and inspected, and of what, if anything, the redoubtable Mrs Barker had managed to conceal. He hoped against hope that the thorough search he was sure they must have conducted was not *so* thorough as to reveal his hidden treasures. How he wished there was some way he could ascertain how much they knew and how much they had been able to piece together from what they had seen. There was nothing for it; he had to ignore the ignominy of being accompanied through his own front door and play along with their little game, act the injured innocent, and hope to God they had not uncovered the extent of his activities.

Meantime, all his attempts to get hold of Ted Manning, the one man who might be able to provide some of the answers, had failed. All he knew was that, for whatever reason, Detective Inspector Manning was locked out of his home too and, since that surprising revelation, was unable to be contacted. He appeared to have gone to ground. Wherever he was, he was so far beneath the radar as to be rendered invisible.

Even that young son of his seemingly had vanished too. Previously never far away when there were errands to run and good money to be earned, Richard was the one who had initially approached the major general, offering his services as scout and runner. He was worldly wise beyond his years, capable of holding and maintaining confidences, sly, dependable, and in no thrall whatsoever to a father he held in contempt, characteristics that made him, in John's eyes, the ideal carrier.

Up till now, the major general had prided himself on being a good judge of men and their potential. What if he had totally misplaced that confidence and those entrusted in part with some of his many secrets and nefarious dealings had themselves succumbed to temptation and revealed whatever they knew or surmised about his various enterprises? It was a disturbing thought and not one he could easily shake off.

The planned return was scheduled for later that day. The major general would be collected and driven to the manor house by the officer who was to accompany him. The major general's only stipulation was that this would be in an unmarked police car. Not that he was in any position to stipulate—that had been made absolutely clear—but his request had been acknowledged and, ultimately, accommodated, all the while emphasis upon his position as a person of interest to the police ensuring that this was seen as a privilege and not a right.

It was two o'clock precisely when the unmarked car pulled into a parking space in front of the country house hotel, the driver remaining behind the wheel while the older man, a detective sergeant who had interviewed the major general immediately following the discovery of the body by the lake, got out of the passenger side of the car, taking a moment to absorb the surroundings. Carefully tended flower beds flanked either side of the gravel forecourt. No trace of any weeds here, he thought, momentarily contrasting it with his own garden, suffering weeks of neglect ever since the start of the current crime wave and the hours of overtime which this had entailed. His reverie was interrupted by a gentle purring as the automatic front doors glided open and the major general stepped out from the porch and descended the steps towards him.

The occupants of the car had made desultory small talk during the short journey to the major general's house, criticising the performance of the English cricket team on tour in Australia and bemoaning the dearth of decent all-rounders and younger players capable of holding their catches.

Acknowledging the duty officers guarding the approach road and front of the house, DS Wilkes unlocked the door and gestured to the major general to follow him into the hall. At this point, neither man had been able to ascertain how much the other knew. Comments were guarded; questions were left hanging; replies were noncommittal. The game of cat and mouse had begun. The major general, veteran of so much military service, had never felt so vulnerable in his life.

CHAPTER 132

Buried Treasure

Elsewhere in the county, the team of SOCOs rested upon their spades and pickaxes, dusty and exhausted after prising every last flagstone from the floor of the ruined lean-to and smashing through the concrete screed below. This had been a painstaking and physically demanding process, as no heavy machinery could be used: not only would getting this to the site of their investigations further compromise the crime scene, where the use of such equipment could all too easily disturb and destroy valuable evidence, but also there was the very real fear that it could bring down the remaining metal trusses onto the men and women working there. And so the task had been a manual one, taking its toll upon the crew, whose shoulders and arms ached from the effort and who, despondently, were about to concede defeat when, methodically lifting and sifting the remaining piece of screed, they discovered a small area which appeared to have been boarded over.

Gently prising apart the rotted slats of wood revealed the narrow gaping jaws of the old well shaft with what seemed to be a rusty ladder attached to one side of the wall, disappearing from view somewhere several feet below. No attempt appeared to have been made to fill this in, and there was no way of guessing its depth. Dean Matthews, one of the younger members of the team, ignored his colleagues urging restraint and attempted to gauge this by the only way he knew. Selecting a smooth round pebble from the garden path, he carefully positioned himself over the shaft and dropped the stone into the well. To the waiting officers, there seemed to be quite a long pause before they heard it hit whatever lay at the foot of the well. There was no splash indicating the presence of any quantity of water, neither was the sound a sharp one as though the pebble had hit the stony floor of the well. Rather, as they gathered round, their ears as close to the well shaft as possible, what they heard, albeit indistinctly, was a slight muffled thump as though the pebble had made contact with something soft.

After minutes of deliberation and uncertainty as to how to proceed, it was Dean, again ignoring protocol, who suggested climbing down the shaft as far as he could to discover what was down there and determine whether they should try to bring it to the surface. "I've probably already contaminated the scene chucking a stone in there, so I might just as well go down myself and have a look-see."

Hesitantly agreeing that he was a more likely candidate for the role than other, more rotund members of the team, his colleagues selected the necessary equipment from the stash they always carried to such a crime scene: climbing ropes and harness, pitons, hooks and claws, powerful torches (handheld and head worn), and slimline breathing apparatus. Some of the older members of the crew recollected the last time *they* were needed was in a desperate attempt to reach a young lad who had been pushed into a disused mineshaft as a punishment by a rival gang several years ago.

Curbing his impetuosity long enough to don the necessary gear and receive his instructions—"First sign that the walls might collapse, or any other danger, pull on the communication cord and we'll haul you out"— Dean clambered over the edge of the well shaft and began his descent. At first the going was relatively easy, his feet finding each rung of the ladder inset into the wall of the shaft, testing each one in turn to be sure they would bear his weight, before inching down, a step at a time. Although the rungs appeared rusty and worn, being distorted with age, those nearest to the surface remained firmly in situ. Dean felt his confidence increasing. The breathing apparatus, although designed for use in confined spaces, nevertheless impeded his progress. He felt tempted to jettison it. However, as his descent progressed, and as the little circle of light from the top of the well grew dimmer and dimmer with each step he took, before disappearing completely, Dean became uncomfortably aware of a change in the atmosphere surrounding him. The air down here smelled stale, and whether from this or from his considerable exertion so far, Dean felt as though his lungs were struggling a little. The light from his head torch, directed downwards towards his feet, illuminated the next few rungs, each seemingly more rusty than the last. A couple of these had rotted right through and had come away from the shaft wall. It was time to make some adjustments.

Breathing more easily now by intermittently using the apparatus, Dean bent down to check the security of his harness clasps where they had rubbed against the wall of the well. It was then that he made the startling discovery. Not only had the lower rungs apparently rusted through and become detached, but also shortly after this they ended completely, almost appearing to have been sawn off. The metal struts forming the sides of the ladder remained, but the horizontal rungs were missing. Feeling gingerly for footholds, Dean part climbed and part abseiled towards the bottom of the shaft.

The stench down here was awful. Dean was relying solely upon the breathing apparatus now, his eyes sore and smarting behind his goggles as he peered round and down, trying to focus and make sense of what he was seeing. He thought his feet had touched the bottom, but this was no solid floor—or even a small pool of water, which could have been expected. Instead, his feet had landed on something soft and mobile. Not wanting to squash whatever it was with his weight, Dean adjusted his harness so that he was suspended inches above the thing his feet had found.

What at first sight had appeared to be bundle of rags was a parcel of some sort, wrapped in fabric, the ends of which were secured in a firm knot. In the narrow confines of the well shaft, there was no way Dean could manoeuvre the bundle in front of him and despatch it to the surface on his climbing rope, leaving him down here to investigate whatever else his toes had detected beneath him. Using the webbing straps from his pack, Dean secured the bundle beneath his harness and gave the signal to his colleagues for his ascent to begin.

Progress was slow as Dean constantly checked that the bundle remained secure. Sometimes it lurched and swung to the side, brushing the shaft wall, and he was fearful its contents might be damaged or might have worked loose inside his improvised sling.

The disc of light above his head was growing brighter—and none too soon. Helpful hands grasped his harness as his colleagues hauled him and his precious bundle over the rim of the well.

"What have we here?" Their excitement was tangible, but common sense and years of training prevailed, so they duly bagged and labelled the bundle for full forensic investigation, should this be warranted.

Gratefully gulping down the bottled water he had been given, Dean told them about the other material he had discovered at the bottom of the well. The bundle already lifted to the surface had prevented him from reaching down to investigate the remaining item, other than feeling it to be soft beneath his feet. Peering round the awkward bundle, and by directing his torch beam so as to sweep the entire width of the shaft at this point, he had formed a brief image of something bulky and amorphous, its irregular rounded contours filling the available space. Whatever lay below, he was unable to tell. All he knew was that he wanted to be the one to get this find up out of the well. And so he argued his case, denying tiredness, refusing to acknowledge his aching limbs. He was already kitted out for another descent; he knew the approximate size of the shaft and had familiarised himself with the hazards. What was more, at this time of year the light failed fast and there was barely time to equip and prepare another member of the crew. In the face of such insistence, his colleagues concurred. With a fresh supply of oxygen and more webbing, hooks, rope, and a camera, Dean entered the well for the second time.

This time he made the descent quickly, certain now that the rungs would hold and knowing exactly at what point to pause and use his harness to take the weight for the remaining few feet. Without the bundle obscuring his vision, he was able to swing round an entire 360 degrees, taking pictures of where the rungs had been sawn from the upright struts, before turning his attention to what lay beneath him.

This time the bundle below him again appeared to occupy almost the entire width of the shaft, but what he had previously thought to be quite a shapeless thing was in fact much more tightly bound than the earlier discovery. It was wrapped in old waterproof sheeting, secured with strong, thin rope of the sort sometimes used to anchor a tarpaulin to the side of a lorry. If these ropes were to hold, there would be no need for the webbing he had brought down with him, but not wanting to leave anything to chance, Dean managed to get one length of this strapping around the bundle and attach it and the tarpaulin rope to the karabiner hanging down from his climbing harness.

Giving the signal for the second ascent, he fervently prayed that his ligatures would hold, wishing there was some way he could have got one round the base of the bundle. As he began the painfully slow ascent to the surface, Dean was only too aware of how close a fit the bundle was proving to be. Shining his torch down, he was unable to see anything beyond the edge of the tarpaulin. He had no way of knowing how long the bundle was or whether there was anything below it at the base of the well. Provided they got this one out intact, the discovery would have to wait for a third attempt, one which Dean ruefully conceded would be beyond him. Every muscle in his body ached. Despite his breathing apparatus, his chest felt tight and his temples throbbed with pain as he peered down at his load, willing it to stay together and not get jammed in the well shaft, as time and time again the edges of the tarpaulin caught against the brick sides and the twisted rungs of the ladder.

It was with profound relief when his head broke surface and the ordeal was eventually over. As he hungrily gasped the first few lungfuls of cool smoky air, the tension drained from his body as his colleagues seized him beneath the arms and lifted him onto the ground. With something bordering upon surprise, Dean realised that he could no longer feel his fingers. His hands, taut and swollen, numb with cold, were futilely fumbling with the fasteners on his harness. He was shivering now in the open air, his teeth chattering against the side of the vacuum mug, the warm liquid spilling out of the side of his mouth. He was only dimly aware of their voices saying, "Well done, lad," before slipping into what seemed like blissful sleep, not knowing or even really caring any more whether the bundle had survived its transit intact.

———•———

It was several hours later when Dean awoke to the unmistakable sounds of a tea trolley being wheeled past his bed. Rubbing the sleep from his eyes, he looked around him, amazed to find that he was not alone. There were five other beds—one either side of him and three opposite. He seemed to be in a hospital ward, but as far as he knew, he had not been ill or been involved in an accident. Maybe he was still dreaming.

The pretty young healthcare assistant seemed real enough, her halting English in reply to his questions and her name badge—reading

"Emika"—suggesting that she was Eastern European. "Brought in last night from A&E, down for observation, you are. Your girlfriend knows. She coming in later? You like tea?"

The morning wore on: basic nursing observations, a little conversation with one of his roommates, and a doctor's round where he was pronounced fit for discharge.

Then the visit he had been dreading: the superintendent in charge of the scene-of-crime team. Dean knew that he had overstepped the mark, electing—no, *insisting*—that he would be the one to go down the well for a second time. By rights he should have rested up and let one of his colleagues make the second descent. That way he would not have ended up in hospital—a waste of man-hours when he should have been at work, especially with the force as stretched as it currently was. His self-flagellation stopped abruptly as the older man approached his bed and, taking him completely by surprise, shook his hand and warmly congratulated him for his "exceptional effort" and the bravery involved, meantime filling in the gaps in Dean's recollection of the previous day's events. Apparently on reaching the surface after the second descent, he had collapsed from sheer exhaustion, hypothermia, oxygen depletion, and dehydration, a formidable combination of factors necessitating immediate medical intervention, but not before he had personally seen the large wrapped bundle safely lifted out of the well on to the ground alongside. The second officer detailed to go down the well had found nothing else of note at the base, apart from a few large scuff marks where the dry sandy soil had been swept aside to reveal the brick base beneath, as though something had been dragged down there. Not wishing to disturb the area, already a putative crime scene, he hovered above the ground in his climbing harness as photographs were taken, along with still shots and a video recording, and a small sample of the soil where it had previously been undisturbed, bagged for subsequent analysis.

Never had the officer been more relieved to have completed his task and return to the surface just as the daylight began to fade. He had found the whole experience terrifying. The long descent was increasingly claustrophobic; he was always fearful that the rungs of the ladder would fail to hold his weight. His eyes were smarting, and his breathing, even with the apparatus to help him, was laboured and inadequate. How Dean had managed it twice, his commanding officer just did not know. Thinking of that first time, Dean's not knowing what he might encounter, and then finding those bundles and somehow managing to make them secure and get to the surface with them, the older man felt nothing but admiration for what the young officer had achieved.

And that was what Dean's senior officer was saying now, with no hint of censure but with words and phrases like commendation, courage, and outstanding commitment to duty, with Dean sitting there feeling nothing but relief and the absolute certainty that this was the only job for him.

CHAPTER 133

Revelations

On a stainless steel trolley in the forensic laboratory lay the first of the bundles retrieved from the well shaft. The fabric around it looked like part of a thin duvet or sleeping bag. It was soiled and worn but still fairly intact, its stuffing seeping from the torn outer nylon in dirty grey clumps. Exercising the utmost care, the presiding pathologist, gowned and gloved, undid the knots securing the bundle and opened out the fabric to reveal what lay within, the entire episode routinely videoed to provide a tangible record of proceedings. The assistant pathologist and two young medical students in attendance gathered round, unable to conceal their collective disappointment as the contents appeared to reveal the badly decomposed body of a large dog. The long-snouted jawbone and wicked incisors protruding beneath the clumps of hair still adhering to parts of the corpse confirmed this. Photographs having been taken, the pathologist gently removed each part of the body, reassembling the skeletal remains on the surface of the trolley until he was satisfied that the corpse was complete. More photographs followed while the assistant pathologist was despatched to fetch a fresh trolley.

It was only then that the waiting audience realised the significance of what they were observing, as the principle pathologist turned his attention again to the grimy bundle and began removing more of the skeletal remains. This time, a tiny long bone—a femur—followed by ribs and a sternum, cartilaginous still, and small plates of bone which he carefully rearranged on the trolley, comprising all the component parts of a minuscule skull. With a united gasp of recognition, his viewers realised what the pathologist had suspected all along: this was no puppy joined in death to the older dog; these were the indisputable remains of a human baby.

The contents of the second bundle were also undeniably human, the shape and contents of the pelvis confirming that this was indeed that of a young woman, and one who was in the early stages of pregnancy. Examination of her remaining bones showed evidence of a childhood fracture of the tibia and associated displacement at the base of the fibula. It had been badly reunited, meaning that this one leg was slightly shorter than the other and must have left her with a permanent limp. There did not seem to be anything else particularly remarkable about the assembled remains, but the actual cause of death had yet to be determined. A battery of further tests was about to be instigated.

CHAPTER 134

Robert

Robert did not know what to do. Glumly collecting up the remains of his meal, the box containing the chicken bones, paper napkins, little packets of salt, and a plastic drinking straw, he tried to take stock of his situation. He had hoped that having something to eat would help him to focus somehow, that the food in his belly would make his mind clearer, but the magic didn't seem to have worked. As he deposited the detritus from his meal into the refuse bin, he realised that he was no nearer to finding a solution to his problems. As he saw it, there were only two choices: either he must return to his home neighbourhood, track down his father, and find out what arrangements had been made for their accommodation, knowing that their house was a crime scene and out of bounds to them, or he could remain on the run, well out of sight, at least until the worst of this nightmare was over.

But what was he to live on? Where could he stay? He sat down again with the paper cup holding the rest of his drink, willing it to last, not wanting to go back outside, relishing the warmth and anonymity of the place.

Previously hardly noticing his surroundings, so totally preoccupied with his own thoughts that he had been oblivious to the noise and bustle around him, Robert was suddenly aware of an escalation in the general racket as a particularly exuberant group of people clustered around his table, jostling for position in the queue. It was a family party: a youngster clutching a balloon, obviously the birthday boy; older children, siblings and cousins possibly; and parents and other adults, aunts and uncles maybe. In that moment, Robert found a solution to his problem.

He would visit his Auntie Mary and hope that she would take pity on him. Theirs had never been a close family. His father had ensured that, antagonising his own brothers by his arrogance and air of superiority, with the result that they had visited less and less over the years, to the point where Robert could barely remember them and had no idea where they lived. His mother's only sister, Mary, saw more of the boys when they were small until she, too, had become the target of Ted's malice and his constant disparaging remarks about their two-up two-down terrace house in one of the least affluent areas of the city, contrasting this with his own executive new build, to the point where she had become virtually estranged from the family. Robert knew that she and his mother talked on the telephone still, always when his father was not in the house, and she always remembered their birthdays and Christmas, having sent presents for them when they were younger but replacing them with Amazon tokens these days. And his mother's tedious insistence upon their sending thank-you letters meant that he knew his aunt's address. He would make his way there first thing in the morning and throw himself upon her mercy. In the meantime, he would stay where he was until closing time, enjoying the warmth, and then find himself somewhere out of the way to spend the remainder of the night—an unlocked garden shed or greenhouse perhaps.

CHAPTER 135

The Major General

The visit to the house had proved inconclusive as far as the major general was concerned. The detectives involved had said little at the time, waiting to share their impressions of what had occurred until they were on the return journey to the police station, having dropped the major general back at the country house hotel.

He, for his part, had appeared disgruntled, having hoped that he might have been permitted to have some time alone in the house. If he was not to be allowed an immediate return to his home, then at least he might have been granted a little time to take stock and reacquaint himself with just what had been on display and no doubt scrutinised by the police during his temporary eviction. Instead of which, it had been a methodical tour of the premises, with very few questions asked. True, there had been some interest in the firearms on display, and he had been able to assert their legitimacy, proving that he held the appropriate firearms certificates and that many of the items were either scale models or had been purposely disabled. It had been an uneasy exchange with his not knowing how much they really knew, their responses noncommittal, their facial expressions studiously bland, giving nothing away.

It had been raining hard when they had left the house, DS Wilkes locking the door and pocketing the key—*his* key—confirmation enough that they were not going to allow him back in just yet. Apparently they *did* want to walk him down to the lake, to the place where the body had been found, but the sky was ominously dark and it had begun to thunder.

"Best leave that for another day," one of them had said, the major general struggling to conceal his fury at the continued banishment.

CHAPTER 136

Karen and Ben

As it transpired, her mother had not been a great deal of help, countering Karen's anxiety with what seemed little more than a kindly meant platitude: "I expect it's just a phase she's going through. Perhaps she's had a bit of a scare, tumbled over in the bath or not liked having water in her eyes when she's had her hair washed, or something." Mention of a possible scare resonated with Karen, who wished in that moment like never before that she could share the little girl's history with her doting grandmother. But such an admission was unthinkable. She pushed aside the thought and all the memories it invoked: the exhilaration of finding her modern-day Moses, the subsequent subterfuge, and how hard she had worked to bring Ben on board with her plans. She was not about to jeopardise her—their—future in a moment of weakness.

CHAPTER 137

Speculation Mounts

The atmosphere in Booth Street police station was electric, all the hours of painstaking work, false leads, and inconclusive findings insignificant now in the light of recent developments. The place was buzzing with gossip; speculation was rife. They had a man in custody, and word had just come in from the forensic team—DNA results positively linking the findings from the well not only with the girl they had rescued from the van but also with the murder victim found by the lake. Further analysis was ongoing. The findings and any correlations between these and the unsolved crimes would be known later, but to the assembled officers, everything they heard pointed to one thing: the murders were the work of one man, the man whose DNA had so far linked him to crimes past and present, the man they felt sure they were close to identifying.

And as if that were not enough, their own much-disliked chief superintendent Ted Manning had been brought in for questioning. Not that they were supposed to know it was anything more than just routine fact-finding following his wife's brutal attack, but their suspicions were aroused when he was escorted off the premises by two very senior officers directly accountable to the regional chief of police. What his subordinates didn't know, they eagerly guessed, their fertile imaginations in overdrive.

As had been so often the case in the past, before he was relegated to light duties, it was Shorty's intervention which brought them back to the present and to the pressing issues which had to be resolved. The man they held in the custody suite, arrested on suspicion of murdering his wife and up until now widely believed to have been responsible for the spate of murdered pregnant women, had yet to be charged. Time was running out for them. They must either charge him or let him go. Until the DNA processing was complete, they had no option but to release him, a person of interest who could be re-arrested and charged once the final link they anticipated was found.

The remaining officers were assembled for a hastily convened briefing by the most senior officer there, Ted Manning's deputy, before being deployed to their duties for the day. Animated conversation lapsed, coffees were collected from the vending machine, reports were read, and tasks were allocated. Shorty returned to his desk, opened his laptop, and deleted the file he had compiled to marry Alex's movements to the current killing spree. It all had seemed to make perfect sense at the time, and Shorty had been riding high, doing what he had done so successfully for so many years: playing a hunch—but more than that, a calculated hunch, one carefully researched, details checked and double-checked, correlations made and solutions found, and then presented to his colleagues with that half-apologetic "I told you so" air of satisfaction, revelling in their surprise and approbation, overtly humble, inwardly rejoicing in their admiration and recognition of the reputation he had achieved.

Except this time it had failed him. All his carefully logged details, the connections he had made, and the conclusions he had reached, trashed. The wasted man-hours that this represented (albeit many of those hours in his own time, tapping away on his laptop in his dreary empty home, food congealing on the plate, coffee cold in the cup, as he sought to unravel the strands of "evidence" he had unearthed). True, there had been disappointments before, promising leads that turned out to be blind alleys, conjecture which could never be proved, but never on this scale. To have been so sure of his facts that they had brought the man in and were about to charge him with multiple murder when all the incriminating evidence related to nothing criminal, only the man's lamentable disloyalty towards his pregnant wife, the days unaccounted for by his work having been spent entertaining his latest mistress. What at the time had seemed like a convenient alibi, Shorty now knew to be the fact. There was no way that Alex would be re-arrested.

Deletion completed, there remained one thing for Shorty to do. His hand sought the envelope in his jacket pocket, transferring it to the tray of internal post. Marked "Private and Confidential" and addressed to the station commander, the envelope contained Shorty's letter of resignation.

CHAPTER 138

Robert

Robert had spent a profoundly uncomfortable night. At 11p.m. he had been unceremoniously ejected from McDonald's, the lad stacking the chairs on top of the tables and mopping the floor having no time for lingerers. Fortunately for Robert, one of the girls behind the counter had been watching him surreptitiously for some time as he toyed with his drink, willing it to last, his eyes downcast, furtively glancing round each time the door opened, shrinking back into his parka, not engaging with anyone. He was a good-looking lad, clearly in some sort of trouble, but he didn't seem like some of the rougher sorts they got in there: druggies or just loud troublemakers. She had seen him eyeing the pile of chips left by a departing customer, sensing his disappointment when the bloke scooped them up and put them in the bin. He must still be hungry, she thought. Perhaps he hasn't the money for anything else. Her mind made up, she waited until the last order had been served, and then, contrary to regulations (but who cared? she wasn't doing it for herself), she put a few of pieces of chicken and a good helping of fries into one of the meal boxes and took it over to the boy. He had smiled at her then, and she was smitten by how sad and tired he seemed. She watched as the sweeper-up ushered Robert out of the door and wondered if she would ever see him again. An hour later, her shift finished, the girl left the restaurant, but there was no sign of the boy.

Robert had made his way along the road, turning off into one of the more affluent estates. At least they had gardens here. Someone was bound to have a shed. Wearily trudging along, he began to think he had made a mistake. It might have been better on the council estate down the road. Here, so many of the houses had their garden gates locked. It took him almost two hours before he managed to find one that was unlocked and not protected by security lights. He felt he could hardly go another step. His head was thumping, his eyes were strained from peering through the dark, and his feet were blistered and sore. Praying they had no dogs to raise the alarm, he crept down the garden path.

Thankfully they had a greenhouse, empty save for a few geraniums in pots. He pulled the door to behind him and sank to the floor, feeling in his pocket for his food. The chicken and chips were cold by now, but he ate hungrily, licking the grease from his fingers and wishing he had something to drink. Then, scrunching a pile of horticultural fleece into a makeshift pillow, he lay down as best he could among the pots and garden tools and settled into an uneasy sleep.

Waking at dawn, aching and stiff from his cramped position, he was mightily relieved to see that none of the house lights was on. He crept out of the garden as stealthily as he had entered, pausing outside the gate just long enough to brush away the worst of the dead leaves and straw sticking to his clothes—tangible evidence of his night on the greenhouse floor. The little rest that he had been able to achieve must have done him some good. Last night's headache, whilst not completely gone, had certainly abated, but his mouth had never felt so dry; his lips were parched and sticking together, and even his throat was sore. Dismissing the tantalising images of steaming cups of coffee, giant bottles of cola, and frothy milkshakes, Robert fingered the few remaining coins in his pocket and prayed they would be enough to cover his fare.

For once it seemed that fate was being kind to him: the bus depot was fairly close, and a helpful driver had directed him to the correct bay. He had never been to his aunt's house and had only a vague idea of the distance involved. Providentially, the driver knew the route well and was able to tell him where to alight. What is more, the little money Robert had was just enough to pay his fare, vindicating his earlier self-denial; he was pleased now that he had not succumbed to temptation and bought a drink. It was all going well—too well—as minutes later, ringing his aunt's doorbell, he received his first shock of the day.

"Sorry, lad, she's not here." His Uncle Geoff, in dressing gown and barefooted, standing in the doorway, legs apart, apparently was not about to let him in. Behind Geoff was an elderly greyhound eyeing the newcomer with undisguised suspicion.

Suddenly, sheer exhaustion and the utter hopelessness of his situation overwhelmed Robert, yesterday's headache back with a vengeance as he swayed and fell forward, his outstretched hand grasping the door jamb for support.

Alarmed now by the boy's pallor, Geoff caught hold of him and, half dragging, half carrying, lifted him over the threshold into the stuffy parlour. Sweeping aside the empty pizza box and crumpled copy of the Racing Post, he laid the boy on the sofa, pulled the door shut, and sat down in the armchair opposite, absent-mindedly lighting a cigarette as he did so, feeling for an ashtray among the detritus on the side table, a number of empty lager tins testimony to the previous night's activity. How to tell the boy? What to tell him? How much did he already know? And what the hell was he doing here anyway?

The earlier fuddle in Geoff's brain was clearing now as he mentally replayed the strange way the events of last night had unfolded. It was an ordinary enough evening, both of them getting in from work. He had stopped off for a pint on his way home, so Mary had got in before him, their evening meal bubbling in the slow cooker, potatoes on the boil. He had come in and washed his hands at the kitchen sink, Mary grumbling good-naturedly, as she did every night, that he was always in her way when she was trying to dish up. "You'd think it was the only tap in the house. What's the bathroom for, I want to know?"

They had eaten together and had just settled down in front of the TV to watch one of Mary's favourite soaps—he wasn't too bothered, busy figuring out the racing form—when the doorbell rang. At that moment, the normality of their evening ceased abruptly.

There were two of them, uniformed police officers, an older man with a pretty young woman, a PCSO she had told him when they introduced themselves, flashing their identity cards as they did so. The confusion was a tangible presence in the room, with the officers safe, solid, and dependable-looking and with Mary shaking and tearful. He was trying to console her, his mind groping, trying to make sense of what they were telling him.

Her sister Pam was seriously injured—attacked, on lifesupport.

Nothing about the husband or the boys. They either didn't know or weren't telling.

He wasn't sure how they had got his and Mary's details or why they were asking about their day: had they both been at work? and where was that? Surely they couldn't have thought that they were implicated. Her own sister?

He had driven May to the hospital, cursing at the inevitable delay—roadworks, traffic management—and accompanied her to the unit where her sister was being cared for following her return from theatre. Surrounded by all the equipment that was keeping her alive, he thought how very small and vulnerable she seemed. To his surprise, Mary, who had sobbed and trembled throughout their nightmare journey, seemed transformed, calmly taking stock of the situation. She was listening closely and apparently absorbing what the ward sister was telling her, accepting the offer of a visitor's guest room for as long as she needed it, then waving Geoff off before taking her place at her sister's bedside. "You need to get home, love. The old dog needs you. You see to her and look after yourself. I'll ring you if there is any change. You can come over and visit tomorrow."

Always a compliant man, Geoff had done as directed. He had driven home and taken the dog on her late night walk, stopping on the way to pick up a takeaway pizza. (All the stress of the last few hours must have given him an appetite, he decided.) He had settled down with his pizza and two cans of lager to watch a bit of telly before bed and pass an otherwise uneventful night.

He certainly hadn't expected this. He wondered what to do next. He wondered what Mary would do.

CHAPTER 139

Leckie

It was OK at first: a room of her own, a lovely comfortable bed, Sandy solicitous, really looking after her. She still wasn't too happy about the dog; he seemed boisterous and untrustworthy, tail wagging with pleasure, but a definite propensity to snarl should she get too close to his food bowl. Still, she was getting stronger now and could move about the house and keep out of the dog's way as much as possible.

And that's when the doubts had begun. She had spent such a long time in her room, looking out at the garden, watching the birds pecking away at the bright orange berries in the hedge, the dead leaves swirling in the wind, the trees skeletal now, the garden bare. What had seemed such a safe haven did not look that way anymore. Where at first it had been secluded, shielded from the prying eyes of passers-by, now it was revealed to her for what it really was: a patch of barren earth, withered shreds of rotting vegetation, open to the skies and to anyone going by. She certainly had no desire ever to go out there. No amount of persuasion succeeded.

She stayed in the house, spending less time in her room, avoiding the view from the windows. But even that had lost its appeal. Despite the cheerful fire crackling in the grate (Sandy had time for such niceties now) and the comfortable furnishings, something felt wrong. Leckie was beginning to feel trapped—and it wasn't just the claustrophobia induced by her surroundings and her self-imposed confinement. No, there was something else that was disturbing her. She was ashamed to admit it even to herself, but she was starting to find Sandy's constant evident concern overpowering. Although she had been grateful enough for Sandy's help with washing and dressing at first, by now she was perfectly capable of doing that for herself. She had begun to shrink away from Sandy's touch, rationalising it to herself as proof of how much more independent she had become. But Leckie felt uneasy. In her book, Sandy was clearly a dyke—and without a partner. In truth, Leckie was beginning to feel threatened, fearful of being drawn into something for which she felt unprepared.

She had follow-up appointment at the hospital next week. Further evidence of the almost suffocating concern, Sandy wanted not only to take her there but also to accompany her at the consultation, acting like an overprotective parent or, heaven forbid, her lover. Leckie was going to have to find a way of giving her the slip. Her mind was made up; she was going to use this appointment to effect her escape.

CHAPTER 140

The Man

The fox was licking his wounds, standing by the door in the dingy room, his few meagre possessions in three neat piles on the bed with a well-worn rucksack alongside. He had told his landlady that he was leaving: "Been offered a better job down south, accommodation thrown in" (he wished!). "No time to tell you more about it just now. I have things to see to before I leave." Speculating that this was possibly the longest conversation he had ever had with the woman he had been paying rent to all these months, the man knew what he had to do next. He turned his attention to the things on the bed. He had retrieved the small dusty suitcase and an old ex-army stuff bag from the top of the wardrobe, smiling to himself as he used the corner of the counterpane to wipe them clean. She would have to wash it this time before letting the room again. He quickly packed the suitcase with the contents of the largest pile—shoes and clothing, and a few toiletries—before turning to the adjacent stack. This demanded greater attention, as he methodically checked each individual item before stowing it in his rucksack, the tools of his trade at the bottom, a change of clothing, and lastly his crash helmet and a beanie hat. The smallest pile remained, a few items of unwanted clothing (the stuff he had worn during his fateful visit to the cottage), which he bundled unceremoniously into the stuff bag, pulling the drawstring tightly across. One last check to make sure he had left nothing behind, then he picked up his things and went out of the room, closing the door quietly behind him.

Without a backward glance, he left the house and walked rapidly down the street before jumping on the first bus that came past. Once in the town centre, he made his way to the railway station, depositing his suitcase in the left luggage office. He had agonised about leaving the stuff bag too, fearing any possible disclosure of such incriminating contents, but finally had decided to take the chance, arguing that it was only for a short time before he could realise the remainder of his plan.

Shouldering his rucksack, he made his way to his first destination, a downtown barber only too happy to oblige. A little while later he emerged, his appearance completely transformed, pulling the beanie from the side pocket of his rucksack to cover his newly shaven, totally bald head.

His next mission involved returning to the street near his old digs where he had parked the motorbike. This was the only part of the plan which caused him actual regret. With that bike, he experienced the nearest thing to love that he had ever felt for anything or anyone. They had been through some taxing times together, and it had always served him well. But he knew that it had to go. With a heavy heart, rucksack on his back, he rode the bike to the only dealer he knew who would take it off his hands, no questions asked, and give him something approaching a fair price for it.

It only remained for him to dispose of the other incriminating stuff. He had wondered how best to do this: either by leaving it where it was in the left luggage office, reclaiming only the suitcase while denying any knowledge of the other bag, or collecting both items and disposing of the stuff bag and its grim contents elsewhere. Regretfully, he had discounted the first idea, fearing the necessary confrontation involved would only serve to draw attention to him and might well be remembered should the police start asking questions there. He would have to devise some other way to rid himself of any items which could place him in the vicinity of the latest crime.

Sometimes fate just plays into your hands.

Retrieving his belongings from left luggage was not only quicker than he had dared to hope, but also pleasingly anonymous thanks to the noisy, vibrant presence in the queue before him: a couple, in full pearly king and queen regalia, having a loud altercation with the harassed railway employee, who apparently seemed unable to locate the cases containing their everyday wear which they were intent upon having for their onward journey. So incensed had they become that the little office rang with their shouts, threatening to summon the security guard. Anxious to serve the other customers before things turned really nasty, the clerk at the counter barely glanced at the man, rapidly exchanging the proffered ticket for the two items in storage.

The man's luck continued to hold; hurrying into the station toilets, he found them to be deserted. Locking himself in the cubicle, he removed his motorbike leathers and changed his clothes, cramming those he had worn into the stuff bag, which was bulging now with unwanted items. He was reluctant to part with his leathers, knowing how much they had cost him, but he knew they had to go. Even to his untrained nose, the pervading smell of smoke remained, placing them (and should he retain them, him too) clearly in the vicinity of some pretty large and recent conflagration.

His biker boots must share the fate of the leathers. As he pulled on a pair of trainers, he wondered how on earth he could get rid of the boots without drawing attention to himself. He could just leave them here, but he knew better than to place too many markers in the same area. Despite his caution, his tracks might lead an astute investigator to the station luggage store—and he had no wish to provide any further information suggesting a change in his appearance. That would be just too careless. There had been too many avoidable mistakes so far: he was not about to compound them by adding another.

A plan had begun to form. Waiting until he heard the approach of the intercity train, slowing to a stop at the station, and the hubbub of jostling crowds pushing along the platform, he slipped out of the toilet block unnoticed and, encumbered by all his possessions, made his way to the vending machine, where he purchased a return ticket to the nearest town, carefully keeping his back towards the train as it pulled out of the station.

He did not have long to wait for the next local train. Once on board, he avoided seats in the carriage, choosing instead to stand by the door conveniently adjacent to the luggage rack where he deposited his biking boots and leathers. He guessed that if they weren't appropriated by someone before then, which would certainly muddle the trail, then they would end the day in a railway lost property office.

His load considerably lighter now, he hopped off the train at the next station and walked towards the town centre, stopping every so often to deposit an item from his discard bag in a roadside rubbish bin. As the bag lightened, so did his mood, to such an extent that he began to notice more about his surroundings. On passing a bonfire pile on a patch of waste ground, he waited until he was sure that he was not being observed before stuffing the remaining contents and the bag into the base of the stack—all except one item. In that moment he couldn't resist the temptation to add his own creative touch as he reached up the bonfire pile and crowned the guy with his motorcycle helmet. He would have liked to take the joke further and ensure the destruction of his belongings by setting fire to the pile. He had always enjoyed the prospect of toying with his pursuers, taunting them and putting on a display, but now was not the time. There was too much riding on his making a clear getaway.

Quickly retracing his steps, he made his way back to the station, crossing platforms to make the return journey. They would not be expecting that, even if they had followed him this far. They would be bound to think he had made the complete journey and travelled to the end of the line, but instead of this, he boarded the returning train and, walking its length, was grateful to find no trace of his biking leathers. He was pretty sure that it *was* the same train, reasoning that sufficient time had elapsed for it to make the return journey while he had been walking the streets and getting rid of his various items of clothing.

Now it was time to put the next phase of his plan into operation. He had already sought to thwart any pursuers by returning to the original station, having clearly pointed them in the direction he had pretended to follow. Now to adopt a completely different tack: not only would he continue inentirely the opposite direction, mingling inconspicuously with the evening commuters as they left the train and made their way towards the railway car park, but also, for the remainder of his journey that night, he would eschew train travel and go by coach. If they had followed his earlier movements as far as the station, they would hardly be expecting that.

It was a good plan. And he prided himself upon his planning. He was bound for a completely new area where with new digs, a different name, and a couple of forged references he would soon find work and rebuild his life yet again. New pastures and a clean start: fresh hunting ground for the wily fox.

CHAPTER 141

Escalating Tensions

The scale of the investigations was unprecedented. Although police forces across the region had been made aware on a need-to-know basis, their involvement until now had remained fairly peripheral, with a concentration of activity only in those areas where the recent murders had occurred. All that had changed with the discovery of the bodies in the well, pointing to a prolonged history of unsolved violence against women, continuing to the present time, and with the horrific injuries sustained by the victim found still barely alive in the burnt-out van. Extra officers had been drafted in, assigned to teams already stretched to capacity in following all the leads in each aspect of the enquiries. Forensic teams were working round the clock assessing and assimilating data. False leads and unsupported speculation were consigned to the back burner. The man, Alex, whilst remaining a person of interest in connection with his wife's murder, was released from custody, and the major general was allowed to return home, where to his fury he discovered that a number of his weapons had been confiscated, pending further certification. On being handed the receipt for these various items, his relief that his collected works of art had remained untouched was short-lived, as further receipts followed and a number of paintings were then removed for further expert scrutiny.

Leonie evinced scant sympathy for his plight, concerned only to reestablish her own connections, firstly ranking up the central heating before turning her attention to the contents of her wardrobe and then to the state of the main rooms, where a hastily summoned Mrs Barker was immediately put to work removing the patina of collected dust. For the time being, access to the grounds beyond the immediate garden remained prohibited, crime scene tape in place, but with no further police presence deemed necessary now.

CHAPTER142

Bedside Vigils

At the bedside of her dying daughter, Mandy's mother sobbed into the soggy tissue held up to her eyes, her husband ineffectual in his support for his wife, tormented by his own grief and bitter regret for the way he had treated his daughter during her developing pregnancy.

Elsewhere, as her sister began the long fight back to recovery, Mary sat by *her* bedside, wondering for the umpteenth time that day why neither Ted nor the two boys had made any effort to be with Pam. She had long thought the family dysfunctional, and was apprehensive over the degree of controlling disinterest evinced by her brother-in-law. Mary hardly knew when she had first begun to feel anxious about her sister. If she were being honest with herself, she'd admit that she had never really taken to Ted, finding him overbearingly arrogant and deploring the supercilious disdain with which he regarded her and Geoff and their "little house". But he and Pam had been together for a lot of years. Surely that counted for something. So why wasn't he here with her now?

At that moment, Mary's speculation was interrupted as two doctors approached the bedside and the nurse caring for Pam suggested that Mary might like to go and have a coffee while her sister was being examined. Retreating to the visitors' suite, Mary took the opportunity to phone Geoff. She was amazed to learn that he was on his way and had the boy Robert with him. However pleased Mary felt that at least one of Pam's close family was coming to see her, she could not shake off the premonition that there was something terribly wrong in all of this.

None of it made any sense to her. She tried desperately to recall what she had been told, replaying the events of the last twenty-four hours. First there was the visit by the police. It had been such a shock, she had barely taken it in. All they seemed to be saying was that her sister had been hurt. In her own home. No, it wasn't an accident. She felt sure someone had told her that, let slip something about her being attacked. But they were being much more cagey about it here at the hospital, just repeating that she had sustained severe head injuries. For the life of her, Mary just did not know what to think.

Geoff, when he arrived, wasn't able to tell her very much more, only that the ashen-faced young Robert had appeared on their doorstep early that morning, seemingly wanting somewhere to stay. Mary glanced across at the boy, who had said nothing since his arrival at the visitors' suite with Geoff. Aware of his aunt's gaze upon him, Robert lifted his head and returned her stare. He had the eyes of a frightened animal caught in the headlights' glare. Instinctively, Mary moved towards him and took him in her arms. In that moment, Robert felt the tension easing from him as he collapsed sobbing in her embrace.

CHAPTER 143

Circularity

Several weeks had elapsed. Ted, suspended from duty whilst enquiries continued, had settled into a lazy routine. Forensic examination of his home completed, he had been allowed to return. With only himself to think of, he slept late into the morning and spent most of his afternoons watching sport on TV or round at his local. He made a point of visiting Pam every couple of days, keeping up the appearance of the caring husband, but he was finding it incredibly boring, so his visits grew progressively shorter. The immediate danger over, she had been moved from the ICU onto the neurological ward, where her gradual progress was being encouraged by a dedicated team of therapists.

Pam's sister Mary visited frequently and stayed a great deal longer, a fact that both irritated him and caused him some concern. He worried that the persona he had created for himself could be shattered by any intimacies about their life together which might be revealed by his wife or her sister. To add to his perturbation, there was the recurring image that haunted his dreams: a slight figure in surgical scrubs. Asian, he thought. Another bloody immigrant who should go back to where she belonged. Left to him, he'd deport the lot of them. Supercilious cow. How dare she question his motives? Peering intently at the bruises on Pam's arms instead of minding her own business and getting on with the job of patching the old girl up.

Families, he thought bitterly, were what held you up. Where once the presence of a pretty young wife by his side, and on his desk a photograph of his smiling toddler sons, had proclaimed his dependability, marking him out as a thoroughly normal, reliable man, one destined for promotion, he now saw them for what they were: a drag, sapping his aspirations, draining his finances, restricting his freedom, and condemning him to a lifetime of suburban servitude. What he would give to be shut of the lot of them. There was no affection there, no pride in their achievements. Why, he acknowledged, he barely knew his boys these days.

He saw very little of his elder son. Robert sometimes accompanied his aunt, and on the rare occasions that their visiting times coincided, Ted no longer felt that he knew how to relate to him, completely failing to understand the boy's decision to move in with her. Robert himself had been surprised by the strength of the unexpected welcome she had given him. In truth, he had found a warmth and genuine affection from her that had long been absent under his father's bullying regime. For her part, Mary was glad to have him there. It was something she could do for her sister. It was something Mary had wanted for a long time. Even Geoff had become reconciled to the idea; the boy was no trouble, and he could see how his wife was enjoying having him there.

Of Richard and his whereabouts, there was no clue. His father might have been concerned, but the investigating team assigned to the incident were even more anxious to locate the boy. His fingerprints had been left all over the cricket bat, unsurprisingly as it was his, but there was no obvious evidence of anyone else's having handled it. Elsewhere in the house there were no signs of anyone other than the immediate family members, apart from such minute traces from casual contact as could be found in any home, such as the odd hair (human or pet) brought in on an outdoor coat that had brushed against someone standing in close proximity on crowded public transport, random fragments of matter from such communal spaces as shops, offices, and work changing rooms, or traces of excrement on their shoes from a dog they did not own.

It was an unsavoury, unsettling truth that everything they had discovered so far pointed to Richard as being the perpetrator of the assault. That a boy could turn on his mother in such an act of appalling brutality beggared belief. Had he acted alone, suffering from some sort of mental breakdown, under the influence of mind-altering drugs. Or had his father been complicit or even compelled him to such an attack? Whatever the cause, Richard had to be their prime suspect. To have carried out such a frenzied attack, he was clearly profoundly disturbed. Whilst he remained at large, he continued to pose a threat, if not to others, then to himself, as the enormity of his actions must surely impinge upon his awareness at some point.

Furthermore, the large cache of extreme pornography found under his bed suggested an addiction beyond his years and a commercial opportunity amongst the criminal underclass, with whom the boy must surely be involved.

CHAPTER 144

Fast Forward

As she watched the girls at play—her beloved Cari, biddable and good-natured, ungrudgingly complying with the demands of her bossy, organising little sister—Karen was beset, not for the first time, by conflicting emotions. All those years of longing and disappointment, anticipation and anguish, had crystallised into something akin to a rogue memory as soon as she had set eyes upon her little Cari Moses, so much so that later, when the surprise conception and uneventful pregnancy occurred, she had felt quite removed from the reality of it all. Ben was delighted, seemingly emerging from the darkness and anxiety that had engulfed him ever since they had first found their water baby and Karen had so determinedly made her their own. Although it was more tangible in the early days, Ben's fear of discovery had never fully abated. He knew that he had been complicit in committing a crime: the child was a constant reminder of that. And although he had grown to love Cari, relishing her trust and the enthusiasm she showed for any of the things they did together, he never felt able to fully relax and enjoy the companionship she offered. He bought her toys and made her playthings, and had always provided well for her, but the constant anxiety he felt had tainted their relationship from the offset. Now, as the years of depression receded, Ben felt as though he had been offered a fresh start. Both sets of grandparents were equally pleased, with Karen's mother secretly harbouring the hope that this new child would deflect some of what she saw as Karen's obsessive, overprotective attitude towards Cari.

Karen herself felt conflicted. Surely this is what she had longed for.

All those years of trying and failing, hoping and despairing, and now, with her body behaving perfectly, with the new child in her arms, she had to admit that she had felt nothing. Nothing. No surge of delight, no instant bonding and devotion, just a slightly surprised air of having successfully accomplished a task. In truth, it was very much like the feeling she experienced when she finished a pile of ironing!

She had told no one, fearing they might attribute it to postnatal depression and dose her with pills or, worse still, put her in hospital. Instead, she had played along with the charade, feigning delight in her child, even suckling the infant, but still her detachment remained. Was it possible, she wondered, that all of her longing, every minute particle of her maternal yearning, had been so utterly satiated with her beloved infant Moses that there was nothing left for this other, unbidden child?

She had persevered with the deception throughout the pregnancy, evincing surprise whenever a perceptive midwife questioned her a little too intently about that earlier birth. They may have had their suspicions, but Karen was in no mood to satisfy their curiosity. It had helped that she seldom saw the same midwife at any of her antenatal checks, and even during the birth itself she had been attended by several different midwives again, fleeting appearances recording her vital signs and the progress of her labour right up to her transfer to the delivery suite. The labour had been slow, slower than they would have expected with a "second" child, but she had given nothing away—neither she nor her body—enduring the undignified invasive examination and maintaining her innocence throughout. But it was hard. She found the continued deception difficult to sustain, so much more than the deception surrounding Cari's "birth". She recalled how she had lied to the health visitor, the registrar, and her family and friends, and how easily it had come to her then. There was so much at stake at the time, so much to lose. The thought of life without Cari, then or now, was too awful to contemplate. And while, as long as she had the child, that threat persisted, there was no such fear where the new baby was concerned. This child was rightfully theirs, a part of her and Ben, something they had planned for and longed for throughout the years of miscarriage and misery, and latterly a stab at the reconciliation they sought within their failing marriage. Yet she felt nothing, no surge of maternal recognition, no overwhelming sense of love and bonding. She had felt more than this when they collected the new puppy, a present for Cari's seventh birthday. It was as though she had used up all her allotted share of maternal emotion when they brought Cari into their lives. This new baby was the alien. That was Karen's guilty secret now.

Nine years had passed since their momentous find on the dismal deserted waterway. Their girls were growing up. Nothing had altered in the way Karen felt. She had tried hard to engage with her younger daughter but had never experienced with her the intensity of love that she had for Cari. It was with limited success that Karen had striven to conceal this from Ben, their families, and the little girls themselves, but scratch the surface and it was clear which child was the favoured one: the child she loved to distraction, the child for whom she lived. And that was why this latest intervention was so unsettling. She had not registered at first that this was anything more than a routine call—enquiries about a traffic accident or a charity collection for the police ball perhaps. But then the questions had started, questions she and Ben had been asked before in those early days when the lies had come more easily, practised and rehearsed, glibly on her part, with Ben's responses always more cautious and measured. They had believed her then, but this time she was less sure.

CHAPTER 145

Cari

All her life she had hated water. Memories surged of the family holidays and her seemingly irrational fear induced by those days on the beach, her mother and Megan wriggling into their bathing suits, racing each other to the water's edge, splashing in the waves, begging her at least to tuck her dress in her knickers and have a paddle or get her bikini wet for a change. She recalled her relief at the days spent inland, the new motorhome and the false expectations aroused by their first touring holiday spent amongst the mountains in Scotland. All those lochs—and not satisfied with admiring them from the safety of the camper van, her father's insistence that they should get out and *enjoy* a walk. Too well she remembered her abject terror as they circuited Loch Etive, the tiny narrow path little more than an animal track gouged into the side of the unremitting grey granite cliff, its claustrophobic proximity rising steeply above them with its sheer drop to the menacing black water below. She had clung onto her father's hand throughout, not daring to look down, as they stumbled their way single file on this walk which seemed to go on forever, screaming as her feet dislodged a pebble, sending it hurtling down the rock face until it splashed into the darkly glistening loch, who knew how many metres below.

She had never learnt to swim, envying Megan's agility in and out of the water, content to cheer her on from the spectators' bench as the younger child cut through the water to gain yet another medal for her team. But as much as Cari hated the water, it held a horrible fascination for her, drawing her reluctant gaze away from the safety of the land into the eddies and swirls. She loved the cascading curtains of the waterfall, the silent drip of rainwater from the trees into the pool below, the rush of the incoming tide surging along the river Severn, and the crashing breakers engulfing the rotting groins on some deserted beach. As her world as she had known it began to implode around her and the dark thoughts intensified, she did not know whether it was solace or affirmation she sought. She only knew in that moment such an affinity with this destructive force of nature that she wanted nothing more than to be a part of it, to lose herself forever in the swirling waters below.

CHAPTER 146

Crime Time Resumed

Ted, fuming at the imposed inactivity, was almost relieved to receive the call summoning him to the major general's home. That the major general invariably wanted something amounting to a favour didn't even rankle with Ted this time. He was grateful for the interruption to what had become his daily routine. Ted was no fool. He knew that their friendship, such as it was, involved only slightly more than a mutual exchange of benefits, but he was happy with that. Never a demonstrative man, Ted enjoyed the masculine solidarity embodied in their relationship and the insights it afforded him into a coveted lifestyle of luxury and affluence. Little was he to know, as he set off that morning to see his friend, of the momentous discovery to be made and just how the day would unfold.

The major general, for his part, had spent a restless morning pacing the corridor alongside his study, pausing now and then to adjust the heavily embossed picture frames lining the walls, irritated by the gaps where some of the paintings had been removed. Here was displayed a range of work, mostly in oils, depicting an array of subjects, portraits, and landscapes. He had a few small watercolours and a particularly striking monochrome pastel of a young woman confronting a ferocious leopard. The entire collection appeared to have been deliberately selected to form an interesting backdrop against the long expanse of white wall, the sturdy ornate gilt frames forming a geometric structure which mirrored the windows and architraves in the great dining hall beyond.

His reverie interrupted by the insistent ringing of the doorbell, the major general struggled to comprehend why it was not being answered.

Shaking off his preoccupation, he remembered why the house was unusually empty. Not wanting her around whilst he dealt with the most pressing issues with which he had to contend, he had given Mrs Barker the day off, "as a gesture of appreciation" for all her hard work in removing the dust and debris that had accumulated throughout the house during their imposed absence when it was being treated as a possible crime scene. With Leonie already safely in town, there was no one there to witness what he was about to do. Alert now, his senses taut with foreboding, he strode smartly back along the corridor and, taking the steps two at a time, almost bounded down the curved staircase to the hall below, and opened the door.

CHAPTER 147

Richard

Unlikely as it seemed, Richard was missing home. It had only taken him a few days to come to the depressing realisation that he was happier on his home turf. Not that he was yearning for the comforts of family life. He felt no nostalgia there. Home had long ceased to mean anything more to him than a place to stay, a base, somewhere he could stash his possessions, grab the odd meal, and return from his nefarious activities to sleep undisturbed in his own bed. Relationships within his immediate family no longer held any sort of meaning for him. He had barely registered his mother's presence throughout the last few years, seeing less and less of her as he followed his own pursuits, glad only that she had a job with irregular shift work and one which frequently seemed to preoccupy much of her thoughts even when she was off duty. His brother he dismissed as being weak and unintelligent, only useful to him as a stooge and occasional provider of a dishonest alibi. Growing up, Richard had both hated and feared his father, and now had begun to despise him too, sensing that beneath the bullying aggressive exterior the man was not as strong as he would like to appear. Richard divined in his father that same fateful flaw which was to lead to his own downfall: the insatiable desire for more and a ruthless determination to sweep aside anyone who stood in the way of achieving that objective.

It was the practicalities within his home terrain that had drawn him back like a magnet, returning to the streets he knew and the network there where he had a purpose and which had paid him well. He pushed aside the uncomfortable memories of the past few nights: selling his body in return for bed and food, one rent boy among many in the grimy subculture of an alien city. He had got by—just—but it was not as easy as he had anticipated. Far from relaxing in the anonymity he had hoped this would have afforded him, he had begun to realise that each fresh encounter brought with it the danger of exposure. Whilst the initial nature of such contacts entailed a mutual degree of secrecy, it was equally likely that the presence of a new face on the block might arouse unwelcome curiosity. That this might (and did) begin to escalate amongst his rivals for existing trade had made Richard all too aware of the difficulties he faced in avoiding the more vicious of his competitors. He did not have their knowledge of the safe places to hide or of where a revenge attack could occur unnoticed and unremarked. It was one such sobering encounter on only the third night of business which had weakened Richard's resolve to start a new life in a different city. At first light he had left his "benefactor's" bed and crept through the silent streets, boarding the first train back home. Little did he know that by far the more immediate danger awaited him there.

CHAPTER 148

Confrontations

It was not what he had been expecting. Opening the door, anticipating the solution to one of his more pressing problems, mentally rehearsing how the projected meeting would unfold, how he would use his acquaintance and get the result he needed, the major general was totally unprepared for the sight before him. It was not the stolid figure of Ted Manning which confronted him but the wiry frame of the young boy he had used as a messenger in some of his illicit transactions. Except there was something different about the boy. Gone was the dapper and well-groomed appearance and the self-confident, almost supercilious manner which had struck such a chord with the older man, his recognising amongst those traits the wily intelligence and a certain single-mindedness which in his eyes denoted definite officer material. The boy had potential, and the major general had known how to exploit it.

But the figure that confronted him now had lost something of the brash exterior, his demeanour somehow more used, more worldly wise. The old soldier recognised the signs. He had seen it often before with troops returning from the battle zone, a lifetime of experiences crammed into a mere few months, days even, the men marked by war, not beaten by it, their resilience shown in their bearing—the better soldiers for it.

The boy should not be here now. He had been expressly told never to come to the house unless he had been sent for. The major general did not want him to bump into Leonie or Mrs B. The less they knew about his business, the better. He was about to reprimand the boy and send him on his way, when the security light flickered, heralding the arrival of his intended guest. He could hear it now, the purr of an engine, gradually increasing in volume as the approaching vehicle rounded the bend in the lane, hesitating long enough for someone to operate the keypad which opened the electric gate to his driveway. A few seconds more and the boy would be seen.

Stepping in front of him to avoid any possibility of this happening, the major general pushed the unprotesting youth into the hall and through the first set of double doors. "Stay here until I come for you," he hissed, closing the doors behind him, before regaining his stance on the front step just as the large black car pulled in alongside.

The scene that was to follow was bizarre. It was only afterwards, when he had time to reflect upon the day's happenings, that the major general realised the complexity of it all: confrontation and retreat, coincidence, timing, crisis management, strategy—all the components of the battleground, the theatre of war played out in his own home, and himself no more than a prisoner of war at the end of it all.

Richard, meantime, had begun to take stock of his situation, dismissing his first, primal instinct to escape, to avoid captivity, to open the doors and creep out of the house as silently as he had arrived. Only the thought of this continued hand-to-mouth existence deterred him. He had come this far; he was not going to leave empty-handed. He would wait and see the major general as he had planned. Meanwhile, he would use this unexpected opportunity to make some discoveries of his own. Prior visits to the manor had seen him ushered unceremoniously into a small downstairs room at the back of the house, walls lined with various shooting prints, a built-in cupboard the length of the room, its doors propped slightly ajar, the contents tweed and Barbour, and always the permeating odour of damp waterproofs. This was his chance to find out more about his sometime employer. You just never knew when such inside knowledge might come in useful!

The large sitting room he now found himself in hosted a continuation of the shooting theme. Cumbersome leather armchairs flanked an open fireplace, with huge sagging sofas and robust coffee tables scattered throughout the rest of the room. A larger table against one wall held an impressive array of decanters, the glass-fronted cupboard above well stocked with cut-glass tumblers, tankards, and wine glasses. In one corner of the room stood a floor-to-ceiling wine rack, and in the other, a handsome longcase clock. Doors at the far end of the room opened upon the most opulent dining room Richard had ever seen. A long, deeply polished dark wood table, each leg terminating in a gilded claw, held a magnificent silver and gilt centrepiece. On either end of the mantelshelf over the ornate marble fireplace stood huge silver candlesticks, and above the shelf hung an imposing portrait of a formidably elegant woman. Three large arched windows on the opposite wall opened onto a paved patio and the lawn and gardens beyond.

Hearing muffled footsteps somewhere above his head, Richard quickly and quietly made his way back to the room where he had been told to wait, but not before he had mentally logged this as a possible escape (and perhaps even a potential reentry) route.

Meanwhile, elsewhere in the house, the meeting with Ted had not gone entirely as the major general had planned. The police officer, acutely aware of the suspicion under which he was currently held, had seemed to be reluctant to do the other man's bidding, agreeing only to provide the necessary authentication for the confiscated weapons, whilst urging the major general once he had secured their release to utilise his gun cabinets and keep them out of sight. About the paintings, he had been less obliging, feigning an ignorance of the proof required to establish them as legitimate acquisitions by the major general. As to the probable whereabouts of those the police had removed for further scrutiny, Ted had been even more evasive. The major general had wanted him to use his authority to intercept their intended progress to the relevant experts and effect their return to the manor, where they too would be locked away until the inevitable frenzy concerning their theft from police custody died down. Reminding the major general of the compromising nature of his current suspension, Ted offered only to make some discreet enquiries on his behalf. Thinking this settled the matter of the paintings for the time being, Ted was prepared to leave, when the major general beckoned him into the corridor.

It was only when the major general quietly removed the first painting from the wall, his fingers nimbly unscrewing the metal fixings then turning the heavy frame round to reveal a second picture behind, that Ted began to realise the enormity of what he was being asked to do and the size of the reward he might command. This put a whole new complexion upon the situation. Ted had only a hazy recollection of the sort of money that might be involved, remembering his disbelief at the cited millions and the force's inability to penetrate the criminal underworld and discover the whereabouts of the stolen masterpieces. And here they were all the time, the major general indicating that this painting was not the only carefully concealed gem in his gallery, hidden from view in the house Ted had visited countless times before and which had been rigorously searched as a possible crime scene.

Ted needed time to think about this, to work out how best to profit from it. If he played his cards correctly, the falsified bills of sale he had somehow to procure for each of these "realistic copies" of famous missing artwork were going to cost the major general a sum the size of Ted's pension several times over. What if at a later stage the major general needed "proof" of provenance; could Ted arrange that too? Suddenly suspension from the force didn't seem too bleak an outlook after all.

Business concluded for the moment, the two men made their way down the stairs and out onto the front porch. Hearing what was unmistakably his father's voice, Richard froze to the spot. He had no idea that he and the major general knew each other. He was going to have to tread very carefully indeed.

CHAPTER 149

The Man

Wiping his blade with elaborate care, the man allowed himself a moment or two of self-congratulation. Standing back to admire the symmetry of his latest creation, he allowed himself a smile of satisfaction. He had been studiously unhurried, clinical in its execution (how he loved that word, savouring again all its most personal connotations). The act was a fulfilment, the culmination of a cycle First there had to be the desire, a coursing in his veins, an accelerating crescendo as he selected and stalked his victim, the heightened anticipation as he sought the ideal location, and then always the procedure to be followed, deviation not tolerated—for that way disaster lay.

Thinking about it now, he could feel the stiffening beginning, so slow, so measured …building, building, growing, hardening, until ejaculating over the tiny body, so tastefully arranged across its mother's naked breast. Wiping himself clean now, emptied, replete, the man took one last lingering look at the tableau he had created before retracing his steps across the springy turf, over the footbridge to where he had parked his van.

CHAPTER 150

Steve

It felt as though he were emerging from some sort of frozen state, a state of permanent darkness where he had felt the loss of Abigail like the loss of a part of himself. He had no sense of purpose then other than to grieve, always asking why. Swimming in a current of uncertainty, swimming against the tide, feeling himself sucked in, he was submerged, totally engulfed in the sickly cloying blackness that was his life without her.

It had not helped that his in-laws, beside themselves with grief and anger, blamed the dreadful sequence of events upon what they saw as Steve's disreputable lifestyle and his inability to provide the luxuries their daughter had been brought up to expect. It seemed inconceivable to them that anyone from their family should have resorted to national healthcare. Had Abigail been looked after in the most expensive private facility that money could buy, then surely none of this would have happened. Their daughter deserved better. They had never accepted Steve, convinced that he had exerted an unhealthy, Svengali-like influence over her, dragging her into a world of poverty and deprivation they despised. So there had been no mutual compassion, no shared moments of remembrance recalling precious memories of happier times. They had gone their separate ways, her parents leaving Steve to grieve alone, abandoned in his shrunken world of sorrow and incomprehension.

Police intervention then had been an unwelcome interruption, only barely impinging upon his utter desolation. He had resented their intrusion, the endlessly repeated questions, their ill-concealed suspicion, and their grudging release back to his lonely fractured world. It didn't even matter to him then whether they caught the man responsible or not. Nothing could bring Abigail back. Steve wasn't even sure that he wanted to see the man punished for his crime. It was as though the profundity of his grief had sapped any desire for retribution. He simply could not muster the strength to inflame hatred.

It was only now, gradually emerging from the quagmire that had enveloped him, that Steve realised what it was he wanted.

CHAPTER 151

Cari—Truths Half Heard

"How?" she asked herself repeatedly, clutching the bedclothes to her chin, staring unseeingly into the blackness beyond, faint patterns forming in the dull half-light as the moon emerged from behind the clouds, the bedroom window open, light summer curtains billowing in the breeze, as the 1970s Artex was momentarily lit by the pale glow in the sky. And still Cari stared, gazing up at the ceiling, aware now of the faintest sound, the distant calling of an owl and somewhere out there, ignorant of its impending fate, its hapless prey. She knew that feeling well. She could identify with it.

Then came another sound, nearer this time, familiar, the same sound that accompanied all her wakefulness. It was the rhythmic contented sound of her sister's breathing, relaxed in slumber, the regular peaceful sleep of an untroubled mind. Cari envied her that, just as she envied her confidence, the younger child blissfully unaware of the night terrors that gripped her sister, only guessing something of the insecurity that had been such a factor in their, her, choice of sleeping arrangements. "No," Cari had protested, when they moved to the bigger house and the girls were each offered a bedroom of their own. Thinking about it now, Cari wondered if it had been mean of her to override her sister and insist that they should continue to share a bedroom just as they always had. Perhaps Megan would have liked to have her own room, but she was an accommodating child. When, as a sweetener, Cari had given her the choice of where to put her bed, Megan did not proffer much in the way of resistance.

That was something else that Cari envied: her sister's calm acceptance of everything that life offered. No, not acceptance, what she displayed was more akin to delight in whatever the circumstances might have been. She wasa thoroughly uncritical child, content and so sure of herself. Yet surely she must have been aware of their mother's ambivalence towards her—mostly indifference, occasionally tempered by an overt display of affection, always, Cari had noticed, when that affection included both of them, Karen proudly declaring that her girls were certain to set the world on fire. Most of the time Karen barely seemed to notice Megan, but when she did, her attitude was likely to be one of disapproval. Despite providing for the child's physical needs, ensuring that she ate well and had the new clothes and shoes she needed, Karen was definitely stricter with her, seldom smiling—and when she did, Cari noticed that the smiles never really reached her eyes. And while Cari could do no wrong, far from relishing her mother's favouritism, she had begun to find it stultifying in its intensity. She almost yearned for the state of apparent anonymity her sister enjoyed, whilst marvelling at the little girl's complete lack of resentment towards her.

Cari's grip on the sheet had begun to relax, her eyes heavy with tiredness now, eyelids fluttering at last as sleep beckoned. Again, in that fitful state neither fully awake nor yet asleep, came that familiar tightening of her chest, almost a paralysis of her limbs, as her nightly terror approached. Then it was crashing, hurtling around her, that awful rushing in her ears. Forcing her head down into her pillows in a futile attempt to drown out the inevitable noise, she heard it as a distant drumming, closer now, the floodgates open. Water. Always it was water, pouring down around her now, threatening to take her with it, her frozen body unable to resist. She opened her mouth to scream for help, knowing that nothing would emerge, her cries stifled by terror and the double jeopardy of an unwillingness, even in her distress, to have her mother fussing over her.

She was wide awake again now, trembling in fear and relief as the moment passed, knowing now for certain that sleep would not come that night. Her vigil with the moon and darkness would last until dawn. Comforted now as she was every night by the sound of her sister's breathing, Cari settled back under the bedclothes and thought back to that earlier eventful day.

She had come in from the garden, where she and Megan had been playing, to fetch them both a drink. Overhearing the unmistakable sound of her father's voice raised in anger, Cari had been curious. Usually very quiet and reserved, he must have really been upset by something to be shouting like that. The sounds came from her parents' bedroom. She couldn't make out the words, but surely that was him, sobbing now. Creeping quietly to the door, she pushed it open and listened at the bottom of the stairs. Always a sensitive child, Cari had not failed to notice a growing tension between her parents, and while she had never been particularly inquisitive, this had caused her some concern and she wished she knew what she could do about it. Now, her ears straining to catch the conversation above, she was startled to hear her own name. "Cari, our Cari. She's mine, Ben. I was meant to have her." His voice was almost unrecognisable now, throaty and broken amongst the sobs: "We have to tell her, Karen."

At this, the child fled, her legs trembling as she stumbled back through the kitchen and out into the yard beyond, all thoughts of a drink forgotten as she heard the conversation played again and again, round and round in her mind. It could only mean one thing: her parents were splitting up and she was to stay with their mother, while presumably Megan would live with their father.

"Hey, Sis, what kept you? Where's my Fruit Shoot?" Megan's voice brought Cari back to reality, and with this came all the weight of responsibility conferred unwillingly by her position in the family as the elder of the two siblings. What should she tell her sister? Looking at her now, carefree and light-hearted, relishing the sunshine and the long hot days of the summer holiday ahead, Cari knew that, for the time being at least, the awful secret would have to be hers alone.

Now, as she lay awake, as she did every night, Cari wrestled again with the awful burden she could not share. As the days had passed with no further indication from either of her parents that they were going to tell her anything of their plans, Cari had determined to find out for herself. She watched them intently, listening to every exchange, noting their body language and sensing the undeniable friction between them. Secretive, sly now, she crept around the house, lingering on the stairs, listening outside their bedroom door, hoping to hear something—anything—that would inform her of their plans. She sensed that she was central to it but could think of no reason why. But always in the whispering fierce exchanges behind closed doors it was her name, never Megan's, that she heard.

Once she heard her mother's hysterical repetition: "Cari, Cari Moses. Oh, my Cari …"

And her father, firm now, authoritative: "But if the police find out, they'll take her from us." Why? What had she done? What were they talking about?

As the days progressed, she had sensed a moving on. Seemingly there was more involved than just dividing up the household. True, her mother's hysterical outbursts were the same—"Cari, my Cari …"—but her father was calmer now, his voice subdued, his responses measured. Until tonight and the latest frightening development. Long after the girls had been sent to bed, Cari had heard them at it again. Slipping quietly from her bed and tiptoeing past her sleeping sister, she had stood shivering in her flimsy nightdress, ears to the door of her parents' bedroom. It was then that she heard it.

"She's not ours, Karen. Never has been. We had no right to keep her. For all we know, she could have a whole family out there, people she *really* belongs to. It's only a matter of time before someone finds out, puts two and two together. The police have been sniffing around again."

"But *we're* her family, Ben—always have been."

It was then that Cari heard a different nuance in her father's voice, insistent and coldly dispassionate now. "If—no, *when*—the police find out, there will be *no* family. You and I will be sent to prison for God only knows how long. The girls will be split up, and while your mum or mine would probably take Megan, Cari will go into care while they try to trace her real relatives. This is the end of the road for us, Karen. No more playing happy family. We've been living a lie ever since we found her. I for one am sick of it, *all* of it: you and your cosseting, your endless fussing over Cari, Megan and I always on the sidelines. This is going to tear us apart, and in a way, I'm almost glad of that. For me, there'll be no going back to how it was before. You and I are finished, Karen."

Stifling her sobs, fingers in her ears, not wishing to hear any more, stumbling, distraught, Cari made her way back to bed and the temporary sanctuary it afforded. Glad now of the wakefulness and the time it left her before having to start the day, she felt herself possessed by a strange calculating calmness. As the enormity of what she had overheard began to impinge, Cari considered the options open to her. Amongst all the uncertainty, there was one indisputable factor: she, and she alone, was the cause of the impending disintegration. And as surely as she was the cause, she had to be the solution. Now that she thought about it, it seemed clear enough. There was a certain ambivalence here. With a clarity beyond her years, Cari discarded all but one of the options before her. Yet it was with the naivety of youth that she thought her decision would solve everything.

CHAPTER 152

Karen

Karen was distraught. Her world had imploded. Everything Ben had said was true. They had been living a lie; she could acknowledge that now. But what she could never accept was any thought that Cari did not belong to her. God knows she had gone through so much before this greatest gift of all had come into their lives. It had been intended from the start.

Without Cari, Karen's life meant nothing. Ben had long ceased to matter to her. Megan meant less, having always seemed an intruder. Karen's life had been perfect without her. It would never be perfect again. Without Cari she could not go on.

Gradually, the turmoil of the preceding night receded, only to be replaced by a forced normality as mechanically, robotically, Karen performed the morning chores: calling the girls and ensuring school bags were packed, their homework found, and their lunch boxes fetched from the fridge where she had put them the evening before—the evening before her whole world fell apart. But no, she mustn't think of that now. There was still the morning ritual to complete. Waving the girls off with an even longer embrace than usual, Karen returned to the kitchen and her plans for the day ahead.

Dispassionately watching as Ben poured milk over his cereal, his hand shaking as he lifted the spoon, she waited for him to gather his things, not speaking. She was slyly observing as he dabbed his eyes, blew his nose hard, and stuffed a handful of tissues into his pocket. All the while Ben was suppressing the urge to take her in his arms and tell her it was all a mistake, that they were in it together and that together they would see it through. All Karen could see was Ben's weakness and how she despised him for it. How could she ever have loved him? There was only one true love in her life, and she had just seen her go. The last time, thought Karen. I won't be around to have her torn from me.

CHAPTER 153

Sandy

Sandy wondered for at least the twentieth time that morning if it had all been worth it. In a moment of madness she had surrendered all she had worked for, all that mattered in her life. She seldom thought of Helen these days, preoccupied as she was with the unfolding disaster she had brought upon herself, but it was with a pang of regret that she realised how much she missed having her beside her now—someone to confide in, someone she could trust implicitly to share the multiple anxieties that beset her every waking moment. Theirs had been a good relationship, Sandy acknowledged that now, but in the same spirit of honesty, she had to admit that, even at its zenith, what she had with Helen occupied second place in her life. First and foremost, there had always been her work. Despite the daily niggles and the petty irritations, it was her life. What if she had been allocated more than her fair share of domestics? She had been part of a greater enterprise. It was all she had ever wanted to do, to join the police force. She had met and overcome so much opposition to achieve her dream job. And what did she do? Just as she was fully integrated, accepted for what she was, and valued for what she could contribute, she had tossed it aside in a fit of pique.

She should have taken their criticism in her stride (it was deserved, after all). She *had* been lackadaisical in her approach to paperwork—well, any administrative details really. Her timekeeping wasn't always the greatest, her witticisms and rejoinders not universally appreciated. But these were the minor details, part of her personality or else flaws that could have been addressed, hardly sackable misdemeanours. Her single indictable offence, the one thing that had determined her fate, was her involvement with Leckie.

The constant visits to the girl's bedside, initially attributed to no more than a conscientious sense of duty and an overenthusiastic determination to pursue the accepted line of enquiry, had begun to attract the attention of her senior officers. They only knew the half of it, thought Sandy, aware that many of her off-duty visits had been deliberately kept under the radar. In fact, they had been about to caution her on the grounds of unprofessionalism before her final incredible debacle.

She had blatantly ignored existing protocol in forming what was seen as an incriminating relationship with a victim and possibly a suspect of crime. She had flaunted this openly by moving the girl in with her. At no point had she consulted with them or confided her intentions with any of her colleagues, nor sought to address the implications in relation to not one but several current major investigations.

Summoned before them, she had been unrepentant, challenging the allegations about her work and defiant in her insistence that her private life was her own concern. Sensing the furore about to explode, she had submitted her resignation, hoping at least to avoid the ignominy of being dismissed from the force.

Now, her life in tatters, for the first time in a long time, Sandy's future looked bleak. She had lost all hope of redeeming herself in the eyes of her superiors. She had no job, no income, no partner, not even a reluctant lodger. There had never been any possibility of a relationship there, she saw that now. She had not even succeeded in what had once been her primary intent: discovering what the girl Leckie knew about the disappearance of Abigail's daughter. What *was* the significance of that little pink blanket in Leckie's rucksack?

Well, there was no point in brooding about that now. What she had to do was to get her life back on track: find a focus and shake herself out of this apathetic self-recrimination. Looking about her now, she was seeking inspiration, seeing the familiar furniture, the cushions piled to one end of the settee, the TV set on stand-by, last night's whisky glass on the little side table, the big table strewn with unopened mail, and the fruit bowl empty save for a couple of rather tired oranges, their wrinkled, withered peel a denominator of the time she had lived in purposeless limbo—this, she realised, is what mattered. Somehow she had to ensure that she could keep her home. Glancing out of the window, she saw her car—mobility, independence. These were the things that counted—attributes of stability and permanence.

Sandy knew what she had to do. Thankful now that she had resisted the impulse to put the house in both her and Helen's names, she acknowledged that repaying the mortgage was her single greatest expense. The direct debit was taken out of her account every month. Until now, this had never been a problem: salary in, mortgage out. The same with her car, but then there were all the associated expenses: insurance (both house and car), council tax …Sandy had only a vague idea of how many other direct debits there were. It had been so easy to order things online, in idle moments, sitting out a dreary surveillance, scrolling the internet on her phone. As for household expenses, any record of these had been Helen's province; Sandy barely knew what regular outgoings there were.

Grateful now, as never before, for Helen's meticulous attention to detail, Sandy scrutinised the box of neatly labelled files: heating, electricity, water, landline telephone and internet, and regular subscriptions. Alongside that was a box labelled "Household equipment, instructions, and guarantees". Staggered that their modest lifestyle could generate quite so much detail, Sandy sensed the familiar fog beginning to cloud her mind. How much of this did she need to know, and where on earth should she start? She knew that they had shared the household expenses, and as she did her banking online, she was vaguely familiar with the regular payments *she* made each month and the hieroglyphs which accompanied them, although they barely registered, as all Sandy really bothered with was the amount left in her current account and how much she could afford to pay off on her credit cards. Thankfully, most of the outgoings had been established in Sandy's name. Throughout their time together, she had contributed her share by bank transfer to Helen's account, but there were a few items which had been Helen's choice and paid for solely by her. Sandy would have to contact the firms concerned and get the payments transferred. Heaven knows how many of their joint commitments had been addressed in the months since Helen left. She supposed that some of the accumulated mail might contain forceful reminders of this, but opening all of that and dealing with whatever horrors it might contain was a hurdle too high at the moment.

No, she would contact the firms she knew about first and deal them. But before that she needed a drink to clear her head. A strong coffee would do it—and a splash of whisky in it. Why not?

Suitably fortified, Sandy rang the first of the firms, that of the quality sound system they had had installed at Helen's instigation, only to discover that Helen had beaten her to it and paid off the remaining debt in full. It was the same with the maintenance contract on their new washing machine and the outstanding balance on the petrol mower. There was nothing more Sandy had to do. Helen had seen to it all. At that realisation, Sandy felt an overwhelming sense of loss and, much to Monty's bemusement, sat on the floor, buried her head in the cushions, and howled.

CHAPTER 54

Months to Years

Months. That is what he had predicted. It would take him months to assiduously compile a new manual. Much as he longed to devote himself to this task with complete singularity of purpose, the rest of life intervened. Not just the rest of life, but a new life. His money would not last forever. Despite years of living frugally, he had encountered significant additional expenditure. There were the necessary wheels: a new (to him) van, another motorbike and the leathers involved, fresh accommodation that would necessitate a down payment, and materials to customise his van. The list seemed endless.

Months. More than two years later, he now looked back ruefully at that optimistic prediction. He was still light years away from completing his task. Finding work in a new neighbourhood had been far more time-consuming than he had anticipated; just forging the necessary documentation had been difficult. He only managed a little at a time as he moved between different guest houses and hostels in the area.

Even with his having secured a job and somewhere eminently suitable to live, the sheer logistics of the challenge confronting him was immense: not only must he complete his manual to his own exacting standards, but he had to find the time to do it. It was not something he could just pick up for the odd hour or two. He needed long uninterrupted periods when he could completely concentrate. So much was recollection as he meticulously logged the details of all his previous murders. Well, not quite *all*—only the ones that fit the criteria for his hobby. This had to be a record of success. There was no way he was going to include the damned woman with the kid. Sneaky bitch, taking him in like that, and all the time a bloody baby in her shopping bag.

He hesitated too about including Mandy in his records, but decided that she fit the criteria he had created for the selection of his "subjects". And up to the time of the fire, the exercise had been a success.

Months. Recreating his manual was not the only thing which was taking so much longer to complete than he'd counted on. Although he had selected an area that he knew in which to pursue his hobby, he had rapidly come to the conclusion that his knowledge was outdated. There had been significant changes over the years since he last spent any considerable time here: country lanes had become subsumed under layers of suburban development, quiet byways had been extended, and the number of roundabouts and one-way systems had increased exponentially.

It had taken him many months to refamiliarise himself with the terrain to the point where he felt confident to resume his stalking activities. It was during this time, almost two years after moving here, that disaster struck. He had been out reconnoitring a stretch of disused canal, a subsidiary branch long since abandoned and completely unnavigable, and became aware of a sudden searing pain in his ankle. Stifling a scream, he parted the undergrowth to discover that he had been caught in a trap which, although illegal, was still widely in use by less than scrupulous landowners and gamekeepers. The return journey was excruciatingly painful; the time until full recovery, tediously slow.

It had also taken much longer than he had anticipated to reconstruct his manual. He had taken pride in it though—and had learnt from last time. *This* time he was going to be even better organised. It had started with the room. He was far more selective in his choice of digs. Rather than settling for the first thing he saw, he had taken his time, staying in cheap B&Bs while he looked around, a different one each night, always paid for in cash, providing a different name each time, not the one he was using for his accommodation now and the one he was using for work.

He knew immediately when he had found it: a large Victorian house with three floors, each one a separate apartment, the two above him both occupied, a young couple in each, all four out at work during the day, and no prying children or noisy dogs who might register his unusual comings and goings. Even better, there was an absentee landlord, his agent disinterested, accepting the deposit and a month's rent in advance, another cash transaction, nothing that could be traced back to him.

His was to be the ground-floor apartment, accessed from a communal hall with only two doors leading from it, one to his apartment and the other to a garden of sorts at the rear of the house. The garden door was locked and firmly bolted, a thick curtain of cobwebs attesting to the fact that it had not been used for some considerable time. And that is how it would stay, he thought. There were ways to circumvent that.

The flat had only recently been vacated. He was lucky to have found it. Housing was cheaper here, and it was a great improvement on his previous lodgings, with a large sitting room, a smaller bedroom, a kitchenette, and a bathroom. The furniture was shabby now but of good quality; he guessed it was mostly the original stuff that came with the house. A sturdy gateleg table gave ample room for his immediate task, namely the rewriting of his instruction manual, and would serve well for the craft activities associated with his hobby, concocting the signage and maintaining his instruments. A hefty sideboard provided ample storage space for these and the various ropes and gags he needed. One of his first tasks was to fit a padlock to this.

A pair of French windows opened out onto the garden—an absolute bonus in providing him with an alternative entrance and exit. He would wait until the people upstairs were out at work and then steal into their rooms (with his background, Yale locks were no deterrent) and familiarise himself with the layout of the house. One never knew when such knowledge would be useful. He wanted to ascertain how much the occupants would be able to see should he use the French windows to get in and out of his apartment.

Satisfied that they would be able to see very little, their bathrooms having been sited in the rooms immediately overlooking the garden, each having only a very small frosted glass window, he realised that the configuration of the rooms was different on these upper floors, with the sitting room overlooking the street at the front of the house and with the kitchens and bedrooms to the side. In the ceiling of the third floor, immediately over the stairwell, was a hatch cover, dusty with age, indicating further useful possibilities.

Happy with his reconnaissance, the man returned to his room and began to list the things he needed to acquire. While a shed at the back of the house could accommodate his new motorbike, he needed to find a garage to let where he could store the replacement van, the ideal vehicle for his pursuits. Thankful that he had always been a thrifty man, he had been able (just) to finance this reinvention of himself. A few more purchases were necessary, and then he must take up the driving job he had found, collecting and delivering sanitary products to businesses across the city. He had purchased a large lever arch file and, unable to resist the lure of fresh material, additional paper, content dividers, and a further selection of pens, telling the unnecessarily inquisitive assistant that he had just been accepted onto a course at night school. Next he sourced the padlock he required from an ironmongers and a couple of strongboxes from a security firm in which to secrete his new manual and the surgical instruments which would be stored inside the sideboard, spreading his purchases to reduce the likelihood of their being remembered as anything significant. He found a shop selling artist and craft supplies, making a mental note of its whereabouts. He would be able to get what he needed here to make the signage for his van, but that would come later. First he had to reconstruct his manual, and he really needed to start work before his money ran out. He fingered the remaining notes in his wallet, those he had intended as payment for the man he had charged with removing the person who represented a link with his past and a possible threat to his future, and wondered if it would be safe to use them yet, realising with a start that not only did they still smell very faintly of smoke but also that he had inadvertently spent some of them already. It must have been when the shop assistant was being so persistent in her enquiries, or perhaps when he had paid the letting agent. There was no point in worrying about that now, but his carelessness in letting it happen rankled. Above all, his new life demanded perfection.

<hr />

It had taken well over another year in the making as he painstakingly relived and documented every aspect of his "case studies" so far, drawing out the details and devising his new matrix, the essential features upon which to base his selection process. He was a patient man—prison eventually had taught him that—but he was becoming apprehensive that his skills might have diminished over such a long period of inactivity. He had to put it to the test—a trial run to ensure that nothing had been overlooked in this new approach to his venture.

The first victim fulfilled every aspect of his criteria. She was young, apparently single, and living alone in a downtown apartment block. She worked regular hours, evening and early morning, cleaning in an office block on his rota for deliveries. She was a pretty girl, a good six months gone he guessed, and carried her pregnancy proudly, *flaunting it,* he thought. She seemed to have few friends and little social life apart from occasional trips across town to see her widowed mother and her married sister, and a weekly grocery shop at a local convenience store. Certainly since the time he had been observing her there had been no boyfriends in evidence and no one visiting her flat.

By now he knew the city well. A driving job ensured that. He had spent the last year familiarising himself with the surface infrastructure and the networks of roads that criss-crossed the area linking the Potteries' six towns and the neighbouring borough of Newcastle-under-Lyme to one another and beyond—Manchester and the North West, Birmingham and the Black Country to the south. And below the giant interchange was the constant allure of the canal.

He had thought that the twin locks below the level of the road would be a splendid place to stage his comeback performance. Shielded from any prying eyes in the houses opposite, it had the added bonus that the constant roar of traffic overhead would drown out the cries of his victim. Exploration of the towpath alongside the locks soon disabused him of this idea. The area was far from salubrious. It epitomised urban dereliction, peppered with the detritus of despair: sodden food wrappers and paper cups, cans and broken bottles, needles and syringes, and a scattering of used condoms. No, he needed to breathe good clean air, nature's perfection. His task was surgical; its display, art.

Just as had been the case with the room, he knew instantly when he found it: a pretty spot, a little glade alongside the bubbling Trent, the water so much clearer now that the factories no longer poured their effluent along its course. It was not a large river here as it meandered through the North Staffordshire countryside, feeding into a series of pools and larger lakes in this area of natural beauty. It was easily accessible from a quiet lane, with a convenient passing place a hundred yards upstream.

He was surprised how naturally he slipped into the familiar routine, stalking the girl, planning his time to catch her unawares as she left the office block after her early morning shift. She had accepted his lift gladly, seemingly unperturbed when they drove past her flat, heading out into the open countryside and pulling into the parking spot beside the river, clearly anticipating a sexual encounter and wondering to herself how much he might be prepared to pay. She had offered little resistance in the struggle that ensued, thinking it some sort of playful precursor, frightened only when the man seemed intent on totally overpowering her. She had left it too late and, unable to escape his clutches, watched in consummate terror as he dragged her, bound and gagged, to the edge of the water before placing both hands around her throat and squeezing the life from her.

It had all been so simple. Looking about him to make sure he was unobserved, he quickly retraced his steps and retrieved his tool bag from the van. The surgery that followed was executed equally effectively, although he had been mildly irritated to find that the posture this entailed caused a dragging sensation in the leg he had injured. Satisfied, however, that he had lost none of his skills, the man stepped back and surveyed his handiwork. Feeling little of the familiar excitement, he was further surprised to find that he was only semierect and had to masturbate hard to achieve an eventual ejaculation. The longer this took, the greater his fear of discovery. It was with mixed relief that he was finally able to gather his instruments and return to the van.

This first attempt since recompiling his manual had merely been a test piece. Next time, he told himself, it will be better.

CHAPTER 55

Ted Manning

Ted's arrest for being in possession of stolen goods had taken him completely by surprise: a humiliating experience unleashing an unpleasant and unfamiliar sense of shame, the ignominy compounded by the fact that his disgrace was witnessed by his erstwhile colleagues, officers beneath him in rank and, until now, subject to his authority. It was only later, released on bail and holed up in the anonymous hotel, that he began to process the events of the day leading up to his arrest. He had always suspected that not every item in the major general's collection of firearms had been acquired through reputable sources—certified dealers, salesrooms, and auction houses—but this latest foray into stolen artwork was something of a revelation. He had recognised the piece as soon as he saw it. Following its theft from a prestigious gallery a year ago (a daring exploit carried out in front of a roomful of visitors and tourist guides expounding the finer points of the paintings to groups of secondary school children), the image had been circulated across the force. He had downloaded it to his mobile as part of the ongoing investigation. The culprit had never been caught, and until today there had been no trace of the painting. Ted knew that he was taking a risk when he had agreed to look after it until the major general felt it was safe to have it returned, but somewhere at the back of his mind was the thought that he might be able to effect its "discovery" and begin to enhance his somewhat tarnished reputation. Ambition was a powerful driver, and he felt little allegiance to his former friend, although it had never really been a friendship, always more of a business relationship, one based on mutual favours, and one where, until now, he had always been the lesser partner. He had been used, he had always known it, but today had offered the opportunity to redress the balance—and if it meant reneging on his former collaborator, then he had little compunction in doing just that!

To have been caught in such compromising circumstances, leaving the premises of a man designated as a person of interest, even potentially a suspect, in a murder investigation, and to have been apprehended with the stolen masterpiece clearly in his possession had been an unmitigated disaster. Already existing on the knife edge of suspicion, Ted Manning speculated upon the odds now stacked against him. His wife was the victim of a brutal attack, until recently his home had been sealed off with his personal belongings inaccessible and probably thoroughly scritinised, and his career had been suspended. Compounding the problem Ted's younger son, sought by the police since the time of the attack on his mother, was missing, his whereabouts unknown. Suddenly everything that had made up the comfortable world of Ted Manning, aspiring chief of police, was falling apart.

It was that glimpse of his son Richard (surely it *had* been him) being hauled, protesting, into an adjacent police car that had haunted him all day. Any attempt by Ted to have his suspicion confirmed had been met with a wall of silence. The officers he had asked—his subordinates, dammit!—had steadfastly refused to respond to his queries. They wouldn't even confirm the lad's identity, saying only that a young person wanted in connection with their enquiries had been apprehended leaving the unauthorised premises.

How they must be laughing at his fall from grace. It had been a day of great results for the Booth Street station. There would be commendations in the pipeline, promotions too, he felt sure of that—personal as well as corporate successes—and he would have no share in it, relegated to the sideline, his contribution to the ongoing investigations ignored, the credit bestowed elsewhere. He knew how it worked. There was no place amongst the accolades for a bent copper.

CHAPTER 156

Richard

Richard, meanwhile, was being held in custody, charged with the assault upon his mother. In the absence of any parental support, social workers and the lawyer assigned to his case had worked hard to get the charge against him reduced from one of attempted murder, but whatever the outcome, when his case came to court it was obvious that a more permanent place would need to be found where work could begin to address the boy's problems. For the time being, he was being held in a secure unit attached to a young offenders' institution, where, despite concentrated attempts by a range of mental health and behavioural specialists, Richard remained obdurately silent, showing little sign of emotion, while stubbornly refusing to answer any of their questions.

CHAPTER 157

Leckie

Looking about her on the street, Leckie felt a pang of conscience. It had all been so easy. She had gone in to see the doctor, leaving Sandy in the waiting room, and was sent from there to the X-ray department, where they were waiting for her still, as she chose instead to leave the hospital as quickly as possible, taking the first bus she saw into the city centre.

And here she was, leaving Sandy in the lurch. She imagined her sitting there with her growing impatience, feeling stupid and embarrassed as she realised that Leckie had gone. Would she have hunted the hospital for her before giving up and returning home? She would find the note then that Leckie had left in her room: just "Thank you for everything you did for me." Leckie knew that if she had tried to say more, it would have only weakened her resolve. And the idea of actually *talking* to Sandy about her intentions—well, that was an absolute nonstarter. She would only have persuaded Leckie to stay, would have offered to do whatever it took to make her happy, while all the time refusing to see that while she kept her there, the more she did for her, the more stultifying it became. Leckie was beginning to feel like a specimen, an experiment to be observed, a captive kept hostage against her will, bereft of identity.

Here in the bustling high street, she felt alive again. This was her natural habitat, although now that she had experienced a taste of better things, she knew there was more to aspire to. But it had to be on her terms, at her own pace. First she must address her immediate needs. She had only the clothes she was wearing (too many, but she had doubled up intentionally), stuffing her remaining underwear and a few toiletries into the canvas shoulder bag she had taken with her to her hospital appointment. She seemed to have mislaid her old rucksack, having hunted for it fruitlessly in Sandy's cottage. She had not dared to ask about it, however casually, for fear it might arouse Sandy's suspicions as to her true intentions. A replacement needed to be found. And while Leckie had a little money, she really wanted to hang on to it. She even had a bank card now, courtesy of Sandy's insistence, and money in the bank from the benefits she had been claiming (again at Sandy's instigation). On their last outing together, Leckie had made a point of withdrawing enough to pay Sandy for her bed and board, deferring the option of establishing a monthly direct debit, which would surely have given the impression that she was going to stay. She fingered the card now: this and the regular benefit money going into her account were her passport to better things.

She could live very economically on the streets until she found somewhere cheap to rent. She would get herself a job—anything to tide her over until she found what she was really looking for. She knew what that was. Her spell in hospital had taught her that. She would be a carer—she'd seen advertisements for that—and perhaps eventually even a nurse, but she knew that jobs like that demanded references. She would have to take whatever she could find and get references from that before she could move on. But it had to be here in the city, amongst the noise and movement, the jostling crowds and constant activity. Even the pungent aroma from the various takeaways and constant exhaust fumes spelled home to Leckie.

CHAPTER 158

Investigations Continue

Fears that the serial killer, now dubbed "the Surgeon" colloquially by the tabloid press, a pseudonym which pleased the man enormously, a recognition of his talents he felt was rightly deserved, had gone to ground while planning further atrocities, that he might have moved the locus of his activities to another part of the country, or that he *had* struck again but the victim or victims had yet to be discovered were keeping senior police officers and a number of local government officials in a state of uneasy anticipation. Paradoxically, it was almost with a sense of relief when the latest attack was disclosed, their enquiries revealing such a similarity both in what they discovered about the victim and in the modus operandi of the crime as to preclude any likelihood that this was a copycat incident. They knew so much about the methods he used, from the abduction of his victims and his choice of venue to the last gruesome detail of the evisceration of the corpse and pathetic display of each unborn child. Yet about the perpetrator they knew so very little. True, the criminal psychologists had put together a possible format, a sort of psychological e-fit, and there was what little forensic evidence amongst the welter of specimens collected from each murder scene that they had been able to assume unequivocally was his, but they were no nearer to knowing who the man was.

That this latest attack had taken place in such a popular local beauty spot surprised them. It was as though he were taunting them, seeing how blatantly he could perform his odious acts and still evade capture. As yet another major incident room was established and police forces

431

across Staffordshire and the Midlands were placed on high alert., all the evidence collected so far was subjected to renewed scrutiny. A local team was designated to investigate this latest crime on their patch. Far from keeping the media at arm's length, this time they actively sought their cooperation. It would have been difficult not to involve them as the crime scene was in an area open to the public and the huge amount of police activity could hardly go unnoticed. The murder had been conducted in breaking daylight as early morning commuters were beginning to cross the city, emerging from homes across the county. Some undoubtedly would take a shortcut across the park, and soon rumour and conjecture would be rife. Far better that the media should give the accepted version of events than leave it to the wildest imaginings of a frightened, titillated public.

And there was always the hope that someone, somewhere, had noticed something untoward—not that there had been many such breaks so far. Since the boys had identified the man in the van with Mandy as "an old guy", nothing useful had been gleaned from the police's contacts with the public. There had been the usual plethora of calls, mostly from those concerned about their safety and that of their wives and daughters, and a number of crank calls, even some claiming to be from the perpetrator they sought, but these callers were so obviously unaware of those identifying features known only to the investigating team and the true culprit that they were rapidly eliminated from the list of possible suspects.

As police teams across the Midlands were being briefed about this latest development, the man returned his van to the garage. After using a full pack of wet wipes to thoroughly clean his hands, his shoes, and the outside of the carpenter's tool bag containing his instruments, he changed out of his waterproof cagoule into a bulky donkey jacket. He would return later and remove every trace of this morning's activity from his van. Satisfied that he would pass as an ordinary workman, he hung his tool bag carefully over his shoulder, locked up, and made his way home, where he let himself in through the French windows and stowed his tools away, once again relishing the facilities here in his flat: a private bathroom where he could not only spruce himself up but also wash and dry his precious instruments.

All that would come later. For now it was imperative to resume his normal routine: a quick shower then a cup of tea and a couple of slices of toast. All that fresh air so early in the morning had given him an appetite. He filled a flask with coffee, locked up, and left the apartment more ostentatiously this time, using the front door, as he did every day, before taking the lane alongside the side of the house to the shed at the bottom of the garden, where he kept his motorbike. Revving it noisily, he turned into the lane and began his journey to work.

CHAPTER 159

John Antrobus

Elsewhere among the commuter traffic, one John Antrobus was still puzzled over something he had seen that morning. It had struck him as odd at the time. Nothing more—nothing he could put his finger on—but he couldn't shake off the feeling that there was something not quite right. A man used to solving puzzles as a release from the monotony of his job in the food factory, every mindless shift spent weighing and recording packaged chicken pieces rolling interminably along the conveyor belt in front of him, John found that this morning's conundrum posed a challenge. He thought about it on and off throughout the day. Sitting in the smokers' hut at lunchtime, the Eastern Europeans around him chatting together in their own language, his thoughts returned to the incident that was troubling him.

Suddenly he had it! The man walking briskly towards his van parked in the passing place, his tool bag over his shoulder, was coming from the direction where there were no houses for miles. In fact, the only dwellings anywhere nearby were the old estate workers' cottages, where John himself lived. There were only four of them—two pairs of semis—and John knew everyone who lived there and recognised the few regular visitors. No, the man he had seen was definitely a stranger. What was more intriguing, the more John considered it, was the van's being parked where it was. He had no idea how long it had been there. He thought he would have noticed it earlier that morning as he let his old dogs out into the garden before getting ready for work and was pretty sure it had not been there the previous night. He would have seen it then as there was seldom any traffic on the lane:

most of it stayed on the main road a good mile from where John caught the bus each day. It was a longish walk, especially after a day's work, so he certainly would have noticed anything parked along the way. Why it was parked there at all was a puzzle. And where had the stranger been with his tools so early in the day? John knew there were pheasant pens in the fields over that way; he kicked himself for not thinking of it earlier. He should have let the gamekeeper know. What if the rearing pens had been tampered with? The man didn't look like an activist, but you never could tell. He had certainly seemed in a hurry to get away from the place, pausing only momentarily to massage the back of his leg before getting in the van and driving off. Damn, John had left his cell phone in his locker. No time to fetch it now; he had to get back on shift. He would do it as soon as he finished work.

But it was a phone call John could never have envisaged, as the gamekeeper regaled him with the events of the day: the momentous discovery of the murdered girl, police all over the area, normal work suspended. They'd even gone with him when he went to feed the birds. Everyone had been questioned, so he was sure John would be, too, once he got home. Reflecting on what he had heard, John ended the call and, absorbed in his thoughts, changed out of his protective coverall and made his way to the bus stop outside the factory gates. Instead of catching the next bus home, he crossed the road and boarded the bus for town. He reckoned it was time to share his suspicions with the police.

CHAPTER 160

Leckie

Hunkered down in the familiar doorway, Leckie felt a frisson of unease. It was a calculated gamble returning here, but since her unscheduled departure from the hospital and the cloying attention of her would-be benefactor Sandy, she was surprised at how insecure she felt. Once the initial surge of adrenaline had receded, her confidence ebbed too. This was not the time to be exploring fresh pastures. She drew comfort from this place, long ago claimed as her own, a fragment of entitlement amongst the bustling anonymity of the city streets. It was a haven of sorts, but she knew it could not last. Should Sandy try to find her, this would be the first place she would look. Leckie would have to stay on her guard, and tomorrow, she promised herself, she would move on. She had no clear idea of what that would entail. She was too tired to think about it now. It had been an exhausting day. Despite her caution, she soon fell into a fitful sleep, waking only when the first of the commuter buses rumbled through the otherwise deserted streets.

Disorientated at first, rubbing her eyes, Leckie peered about her, detecting familiar landmarks, the remembered odours of the street. She knew where she was now and what she had to do: get out of here fast and lose herself amid the early morning flurry. Then, once the shops were open, she should find something to eat before moving on with her plan.

Making her way towards the outskirts of the town, Leckie considered her options. For the first time in years, she had money in her pocket and could afford to buy herself a breakfast. There were times in the past when she had longed for that. Safe in the knowledge that no one would recognise her here, or even be likely to remember seeing her, Leckie stifled her lifelong instinct just to steal what she needed to eat and found a nondescript café, where she bought her first meal as a free woman. Attracting scant attention from the girl behind the counter or from the scattering of other customers, reassured, she chose a table in the corner and picked up a discarded copy of the Metro, several days old, stuffing into her bag to look at later as her food arrived more quickly than she had anticipated.

Later that morning she boarded a train to the south, again resisting the urge to travel illegally. She was starting her new life as she meant to go on. That morning had sown the seeds of an idea. She would make her way to the coast and find work, waitressing, barwork, cleaning—anything to keep her afloat while she thought out what to do next. She would need to find lodgings too, although with a bit of luck she might even find they came with the job. Buoyed by the feeling of hope and an uncharacteristic optimism, Leckie settled back into her seat and opened the paper.

It was amazing how quickly that mood was to disintegrate. Spreading out the crumpled newspaper, smoothing the creases, the better to decipher the text, Leckie found herself confronted with her worst imaginings as the face that gazed back at her in grainy black and white was one she had never wanted to see again. Stifling a scream of terror, the bile rising in her throat as she fought the waves of nausea, Leckie stuffed the newspaper back in her bag and waited for the awful dread which had engulfed her to recede.

Hers was a terrible knowledge. What she would do with it threatened to abort the remaking of herself and the new life she had only just begun. In the long hours ahead of her, as the train rattled towards its destination, Leckie confronted her fears and considered what she should do next.

Disembarking at Brighton, she looked around her for a railway official and asked directions to the nearest police station. Intrigued, a member of the British Transport Police was summoned who insisted on taking her there himself. Had she been less absorbed in her own thoughts, Leckie would have recognised in his immediate offer of help more than mere dissatisfaction with the mundanity of his job, but a vicarious desire to be part of some sensational news he felt was about to unfold.

And sensational it was. Although the desk sergeant at first was inclined to be sceptical, something about the girl's intransigence convinced him sufficiently to decide to take her into a quiet room away from the public gaze (much to the transport policeman's disappointment), where she was interviewed at length by two detectives. Several intense telephone conversations ensued with officers from the Staffordshire force, to which Leckie was not privy, although one of the detectives would return from time to time asking her to verify a particular point. Leckie had been left in the interview room in the care of a WPC while they determined her immediate fate. Clearly not free to go, she was experiencing a growing and all too familiar distrust of authority, beginning to wonder if she had been mad to come here. The discussions went on until late into the night. When she was finally released, it was not to find lodgings herself, as she was ensconced in a hotel suite accompanied by two female officers, one of whom she felt sure was armed.

CHAPTER 161

The Man

In the intervening days since committing what he intended as his test piece murder, the man had been forced to abandon his plans and revert once more to a state of anonymity. It was a supreme irony that in performing a piss-perfect operation, he had been caught out by an accident of timing. Not once during his prior surveillance had he encountered the man on his way to work. But then, he had not reckoned on the time it had taken to achieve his orgasm. He, a man who prided himself on preparation and accuracy, had made a crucial error of estimation by detailing each element of his operation on previous experience. He did not know if it was an unexpected and thoroughly unwelcome aspect of ageing or the result of the prolonged period of abstinence whilst he had rebuilt his manual, but the extra minutes had been his downfall.

He was not sure how much the man had noticed, but he was taking no chances as, once again, he packed his belongings into his van, locking it and the contents securely in the garage, then retrieving his motorbike from behind the apartment. He would have to move again and start afresh in another area. The thought saddened him. It was such an ideal location; he doubted he would ever find its equal. And all the while there was the nagging doubt as to the necessity of such a drastic move. The man might not even remember seeing him, but he could not afford to risk it.

Always keen to follow the media reports of his crimes, he found that this time it was less to revel in the perfection of his art and mock the futile efforts of the authorities to trace the perpetrator and more a vital necessity to learn how much they knew about him and how near they were to catching him. As he moved through the shadowy suburbs of another town, looking for somewhere to resume his mission, he watched with mild amusement as the A-frames outside the newsagents screamed their sensational headlines: "Waterside Killer Returns"; "Pregnant Women Beware"; "Serial Killer Strikes Again". Later editions carried a far more worrying message: "Have You Seen This Man?"; "Is This the Face of the Killer?"; "Police Issue E-fit of Man Sought in Connection with Murders".

It was a commanding likeness; that much he had to concede. He had not bargained with the man being quite so observant (a skill honed by working out the countless puzzles with which he occupied the long winter evenings, always preferring those with an optical element, calling for a discerning eye and attention to detail). But it was only a sketch after all, and he doubted how recognisable members of the public would find it. The estate agent and the residents of the other apartments in the house might just be able to do so, but all they knew of him was a false name and possibly details of the motorbike he used. He had deliberately kept a very low profile at work and doubted anyone there would be able to pick him out from that drawing. He had seldom used the van, either in the vicinity of the house or that of his workplace, and even if his motorbike had attracted attention, it was nothing that a set of false plates could not conceal. No, he felt relatively safe where that was concerned.

It was, however, a confidence that was to be short-lived. By evening, a new headline had appeared, and it was one that gave him considerable cause for alarm :"The Face of the Killer". Surely this was a scoop for the paper involved, the first of many to carry this picture of a much younger version of him, warning the public not to approach him but to immediately contact the police.

How the hell could they have got that? he wondered. It could only have been from a prison mugshot taken years ago. Well, it won't do them much good, he thought, as he considered his reflection in the public lavatory mirror. His features had altered since then; his was a leaner look now, and the thinning hair had given his face a sharper profile. Gone were the rosy plump cheeks of the younger man. His face was sallow now with a veritable delta of lines, tributaries from the deep creases below his eyes, tufts of dark hair protruding from his nostrils and ears, the marks of maturity. And there was that ragged scar above his lip, livid once, now faded to a faint white line. Courtesy of the bloody dog. Well, that had got its comeuppance for sure!

He was satisfied that there was little to immediately identify him in that picture, but he had to act fast. He knew they were capable of digitally ageing images of missing kids and wondered how reliable that technology was when applied to the features of an adult. He was taking no chances; he would make himself a new face. Grateful now for the drama workshops which had been a transitory distraction during one of his early spells in prison, the man made his way to the nearest bargain shop, ostensibly selecting a couple of cigarette lighters whilst secretly pocketing a stick of mascara and a packet of children's face paint. That should be enough, he thought—enough to render some subtle changes to his appearance. For now, he had new territories to explore.

CHAPTER 162

Brighton Nick

The girl coming forward like that was a godsend. Early disbelief had given way to incredulity as her story unfolded. As more and more of what she was able to tell them tallied with the nationwide investigations so far, the more they were inclined to trust her account. At first the girl had seemed incredibly reticent, wary, and almost aggressively defensive in response to their questions, only becoming calmer and more compliant when the female detective took over and was able to elicit from Leckie the girl's full name and relationship with the man she thought she had recognised from the drawing. Gradually a few details of her early life emerged: a distressing story of neglect and, the detective suspected, abuse at the hands of the father.

Leckie was wracked with sobs now as the story unfolded, remembering an all too brief period of comparative calm, just her and her mother and little brother, her father "working away". Only later, in one of her drunken rambles, had Leckie's mother told her the truth: their father had been in prison for assault.

Leckie, the child of seven, wondered what had happened to the scary family dog which had mysteriously disappeared, why they no longer saw her older brothers, and how it was left to her to look after herself and little Gregory when her mother was too tired looking after the new baby or too ill to care for them. There had been an older sister too, but Leckie could not remember ever seeing her, only her father saying hateful things about her and making their mother cry. She did not know where any of them were now, only that her mother was dead. Little Gregory was the one she missed most, but they had both been sent away and rarely saw each other after that, certainly never as adults.

Clearly the girl was exhausted now, emotionally drained, her slight frame trembling, her hands grasping the mug (the latest offering of hot strong tea) and shaking like those of an old person with Parkinson's disease. Leaving her under the watchful eye of a WPC, the two detectives conferred. Could this be the breakthrough they so desperately sought? The urge to continue questioning her was intense, but how much more could she take? She had come to them of her own free will; they dared not risk losing her now. They would have to take her into custody for her own protection. Accommodation was hastily arranged and two officers detailed to accompany her, one being the female detective who had managed to establish some sort of rapport with the girl during the long hours of her interview.

The following day, the questioning resumed, Leckie more guarded now, trying to recollect what she had told them the previous night, hating being held here now, no longer of her own choosing, already afraid that she may have said too much. Once again she had spent a restless night, despite being so desperately tired, and was awake again at first light, contemplating making a break for it, returning to the welcome anonymity of the streets. Her resolve floundered under the watchful eye of the detective; she reluctantly accepted the proffered breakfast before being taken back to the police station, where the grilling resumed.

Something was different; Leckie felt it. The officers conducting the interview were the same, but it was as though their attitude towards her had changed—subtly, imperceptibly. The interrogation was just as relentless, but it felt less aggressive somehow. It was almost as though they believed her—respected her even.

The intervening hours had seen a frenetic bout of activity inside Brighton police station. Numerous telephone calls had been made, emails sent and received, and, crucially, photographs of prison inmates across the country during the years specified in Leckie's statement, then downloaded onto the interviewer's PC. It was a long shot and they knew it. There were hundreds of them. But it had to be worth a try. They had the suggested name, of course, but that in itself constituted a somewhat slender lead.

What they sought was confirmation. If only the girl could supply it. And confirmation when it came was dramatic and unequivocal.

Leckie was cooperative now. Bolstered by their apparent confidence in her, she set about her task with something approaching enthusiasm (the sooner this was over, the sooner she could get on with her life). But the display seemed endless, picture after picture, face after face: young ones, boys almost, then older ones, middle-aged and worldly wise, calm features, sullen, defiant, most showing no emotion at all. It had become infinitely tedious. Leckie was stalling now. After a tea break—strong tea and a couple of biscuits—it was back to the job in hand. And suddenly, there it was: the face of the man she hated, the man she had once thought had loved her, the man who had made her do all those terrible things. She was shaking uncontrollably, with fingerlike icicles the length of her spine, her limbs no longer her own, jellylike, collapsing beneath her. "That's him," she spluttered. "That's my father."

No longer hiding from them, disappearing, melting into the crowds, or employing her well-honed evasion tactics at the first sight of a uniformed officer or at the first sound of a siren, Leckie could hardly believe this volte-face. Here she was, cast in a wholly new light, helping the police. Still not totally comfortable with the concept, she could not help wondering how much they really knew. How close were they to catching him, and how safe was she?

After all, that horrible friend of her father's, Martyn, was still out there. The sudden recollection momentarily stunned her. His, not her father's, was the face that had haunted her dreams. Only now did she realise it. This was the embodiment of the malevolent shifting shape, the face behind the wheel of the car that had smashed into her that night. The fog that still clouded her brain was lifting now. He had meant to kill her, she was certain of that. The thought of it chilled her, but what was even more terrifying was the realisation that he knew he had failed. That is why he had come back to her. Time and again she had sensed his presence there, and although she had not been aware of it then, it was him she was scared of all the time she had lived with Sandy. Whatever her father was mixed up with, she felt sure that Martyn would be involved too.

Her positive identification had had an electrifying effect upon the detectives interviewing her. They had a name and a photograph now.

444

Already multiple copies were being made and an officer despatched to the home of John Antrobus, hoping he would be able to confirm that this was the man he had seen on the morning of the murder carrying his tools to his van. In the ensuing excitement, Leckie's presence had been almost overlooked. Turning to her now, DC Watts, the detective who had been the first to feel any empathy for the girl, was shocked to find her still sitting there, staring at the monitor. Gone were the prison photographs, and in their place the usual wallpaper: a depiction of the police logo with the caption "Serving the Community". The girl seemed in a trance: her eyes unnaturally wide open, her pupils dilated, the pulse at her temples visibly throbbing, and her fists clenched so tightly that her fingers had turned white. She was clearly traumatised. Though technically free to go, having supplied the necessary statement, she was in no state to be turned out into the streets. DC Watts was well versed in the safeguarding procedures. They had a duty of care, and she, for one, was about to implement it. Pulling up a chair to sit beside Leckie, gently turning to the girl, their eyes level now, she waited to see if she would speak. As a serving police officer, she had seen many people in shock. Where there had been loss of life or injury, she had comforted and consoled—had even tried to be supportive to those they had apprehended for some criminal act. She was a perceptive woman, and Leckie's story had had a profound effect. Instinctively she felt that this was only part of what was troubling the girl.

Hesitantly at first, not really wanting to prolong her time in this, such an alien terrain, yet driven by some inner compulsion to continue unburdening herself, Leckie began to talk. She told of her fears and how the man she only knew as Martyn had come into her life. He was a friend of her father's, and it had been her father who had encouraged him do horrible things to her. Initially she had hoped that her father would protect her, that the things *he* did to her were because he loved her, that what they did was special. But she soon learnt that he had been working up to this, preparing her. And far from intervening to stop Martyn, he seemed to be giving her to him, as a gift almost, or, as she later discovered, as the repayment of a debt. She hated her father for that, and seeing how much in thrall to Martyn he seemed, she despised him for his weakness. She was scared of Martyn, never knowing to what depths of depravity he would take her, scared of his touch, and terrified when he began really hurting her, leaving her bleeding and sore for days.

DC Watts sat silently, never interjecting, merely keeping her gaze constant, nodding approval from time to time, showing that she was really listening. Inwardly, her thoughts were in turmoil. She had heartfelt sympathy for the girl and such feelings of rage towards the man—men—involved in this all too familiar story of sexual abuse. The palpable impotence of the little girl subjected to such pain and degradation and the destruction of yet another childhood appalled her. She longed to bring the perpetrators, not just of this crime but also of those that had ruined so many lives, to justice. But for now, she had to keep her emotions in check: professionalism dictated as much. She must hear the girl out and only then determine what, if any, action she could initiate.

For Leckie, it was as though the floodgates had opened. Unleashed upon her story, as the recollection of so many atrocities unfolded, she relived the fear and unhappiness at the disintegration of her family, her years in foster care, and her eventual life as a rough sleeper. Even then she had not felt safe because the man, Martyn, had discovered where she was living. Not content with humiliating her when she was at her lowest ebb, penniless and starving, by posing as a punter, "buying" her sexual favours before revealing himself to her, he had taunted her with her past and refused to pay her.

Because she had been shaken by the experience, it was days before she plucked up the courage to try again, returning to her spot beneath the lamp. It had been a case of hunger versus degradation. What had she, who was spoiled goods anyway, to lose?

But Martyn had found her again, and this time he had tried to kill her. She did not understand why, but she knew it *was* him. In the split second before the car hit her, she recognised his face. It was the same black car that he had been in before—and he was driving it straight at her.

Startled by this revelation, DC Watts struggled to maintain her composure, her excitement mounting as she realised the implications of what she was hearing. Something about the girl's story had begun to ring a few bells. There had been a hit-and-run somewhere up north several months ago. She remembered reading about it at the time, also recalling the appeal that had been circulated to police forces across the country in an attempt to identify the comatose victim. She had no idea if this was a closed case or whether the police in that area were still investigating it. This could be the breakthrough they sought, and she was the one to have secured it.

DC Watts was ashamed at the elation she felt and the prospect of acclaim from her superiors while the cause of her self-satisfaction sat trembling before her, lost and vulnerable, already fearing that she had said too much and desperately wanting to get out of there. They must not let her go. Sensing the girl's unease, DC Watts made a decision. Right now the priority must be to find the girl a place of safety, some place where surveillance could be maintained whilst all these emerging threads of her story could be investigated. Leckie was far too valuable a witness to lose.

CHAPTER 163

Staffordshire Police

In other police stations across the country, the sense of elation was shared: with this latest revelation from their colleagues in Brighton, they had a positive ID of a man seen acting suspiciously near to the latest serial killing—the perpetrator nicknicknamed, among those in the know, as the "Tableau Murderer"—an ID made by the man's daughter no less and confirmed on being shown the photograph by a dispassionate witness, a stolid and ostensibly reliable man living near to the murder scene. Hopes were running high that at last they had what seemed to be a promising lead in a series of cases that had baffled and frustrated them for years. Detectives from the North West who had travelled down to interview the girl in Brighton had double the excitement on learning from their colleagues that this was the mystery victim of the hit-and-run which had happened on their patch and about which, up to now, they had drawn a blank.

The girl had been reticent at first, only agreeing to speak to them if DC Watts could be there too. Leckie felt secure in her presence. Strangely, it reminded her of another time, dimly remembered now, when she had awakened from troubled sleep to find the comforting shape-shifter sitting beside her bed. Cautiously she began to recount the events leading up to what she clearly thought had been a deliberate attempt to kill her. She hated having to repeat her story, the degradation and shame she had felt at the time reasserting itself in the presence of these two unfamiliar officers, causing her to feel exposed and vulnerable again. And anger, anger at all that had happened to her, everything that had been done to her—anger with an intensity she had never known before. This was her opportunity, she saw it now—her opportunity to retaliate, to snatch something back, to regain some dignity and her sense of self-worth. She had led them to her father. If only she could remember something about Martyn that would put him behind bars too. Dammit, she knew so little about him. She didn't even know his surname.

Suddenly she had it, a fragment of dialogue, a barely remembered conversation she had overheard as a child. It was between her father and Martyn, something about their time together, how they had met. She had not understood the significance of it then; it was only later that she learnt what they meant. There had been words like screws, landings, wings. In her naivety, she thought they had been in the air force together, serving their time, mending aeroplanes perhaps. Even the name Parkhurst had not meant anything to her then.

She was not to know how useful that knowledge was to prove, but she had told them anyway and they had quizzed her relentlessly, trying to get her to remember more. Could she give them dates? Approximately even. How old was she at the time? How often had her father been "working away"?

And so it was that she found herself seated once again in front of a computer screen being shown a series of prisoner ID photographs from the same period as those of her father. This time she had no difficulty in picking out the ones of Martyn—and this time the only emotion she felt was of revenge.

CHAPTER 164

Ben and Karen

Police activity across the country was reaching unprecedented levels now that they had a name and a picture of the prime suspect in this latest atrocity, linking him with all the other unsolved murders attributed to the serial killer the media had dubbed "the Surgeon". Old leads where they had previously drawn a blank were revisited; case notes were reopened; and investigating teams were briefed.

The knock on the door that Ben had so long dreaded occurred early on the Monday morning, disturbing the family's routine. Ben was just about to leave for work. He was already running late, having spent a frustrating time persuading Megan to put down her toys and finish her breakfast. One of his chores was preparing the children's lunch boxes. To his irritation, he discovered that the butter had been left in the fridge and was rock-hard. Spreading their sandwiches was a chore. He wished he had done them the previous evening, but it was too late to worry about that now. Another few minutes had been wasted hunting for the child's boots, before finally running them to earth in the toy box. He only had to strap her in her car seat and then he would be able to go, stopping only long enough to drop Megan off at the day nursery on his way to work. Meantime, Karen was getting Cari ready for school, delighting in her smart new uniform, brushing her hair until it shone, then securing it in two neat plaits held in place with matching scrunchies. The child was a credit to her, so much better turned out than many of the children in her class. Karen would walk to school with her (despite Cari's protestations that, at eight years old, she was perfectly capable of going there on her own) and would linger at the school gates, hoping to attract admiring glances from the other mothers there, savouring the comment once made to her: "She always looks so pretty. I don't know how you do it. It takes me all my time to tear Jess away from the telly and put her clothes on. As for her hair, well, you'd think I'd put the tangles there on purpose!" Once the school bell rang, Karen would return home and have a leisurely coffee while she scrolled through the messages (predominantly advertisements) on her phone before starting on the housework for the day.

It was a routine that had developed as their family grew: predictable and repetitive, varying only should the schools be closed for teacher training or one of the children fall ill. But today that routine was about to be shattered. Cursing under his breath, Ben answered the door.

Several hours later, he sitting opposite Karen at their kitchen table, both of them clutching mugs of coffee, they had their first proper conversation in months. After the police had gone, Ben had grimly set about restoring some sense of normality, loading both children into the car, intending to drop them off respectively at the day nursery and middle school. Karen, much more the calm and collected one, would speak to the teachers, apologising for the girls' lateness, while Ben would use the time to telephone his workplace and tell them he was taking the day off. He was certainly in no fit state to work. The visit by the police had unnerved him. He had found himself stuttering, muddling his answers to their questions, certain that he sounded every bit as guilty as he felt. Karen had been amazing though, remaining composed throughout, recalling details of their trip with a clarity and accuracy that astounded him, deflecting difficult questions, and blatantly lying with such ease and charm that he had almost believed her himself!

The two police officers had seemed satisfied. For now. But this renewed interest in the case frightened him. The picture that they had been shown meant nothing to either of them. They had not seen this man anywhere near to where they were told the body had been found. They did not recognise him at all. He rather wished they had: it might have diverted the interest away from them. Ben had this ominous feeling that he and Karen remained persons of interest.

CHAPTER 165

Further Revelations

Staff at the Brighton police station were surprised by the change in the girl's demeanour. No longer cowed, no longer the trembling terrified victim or the sullen detainee resentful of the forced constraints of protective custody, Leckie had a fresh confidence and an air of determination as she outlined the events leading up to the accident. She told them of the journey north in the hope of a better life and of recognising Martyn and hiding from him on the train. She spoke of how the promising future they had envisaged had failed to materialise as her friend Rosie left her to fend for herself in a strange city. Life on the streets was tough, and she seldom made enough money to afford a bed in the hostel at night. Rootless and destitute, she had no way to get any paid work. Begging and, yes, occasionally prostitution had been her only resort. She was not telling them her story in the hope of attracting their sympathy. Rather, she knew that if she wanted the two monsters in her life, her father and Martyn, to be brought to justice, then she had to be completely honest.

So it was that she described again the sequence of events leading to her current situation, omitting nothing, determined at last to set the record straight. She even told them how she and Rosie had stowed away on the train, how she had stolen bread to survive and even contemplated kidnapping a baby. If the detectives interviewing her realised the enormous significance of this disclosure, they were well-trained and proficient at not letting this show. They needed to hear her story out. Any interruption now could jeopardise that. Their questions could come later.

Shuddering with disgust at the depths of depravity to which she had succumbed, Leckie recalled the encounter with Martyn, the punter who had recognised her, used her, refused to pay her, and threatened to do so again and again now that he had found her. He had her in his thrall, and she had every reason to believe him, so it was an utter shock when she recognised him as the driver of the car which had careered towards he, She had no doubt that he had deliberately tried to kill her.

Her recollection of her time in hospital was hazy, but she knew he had been there too. Her fear of him was palpable even now. Leckie was grateful for the protection Sandy had afforded her, along with her care and concern, and how kind Sandy had been to give her a home. She did not know it at the time, but she recognised now that it had probably cost Sandy her job. Leckie cringed at the recollection of how badly she had repaid that debt by absconding from the outpatient appointment and making her way here. It was her fear of Martyn that had driven her; she saw that now. She did not know then of the hunt for her father and had only learnt of it from the old newspaper, but whatever he had done, she felt sure that Martyn was mixed up in it too.

Her story over, for now, and back in protective custody, Leckie felt an overwhelming sense of relief. More questions would come, she knew, but for now it was over. Tonight she would sleep in peace, and tomorrow …tomorrow she could begin to think about her future.

CHAPTER 166

Ben and Karen

The decision had been sudden. They would take a holiday.,Get away from it all for a while—a chance to recalibrate their relationship, away from the prying eyes of the police and without the constant fear of discovery.

Megan was overexcited, cramming more toys than underwear into her little ride-on suitcase. Cari was altogether more cautious, suspicious of this new sense of optimism within the family, sensing an ulterior motive.

She had overheard snippets of conversation, her ear to the ground, always listening to them, unobtrusive, silently going about the day's activities.

"If we go back there …I mean, it's been a long time …"

"Not actually doing the boat thing …"

"Staying somewhere near …familiarise ourselves with the lie of the land …"

"Make our story more convincing."

Karen wasn't sure, wanting to forget the entire incident, relegating thoughts of it to another Karen, another life. Cari was *theirs*. There was no need to focus on her arrival in their lives, not after all this time. But if it would put Ben's mind at rest, make him a more convincing liar should the need arise, then it had to be worth it. They would go, take in the sights, and come back refreshed and fluent in their make-believe.

CHAPTER 167

Brighton Nick, Day Three

The girl was pure gold dust: not only had she given them a name, but also she had identified a picture, albeit dated, of the man sought countrywide in connection with what some of the papers now referred to as the "Maternity Murders". That she had also turned out to be the previously unidentified victim of a hit-and-run and had been able to name the perpetrator and suggest a link between him and the serial killer was an unexpected bonus. This latest piece of information tied in with what they had already surmised: that someone other than themselves was interested in the killer, the man caught up in the terrible inferno at the derelict cottage where they had found the kidnapped Mandy and the gruesome remains in the well. He had been fleeing from the flames, they were sure of that, but had died from his burns before they were able to learn anything from him. All their attempts to identify him had so far failed. Now, as they studied the two images side by side, the prison mugshot of the man known to the girl only as Martyn, and the mortuary photographs of the burns victim, they hoped that at last they could put a name to him.

The initial comparison was frustratingly inconclusive, the ravages of the fire having virtually destroyed the right-hand side of the man's face, while the remaining features were bloated and distorted beyond recognition. It was only when they clicked on the image of the left side in profile that the similarities became apparent. He had been found lying face down among the trees, his head turned so that his left cheek was pressed into the earth, partially protected from the searing heat, his nose and the shape of his face distinguishable still. The technician's wax reconstruction had produced an image that could easily be a match for the ex-convict identified as Martyn. At last they had a name for John Doe.

Returning to the girl's statement to see if there were any other clues they might have overlooked, they were struck by a sense of familiarity within the narrative. It was DC Watts who first realised the significance. They would have to bring the girl in for further questioning.

———◆———

Frustratingly, the more they discovered, the more questions arose. Even presuming the tentative ID was correct and the burnt man was indeed this Martyn of whom the girl spoke, they were no nearer to discovering his involvement with the killings. Ever since the fire, he had been their prime suspect as he'd been found in suspicious circumstances fleeing the scene of Mandy's abduction and the incriminating contents of the well. The period of calm which followed the man's death appeared to confirm their suspicions. Until this latest outrage, there had been no further murders of vulnerable pregnant women. Even the media interest in the case had waned. To date, they had made little progress in identifying the bodies from the well, only discovering from the DNA evidence that they were closely related—probably a mother and her little son. The knowledge that she had been pregnant was surely significant, but it contributed nothing tangible to the ongoing investigations into these scattered serial killings.

This latest murder completely overturned that presumption. With the likelihood of a copycat killing ruled out (the MO was strikingly similar and contained elements known only to the man himself and the murder squad involved in each of the earlier instances), all the evidence pointed to the disturbing fact that the serial killer was still at large. The man they had now tentatively identified as Martyn Conroy had moved from being the prime suspect to being someone of particular interest. Just what was his connection with the murderer, or at least with the conflagration at the scene of so many atrocities? And if it actually was him, why had he chosen to terrorise and try to kill Leckie Zabot?

And then there was the girl herself: just how much did she really know? Was she the innocent victim she purported to be? And why did elements of her story continue to puzzle and intrigue them?

At that moment, DC Watts came into the room and, as though

divining their thoughts, provided the elusive lead they wanted. She had studied the girl's statement afresh and was amazed that they had failed to see it before. This had to be the girl they had sought in connection with the failed abduction of a child, the girl who admitted to entering childcare facilities in her pursuit of a target and who had paid numerous visits to the maternity department of the local hospital—the very unit where the victim of another waterside murder had last been seen alive. It was a long shot, and she knew it, but could the girl have seen anything there which could shed some light on the mystery of Abigail Lamont's disappearance and the possible fate of her baby daughter?

Sceptics on the team wondered how much credence could be ascribed to the girl's story. Just how reliable a witness was she? After all, she had been injured and severely traumatised by what she was claiming was a deliberate attempt upon her life. She had spent several weeks in a coma, and by her own admission, her memory had only recently begun to return. After so many months of intensive investigation and hard work, and the innumerable man-hours involved—the countless dead ends and blind alleys explored and discarded—the excitement among their peers was understandable, but it needed to be tempered by caution. There was a danger in attributing too much weight to these latest revelations, so much seemingly speculative at best. What was needed was some sort of proof of the girl's reliability, evidence that she was whom she purported to be and that she had been where she claimed to have been.

CHAPTER 168

Sandy

Initially exhilarated by the police visits, her first contact with her former colleagues since her resignation and the tedious months she had been working as a security officer in a downtown department store, Sandy felt a wave of nostalgia for what had been her former life. But the interviews, because that is what they were, were conducted entirely on her former colleagues' terms, ignoring Sandy's pleasantries and enquiries about how life was treating them since the spectacular arrest of Ted Manning on charges of assault against his wife (which he had blatantly denied) and involvement in the firearms and fine art theft (for which there could be no denial as he had been caught with one of the prized antiquities in his hands). It had attracted headlines in both local and national press and had given Sandy a moment or two of profound satisfaction as she recalled the ignominy to which he had subjected her. It was as if her former coworkers had never known her. There was no response to any of her questions, but while the interviews so far had not been conducted under caution, *their* questions had been relentless.

"What did you learn about Leckie during your time together? Why did you show so much interest in her right from the start?" Sandy wondered if she detected snide innuendo here. Were they implying that theirs had been a lesbian relationship? Prejudice in the force was alive and well, thought Sandy, resentful that this was all her former colleagues seemed to remember from their previous years of service together.

Before she could even challenge their assumption, the questioning moved on, going back in time now. "When did you first realise that you knew the girl? Why did you hand her rucksack over as evidence? What do you know about the pink baby blanket?"

Well, that did it! Sandy recalled the complete disinterest shown in her find, even when the failed abduction of a child, or possibly children, in their territory should have been one of prime concern, and how all the attention was focused upon the spate of grisly murders. Back then they were all disparaging about her contribution and were only interested in what she could tell them now, to cover their inadequacies in the past: it was nothing more than a face-saving exercise. The realisation hurt her to the core and definitely dispelled any illusions she may have had about rejoining the force. The nostalgia she felt was not for the organisation; it was for the actual work. She had no need to give that up. She could use the remainder of Aunt Julia's legacy to set up her own business. She would become a private investigator, advertising her particular interest in tracing lost relatives, using her knowledge of homelessness and life on the streets in a way that was positive and restorative.

CHAPTER 169

Ben and Karen

This latest trip to Wales was proving no more conducive to settling the growing rift between the couple than their first one had been. It had started off badly: the impetuous decision to go, Karen a whirlwind of activity, rapidly packing their things, emptying the fridge, organising the children, all accomplished with such frenetic haste that it had left Ben feeling even more unsettled. He was aware of his hands shaking as he started the car, his head throbbing, Megan's excited chatter a source of disproportionate irritation. Glancing at the children through the rear-view mirror, he was struck by the difference in their demeanour: Megan clearly delighted at the prospect of this impromptu holiday, her face a picture of gleeful anticipation, and Cari quiet, almost sullen by comparison. No, that was unfair: more distant and withdrawn, her look of profound unhappiness momentarily distracting him from driving. Wrenching his gaze back to the road, Ben experienced an unprecedented surge of empathy and affiliation with the little girl, who was obviously as disturbed as he was by this latest turn of events.

They had no fixed plans. Karen, always the organiser, confidently asserted that they would have no trouble in finding a B&B, possibly a different one each night, allowing them the freedom to explore the area more comprehensively. Her assurance had proved unfounded. After what seemed like miles and miles of winding country lanes and countless villages and tiny hamlets, all with the accommodation displaying No Vacancies signs, they had finally alighted upon a small B&B, the middle cottage in a rather grim grey stone terrace. It had a communal bathroom, no en suite—the girls sharing a room—and no catering facilities until breakfast the following morning. At least the bed linen was clean, although so old and well-washed that it had assumed a uniform grey tinge, perfectly toning with that of the walls and woodwork, once long ago probably the ubiquitous magnolia, now the colour of very old underwear.

Ben was exhausted. Karen, stubbornly defiant, insisted that things could only get better. Even the normally equable Megan was becoming fractious. They clearly needed to eat. Wearily, Ben locked the rooms behind them and they set out once again to find a meal. No cafés or restaurants out here in the sticks; their only hope would be a village pub serving food.

Only Cari seemed unaffected by the frustrations of the day. Silent, locked in a world of her own, she accompanied the family, disinterested, compliant with their plans, seemingly oblivious to the tensions surrounding her. She alone knew the real reason for this visit. Sure, her parents had a purpose behind the trip, but Cari knew without a doubt what had driven them to seek out these unassuming villages, the narrow lanes little more than cart tracks from long ago, winding incongruously around the perimeters of the fields, criss-crossing the countryside, bridge after bridge over the silent canal, the artery feeding their futile search for resolution. The neat compactness of the bridges and the narrowness of the waterway below epitomised all that was small and small-minded in their search for answers. While her parents were determinedly pursuing their quest, Cari had her mind set on something greater. She would know when she had found it.

She had thought about it often, seeing the place so vividly in her increasingly troubled dreams. It lacked the chocolate box prettiness of the little stone bridges over the still waters of a rural canal or a rickety wooden construction over a bubbling stream: this was an architectural beauty, a feat of civil engineering unlike anything she had encountered in the world beyond her dreams. She wondered if she had seen a picture of it somewhere, in a geography lesson or perhaps something on the television, YouTube maybe. Wherever it had been, she knew she would find the place soon.

This was her destiny. It had been from the start.

CHAPTER 170

Leckie

Something in their attitude had changed. Leckie sensed it immediately. In a matter of days she had gone from feeling a trusted confidante to becoming a suspect again. Their questioning was more aggressive somehow. Gone was the gentle probing, allowing her time to consider her responses; this was quick-fire stuff, her answers seized and torn apart, never satisfying them, spawning more questions, the demand for more proof. She should never have come here. Having disregarded her instinctive distrust of authority, she was paying for it now. Even DC Watts seemed less approachable, remaining aloof throughout, contributing little, and avoiding any eye contact with Leckie. She was on her own now. There was no one on her side.

If only they wouldn't keep tossing dates at her, asking when had she done this or that, or how many times she had been up to the day nursery. How many visits had she made to the hospital? When was that; how long ago? Did she see anyone she knew? Was there anyone who could vouch for her? Was there any proof that she had been there at all?

And then she remembered seeing the woman emerge, dropping the card in her hurry to leave, and her own elation at being able to retrieve it and use it, actually getting inside the unit. She recalled how no one had even noticed her as she found her way into the nursery and, still unchallenged, was able to lift one of the babies from its cot. Sobbing, she told them of the awful moment of realisation that she could not go through with her plan. Angry with herself and with them, the people who should have been caring for these little babies, she had put the child down, deliberately choosing the other empty cot, hoping the exchange would be recognised and that at least someone would be in trouble for not having protected the children in their charge.

Leckie paused. Should she tell them about stealing the blanket? She knew that if she didn't, they would probably drag it out of her anyway. So she told them about choosing a pink one and stuffing it into her backpack. No, she didn't have it now. She had no idea what had happened to it, to any of her things. If only she had, she could prove that she was telling the truth. Perhaps if she had it, they would believe her and let her go.

CHAPTER 171

Almost There

She had found it. There had been false leads along the way, but surely this was it.

Halfway through their holiday, they had been taken to see the Pontcysyllte Aqueduct, Karen tightly clutching Cari's hand as they walked along the concrete towpath high above the river valley, Megan held as firmly by her father. True, there was a guard rail on this side of the canal, but their parents were taking no chances. The view was breathtaking. Cari had felt a frisson of excitement. This may not be the bridge of her dreams, but she sensed that she was getting very close to finding it.

The remainder of the holiday had passed in a blur: long days spent driving around the countryside, pervading uncertainty as to where they would spend each night, a succession of different guest houses and often the only family there, and just once, the luxury of a small hotel, a welcome alternative to the threatened prospect of having to spend the night in the car. During these last few days, Cari had been barely aware of the changing scenery and had paid scant attention to the towns they visited. She was sleeping badly and had little interest in food, doggedly accompanying her family whilst locked in a world of her own. By now the novelty of the trip had waned. Even Megan was more subdued as her idea of a holiday—buckets and spades and paddling in the sea—did not seem to be materialising. Their parents rarely spoke except to bicker. Cari was beginning to feel claustrophobic.

They had stopped again for something to eat, a pretty café clearly catering for tourists, gingham tablecloths and cream teas, and a display stand of brochures advertising various local attractions. Selecting a few of these at random, Cari took them over to their table and scanned them in a desultory fashion. It was something to do while they waited to be served.

It was then that she saw it: a picture of the bridge, *her* bridge, the bridge she had dreamt about ever since that fateful day when she made her discovery. Glancing furtively at her parents, Cari was aware that they were momentarily distracted, watching the smiling waitress approaching their table carrying a laden tray. Hastily stuffing the brochure into the pocket of her jeans, Cari pushed aside the remaining pile of leaflets to make space for her plate and helped herself to jam and cream, a gratifying sight for Karen, who had begun to fear that her favoured child was becoming anorexic.

Cari would look at it later, away from prying eyes. And then she would make her plans.

CHAPTER 172

The Man

They were searching garages and lock-ups across the town. He had been aware of the increased police activity since dawn, having spent an uncomfortable night in his van, trying to figure out his next move. At first light, he had packed his instruments, his instruction manual, and a few clean clothes into the panniers on his bike. It was time to make his getaway.

Locking the garage behind him and dropping the keys into the nearest drain, he set off on his journey. Using side streets and back alleys, he reached the bypass without incident and was soon enjoying the exhilaration of the open road, becoming more confident and relaxed with every mile behind him.

He had got away with it again. It was time to move to a new hunting ground; virgin territory, a fresh victim pool. He liked the sound of that, the oxymoron playing over and over in his mind, as his victims were far from virginal. There was no challenge for him in that.

During the hours of darkness he had pondered his options: with his new manual complete and the recent confirmation that he had lost none of his surgical skills, he felt elated at the prospect of resuming his hobby. He would perfect his disguise and assume a new identity in a different town, one that matched his criteria. It had to be somewhere he had visited extensively on his travels, where his deliveries had provided him with a good working knowledge of the terrain. There had to be water as a backdrop for his art. As for potential victims, well, provided it wasn't a retirement hub, there was never going to be a shortage of pregnant women.

The thought excited him, and with it came the familiar stirring, his leathers tight now, constricting. He needed to pull off the road and deal with that. Distracted, glancing at the fields as he passed, hoping for an open gate, somewhere to give him the privacy he craved, the man was almost upon them before he became aware of the two stationary cars slanted across both lanes of the carriageway. Any lustful thoughts he had been harbouring immediately deserted him, replaced by initial panic as he recognised this as a police roadblock. Hoping like hell that it was only because of an accident ahead (although surely he would have heard an ambulance by now), he had no choice but to stop.

With all the charm of a snake oil salesman, he bade the two officers a good morning, politely enquiring as to the cause of the problem. His question hung in the air as one of the officers studied something on his phone. The two seemed to be conferring over something. This was his chance to make his escape. Glancing furtively around him, he realised the futility of the idea: the way forward was impassable, there was no way he could cross the barrier to the opposite carriageway, and if he were to try to return the way he had come, he would be driving headlong into any oncoming traffic—besides which, should the police set off in pursuit, his laden motorcycle would prove no match for the powerful cars at their disposal.

Stunned, he was ordered to surrender his keys before being handcuffed and led away to one of the waiting vehicles, where he could only watch helplessly as the officers began their inspection of his motorbike, searching through the contents of his luggage. He was being cautioned, arrested on suspicion of murder, but they were addressing him by name, his real name, one he had not used for years.

It was then that he saw it: a screen on the dashboard, backlit, its fluorescent glow illuminating the interior of the car. The display transfixed him. No traffic information or selection of radio stations, the picture on the screen was of *him*—an earlier version, a prison mugshot, but unmistakably him. As he watched, the picture faded, only to be replaced by a moving image: the interior of some cheapskate shop, a lone customer moving through the aisles, stopping, and picking something up—and then a close-up, full face, of the man at the checkout.

He, who prided himself upon his skill at evasion, had been caught on the shop's security camera. That is what happens, he thought, when you deviate from the plan.

CHAPTER 173

Cari Moses

She hadn't bargained on her father barging in on her like that. Waiting until she thought the rest of the family was asleep, Cari had taken her torch and crept along the landing to the bathroom. Not wanting to attract any attention, she decided against putting on the light or struggling with the antiquated lock on the door. Sitting on the lid of the lavatory, she spread the crumpled brochure across her knees and began to study it, her eyes drawn irrevocably to the picture of the bridge, wondering just how far away it was and how she could get to it.

So intent she had been that she had failed to hear the approaching footsteps or the cautious opening of the bathroom door, only becoming aware of his presence when the shadow fell across her, obliterating the picture on her lap. In her sudden fright at being discovered, she scrambled to her feet, dropping her torch and the precious brochure. Panicked now, scrabbling to retrieve her things as her father clicked on the bathroom light, Cari turned to him with a furious "You could have knocked!"

Taken aback by the unaccustomed venom of her tone, Ben took her gently by the shoulders and sat down beside her on the edge of the bath. Something was troubling the girl. He knew that now. Although he had never subscribed to Karen's latest theory that Cari was developing an eating disorder, Ben had been so distracted by his own concerns—the constant fear of discovery, the endless tissue of lies, and the precarious state of his marriage—that he had failed to realise how withdrawn she had become. Perhaps she was as sick of this charade of a holiday as he was. The perpetual aimless meander through countryside, which aroused nothing more than frightening memories for him, must have seemed boring and quite meaningless to his children. It had long since satisfied Karen's desire to reappraise themselves with the route and topography of the Llangollen Canal. The last few days had been pointless in the extreme.

What had the girl been poring over with such profound concentration that she had failed to hear him coming along the landing? Gently prising her fingers apart, Ben took the crumpled leaflet from her hand. Surprised that she offered no resistance to this, he looked at the girl and saw in her expression a look of such utter weary resignation that it could have been his own, mirroring his feelings so exactly that he felt an immediate surge of empathy with the child. Again he berated himself at his—no, *their*, as he and Karen were equally culpable—selfish pursuit of their own agenda with only scant and cursory consideration for their children.

Ben knew that from the very beginning of their relationship he had been driven by Karen's wishes, submissive to the point where he had begun to question his own identity. And now she was doing the same to the girls. This whole ill-founded trip had been her idea, whereas Ben wanted nothing more than to return home, put the whole sorry business behind him, and go to work as usual on Monday morning.

They had one full day left, not long enough to redress the balance, but at least he could make a stand. *He* would determine how they would spend the day. Cari's brochure had given him the idea. It obviously appealed to the child. On studying further, he found that the magnificent bridge lay just beyond a historic market town with castle grounds and an adventure park—something they could all enjoy.

"Go back to bed now, love. We'll go and find this tomorrow, shall we?"

CHAPTER 174

The Bridge of Dreams

It had been a strange day, their father, eager to make amends to his daughters for the tedium of the past week, setting off straight after breakfast to find the advertised attraction, Karen sullenly agreeing to this deviation from their continued meander through the countryside around the canal, and Megan excited at last by the prospect of a real holiday outing. Cari herself harboured mixed emotions; she was both exhilarated and scared. This expedition promised a fulfilment of her consummate yearning to see the place of her dreams, but she had never envisaged it being such a public occasion. Deeply afraid of how she might react, she longed for the opportunity to face this alone. It was *her* bridge; she did not want to share it.

She was so preoccupied that she was not aware of the car stopping. It was only when her father turned to her, saying, "Here we are, love, the place you wanted to visit," that she realised the moment she had both longed for and dreaded had come. It was stunning, every bit as beautiful as it was in her dreams. As the family walked around admiring the views, Ben was gratified to see the look of deep satisfaction on his elder daughter's face. She looked radiant and, it seemed to him, almost ethereal. Not a man given to wild imaginings, Ben shrugged off the thought and turned his attention to the others. Megan was skipping along, chattering to her mother and already tiring of the sights, demanding to know if they were going to walk to the castle next and how near they were to the adventure playground. Even Karen looked happier now, accepting Ben's plans for a family fun day and the prospect of spending the last night of their holiday in a charming nearby hotel. Ben had sourced it online and made the booking that morning over breakfast.

CHAPTER 175

The Final Act

She could prolong their stay no further. With a sigh of longing and a backward glance at the bridge, Cari followed her family back to the car. The remainder of the day passed in a haze of emotion, her participation in the various activities no more than a distraction from the thoughts that filled her mind, eddying round and round, before crystallising eventually into a determined plan.

She could hardly wait until dinner was over, demolishing her food with a rapidity which delighted her mother: the child was not anorexic after all. She must have been "just going through a phase", as Karen's own mother would have said. The events of the day must have tired her, though, as she begged to go to bed at the same time as her little sister, Ben reassuring Karen that this was nothing to worry about, merely the consequence of her previous night's broken sleep.

How long she waited she did not know, lying fully clad on the unfamiliar bed, conscious that the traffic sounds had diminished. Even the hotel seemed quiet. Her parents must have gone to bed by now. She had pulled the covers over herself and feigned sleep as they peeped into the bedroom, whispering goodnight to the girls. Tiptoeing past her sleeping sister, Cari drew aside the bedroom curtains and watched as, one by one, the house lights in the little town went out. Only a very few street lights remained, until eventually these too were extinguished.

This was her moment. Blowing her sister a kiss, Cari silently crept from the room and made her way downstairs, walking past the empty reception desk and out through the heavy front door, quietly drawing it closed behind her. It was easier than she had imagined: she had not encountered a soul, had not been challenged, and had even managed to draw the bolt on the inside of the door and turn the key without alerting anyone. It was as though it had been intended. All she had to do now was to retrace her footsteps, following the map in her mind.

It had taken longer than she had anticipated She had only a hazy concept of the distance involved as they had made the earlier journey by car. She had committed the route to memory and knew when she was nearly there.

Her bridge. As she had seen it so often in her dreams, there it was, stark in the moonlight, bidding, foreboding, enticing, repelling. And yet she was drawn to it, feeling its enormous strength, pulling her like a magnet.

CHAPTER 176

Samaritans

"Samaritans. Can I help you?"

It was the second silent call of the night. The first had lasted only a few seconds before the call was ended. This time it was longer.

"Just take your time. . . . I know it can be very difficult to talk sometimes." The listener was gently coaxing, letting the caller know that however long it would take, the Samaritans were there for whoever happened to be on the line. No pressure. The listener gave her name, trying to establish some sort of rapport, asking again how she might help.

The concentration was intense, the listener straining to pick up what might only be the faintest response, knowing from experience that silence is seldom complete, that there are often sounds in the background which can be useful in initiating some interaction with the caller—music perhaps, traffic noise, a dog barking.

Then she heard it, almost imperceptible: a stifled sob. And in the background, very faintly, could she detect what seemed to be the sound of water flowing.

CHAPTER 177

Cari Moses—Back to Black?

An act of such finality. An end to the charade. Not an ending of it all; more a beginning. Once that she'd been freed from the shackles of her mother's cloying affection, the family would at least have a chance.

And Megan. Megan. How she loved her little sister. Without the alien in their midst, the usurper, Megan would have her rightful opportunity to shine.

Staring down at the water, Cari knew what she had to do.

———◆———

It was a sound unlike anything the Samaritan listener had heard before: distant watery noise replaced by something akin to background static, then the faintest of whistles. It sounded like air rushing past, louder and quicker now, and then just as quickly the whistling stopped. And then she heard it: a muffled plop and an all-encompassing silence, as even the sound of what might have been water was totally subsumed beneath the purr of the handset and her own sharp intake of breath.